Praise for

ELMORE LEONARD

"As welcome as a thunderstorm
in a dry spell."
—*Dallas Morning News*

"Well-developed characters and
dialogue with a perfect pitch . . . this is
Elmore Leonard territory."
—*Chicago Tribune*

"Before Leonard's contemporary cadre of
urban cowboys, there was an impressive
lineup of the real thing. Bounty hunters,
Indians, stagecoach drivers, bank robbers,
sheriffs, and cowpunchers peopled the pages
of his novels in a gritty mix rich in the flavor
and individualism of the old west."
—*Florida Times-Union*

"Leonard knows his way onto a horse and
out of a gunfight as well as he knows the
special King's English spoken by his patented,
not-so-lovable urban lowlifes."
—*Milwaukee Journal Sentinel*

GUNSIGHTS

AND

FORTY

LASHES

LESS ONE

By Elmore Leonard

Fiction

Nonfiction

GUNSIGHTS

AND

FORTY LASHES LESS ONE

Two Novels by

ELMORE LEONARD

WILLIAM MORROW

An Imprint of HarperCollinsPublishers

Excerpt from *Valdez Is Coming* copyright © 1970 by Elmore Leonard, Inc.

GUNSIGHTS. Copyright © 1979 by Elmore Leonard, Inc.
FORTY LASHES LESS ONE. Copyright © 1972 by Elmore Leonard, Inc.

First William Morrow mass market printing: September 2018

Print Edition ISBN: 978-0-06-287711-6

Cover design by Adam Johnson
Cover image from On the Skirmish Line *by Charles Schreyvogel, courtesy of Yale Collection of Western Americana, Beinecke Rare Book and Manuscript Library*

CONTENTS

GUNSIGHTS

1

The gentleman from *Harper's Weekly*, who didn't know mesquite beans from goat shit, looked up from his reference collection of back issues and said, "I've got it!" Very pleased with himself. "We'll call this affair . . . are you ready? The Early-Moon Feud."

The news reporters in the Gold Dollar shrugged and thought some more, though most of them went on calling it the Rincon Mountains War, which seemed to have enough ring to it.

Somebody said, "What's the matter with the Sweetmary War?" Sweetmary being the name of the mining town where all the gawkers and news reporters had gathered to watch the show. The man from the *St. Louis Globe-Democrat* wanted to call it the Last of the Great Indian Wars. Or—he also mentioned to see how it would sound—the Great Apache Uprising of 1893. Or the Bloody Apache Uprising, etc.

The man from the St. Louis newspaper was reminded that, first, it wasn't an uprising and, second, there weren't just Apache Indians up in the mountains; there were also some niggers. The man from St. Louis, being funny, said, "Well, what if we call it the Last of the Great Indian-Nigger Wars?" A man from Florence said, "Well, you have got the chili-pickers in it also. What about them?" Yes, there were some Mexican settlers too, who had been farming up there a hundred years; they were also involved.

What it was, it was a land war.

The LaSalle Mining Company of New Jersey wanted the land. And the Indians from the White Tanks agency, the colored and the Mexicans—all of them actually living up there—wanted it also.

Dana Moon was the Indian Agent at White Tanks, originally established as a reservation for Warm Springs Apaches, or Mimbreños, and a few Lipan and Tonto-Mojave family groups. The agency was located sixteen miles north of Sweetmary and about the same distance west of the San Pedro River. The reservation land was not in dispute. The problem was, many of Moon's Apaches had wandered away from White Tanks—a bleak, young-desert area—to set up rancherías in the mountains. No one, until now, had complained about it.

Brendan Early worked for LaSalle Mining, sort of, with the title Coordinating Manager, Southwest Region, and was living in Sweetmary at the time.

It was said that he and Dana Moon had been up and down the trail together, had shared dry camps and hot corners, and that was why the *Harper's Weekly* man wanted to call it the Early-Moon Feud; which, as you see, had nothing to do with the heavens or astrology.

Nor was there any personal bitterness between them. The question was: What would happen to their bond of friendship, which had tied them together as though on two ends of a short riata, one not venturing too far without running into the other? Would their friendship endure? Or would they now, holding to opposite principles, cut the riata clean and try to kill one another?

Bringing the land question down to personalities, it presented these two as the star attractions: two well-known, soon-to-be-legendary figures about to butt heads. It brought the crowds to Sweetmary to fill up both hotels, the Congress and the Alamosa, a dozen boarding houses, the seven restaurants and thirteen saloons in town. For several weeks this throng swelled the normal population of about four hundred souls, which included the locals, those engaged in commerce, nearby farmers and ranchers and the miners at the Sweetmary Works. Now there were curiosity seekers, gawkers, from all over the Territory and parts of New Mexico.

(Not here yet were the hundred or more gunmen eventually hired by the company to "protect its leases" and quartered at the mine works. These men were paid, it was said, twenty dollars a week.)

There were newspaper representatives from the *Phoenix Republican, Phoenix Gazette, Yuma Sentinel, Safford Arizonian, Tucson Star, Florence Enterprise, Prescott Courier, Cococino Sun, Clifton Copper Era, Graham County Bulletin, Tombstone Prospector, St. Louis Globe-Democrat, Chicago Times* and the *New York Tribune.*

Harper's Weekly had hired the renowned photographer C.S. Fly of Tombstone to cover the war with his camera, the way he had pictorially recorded Crook's campaign against Geronimo and his renegade Apaches.

C.S. Fly set up a studio on LaSalle Street and there presented "showings" of many of his celebrated photographs of Indians, hangings, memorial parades and well-known personages, including Geronimo, former president Garfield and several of Brendan Early and Dana Moon. The two photos that were perhaps best known showed them at Fort Huachuca, June 16, 1887, with a prisoner they had brought in that day.

There they were, six years ago:

Brendan Early, in his hip-cocked cavalry pose. First Lieutenant of the 10th at Huachuca but wearing civilian dress, a very tight-fitting light-colored suit of clothes; bare-headed to show his brown wavy hair; a silky-looking kerchief at his throat; a matched pair of Smith and Wesson .44 Russians, butt-forward in Army holsters, each with the flap cut off; cavalry boots wiped clean for the pose; Brendan holding his Spencer carbine like a walking cane, palm resting on the upraised barrel. He seems to be trying to look down his nose like an Eastern dandy while suppressing a grin that shows clearly in his eyes.

In contrast:

Dana Moon with his dark, drooping mustache that makes him appear sad; hat brim straight and low over his eyes, a bulge in his bony countenance indicating the ever-present plug of tobacco; dark suit of clothes and a polka-dot neckerchief. Dana's .44 Colt's revolver is in a shoulder rig, a glint of it showing. He grips a Big-Fifty Sharps in one hand, a sawed-off 12-gauge Greener in the other. All those guns for a man who looks so mild, so solemn.

Between the two:

Half a head shorter is a one-eyed Mimbreño Apache named Loco. What a funny-looking little man, huh? Black eyepatch, black stringy hair hanging from the bandana covering his head, he looks like a pirate of some kind, wearing an old dirty suitcoat and a loincloth. But don't laugh at him. Loco has killed many people and went to Washington to meet Grover Cleveland when times were better.

The caption beneath the photo, which appeared that year in *Harper's Weekly*, reads:

> *Lt. Brendan Early Loco Dana Moon*
> *Two Famous Heroes of the West with a Captive*
> *Red Devil*

There was also a photo of the Two Famous Heroes standing on either side of an attractive fair-haired young lady in a torn and dirty cotton dress; she is wearing a man's shirt over her quite filthy attire, the shirt unbuttoned, hanging free. The young lady does not seem happy to be posing for her picture that day at Fort Huachuca. She looks as though she might walk up to the camera and kick it over.

The caption beneath this one reads:

> *Lt. Brendan Early Katherine McKean Dana Moon*
> *Following Her Ordeal, Katy McKean*
> *Gratefully Thanks Her Rescuers*

In the *Harper's Weekly* article there was mention of a 10th Cavalry sergeant by the name of Bo Catlett, a Negro. Though he did not appear in either of the photographs, Sergeant Catlett had accompanied the Two Famous Heroes in their quest to apprehend the Apache warchief, Loco, and shared credit for bringing him in and rescuing the McKean girl. In the article, Sergeant Catlett was asked where he had gotten the name Bo. "I believe it short for 'Boy,' suh," was his reply.

Not many days before the photographs were taken by C.S. Fly, the five principals involved—Early, Moon, the McKean girl, Loco and Bo Catlett—were down in Old Mexico taking part in an adventure that would dramatically change their lives and, subsequently, lead to the Big Shootout known by most as the Rincon Mountains War.

2

Dana Moon had come down from Whiteriver to guide for Lieutenant Early and his company of 10th Cavalry out of Huachuca. They met at St. Helen, a stage stop on the Hatch & Hodges Central Mail Section route, where the "massacre" had taken place: the massacre being one dead swamper, shot several times and his head shoved into his bucket of axel grease; the driver of the stage; his shotgun rider and one passenger, a Mr. R. Holmes of St. David. Four were dead; two passengers caught in the gunfire and wounded superficially; and one passenger abducted, Miss Katherine McKean of Benson, on her way home from visiting kin in Tucson.

Loco was recognized as the leader of the raiding party (How many one-eyed Apaches were there between San Carlos and Fort Huachuca?) and was last seen trailing due south toward the Whetstone Mountains, though more likely was heading for the San Pedro and open country: Loco, the McKean girl and about twenty others in the band that had jumped the reservation a few days before.

"Or about ten," Dana Moon said. "Those people"—meaning Apaches—"can cause you to piss your britches and see double."

Brendan Early, in his dusty blues, looked at the situation, staring south into the sun haze and heat waves, looking at nothing. But Brendan Early was in charge here and had to give a command.

What did they have? In the past month close to 150 Warm Springs people had jumped the San Carlos reservation, women and children as well as bucks, and made a beeline down the San Pedro Valley to Old Mexico and the fortress heights of the Sierra Madres. Loco's bunch was the rear guard, gathering fresh mounts and firearms along the way. Maybe Bren Early's troopers could ride like wild men a day and a night, killing some horses and maybe, just maybe, cut Loco off at the crossing.

Or, a lieutenant in the U.S. Cavalry might ride through the scrub and say, "What border?" even after ten years on frontier station, cross leisurely with extra mounts and do the job.

Dana Moon—sent down here by Al Sieber, Chief of Scouts at San Carlos—waited, not giving the lieutenant any help. He sat his chestnut gelding, looking down from there with the tobacco wad in his jaw. He didn't spit; he didn't do a thing.

While Lieutenant Early was thinking, Then what? Track the renegades, run 'em to ground? Except his troop of U.S. Cavalry would be an invading army, wouldn't it? having crossed an international boundary contrary to treaty agreement and the mutual respect of foreign soil, customs, emigration, all that bullshit.

"Lord Jehovah protect us from dumb-ass officialdom," said the lieutenant out loud to no one in particular.

All soil west of the Pecos looked the same to Bren Early—born and raised in Monroe, Michigan (adopted home of George Armstrong Custer), before matriculating at West Point, somehow getting through, one hundred seventy-ninth in a class of one ninety-two—and there was no glory standing around a wagon yard watching civilians bleed.

Dana Moon read signs—grain shucks in horse shit, and could tell you where the rider had come from and how long ago—and sometimes he could read Bren Early's mind. He said, "You're gonna hurt your head thinking. You want to do it, I'll take you four and a half days' ride southeast, yes, across the line toward Morelos, and on the sixth day Loco and his fellas will ride up to our camp. But not with all your troopers. You and me and Bo Catlett to handle the cavvy if he wants to come, six mounts on the string, grain and water. If you don't want to do it I think I'll quit government work; I'm tired of looking over the fence and watching dust settle."

"On the sixth day," Bren Early said, nodding. "And on the seventh day we'll rest, huh?"

He bought the tight-fitting suit of clothes off the St. Helen station agent for seven dollars, and for three more got Bo Catlett a coat, vest and derby hat. Hey, boy, they were going to Old Mexico like three dude tourists:

Rode southeast and crossed into Sonora at dusk, guided by the faint lights of a border town, against the full-dark moonside of the sky.

2

Dana Moon's plan: ride straight for a well he knew would be on Loco's route; get down there in the neighborhood, scout the rascal and his band to make sure they were coming; then, when they arrived, parley with the thirsty renegades, keeping their guns between the Apaches and a drink of water. Talk them out of the McKean girl first—if she was still alive—then talk about the weather or whatever they wanted, gradually getting the discussion around to a return trip to San Carlos for everybody, all expenses paid.

Or commence firing when they draw within range, Bren Early thought, seeing it written up as a major skirmish or, better yet, the Battle of . . . whatever the name of this rancho used to be, sitting in the scrub oak foothills: three weathered adobes in a row like a small garrison, mesquite-pole out-building and corral, part of an adobe wall enclosing the yard.

Out fifty yards of worn-out pasture was a windmill rigged to a stock tank of scummy water. From the end house or the wall, three men could cover the tank and a thirsty traveler would have to get permission to drink if the three men didn't want him to.

The Battle of Rancho Diablo. Give it a hellfire exciting name. Who'd know the difference?

On the sixth day Dana Moon rode in from his early-morning scout, field glasses hanging on his chest. He said, "What ever happens the way you expect it to?" He did spit right then.

Bren Early saw it. He said, "Duty at Huachuca."

"They split up," Dana Moon told him and Bo Catlett. "It looks to be Loco and the young lady coming ahead. They'll be here by noon, the ones with the herd maybe an hour behind. And some more dust coming out of the west."

"Federales," Bo Catlett said.

"Not enough of 'em," Moon said. "Some other party; maybe eight or ten."

They brought the spare horses and feed into the middle adobe, three saddled horses into the building closest to the stock-tank end of the yard, and went inside to wait.

Hoofprints out there meant nothing; people came through here all times of the year traveling between Morelos and Bavispe and points beyond, this being the gateway to the Sierra Madres.

Still, when Loco came, leading the second horse and rider they took to be the girl, he hung back 300 yards—the horses straining toward the smell of water—and began to circle as he approached the rancho again, coming around through the pasture now, keeping the wall between him and the adobes.

"We'll have to wing him," Bren Early said, flat against the wall with his Spencer, next to a front window.

Moon watched through the slit opening in the wooden door. He said to Bo Catlett, "Mount up."

Bo Catlett did and had to remain hunched over

in the McClellan, his derby hat grazing the low roof.

"That one-eyed Indian is a little speck of a target, isn't he?" Bren Early said.

"Tired and thirsty," Moon said. "I'm going out." He looked up at Bo Catlett. "He flushes when he sees me, run him down. There won't be any need to shoot."

Bren Early, dropping the stock of his Spencer to the dirt floor, said, "Shit. And parley awhile." He didn't like it; then thought of something and squinted out past the window frame again.

"I wonder what that girl looks like," he said. "I wonder what the one-eyed son of a bitch's been doing to her."

Moon said, "Probably looks at her and thinks the same thing you would." He glanced up to see Bo Catlett showing his yellow-white teeth, grinning at him, and Moon thought of his mother telling him a long time ago why colored people had good, strong teeth: because they ate cold leftovers in the kitchen and couldn't afford to buy candy and things that weren't good for you.

Outside, Moon raised his arm. He saw Loco stop about a hundred yards off: the Apache deciding how much he wanted water or if he could win a race if he turned and ran. He saw the roan horse behind coming up next to Loco—yes, blond hair stirring, the McKean girl. Then saw something he didn't expect: the girl twisting in her saddle and shoving the Apache hard with both hands, sending him off his horse to land hard and lie there a moment while the girl reached to unhitch the lead line from the Indian's saddle; and now she was kicking her roan out of there, not bothering to look back as Moon yelled at her, "Wait! . . . Hey, come on back!" Then turning, getting out of the way as he called to Bo, "Get her!"

Bo Catlett came out of the door chute, chin pressed into the horse's mane, rose up in the yard and pressed down again as the horse cleared the four-foot adobe wall—Loco standing now, watching for a moment, then gathering his reins and coming on, not interested in the two horses racing across the pasture toward a haze of mountains.

3

They sat inside the doorway of the house with no furniture: Dana Moon and Loco with cups of sweet black coffee, the square of outside light between them on the earth floor. Bren Early came over from the fireplace where the coffee pot sat on a sheet of tin over the smoldering mesquite sticks. He stood looking out the window that was behind the Apache.

Loco said in Spanish, "Tell him I don't like him there."

Moon looked up at Bren. "He asks you to join us."

"Tell him he smells."

Moon motioned to him. "Come on, be sociable." To Loco he said in Spanish, "So, here we are."

Squatting down, Bren Early said, "Ask him, for Christ sake, what he did to the girl."

The Apache's one eye shifted. "Did to her? Did what?" he said in English.

"Is she all right?" asked Moon.

"She needs to be beaten," the Apache said. "Maybe cut off the end of her nose."

"Jesus Christ," Bren Early said. He got up and stepped to the window again.

"He speaks of Hey-soo Cristo." The Apache paused and said, using Spanish again, "What is the matter he can't sit down?"

"He wants to do battle," Moon said.

The Apache stretched open his one eye, raising his brow as if to shrug. "Wouldn't it be good if we could have what we want? I take all the mountains sunrise of the river San Pedro. You take all your people and go back to Washington"—pronouncing it Wasi-tona—"be by your big chief, Grover Cleveland. Man, he was very fat, do you know it?"

"He eats good," Moon said.

"Yes, but he gave us nothing. We sat in a room in chairs. He didn't seem to know why we were there."

"You liked Washington?" asked Moon.

"Good water there," Loco said, "but no country or mountains that I saw. Now they are sending our people to Fort Sill in Oklahoma. Is it like Washington?"

"I don't know," Moon said. "*He* served there one time," looking up at Bren Early.

"I believe it," the Apache said.

"It's like San Carlos, but with more people and houses."

"With mountains?"

"I don't think so," Moon said. "I've never been there. I've never been to Washington either. I've been to Sonora . . . Santa Fe, in the New Mexico Territory."

"The buildings in Washington are white," Loco said. "There are men made of iron on horses also made of iron. Many buildings and good water. You should go there and live if that's what your people like."

"I like mountains, as you do," Moon said. "I was born here, up on Oak Creek. I want to stay here, the same as you do. But there's a difference. They say, 'Put Loco and his people on the train to Fort Sill.' I can say, 'Put him on yourself, I won't do it.' And somebody puts you on the train. It's too bad, but what can I do about it?"

"Jesus Christ," Bren Early said, listening to them talking so seriously and understanding the drift but not the essence of what they were saying and feeling.

Moon raised his eyes. "We're looking at the situation."

Bren Early made a gun out of his right index finger, aimed it at the back of Loco's head and said, "Pow. That's how you solve it. You two're chatting—last week he shot four people dead. So we send him to Oklahoma for a vacation."

"It's the high part of his life to raid and steal horses, since the first Spaniard came up this valley," Moon said. "What else does he know? What's right and what's wrong on his side of the fence?"

"My life is to meet the hostile enemy and destroy him," Bren said. "That's what I know."

"Listen to yourself," Moon said. "You want a war, go find one." He began gathering Spanish words again and said to Loco, "When your men arrive, tell them to get all of your people here in the mountains and bring them back to San Carlos. You go with us. It's the way it has to be for right now."

"Maybe it won't be so easy," Loco said. "There are others coming too."

Yes, the dust from the west, eight or ten riders. "Who are they?" Moon asked.

Loco touched the dirty red pirate bandana covering his head. "The ones who take hair."

"You're sure of it?"

"If they're not of you, or not the soldiers of Mexico, who are they?" the Apache said.

4

Bo Catlett came back with Katy McKean, the girl eyeing them with suspicion as she rode into the yard, sitting her roan like they'd have to pull her off it. Then sitting up there feeling left out, because they didn't have time for her those first moments. Bo Catlett began telling them about the riders coming. He said it looked like they had scattered the Indian herd and the two sides had exchanged gunfire, Bo Catlett hearing the reports in the distance. Now some of them for sure, if not all, were coming this way and it wouldn't be too long before they'd see the dust.

Bren Early studied the girl as he listened, thinking to himself, My, my, my, the poor sweet young thing all dirty and tattered, like the savages had rolled her on the ground and torn at her dress to get it off.

He said, "Miss," helping her down, taking her by the arm, "come on inside out of the hot sun." She pulled her arm away, giving him a mean look, and Bren said, "What're you mad at *me* for? I just want to give you some coffee."

"I ain't going in there with him," the McKean girl said, looking at Loco standing in the doorway. "Less you want to loan me one of your guns."

"Don't worry," Bren said. "He gets familiar with you again, I'll make the little heathen marry you. But how are you, all things being equal?"

The girl said, "What do you mean *again*?"

"I was just teasing," Bren said, "showing you there's nothing to worry about."

"He tried things," the McKean girl said. "I hit him in his good eye and kicked him up under his skirt where it'd do the most good. But I ain't going in that room with him. I still got his smell in my nose."

Dana Moon took her gently by the arm. She looked at him but didn't resist as he said in his quiet tone, "You been through something, lady, I know; and we're going to watch over you."

"Thank you," the girl said, subdued.

"But you got to do what I tell you for the time being, you understand? You can kick and scream when you get home, but right now try and act nice."

5

Who were they? was the question: Watching from the windows as they had waited for the Indian, Moon and Bren Early with their glasses on the riders raising dust across the old pasture.

"Seven, eight," Bren Early said. "Like cow-punchers heading for town."

"Starting to hang back, sniff the air," Dana Moon said. What did those people out there know, looking this way? First, trailing Apaches with a horse herd and a white woman. Then, seeing a man in a derby hat riding off with her. They would have to be confused.

"They traded shots," Bren Early said and paused, thinking, Then what? "If they wanted the horses, why didn't they take 'em?"

Which was about where Moon was in his own mind. "Say they did, and left somebody with the herd. How many you count, Bo?"

"Ten," Bo Catlett said. "Coulda been another one."

"And they saw you for sure."

"Couldn't miss us—time I got the lady turned around."

"They're cowhands," the McKean girl said, with that edge to her tone again, not feeling very rescued crowded into this adobe room with four men and animals. She had moved up by Moon's window and stood close to him, seeing the hard bump in his jaw, wondering if he would ever spit; then would look over at Bren Early, maybe admiring his long wavy hair, or the tight, shrunk-looking suit molded to his tall frame. Squinting out the window, she said, "You can tell by the look of them, the way they ride."

Still, the McKean girl had to admit—without saying it aloud—it was a bunch of riders for not having any cows, and moving south at that, not like they were heading home from a drive.

"There was a man used to sell us beef at San Carlos," Moon said. "I believe the name was Sundeen." Still watching through his glasses, seeing the riders at four hundred yards now, spreading out more as they came at a choppy walk, not a sound from them yet.

"I used to know him," the McKean girl said, a little surprised.

Maybe they didn't hear her. Bo Catlett said, "The same man supplied meat to Huachuca. Look in his war-bag you see a running iron, it's Phil Sundeen. Used to bring his beef in vented every which way; cows look like somebody was learning to write on 'em."

Moon said, "If I remember—hired vaqueros he paid twenty a month and feed. And we see some Mexican hats, don't we?"

"Which one's Sundeen?" Bren Early asked.

As Moon studied the bunch through his glasses, the McKean girl, squinting, said, "That stringy one on the sorrel—I bet he's got a hatband made of silver conchas."

"Something there's catching the light," Moon said.

"And forty-fours in crossed belts with silver buckles?"

"You got him," Moon said.

"Don't anybody listen to me," the McKean girl said. "I used to know him when his dad was still running things, before they sent Phil Sundeen to Yuma prison."

"That's the one," Moon said. "You knew him, huh?"

"I was *acquainted* with him," the McKean girl said. "I wasn't to have nothing to do with him and that was fine with me. He was cheeky, loud and had ugly ways about him."

Bren Early said, "What was he in prison for?"

"As this colored man said, for using his running iron freely," the McKean girl answered. "It might be he run a herd down here to the Mexicans. On the way home he sees One-Eye here and decides to go for the bounty trade. Ask the Indin. He wouldn't have given himself up otherwise, would he?"

The men in the adobe room looked at this girl who seemed to know what she was talking about. How old? Still in her twenties, a healthy-looking girl, though dirty and sunburned at the moment. Yes, she knew a few hard facts of life.

Bren Early, leaning against the wall by his window, looked from the girl to Loco. "You must be worth plenty, all these people coming to see you."

"Make 'em bid high," the McKean girl said, "and look at the scrip before you hand him over, or that son of a bitch Sundeen will try and cheat you."

The men in the room had to look at that girl again.

Moon saw the waiting expression in Loco's eye and said, "He ain't going with them, he's going home."

"I know he's going home," Bren Early said. "I didn't come six days for the ride."

"If it means an argument, what difference does it make who takes him?" the McKean girl asked. She was serious.

Bren Early said, "Because he belongs to me, that's why."

And Moon said to her, going over to his horse, "I'll try and explain it to you sometime."

Bren Early was watching the riders, two hundred yards now, still coming spread out. "We got blind sides in here," he said. "Let's get out to the wall."

Moon was bringing a spare revolver out of his saddle bag, a Smith & Wesson .38 double-action model. He said, "You don't mean everybody."

Bren Early looked at him. "I'm referring to you and me only. Shouldn't that do the job?"

Moon pulled his sawed-off Greener from inside his blanket roll. Coming back to the window he handed the .38 to the McKean girl, saying, "You don't have to cock it, just keep pulling on the trigger's the way it works. But let me tell you something." Moon paused, looking at the Apache only a few feet away. "He's with us, you understand? He's ours. Nobody else's." Moon looked at Bo Catlett then and said, "Bo, give him his gun. Soon as it's over, take it back."

Walking out to the adobe wall, carrying their firearms, they watched the riders coming on, the riders looking this way but cutting an angle toward the stock tank.

"We'll let 'em water," Bren Early said.

"You give 'em too much they'll camp there," Moon said.

"We got no choice but have a talk first, do we?"

"No," Moon said.

"So they'll water and stretch first, take a pee and look the situation over. I hope they don't use dirty language and offend the girl's ears."

"Don't worry about *her*," Moon said.

He laid his Greener on the chest-high crumbling wall, leaned the Sharps against it, cocked, in front of him, loosened the Colt's in his shoulder rig, then decided to take his coat off: folded it neatly and laid it on the wall a few feet away.

"They're watching us," he said.

"I hope so," Bren Early said.

Bren had leaned his Spencer against the adobe wall. Now he drew his big .44 S & W Russians, broke each one open to slide a bullet into the empty sixth chamber and reholstered his guns.

Sundeen's bunch was at the stock tank now, fifty yards off, stepping down from the saddles.

Bren Early said, "At Chancellorsville, a Major Peter Keenan took his Eighth Pennsylvania Cavalry, four hundred men and—buying time for the artillery to set up—charged them full against ten thousand Confederate infantry. Talk about odds."

Moon turned his head a little. "What happened to 'em?"

"They all got killed."

6

The Mexican in the straw Chihuahua hat who came over to talk looked at first like he was out for a stroll, squinting up at the sky and off at the haze of mountains, inspecting a cholla bush, looking everywhere but at Moon and Early until he was about thirty feet from the adobe wall, then giving them a surprised look: like, what're you doing here?

The riders back of him, small figures, stood around while their horses watered in the corrugated tank and in the slough that had formed from seepage. One of the figures—it looked to be

Sundeen—had his peter out and was taking a leak facing this way: telling them what he thought of the situation.

The Mexican touched his hat, loosening it and setting it again. Even with the revolver on his leg and the cartridge belt across his chest he seemed friendly standing there.

He said, "Good afternoon. How are you today?"

Moon and Bren Early watched him, Bren murmuring, "Jesus Christ," under his breath.

"It's good to reach water on a hot day," the Mexican said. "Have you been here very long?"

Moon and Bren Early seemed patient, waiting for him to get to it.

"We looking for friends of ours," the Mexican said. "We wonder if you see anybody ride by here the past hour."

Bren Early said, "Haven't seen a soul."

The Mexican took time to look past them and study the adobes, seeing the white smoke rising from the first chimney and vanishing in the glare.

"Where your horses?"

"Out of the sun," Bren Early said.

"You good to them," the Mexican said. "What else you got in there?"

"Troop of cavalry," Bren Early said and called out, "Sergeant!"

Bo Catlett, with a Spencer, appeared in the doorway of the first adobe, calling back, "Suh!"

The Mexican began to shake his head very slowly. "You got the Uninah States Army in there? Man, I like to see that." His gaze returned to Bren Early and Moon. "Soldiers . . . but you don't have no uniforms on." He paused. "You don't want nobody to know you here, huh? Listen, we won't tell nobody."

"You don't know what you've seen, what you haven't seen," Bren Early said. "Leave it at that."

The Mexican said, "You don't want to invite me in there?"

Moon drew his Colt from the shoulder rig and put it on the Mexican. "You got a count of three to move out of here," he said. "One . . . two . . . three—"

"Espere," the Mexican said. "Wait. It's all right with me." He began to back away, his gaze holding on Moon's revolver. "You don't want to be friends, all right, maybe some other time. Good afternoon to you."

7

The Mexican, whose name was Ruben Vega, forty-four years of age, something like seven to ten years older than the two men at the wall, said to himself, Never again. Going there like that and acting a fool. Good afternoon. How are you today? They knew, those two. They knew what was going on and weren't buying any of that foolish shit today. Never again, Ruben Vega said to himself again, walking back to the stock tank . . . Sundeen waiting for him.

Sundeen with his eyes creased in the sun glare, pulling the funneled brim of his hat down lower.

"He was bluffing you. Don't you know when a man's bluffing?" Like the joke was on Ruben Vega and Sundeen had seen through it right away.

"Sometimes I don't see the bluff if the man's good at it," Ruben Vega said. "These two mean it. Why is it worth it to them? I don't know. But they mean it."

"Eight to three," Sundeen said. "What difference is it what they mean? The Indin's ours."

"I don't know," Ruben Vega said, shaking his head. "You better talk to them yourself."

Sundeen wasn't listening now. He was squinting past the Mexican and touching his two-week's growth of beard, fondling it, caressing himself, as he studied the pair of figures at the wall. One of them had yelled, "Sergeant," and the booger had stuck his head out. Soldiers—chased after the Apache and now had him in there. That part was clear enough. The girl, she must be in there, too. But eight guns against three was what it came to. So what was the problem? Ask for the Apache. Ask at gunpoint if need be. Those people would have no choice but to hand him over and be happy to do it.

He said to the Mexican, "Send two around back to make 'em nervous. The rest of us'll walk in." The Mexican didn't say anything and Sundeen looked at him. "What's the matter?"

"It isn't the way to do it."

Sundeen looked at the Mexican's old-leather face, at the thick, tobacco-stained mustache covering his mouth and the tiny blood lines in his tired-looking eyes.

"You're getting old, you know it?"

"I think that's it," Ruben Vega said. "I'm getting old because I'm still alive."

Sundeen wanted to push him and say, Goddamn

it, quit kicking dirt and come on; there's nothing to this. But he knew Ruben Vega pretty well. He paid him fifty dollars a month because Ruben Vega was good with men, even white men, and was one trail-wise first-class segundo to have riding point with a herd of rustled stock, or tracking after a loose Apache with a Mexican price on his head. Like the one-eyed Mimbre, Loco: 2,000 pesos, dead or alive.

When Ruben Vega spoke, Sundeen generally paid attention. But this time—Ruben had been bluffed out, was all, and was trying to save his face, sound wise, like he knew something as fact; whereas it was just an off-day for him and his back ached or his piles were bothering him.

Sundeen looked over at his riders, part of them hunkered down in the stingy shade of the stock tank: four Americans and two skinny Mexicans with their heavy criss-crossed gunbelts. He said to Ruben Vega, "I'll show you how white men do it," grinning a little. "I'll send your two boys around back where it's safe, and march in with the rest of these ugly bronc stompers myself."

"I'll watch you," Ruben Vega said.

Sundeen looked over at the riders again, saying, "Who wants to earn a month's wages this fine afternoon?"

8

"Now we're getting to it," Bren Early said, seeing the five men assembling, starting to come out from the tank, spreading out in a line. "I don't see a rifle amongst them; so they intend to come close, don't they?" And told himself not to talk so much, or else Dana would think he was nervous.

"The other two," Dana Moon said. "Leaving or what?"

Two with Mexican hats, mounted, were moving away from the tank, off to the right, heading out into the scrub.

"Do we want them behind us?"

"Uh-unh," Bren Early said. He picked up his Spencer as Moon hefted his Sharps, watching the two Mexican riders swinging wide, going out to nearly two hundred yards as they began to circle at a gallop.

"The horses first," said Moon, "if that's agreeable."

"I suppose," the cavalryman answered, "but it's a shame."

"If they keep coming, you finish it. I'll tend to the others."

Moon stole a look at the five on foot coming out from the tank, taking their time, one remaining back there with the horses.

He said, "When you're ready."

They pressed Spencer and Sharps to their shoulders and almost instantly the hard, heavy reports came BAM-BAM in the stillness and the two running horses two hundred yards out stumbled and went down with their riders in sudden burts of dust, the tiny figures flying, tumbling.

Moon turned his empty Sharps on the line of five, saw them stop dead.

Bren Early called, "Sergeant!"

Moon didn't look around. He heard off behind

him, "Suh!" And Bren Early calmly, "Two on the flank. Keep 'em there. They move, shoot 'em." And the black voice saying, "Suh!" and that was done.

The five had broken line and were looking out that way, losing some of their starch maybe. But the one with crossed gunbelts and silver buckles was saying something, getting them back in business and they were coming again, the line of men about fifteen feet wide—Sundeen in the middle—every one of them shaggy and scruffy, rannies with hard squints trying to look mean, and they did.

The last exchange made between Moon and Bren Early was Moon saying, "If it comes to it, work from the ends," and Bren Early saying, "And meet at the silver buckles."

Now the floor was Sundeen's, bringing his line to a halt at a distance Moon's eyes measured as a long stride short of forty feet. A good working range: close enough for a sawed-off, far enough you'd have to aim a revolver if you had nerve enough to take the time. Who were these brush poppers? Were they any good? Moon and Bren Early were about to find out.

Sundeen said to the two at the wall, "Are you nervous or something? We come to talk to you is all."

He waited a moment, but they didn't say anything. Then looked off into the distance at the two dead horses and the riders stranded out there before bringing his gaze back to the wall.

"Like shooting a buck, that range. I guess you've done it in your time. But here looking at it close to earth is different, huh? You see what you got on your hands? Now then," Sundeen said, "you also got that red nigger in there by the name of Loco we want you to hand over to us. Do you see a reason to discuss it any?"

"He's mine," Bren Early said. "He goes home with me."

"Oh, are you the gent in charge?" asked Sundeen. "Then tell me something. What difference does it make who takes this Indin, long as we rid the earth of him?"

"I was sent to get him," Bren Early said, "and I did."

"A long piece from home without your uniform on, soldier boy. I bet you shouldn't even be 'cross the border here. What I'm saying, it looks like I got more right to the red nigger than you have. I got the law on my side."

"But I've got the Indian," Bren Early said. "What remains is how dearly you want to pay for him."

"Turn it around," Sundeen said. "Why would you put up your life to keep him? I'm gonna ride out with him, one way or the other."

Moon said then, "You ever mount up again you'll do it bleeding to death."

Sundeen shook his head. What was the matter with these two?—and had to make himself calm down. He said, "Listen to us grown men arguing over a little one-eyed Indin."

"What's he worth," asked Moon, "couple thousand pesos?"

"Sure, there's something in it, or we wouldn't be talking," Sundeen answered. "But you can't hand him in and collect the bounty, not if you're U.S. Army. They find out back home, they'll cut your buttons off, won't they? Drum you out. It may be duty with you, if you say it is; but it's pure business with me. Way to make a living." Sundeen paused. He said then, "It gives me an idea. What we might do is divvy him up. You give me his hair and his eye patch, something to identify him to the Mex gover'ment, and you take the rest of him back where you came from. And if that ain't a deal I never heard one."

Sundeen glanced both ways at the pair of riders on either side of him, then looked at the two behind the low wall again, pleased with himself, his display of wisdom and generosity.

Bren Early did stop and think a moment. Yes, if they'd had to shoot the Indian they'd be bringing him back dead anyway. But how would they explain his tonsured head, the scalplock ripped from his skull? Then realized, No, that wasn't the point at all. It was a question of principle, beyond reason or even good sense. A question of standing at the drawn line and never backing off.

Bren Early said to Moon, but for all to hear, "Do you want to tell him to stick it in his horse, or should I?"

Sundeen was a grunt away from giving in to his violent nature; but knew his men had to look at him or hear him and all of them pull at the same time to do the job right. Put the two off guard and then hit. It wasn't gong the way he thought it would—that goddamn Ruben Vega telling him, knowing something. With the hook still in his belly but holding on to good judgment, Sundeen said, "I'm gonna go talk to my partner a minute. See if we can think of a way to satisfy us."

Moon and Bren Early watched him turn away from them, his rannies looking at him like, What's going on? Sundeen dropping a word as he glanced left and right, all of them moving off now.

Bren said, "He's used to having his way."

Moon said, "But he didn't come prepared, did he?"

"I'll give them three more steps," Bren said and pulled his matched Smith & Wesson .44s. Moon drew his Colt's, gathered the sawed-off Greener from the wall in his left hand.

Three more strides—that was it.

The five came around with weapons in their hands, Sundeen hollering something, and his two men on the ends fell dead in the first sudden explosion from the wall, before they were full around, Bren Early and Moon with revolvers extended, aiming, firing at the scattering, snap-shooting line, Bren holding both the big .44 Russians out in front of him and moving his head right and left to look down the barrels and fire; Moon holding the Greener low against its hard buck and letting go a Double-O charge at a half-kneeling figure and seeing the man's arms fly up with the big-bore report, swinging the Greener on Sundeen and raking his boots with a charge as Sundeen stumbled and Bren Early fired, shooting his hat off, firing again and seeing the man let go of his revolvers and grab his face with both hands as he sank to the ground.

They went over the wall and walked out to where the five lay without moving.

"Four dead," Bren Early said.

Moon nodded. "For no reason. This one looks to be right behind."

Sundeen was still alive, lying in the sun as his life drained from shotgun wounds in both legs, bullet wounds in his neck, through his left cheek and where part of his left ear had been shot away.

Ruben Vega came out to them, looking at the men on the ground. He said, "Well, I tried to tell him."

The Mexican began to think of how he would get Sundeen to Morelos, or if he should try; and if he should take the others over their horses or leave them here. He walked around them, nudging one and then another with his boot, making sure they were dead; then began to recite the names of these men, as though saying last words over them:

Lonnie Baker.

Clement Hurd.

Dick Maddox.

Jack McWilliams.

Moon and Bren Early heard him, but they were looking toward the adobe now, seeing the girl and the sergeant and the Indian in the yard, and they didn't listen to the names carefully and store them away. It could have helped them later if they did.

3

1

When the news reporters first came here to cover the War they had to look for the "angle." The Big Company trying to run off the little homesteaders was good stuff; they could write it as factually as need be from both sides. But it would be far better if Personalities were involved: names of newsworthy individuals that readers would recognize, or, feel dumb if they didn't after the news articles described their colorful and exciting past histories.

What could you do with William A. Vandozen, the LaSalle Mining vice-president who was completely lacking in color, appeared in town once in awhile but would not talk to anyone when he did?

What kind of story would you get from an Apache Indian homesteader named Iskay-mon-ti-zah who didn't speak English anyway?

This was, in part, the reason Dana Moon and Brendan Early were elected to be the principal antagonists, bound to come together sooner or later, which would be the climax, the Big Story: two living legends in a fight to the finish.

Fine, the editors of the newspapers would wire back to their reporters. But who are they? What did they do? GET TO WORK AND DIG UP SOME BACKGROUND! was the tone of the wires if not the actual words.

The news reporters hanging out at the Gold Dollar would shake their heads. Just like a goddamn editor—like asking what Wild Bill Hickok did for a living. (What *did* he do? No one asked.) They all nodded their heads in agreement as to editors.

All right, they'd go talk to the principals involved.

But try to get a straight answer from Brendan Early, who was stuck-up, high-and-mighty, vain and rude when interviewed. They would ask him questions such as: "What is it like to kill a man?" He would stare back at them and not answer. "Do you think you will die by the gun?" Answer: "If you don't leave, somebody will." Or they would ask a question in a group none would dare ask alone: "What turned you against humanity?" The famous Bren Early: "Pains in the ass like you people." They would see him drinking whiskey and playing faro, then not see him for days while he remained holed-up in his room in the Congress Hotel or visited the mysterious Mrs. Pierson who lived in a house on Mill Street without any visible means of support.

Or try to locate Dana Moon, having to go all the way up into the mountains on a two-day pack. Finally, there he was. Ask him a list of shrewd questions and have him say, "You people don't know what you're talking about, do you?"

So the reporters filed embroidered stories based on heresay and sketchy information they accepted as fact. They wrote that Bren Early had been courtmartialed following the Sonora Incident and cashiered out of the Army. Since then he had been:

A hunting guide.

Road agent.

Convict in a work gang.

Gold prospector.

Had shot and killed anywhere from ten to twenty men.

All this before selling his claim to LaSalle Mining and joining the company. Great stuff, plenty of material here to work with.

Dana Moon's background wasn't as colorful, though it was solid ground to build on. After Sonora he had been fired from his position as Assistant Supervisor, San Carlos Indian Reservation, and had entered the business of mustanging: supplying remounts to Fort Huachuca and stage horses to Hatch & Hodges, before they shut down their lines. He was known to be a rough customer who had shot and killed a few men himself. Now, and for the past few years, Dana Moon was in charge of the Apache sub-agency at White Tanks.

Yes, Moon and Early had crossed paths several times since the Sonora Incident, which is what made the "angle" of these two eventually tearing into each other a natural. Headlines, with facts slightly bent, practically wrote themselves.

PERSONAL FEUD SETS STAGE FOR LAND FIGHT
MOON AND EARLY FACTIONS LINE UP FOR BATTLE

Great stuff.

While all the "color" was being written, a young

Chicago Times journalist by the name of Maurice Dumas, who had not yet mastered a pose of cynicism or world-weariness, did talk to both Bren Early and Dana Moon. Young Maurice Dumas asked straight questions and didn't know any better when he got direct answers.

Beginner's luck, the other news reporters said.

2

Was it luck? Or the fact Maurice Dumas had trained himself to jump out of bed each day at 6:30 A.M. and immediately check his list of THINGS TO DO. At seven he walked into the Congress Hotel dining room and there was Brendan Early, alone: the first time Maurice Dumas had ever seen the man without a crowd around him.

"Excuse me, but would you mind if I interviewed you?" Nervous as hell.

Brendan Early looked up from his T-bone steak, tomatoes and scrambled eggs. He looked different than he did in the C.S. Fly photos: his face was thinner and he now wore a heavy mustache that curved down around his mouth and was darker than his hair.

"Let me hear your first question."

"Well—were you chucked out of the Army or did you retire?"

"You mean you are asking instead of telling me?" Brendan Early said. "Sit down."

Both surprised and encouraged, Maurice Dumas took off his cap and did as he was told. He couldn't believe it.

"I quit, resigned my commission," Bren Early said.

"What did you do right after that?"

"I rested."

"Thought of what you would do next?"

"Thought of staying alive. I thought quite a lot about it."

"Meaning you had to make a living?"

"I thought of ladies somewhat. But most often I thought of staying alive."

"I believe you advertised your services to lead western hunting expeditions. In Chicago and other eastern papers?"

"It's true. The advertisement said, 'Ladies welcome . . . Your dear lady will be well protected and taken care of.'"

"How long were you a hunting guide?"

"I wasn't a guide, I *hired* guides to do the work while I led the expeditions."

"How long did you do that?"

"Till I got tired of smiling."

The news reporter wasn't sure he understood that; but he preferred to cover ground rather than clear up minor points. He watched Mr. Early take a silver flask from inside his dark suitcoat and pour a good slug into his coffee.

"Is that whiskey?"

"Cognac. I don't drink whiskey in the morning."

"May I continue?"

"Please do."

"It's said you've killed between ten and twenty men. How many exactly did you?"

"That's not the question to ask."

Maurice Dumas thought a moment. "Did you know their names?"

And saw Mr. Early pause over his breakfast and look at him with interest.

"That's the question. How did you know to ask it?"

"It seemed like a good one," the reporter said.

Brendan Early nodded, saying, "It's interesting that some of them—I don't mean the backshooters, of course—would announce themselves with the sound of death in their tone. 'Mr. Early . . . I am R. J. Baker.' Then stare with a hard, solemn look, like I was supposed to faint or piss my britches."

"Really? What happened that time? The one said his name was Baker."

"Don't you want some breakfast?"

"I'll just have some of this coffee, if I may."

Eating his steak, watching the young reporter pour himself a cup from the silver pot on the table, Brendan Early said, "Are you sure you're from a newspaper? You aren't like the rest of that snotty bunch at all."

"*Chicago Times*," Maurice Dumas said. "There are so many things I want to ask you about." Including the mysterious Mrs. Pierson, who lived over on Mill Street. Was she just a friend or what?

"Don't be nervous." Brendan Early looked through the doors to the railroad clock in the hall. "We got till I get tired of talking or you decide you know more than I do. This morning I'm going shooting."

"You mean—up there?"

"No, I'm gonna step out into the desert and limber up my revolvers and test my eyesight."

"Getting ready for the showdown," Maurice Dumas said, squirming in his chair a little.

"You're starting to sound like the others," Brendan Early said. "Don't tell me things. Ask me."

"I'm sorry. How come you're going out to limber up your revolvers?"

"Today and tomorrow. I intend to shoot off several boxes of forty-fours. Because sometime soon, I've been told, an acquaintance from long ago will arrive in Benson by train, get here somehow or other, and I don't know his present frame of mind."

"You mean somebody who wants to kill you?"

"Ask him that one. Fella by the name of Phil Sundeen, come back from the dead."

Maurice Dumas frowned. What was going on? He said, "Sundeen. I don't believe I've heard that name before."

"Well, write it down. It could be an item for your paper."

4

1
Dragoon Mountains: April, 1888

The smell of the mares was on the wind, but the stud did not seem to like this graze as a place to breed. He lowered his head, giving the signal, and the mares and the stallions skitting around them followed after as the lead mare moved off.

Seven days Dana Moon had been tracking this herd, gradually, patiently moving the wild horses toward a barranca they'd fenced off with brush; a week of watching, getting to know them, Moon thinking on and off: If you were the stud, which one would you pick to mount first?

It would be hard. There were some good-looking mares in that bunch. But each time he wondered about it Moon found his gaze cutting out the palomino, the golden-haired girl, from the rest of the mares. She attracted the most overtures from the stallions who'd come sniffing her flanks. Moon would watch the palomino jump gracefully and give the boys a ladylike kick in the muzzle—saving it for the stud.

Out here a week tracking with his six Mimbre riders, former members of the Apache Police at San Carlos, now mustangers working for the Dana Moon Remount & Stage Team Supply Company—if anyone were to ask who he was and what he did.

Though it was not the answer he gave the fool who came riding upwind out of the sun haze. There he was, a speck of sound and smell and the herd was *gone*, like it would run forever, the Mimbres gathering and chasing off through the dust to keep them located. The fool, two black specks now, came clopping across the scrub waste, *clop clop clop clop*, leading a pack animal, not even knowing what a goddamn fool he was.

Yet he appeared to be a rider himself, sweat-dirty Stetson down on his eyes, someone who should know better.

A little bell rang inside Moon's head.

Pay attention.

"Are you Dana Moon?"

An official tone. A policeman verifying the name before saying you're under arrest. Or a messenger boy from somewhere.

"You just wiped out a week of tracking," Moon said. "You know it?"

"I guess it ain't your day," the man said and drew a pistol and immediately began firing at Moon, shooting him in the thigh, just above his right knee, shooting his horse through the neck and withers, the horse screaming and throwing its head as Moon drew his Colt's and shot the man twice through the chest.

He was a fool after all, not as real as he appeared. But who was he?

One of Moon's Mimbre riders, who was called Red, came back to find his boss sitting on the ground twisting his polka-dot scarf around his leg. The leg looked a mess, the entire thigh bleeding where the bullet had dug its way through Moon's flesh to come out just below his hip bone.

"I never even saw him before," Moon said. "See if he's got a wallet or something." He knew the man lying by his horse was dead; he didn't have to ask that.

There were seventeen dollars in a wallet and a folded soiled letter addressed to Asa Maddox, c/o Maricopa Cattle Company, Bisbee, Arizona Territory. The tablet-paper letter said:

Asa Maddox:

    That was good news you sent that you have finally got him located. If you do not want to wait for us I cannot stop you, but then we will not wait for you either and will proceed with our plan to get the other one. I think you are wrong in doing this alone instead of with us, but as I have mentioned I cannot stop you nor do I blame you much for your eagerness.
    Good luck.

(Signed)
J.A. McWilliams

Moon said, "Who is Asa Maddox? Who in the hell is J.A. McWilliams?"

Red, hunkered down next to Moon, looked at him but did not say anything.

"Well, shit," Moon said. "I guess I'm going to Benson a week early."

2
Florence: May, 1888

The cowboy standing at the end of the Grayback Hotel bar said, "Are you Captain Early?"

From his midpoint position, Bren Early's gaze moved from his glass of cold beer down in that direction.

"I am."

"There is a man here looking for you."

The man who stepped out from behind the rangy cowboy, a large-framed man himself, wore a dark business suit, a gold watch chain across the vest, a gray Stetson that looked like it had just come out of the box.

"Are you Mr. Johnson?" Bren Early asked. It was the name of the party he was supposed to meet here in Florence.

Instead of answering, the man walked over to a Douglas chair against the back wall where a maroon felt traveling bag sat waiting.

Bren Early liked businessmen hunters who were conscientious about the clause "Fee in Advance" and handed it over before they shook hands and said how much they'd been looking forward to this expedition. Raising his cold beer, Bren Early looked up at the clock on the wall between the back-bar mirrors. It was 11:48 in the morning. He liked the idea of putting five hundred dollars in his pocket before noon. He liked the quiet of a morning barroom—the heat and heavy work left outside with Bo Catlett and the light-blue hunting wagon. He'd bring Bo out a glass of beer after.

The cowboy was still sideways to the bar, facing this way. Like making sure he wasn't going to leave. Or so that he'd see the pistol stuck in the cowboy's belt. Why was this cowboy staring at him?

The man in the business suit was bending over his open traveling bag, taking a lot of time. Why wasn't the money on his person?

Bren Early put down his glass of beer. He heard the man in the business suit say, as the man came around, finally, with the pistol:

"This is for Jack McWilliams, you Indin-loving son of a bitch—"

(Though, the bartender testified at the Pinal County Sheriff's Inquest, the gentleman never got to say the last word.)

Bren Early shot the man with a .44 Smith & Wesson, the slug exploding from the barrel, obliterating the word and taking the man cleanly through the brisket . . . shot the cowboy dead through the heart, heard him drop his weapon and fall heavily as he put the Smith on the man in the business suit again, not 100 percent sure about this one.

The man was slumped awkwardly in a pole-axed daze, half-lying-sitting on the maroon travel bag, bewildered, wondering how his plan had suddenly gone to hell, staring up at Bren Early with maybe ten minutes of life remaining in him.

"You rehearsed that, didn't you?" Bren Early said. "I'll bet it sounded good when you said it to a mirror."

Blood seeped out between the man's fingers

pressed to his rib cage, trying to hold himself together, breathing and hearing the wound bubble and breathe back at him, sucking air, the man then breathing quicker, harder, to draw air up into his mouth before the wound got it all.

"You should not have begun that speech," Bren Early said. "But a lot of good it does advising you now, huh? . . . Has anybody an idea who this man is?"

J.A. McWilliams of Prescott, a supplier of drilling equipment and high explosives, according to identifying papers. The cowboy with him remained nameless—at least to Bren Early, who left Florence with Bo Catlett and their blue hunting wagon as soon as he was cleared of any willful intent to do harm.

McWilliams. It was a somewhat familiar name, but did not stir any clear recollections from the past.

3
Benson: May, 1888

For nearly a month Dana Moon lived in Room 107 of the Charles Crooker Hotel, waiting for his wound to heal. With the windows facing east it was a hot room mornings, but he liked it because it gave him a view of country and cottonwoods along the river. In the evening he listened to train whistles and the banging-clanging activity over in the switch yard.

He had planned to come to Benson a week later to visit the whorehouse and maybe call on Katy

McKean and see if there was a future respectable possibility there.

Now Katy McKean was calling on him. The first time she came he wondered: Will she leave the hotel room door open?

No, she didn't. She sat in the big chair between the windows, and Moon, sitting upright in bed, had to squint to see her face with the sun glare on the windows. He couldn't ask her to pull the shades. After her second visit he got up and struggled one-legged with the horsehide chair, moving it all the way around the bed and after that, when she came, the good view was to the west.

Well, how have you been? . . . Fine . . . I hardly recognize Benson the way it's grown . . . Has it? . . . You live with your folks? . . . Yes, and three young brothers; a place down the river a few miles . . . Bren ever come by to see you? . . . Now and then.

It required three visits from her before he asked, "How come you aren't married with a place of your own?"

"Why aren't you?"

"It hasn't been something I've thought about," Moon said. "Up till now." (Why was he saying this? He had come to town to visit the whorehouse and look at possibilities only.)

"Well, I haven't met the man yet," the McKean girl said. "They come out, my dad looks them over. The best he gives is a shrug. The drag riders he won't even speak to."

"Your dad," Moon said. "Whose choice is it, yours or his?"

"He knows a few things I haven't learned yet," the McKean girl said. She wore boots under her cotton skirt, the toes hooked on the sideboard of Moon's bed, her knees raised and a little apart. He couldn't see anything, but he was aware of her limbs and imagined them being very white and smooth, white thighs—Jesus—and a patch of soft hair.

Moon sat up straight in bed, the comforter pulled up to his waist over his clean longjohns, his hair and mustache combed, bay rum rubbed into his face and wearing his polka-dot scarf loosely for her visit. He was seasoned and weathered for his thirty-four years, looking closer to forty. The McKean girl was about twenty-three, a good-looking woman who could have her pick but was in no hurry; knew her own mind, or her dad's. Bren Early was thirty one or thirty two, closer to her age, liked the ladies and they liked him. Why, Moon wondered, did he always think of Bren when the McKean girl was here? Hell, ask her.

"Are you interested in Bren?"

"*In*terested? You mean to marry?"

"Yes."

"What's he got to offer? A wagon painted blue to look like a Conestoga, a string of horses . . . What else?"

"I wasn't thinking of what he owns."

"He's full of himself."

"He's got potential."

"Who hasn't?"

"What's your dad think of him?"

"My dad says time's passed him by."

"What's your dad do, whittle and say wise things?"

"He runs a cattle outfit and drives here twice a year," the McKean girl said. "When I got home from Old Mexico he rode up to San Carlos to shoot that one-eyed Apache dead, but they'd already shipped him off to Indian Territory."

"You have a deep fondness and respect for your old dad, haven't you?"

"He's the only one I got and he isn't that old."

"Man that marries you has to measure up to him?"

"I'd be a fool to choose less, wouldn't I?"

"I got to meet this dad of yours," Moon said.

"I'll fetch you in a buckboard," the McKean girl said.

During his third week Moon went downriver to a cluster of adobes, the McKean homestead, and sat out under the ramada in the early evening with her dad. They discussed gunshot wounds, reservation Indians, cattle, graze and wild horses. After a little while McKean invited Moon to share some corn whiskey with little specks of charcoal in it.

"You want to marry my daughter?"

Maybe important decisions were made like any other. Without thinking too much. "Yes, I do."

"I don't see what in the hell you got to give her."

"Me," Moon said.

"Well, you present more in person than any I've seen, including Captain Early; but what does she do, camp with your Mimbres and eat mule?"

"I'll think of a way," Moon said.

The next day when the McKean girl came to visit, and before she could sit down, Moon pulled her to him, felt her hold back till he got her down on the bed, lying across it, felt a terrible pain in his wounded thigh from the exertion and sweat break out on his forehead.

She said, "How're you going to do it?"

He thought she meant perform the act of love. "Don't worry, it can be done."

"You're gonna leave mustanging?"

"Oh," Moon said.

"And settle someplace?"

Moon nodded solemnly and said, "I love you," the first time in his life hearing the actual statement out loud.

"I hope so," the McKean girl said. "We can kiss and you can touch me up here if you want, but that's all till I see what my future is."

"It's a deal," Moon said.

He never did make it to the whorehouse. In fact, he swore he would never visit one again as long as he lived.

4

Apache Pass Station: September, 1888

This trip Bren Early had taken a party from Chicago, three men and the wife of one of them, south of the Pass into the Chiricahua Mountains for mule deer and a look at some authentic Apache Indians. The eastern hunters remained in camp while Bren and Bo Catlett drove the blue wagon to Apache Pass to pick up whiskey and supplies shipped down in the stage from Willcox. Bren was happy to get away from his five-hundred-dollar party.

He was in the back of the wagon, yawning and stretching, waking up from a nap, as Bo Catlett pulled the team into the station yard, Bo yelling at the agent's three kids to get out of the way. There were riding horses in the corral and, on the bench in front of the adobe, three saddles where they usually kept the wash basins. An olla of water hung from the mesquite-pole awning. Going inside, Bo Catlett noticed the saddles.

Three men who looked to have been sleeping as well as traveling in their suits of clothes were playing cards at the near end of the long passenger table. Edgar Watson, the station agent, said, "Where's the Captain?"

Bo Catlett didn't answer him. One of the men at the table stood up and moved to the door to look out. Edgar Watson was at the window now. He said, "There he is."

Looking past the man in the door, Bo Catlett could see Captain Early coming out of the wagon, climbing over the tailgate. The man in the doorway said to Edgar Watson, "Tell your kids to come inside." The other two were also standing now, both holding rifles. A shotgun lay on the table.

Pretending not to notice anything, Bo Catlett said, "Mr. Watson, draw a glass of beer if you will, please."

Edgar Watson, seeming bewildered, said a strange thing, considering what was going on in this close, low-ceilinged room. He said, "You know I can't serve you in here."

Bo Catlett believed he was born in Arkansas or Missouri. He was liberated by Jayhawkers and, at age fifteen, joined the 1st Kansas Colored Volunteers at Camp Jim Lane in February, 1863; saw immediate combat against Rebel irregulars and Missouri bushwhackers and was wounded at Honey Springs in June of '63. He guarded Confederate prisoners at Rock Island; served with the Occupation at Galveston and saw picket duty on the Rio Grande before transferring to the Department of Arizona where he drew the 10th Cavalry, Fort Huachuca, as his last regimental home in a twenty-four-year Army career. Some white officer—before Bren Early's time—dubbed Benjamin Catlett the *beau sabruer* of the nigger outfit and that was how he'd gotten his nickname. Bo Catlett was mustered out not long after the Sonora Incident—which did not affect his record—and had been working for Captain Early Hunting Expeditions, Inc. almost a year now. He liked to hear Bren Early talk about the war because the Captain was like a history book, full of information about battles and who did what. It didn't matter the Captain was still a little seven-year-old boy when fifteen-year-old Bo Catlett was getting shot through the hip at Honey Springs, or that the Captain didn't get his commission till something like ten years after Appomattox Court House. The Captain knew his war. He told Bo Catlett that he had never objected to colored boys being in the Army or killing white men during the war. But he would admit with candor his disappointment at being assigned to the Colored 10th rather than the "Dandy 5th," George Rosebud Crook's fighting outfit. No, the Captain had nothing against colored people.

There were sure some who did, though.

And there were some who had it in for the Captain, too.

Bren Early, standing by the tailgate of the wagon, wasn't wearing his revolvers. But as soon as he saw the three saddles on the wash bench and heard Edgar Watson call to his kids, Bren reached over the wagon gate, pulled his gunbelt toward him and was in that position, left arm inside, his fingers touching one of his revolvers, when the man's voice said, "We didn't expect you for a couple more days."

Bren looked over his right shoulder at the three coming out from the adobe, two rifles, a shotgun in the middle, and said to himself, Shit. There wasn't any way to mistake their intention.

The man with the shotgun, wearing a hat, an old suit and no collar or tie, said, "I'm R.J. Baker."

Bren Early waited. Yes? Why was that supposed to tell him anything? He said, "How do you do?" seeing Bo Catlett coming out of the adobe behind them: his dear friend and fellow cavalryman, the twenty-four-year seasoned campaigner he hoped to hell was at this moment armed to his teeth.

The man with the shotgun said, "It's time to even a score, you wavy-haired son of a bitch."

Wavy-haired, Bren Early thought and said, "If you intend to try it, you better look around behind you."

"God Almighty, you think I'm dumb!" the man named Baker said, as though it was the final insult. He jammed the shotgun to his shoulder; the barrels of the two rifles came up, metal flashing in the afternoon sunlight, and there was no way to stop them.

Edgar Watson, the station agent, had told his wife and children to stay in the kitchen. He heard the gunfire all at once, at least four or five shots exploding almost simultaneously. Edgar Watson rushed to the window by the bar and looked out to see the three cardplayers lying on the hardpack, Bren Early standing out by his wagon with a smoking revolver; then the colored man, Bo, who must have been just outside the house, walking out to look at the three on the ground.

When they came in, Edgar Watson drew a beer and placed it on the bar for Bren Early. He was surprised then when the colored man, Bo, raised an old Navy Colt's—exactly like the one kept under the bar—and laid it on the shiny oak surface. The colored man said, "Thank you for the use," before Edgar Watson realized it *was* his own gun. Bren Early told him to draw a beer for his friend Bo and Edgar Watson did so. Upon examining the Colt's, he found two rounds had been fired from the gun. Still, when Edgar Watson told the story later—and as many times as he told it—it was Bren Early who had shot the three cardplayers when they tried to kill him.

5
McKean's Ranch on the San Pedro: October, 1888

Moon rode up in the cool of early evening leading the palomino on a hackamore. He dropped the rope and the good-looking young mare stood right where she was, not flicking a muscle.

"She reminded me of you," Moon said to the McKean girl, who replied:

"I hope not her hind end."

"Her hair and her eyes," Moon said. "She answers to Goldie."

The McKean girl's mother and dad and three brothers came out to look at the palomino, the horse shying a little as they put their hands on her. Mr. McKean said the horse was still pretty green, huh? Moon said no, it was the horse had not seen so many people before at one time and felt crowded. They kidded him that he was bringing horses now, courting like an Indian.

Moon told them at supper he had been offered a government job as agent at White Tanks, working for the Bureau of Indian Affairs. He would be paid $1,500 a year and given a house and land for farming.

All the McKeans looked at Katy who was across the table from him, the mother saying it sounded wonderful.

Moon did not feel natural sitting there waiting for approval. He said, "But I don't care for flat land, no matter if it has good water and will grow anything you plant. I'm not a grain farmer. I told them I want high graze and would pick my own homesite or else they could keep their wonderful offer."

The McKeans all looked at Katy again.

"They're thinking about it," Moon said. "Meanwhile I got horse contracts to deliver."

"When'll you be back?" Mr. McKean asked.

"Not before Christmas."

"You wait too long," McKean said, "this girl might not be here."

"It's up to me when I get back and up to her if she wants to wait." Moon felt better as soon as he said it.

6
St. Helen: February, 1889

Bren Early said hadn't they met here one time before? Moon said it was a small world, wasn't it?

Moon here delivering a string of horses to the Hatch & Hodges relay station. Bren Early here to make a stage connection, out of the hunting expedition business and going to Tucson to sleep in a feather bed with a woman and make all the noise he wanted.

He said, "Do you know what it's like to make love to a woman dying for it and have to be quiet as a snake lest you wake up her husband?"

"No I don't," Moon said, "but I'm willing to hear about it."

There was snow up in the Rincons, a wind moaning outside, a dismal, depressing kind of day. But snug inside the relay station. They stood at the bar and had whiskey before Bren shed his buffalo overcoat and Moon peeled off his sheepskin and wornout chaps. Then sat at the plank table with a bottle of whiskey and mugs of coffee, smelling meat frying; next to them were giant shadows on the plaster wall, dark twin images in a glow of coal-oil light. Like two old pards drinking and catching up on each other's life, wondering how they could have spent a whole year and a half apart. Neither one of them mentioned the McKean girl.

The main topic: Was somebody shooting at you? Yeah—you too? And getting that business finally cleared up. Bren saying he had come out here to be

an Indian Fighter and so far had killed nine white
men, counting the first two from the bunch in
Sonora (the two Bo Catlett had shot), and two he
would tell Moon about presently. Moon, not digging up any bodies from the past, said, Well, you're
ahead of me there.

But what about this loving a woman and not
making any noise?

"Something happens to those women when they
come out here," Bren said. "Or it's the type of
woman to begin with, like to put a Winchester to
her shoulder and feel it kick."

"Or the wavy-haired guide giving her his U.S.
Cavalry look," Moon said. "You wear your saber?"

Bren straightened a little as if to argue, then
shrugged, admitting yes, there was a point in that
he was a man of this western country; and the
woman's husband, out here with his gold-plated
Henry in a crocodile case, was still a real-estate
man from Chicago or a home builder from Pitts-
burgh.

"Get to the good part," Moon said.

Bren told him about the party he took up into the
Chiricahuas: the man named Bert Grumbach, mil-
lionaire president of Prudential Realty in Chicago;
his colored valet; a young assistant in Grumbach's
company who wore a stiff collar and necktie, as
the man did; and the man's wife Greta, yes indeed,
who was even rounder and better-looking than
that French actress Sarah Bernhardt.

As soon as he met them at Willcox with the
wagon and saddle horses, Bren said he could see
what kind of trip it was going to be: the man, Bert
Grumbach, one of those know-it-all talkers, who'd

been everywhere hunting and had a game room full of trophies to prove it, considered this trip not much more than going out back to shoot rabbits. The wife, Greta, was quiet, not at all critical like other wives. ("How many times you gonna tell that tiger story?" Or, "You think drinking all that whiskey proves you're a man?") No, Bert Grumbach would be talking away and Bren would feel Greta's eyes on him. He'd glance over and sure enough, she'd be staring, giving him a calm, steady look with her eyes. Christ, Bren said, you knew exactly what she wanted.

She did not try to outdo her husband either, though she was a fair shot for a woman, dropping a mule-deer buck at two hundred yards with a clean hit through the shoulders.

Moon asked if they left deer laying all over the mountain and Bren said no, the guides took most of the meat to the fort Indians at Bowie.

It wasn't all hunting. Time was spent sitting around camp drinking, eating venison steaks, talking and drinking some more, Grumbach belittling the setup and the fare. Bren said he would perform a routine with his .44 Russians, blowing up a row of dead whiskey bottles, which the Eastern hunters usually ate up. Except Grumbach wasn't impressed. He had a matched pair of Merwin & Hulbert six-shooters, beauties he took out of a rosewood box, nickle-plated with carved ivory grips. He'd aim, left hand on his hip, and fire and hit bottles, cans, pine cones at twenty paces, chipmunks, ground squirrels, ospreys and horned owls. He was a regular killer, Bren said.

"And he caught you with his wife," Moon said.

"Not outright," Bren said. "I believe he only suspected, but it was enough."

What happened, Greta began coming to Bren's tent late at night. The first time, he tried in a nice way to get her to leave; but as she took her robe off and stood bare-ass, she said unless he did likewise she would scream. There was no choice but to give in to her, Bren said. But it was ticklish business, her moaning and him saying shhh, be quiet, his nerves alive as another part of him did the job at hand. Five or six nights, that was the drill.

The morning of the final day of the hunt, Bert Grumbach walked up to Bren, slapped his face with a glove and said, "I assume you will choose pistols. May I suggest twenty paces?"

Moon had an idea what happened next, since Bren was sitting here telling it; but he did not interrupt or even pick up his whiskey glass as Bren continued.

Bren said to the man, Now wait a minute. You know what you're doing? The man said he demanded satisfaction, his honor being abused. Bren said, But is it worth it? You might die. Grumbach gave him a superior look and had his assistant draw up a paper stating this was a duel of honor and if one of the participants was killed or injured, the other would not be legally culpable, hereby and so on, attesting with their signatures they were entering into it willingly and pledging to exonerate the other of blame whatever the outcome.

Bren said they stood about sixty feet apart, each with a revolver held at his side. Bo Catlett would fire his own weapon, the assistant holding a rifle on Bo to see he fired up in the air, and that would be the signal.

"Yeah?" Moon said, hunching over the plank table.

"Aiming at a man and seeing him drawing a bead on you isn't the same as shooting chipmunks," Bren said, "or even wilder animals."

"No, it isn't," Moon said. "He hurried, didn't he?"

"He dropped his hand from off his hip, stood straddle-legged and began firing as fast as he could. Having to protect myself, I shot him once, dead center."

"What did Greta do?"

"Nothing. We rolled Grumbach up in a piece of canvas, had a coffin made in Willcox and shipped him home with his legal papers. Greta said thank you very much for a wonderful and exciting time."

"Well," Moon said, "you have come to be a shooter, haven't you?"

"Not by choice," Bren said. "There was another fella at Bowie tried his luck when I sold my wagon and string. Announced he was an old compadre of one Clement Hurd. How come they all tracked after me and only one of them tried for you as a prize?"

"You advertise," Moon said. "Captain Early, the great hunter and lover. When did you get promoted?"

"I thought it sounded like a proper rank to have," Bren said. "Well, I've bid farewell to the world of commerce and won't be advertising any more. It's a good business if you have an agreeable nature and can stand grinning at people who don't know hotcakes from horseshit."

"I'm leaving my business, too," Moon said. "Gonna try working for the government one more time."

Bren Early was off somewhere in his mind. He sighed, turning in his chair to sit back against his shadow on the plaster wall.

"Down in Sonora that time, we stood at the line, didn't we?"

"I guess it's something you make up your mind to," Bren Early said, "if you don't care to kiss ass. But my, it can complicate your life."

⇥ 5 ⇤

1

Young Maurice Dumas of the *Chicago Times* looked at his list of THINGS TO DO:

Interview W.A. Vandozen, LaSalle Mining v.p. staying at Congress.

How? The only chance would be to run into the man accidentally, as he did with Early, and show the man he was courteous (took his cap off), industrious and did not ask personal or embarrassing questions or make brash assumptions.

And then kiss his heinie, why don't you? Maurice Dumas thought.

It had been pure luck with Brendan Early, the timing, catching him in a talkative mood. Then being invited out to the desert to watch him shoot: amazing, studying the man as he calmly blazed away with two different sets of matched revolvers: one pair, Smith & Wesson, big and mean-looking; the other, ivory-handled, nickle-plated Merwin & Hulberts that Early said were given to him by a wealthy and grateful lady from Chicago. Not saying why she had been grateful. At first—

out there shooting at saguaro and barrel cactus that were about the girth of a man—Early seemed troubled about the accuracy of his weapons. But within an hour his confidence was restored and as they rode back to Sweetmary Early told about the Sonora Incident and what he knew of Phil Sundeen. Which covered the next item on Maurice Dumas' THINGS TO DO.

Find out about this Sundeen.

Early said he had assumed the man was buried beneath Mexican soil and was surprised to learn he was alive and kicking. Different other LaSalle Mining people said that Sundeen had been hired by the company as Supervisor in Charge of Protection and Public Safety and was to see that no one infringed on company leases, destroyed company property or exposed themselves to harm or injury in areas related to company mining operations.

What?

The news reporters in the Gold Dollar said what it meant in plain English: Phil Sundeen had been hired to bust heads, shoot trespassers and run them off company land. And that included all the Indians, niggers and Mexicans living up in the Rincons. For months the two sides had been threatening and calling each other names. Finally, as soon as Sundeen arrived, there would be some action to write about. Yes, the company had called him in, a spokesman said, as an expert in restoring order and maintaining peace.

Good, the newsmen said, because it certainly wasn't much of a war without any shooting.

"I said restore peace," the company spokesman

said. And a reporter said, "We know what you mean."

But wait a minute. Why hire Sundeen? Why not let Bren Early, known to be a shooter, restore order and maintain peace?

Because Mr. Early had his own responsibilities as Coordinating Manager of the Southwest Region, the company spokesman said.

According to the journalists that was a pile of horseshit. Not one of them, including Maurice Dumas, had yet to see Bren Early sitting at a desk or coordinating much other than a draw poker hand. Bren Early had been hired as part of the deal when the company bought his claims, and his executive title had been made up out of thin air. They *could* put him to work if they wanted. Otherwise Early was to keep himself available to show visiting dignitaries and politicians the Works: which meant the local whorehouses and gambling parlors and— if the visitors were inclined—take them out hunting or to look at some live Indians. It was said the company was paying Early a guaranteed $100,000 over ten years, plus a one-percent royalty on all the milled copper sent to market. He was a rich man.

O.K., but now Early and Sundeen were on the same side. What about the bitterness between them—as reported by Maurice Dumas? How would it affect the Early-Moon Feud? Would it be like a preliminary event, winner getting to go against Dana Moon?

The journalists sat down to have a few drinks and think about that one, see if they could develop a side issue cross-plot to lay over the main action. They fooled with possible headline themes such as:

Prospect of Preliminary Showdown Delays War
Will New Man Live to Take Command?
Shoot-Out Expected on LaSalle Street

All this even before Phil Sundeen arrived in town. If he had the least intention of gunning for Bren Early he would find the atmosphere most conducive.

Meanwhile, Maurice Dumas was working on the third item on his list of THINGS TO DO.

Interview Dana Moon.

2

When Maurice Dumas arrived at White Tanks he didn't know what was going on: all these Apaches, about a hundred of them out in the pasture near the agency buildings and stock pens, sitting around campfires, roasting chunks of beef while others were chanting and a line of women were doing some kind of shuffle dance. Like it was an Indian Fourth of July picnic or some kind of tribal pow-wow. Some of the men wore hats and parts of white men's clothes, a pair of trousers, a vest; though most of them still wore skirts and high moccasins and thick headbands wrapped around their coarse hair.

Maurice Dumas found out it was Meat Day. When the beef allotment provided by the government was delivered, the Apaches always butchered a few head on the spot and had a feast. They would stuff themselves with meat, eating it straight, drink some corn beer, or tulapai, as it was called, spend the night here in the agency pasture and, in the morning, drive their skimpy herd up into the mountains to their rancherías. Maurice Dumas remembered being told that Apaches always camped high and wouldn't be caught dead living down in the flats. It was part of the problem in this land dispute which he wanted to discuss with Dana Moon—if he could find him.

Well, it seemed he was getting luckier all the time—just by chance arriving on Meat Day—dismounting his hired horse in front of the Indian Agency office, a one-story adobe building with a wooden front porch, and there was Moon himself sitting in a straight chair tilted back, his boots up on the porch rail, at rest. Perfect, Maurice Dumas thought. The Indian agent in his seat of governmental authority, while his charges performed their tribal rites.

Moon looked exactly as he did in the C.S. Fly photos, though not as buttoned up and strapped together. He did not appear to be armed. His belt buckle was undone and he was smoking a cigar. When Maurice Dumas introduced himself, Moon asked if he would like something to eat. The news reporter said no thanks. He handed Moon a paper bag saying, "A little something for you," and watched as Moon took out the bottle of Green River bourbon whiskey and read the label unhurriedly before placing the quart on the plank floor next to him. "Thank you," he said.

"I just wanted to talk to you a little," Maurice Dumas said. "Ask your opinion of a few things."

"Ask," Moon said.

"I didn't think you lived here at the agency."

"I don't. I'm a few miles up that barranca,"

lowering his head and looking west, beyond the pasture and the gathering of feasting Indians. "I'm here for Meat Day and will leave soon as I'm able to." He seemed full but not too uncomfortable.

"Do you live up there alone?"

"My wife and I."

"Oh, I didn't know you were married."

"Why would you?"

"I mean nobody's mentioned it."

"Does it make a difference in how you see me?"

"I mean I'm just surprised," Maurice Dumas said. "If there's gonna be trouble and all—I was thinking, having your wife there could make it harder for you."

Moon said, "Do you know how many wives are up there? How many families?"

"I guess I hadn't thought of it."

"You call it a war, you like to keep it simple," Moon said. "These men against those men. Line 'em up, let's see who wins. Well, to do that we'd have to get rid of the women and children. Where should we send them?"

"As I said, I hadn't thought about it."

"What do you think about?" Moon asked. The front legs of the chair hit the plank floor as Moon got up and went into the agency office.

Now what? Was he offended by something? No, Moon came out again with two glasses, sat down and poured them a couple of drinks.

Maurice Dumas pulled a chair over next to Moon's. "I'm only an observer," he said, sitting down and carefully tilting back. "I don't take sides, I remain objective."

"You're on a side whether you like it or not,"

Moon said. "You're on the side of commerce and, I imagine, you believe in progress and good government."

"What's wrong with that?"

"Copper is progress and the land has been leased to the mine company by the government."

Maurice Dumas didn't like the insinuation. "That doesn't mean I'm on the side of the company. But if we're talking about legal rights, I'd have to say *they*, the legal right, are. The company owns mineral rights to the land for a hundred years."

"You feel that's long enough?"

"I don't know how long it takes."

Moon took a sip of whiskey and drew on his cigar. "You happen to know what the mine company's doing up there?"

"Right now they're surveying," Maurice Dumas said, "trying to locate veins and ore loads that look promising."

"And how are they doing that?"

"As I understand, they set off dynamite, then pick around, see what they've got."

Moon waited.

"So far, I guess they haven't found anything worth sinking a shaft in."

"But they spook the herds, scatter 'em all over, kill what they want for meat," Moon said. "They've blown up stock tanks, ruined the natural watershed, wiped out crops and some homes in rock slides. They tear up a man's land, clean him out, and leave it."

"It's theirs to tear up," the news reporter said.

"No, it isn't," Moon said, in a quiet but ominous tone.

The whiskey made Maurice Dumas feel confident and knowledgeable. He said, "I'd like to say you're right. Good for you. But the fact remains your Indians are off the White Tanks reservation by several miles. And the other people up there, whoever they are, are living on land without deed or title. So LaSalle Mining, legally, has every right to make them leave."

"You asked my opinion," Moon said. "Are you gonna print it in the paper?"

"I hope to, yes."

"You're not writing anything down."

"I have a good memory," Maurice Dumas said.

"Well, remember this," Moon said. "The Mimbre Apaches were hunting up there before Christopher Columbus came over in his boat, and till now nobody's said a word about it, not even the Indian Bureau. There's a settlement of colored people, colored soldiers who've taken Indian wives, all of them at one time in the United States Tenth Cavalry. You would think the government owed them at least a friendly nod, wouldn't you? The Mexicans living up there have claims that go back a hundred years or more to Spanish land grants. The Mexicans went to Federal Claims Court to try to protect their property. They got thrown out. I wrote to the Indian Bureau about the Apaches up there—it's *their* land, let 'em live on it. No, they said, get your people back to White Tanks or you're fired. You see the influence the company has? Generations they've hunted, roamed through those mountains. Government doesn't say a word till the big company kneels on 'em for a favor. Yes sir, we'll see to it right away, Mr. LaSalle—"

"Is there a Mr. LaSalle?" Maurice didn't think so.

"I went to Federal District Court to get an injunction. I wanted to restrict the mine company to certain areas—they find ore, O.K., they pay a royalty on it to any people that have to move. They don't find any ore, they clean up their mess and get out. The judge held up my injunction—cost me fifty dollars to have written—like it was paper you keep in the privy and threw it out of court."

"Legal affairs get complicated," the news reporter offered.

"Do you want to tell me how it is," Moon said, "or you want to listen."

"I'm sorry. Go on."

"All these people I've mentioned number only about two hundred and sixty, counting old ones, women and young children. Fewer than fifty able-bodied men. And they're spread all over. By that, I mean they don't present any kind of unified force. The mine company can send a pack of armed men up there with guns and dynamite to take the land, and you know what will happen?"

"Well, eventually—" the reporter began.

"Before eventually," Moon said. "You know what will happen? Do you want to go ask the people what they'll do if armed men come?"

"Will they tell me?"

"They'll tell you it's their land. If the company wants it, the company will have to take it."

"Well," the news reporter said, a little surprised, "that's exactly what the company will do, take it."

"When you write your article for the paper," Moon said, "don't write the end till it happens."

6

1
White Tanks: May, 1889

Moon and four Mimbre Apaches were white-washing the agency office when the McKean girl rode up on her palomino. They appeared to have the job almost done—the adobe walls clean and shining white—and were now slapping the wash on a front porch made of new lumber that looked to be a recent addition.

The McKean girl wore a blue bandana over her hair and a blue skirt that was bunched in front of her on the saddle and hung down on the sides just past the top of her boots.

Sitting her horse, watching, she thought of India: pictures she had seen of whitewashed mud buildings on barren land and little brown men in white breechclouts and turbans—though the head-pieces the Apaches wore were rusty red or brown, dark colors, and their black hair hung in strands past their shoulders. It was strange she thought of India Indians and not American Indians. Or not so strange, because this place did not seem to belong in the mountains of Arizona. Other times looking at Apaches, when she saw them close, she thought of gypsies: dark men wearing regular clothes, but in strange, colorful combinations of shirts made from dresses beneath checkered vests, striped pants tucked into high moccasins and wearing jewelry, men wearing beads and metal trinkets. The Mexicans called them barbarians. People the McKean girl knew called them red niggers and heathens.

Moon—he was saying something in a strange tongue and the Apaches, with whitewash smeared over their bare skin, were laughing. She had never heard an Apache laugh, nor had even thought of them laughing before this. Coming here was like visiting a strange land.

One of the Apaches saw her and said something to Moon. He turned from his painting and came down from the porch as the Apaches watched. He looked strange himself: suspenders over his bare, hairy chest, his body pure white but his forearms weathered brown, like he was wearing long gloves. He was looking at her leg, her thigh beneath the skirt, as he approached.

She expected him to pat the mare and pretend to be interested in her, saying how's Goldie. But he didn't. He looked from her leg up to her face, squinting in the sun, and said, "You getting anxious?"

"It's been seven months," Katy McKean said. "If you've changed your mind I want to know."

"I've been building our house," Moon said.

The McKean girl looked at the whitewashed adobe, and the stock pens, the outpost on the barren flats, dressed with a flagpole flying the stars and stripes. Like a model post office.

"That?" she said.

"Christ, no," Moon said. "That's not a house, that's a symbol. Our house is seven miles up the draw, made of 'dobe plaster and stone. Front porch is finished and a mud fence is being put up now."

"You like front porches," the McKean girl said. "Well, they must've given you what you wanted. What do you do in return?"

"Keep the peace. Count heads. I'm a high-paid tally hand is what I am."

"Tell them jokes, like you were doing?"

"See eye to eye," Moon said. "A man catches his wife in the bushes with some other fella—you know what he does? He cuts the end of her nose off. The wife's mother gets upset and tells the police to arrest the husband and punish him and the police dump it in my lap."

"And what do you do?"

"Tell the woman she looks better with a short nose—I don't know what I do," Moon said. "I live near them—not with them—and try not to change their customs too much."

"Like moving to a strange heathen land," the McKean girl said, unconsciously touching her nose.

"Well, Christian people, they caught a woman in adultery they used to stone her to death. Customs change in time."

"But they never do anything to the man," the McKean girl said.

"Ask your dad, the old philosopher, about that one," Moon said. "Ask him if it's all right for you to come live among the heathens."

"When?"

"Next fall sometime," Moon said. "October."

"Next month," the McKean girl said, "the third Saturday in June at St. John the Apostle's, ten A.M. Who's gonna be your best man, one of these little dark fellas?"

The wedding took place the fourth Saturday in June and the best man was Brendan Early: Bren looking at the bride in church, looking at her in the dining room of the Charles Crooker Hotel where the reception was held, still not believing she had chosen quiet Dana Moon. It wasn't that Bren had sought her hand and been rejected. He had not gotten around to asking her; though it had always been in the back of his mind he might easily marry her someday. Right now, as Dana's wife, she was the best-looking girl he had ever seen, and the cleanest-looking, dressed in white with her blonde hair showing. And now it was too late. Amazing. Like he'd blinked his eyes and two years had passed. They asked him what he was doing these days and he said, well (not about to tell these industrious people he was making a living as a minecamp cardplayer), he was looking into a mining deal at the present time—saying it because he had in his pocket the title to a staked-out claim he'd won in a $2,000-call poker game. Yes, he was in mining now.

And told others on the Helvetia stage—pushed by a nagging conscience or some curious urge, having seen his old chum settling down with a wife he thought *he* would someday have. Time was passing him by and it wasn't the ticket for a gentleman graduate of the U.S. Military Academy to be making a living dealing faro or peaking at hole cards. Why *not* look into this claim he now owned? He had title and a signed assay report that indicated a pocket of high-yield gold ore if not a lode.

Starting out on that return trip to nowhere he was in mining. Before the stage had reached its destination, Bren Early was in an altogether different situation.

2
The Benson-Helvetia Stage: June, 1889

Three very plain-looking ladies who had got off the train from an Eastern trip had so much baggage, inside and out, there was only room for Bren Early and one other passenger: a fifty-year-old dandy who wore a cavalry mustache, his hat brim curved up on one side, and carried a cane with a silver knob.

Bren Early and the Dandy sat next to each other facing the plain-looking, chattering ladies who seemed excitable and nervous and were probably sweating to death in their buttoned-up velvet travel outfits. Facing them wasn't so bad; Bren could look out the window at the countryside moving past in the rickety, rattling pounding of the stagecoach; but the Dandy, with his leather hatbox and travel bag, lounged in a way that took up more than half the seat, sticking his leg out at an angle and forcing Bren Early to sit against the sideboards. Bren nudged the Dandy's leg to acquire more room and the Dandy said, "If you don't mind, sir," sticking his leg out again.

"I do," Bren Early said, "since I paid for half this bench."

"And I paid in receiving a wound to this leg in the war," the Dandy said. "So, if you don't mind."

The ladies gave him sympathetic looks and one of them arranged her travel case so the Dandy could prop his leg on it. The Dandy had a cane, yes, but Bren Early had seen the man walk out of the Benson station to the coach without a limp or faltering gait. Then one of the ladies asked him whom he had served with.

The Dandy said, "I had the honor of serving with the Texas Brigade, Madam, attached to General Longstreet's command, and received my wound at the Battle of the Wilderness, May 6, 1864. Exactly twenty-five years ago last month."

Bren Early listened, thinking, Ask him a question, he gives you plenty of answer. One of the ladies said it must have been horrible being wounded in battle and said she was so thankful she was a woman.

"It was ill fate," the Dandy said, "to be wounded in victory while giving the enemy cold steel, routing them, putting to flight some of the most highly regarded regiments in Yankeedom. But I have no regrets. The fortunes of war sent a minié ball through my leg and an Army wagon delivered me to the hospital at Belle Plain."

"Whose wagon?" Bren Early said.

The Dandy gave him a superior look and said, "Sir?"

"You are only half right in what you tell these ladies," Bren Early said. "You did meet six of the most respected regiments in the Union Army: the Second, Sixth and Seventh Wisconsin, the Nineteenth Indiana and the Twenty-fourth Michigan.

You met the men of the Iron Brigade and if you ever meet one again, take off your hat and buy him a drink, for you're lucky to be alive."

"You couldn't have been there," the Dandy said, still with the superior look.

"No," Bren Early said, "but I've studied the action up and down the Orange Plank Road and through the woods set afire by artillery. The Iron Brigade, outnumbered, fought Longstreet to a standstill and *you*, if you were taken to Belle Plain then you went as a prisoner because the Confederate line never reached that far east."

The Dandy looked at the ladies and shrugged with a weary sigh. See what a wounded veteran has to put up with?

Bren Early had to hold on from grabbing the mincing son of a bitch and throwing him out the window. With the ladies giving him cold-fish looks he pulled his new Stetson down over his eyes and made up his mind to sleep.

Lulled by the rumbling racket of the coach he saw himself high on a shelf of rock against a glorious blue sky, a gentle breeze blowing. There he was on the narrow ledge, ignoring the thousand-foot drop directly behind him, swinging his pick effortlessly, dislodging a tremendous boulder and seeing in the exposed seam the glitter of gold particles imbedded in rock, chunks of gold he flicked out with his penknife, nuggets he scooped up from the ground and dropped into canvas sacks. He saw a pile of sacks in a cavern and saw himself hefting them, estimating the weight of his fortune at $35 an ounce . . . $560 a pound . . . $56,000 a hundred pounds . . . He slept and awoke to feel the coach swaying, slowing down, coming to a stop, the three ladies and the Dandy leaning over to look out the windows. The driver, or somebody up above them, was saying, "Everybody do what they say. Don't anybody try to be brave."

The ladies were now even more excitable and nervous and began to make sounds like they were going to cry. The Dandy gathered his hatbox and travel bag against him and slipped his right hand inside his waistcoat.

The voice up top said, "We're not carrying no mail or anything but baggage."

And another voice said, "Let's see if you can step off the boot with your hands in the air."

Shit, Bren Early thought.

His revolvers were in his war-bag beneath his feet, stowed away so as not to upset the homely, twittery ladies, and, for the sake of comfort. What would anybody hope to get robbing this chicken coop? The only important stop between Benson and points west was Sweetmary, a mining town; and he doubted a tacky outfit like this stage line would be entrusted to deliver a payroll. No—he was sure of it, because there was just the driver on top, no armed guard with him, not even a helper. Cheap goddamn outfit.

A rider on a sorrel came up to the side of the coach, Bren seeing his pistol extended, a young cowboy face beneath an old curled-brim hat.

"You, mister," the young rider said to the Dandy, "let me see your paws. All of you keep your paws out in plain sight."

Another one, Bren Early was thinking. Practiced it and it sounded good. Times must be bad.

Looking past the sorrel Bren could see two more riders beyond the road in the scrub, and the driver standing by the front wheel now, a shotgun on the ground. The rider on the sorrel was squinting up at the baggage, nudging his horse closer. He dismounted then and opened the coach door to look in at the petrified ladies in velvet and the two gentlemen across from them. Someone behind the young rider yelled, "Pull that gear offa there!"

Making him do all the work while they sit back, Bren thought. Dumb kid. In bad company.

The young rider stepped up on the rung and into the door opening, reaching up to the baggage rack with both hands. His leather chaps, his gunbelt, his skinny trunk in a dirty cotton skirt were right there, filling the doorway. Bren thinking, He's too dumb to live long at his trade. Hoping the kid wasn't excitable. Let him get out of here with some of the ladies' trinkets and the Dandy's silver cane and think he's made a haul. Bren had three twenty-dollar gold pieces and some change he'd contribute to the cause. Get it done so they could get on with the ride.

Sitting back resigned, letting it happen, Bren wasn't prepared—he couldn't believe it—when the fifty-year-old Dandy made his move, hunching forward as he drew a nickle-plated pistol from inside his coat and shoved the gun at the exposed shirtfront in the doorway, pointing the barrel right where the young rider's shirttail was coming out of his pants as he reached above him.

Bren said, "No!" grabbing at the Dandy's left arm, the man wrenching away and coming back to swat him across the face with his silver-tipped cane—the son of a bitch, if that was the way he wanted it . . . Bren cocked his forearm and back-handed his fist and arm across the man's upper body. But too late. The nickle-plate jabbed into the shirtfront and went off with a report that rang loud in the wooden coach. The young rider cried out, hands in the air, and was gone. The women were screaming now and the Dandy was firing again—the little dude son of a bitch, maybe he *had* raised hell at the Wilderness with his Texas Brigade. He was raising hell now, snapping shots at the two riders until Bren Early backhanded him again, hard, giving himself room to get out of the coach.

He saw the young rider lying on the ground, the sorrel skitting away. He saw the driver kneeling, raising the shotgun and the two mounted men whipping their horses out of there with the twin sounds of the double-barrel reports, the riders streaking dust across the scrub waste, gone, leaving the young rider behind.

Kneeling over him, Bren knew the boy was dead before he touched his throat for a pulse. Dead in an old blood-stained shirt hanging out of his belt; converted Navy cap-and-ball lying in the dust next to him. Poor dumb kid, gone before he could learn anything. He heard the Dandy saying something.

"He's one of them."

Bren Early looked up, seeing the driver coming over, reloading the shotgun.

"I had a feeling about him and, goddamn it, I was right," the Dandy said. "He's the inside man. Tried to stop me."

Bren said, "You idiot. You killed this boy for no reason."

The driver was pointing his shotgun at him, saying, "Put your hands in the air."

3
Sweetmary: June, 1889

Mr. and Mrs. Dana Moon got out of the Charles Crooker Hotel in Benson after two honeymoon nights in the bridal suite and coming down to breakfast to feel everybody in the dining room looking at them and the waitress grinning and saying, "Well, how are we this morning, just fine?" They loaded a buckboard with their gear, saddles, two trunks of linen, china and household goods, and took the old stage road west, trailing their horses. Why stay cooped up in somebody else's room when they had a new home in the mountains with an inside water pump and a view of practically the entire San Pedro Valley?

In late afternoon they came to Sweetmary, a town named for a copper mine, a town growing out of the mine works and crushing mill high up on the grade: the town beginning from company buildings and reaching down to flatland to form streets, rows of houses and business establishments—Moon remembering it as a settlement of tents and huts, shebangs made of scrap lumber, only a year before—the town growing out of the mine just as the hump ridges of ore tailings came down the grade from the mine shafts. LaSalle was the main street and the good hotel was in Congress. One more night in somebody else's bed. In the morning they'd buy a few provisions at the company store and head due north for home.

During this trip Moon said to his wife, "You're a Katy a lot of ways; I think you'll always look young. But you're not a bashful girl, are you? I think you're more of a Kate than a Katy, and that's meant as a compliment."

In the morning, lying in the Congress Hotel bed with the sun hot on the windows, he said, "I thought people only did it at night. I mean married people."

"Who says you have to wait till dark?" She grinned at him and said then, "You mean if you're not married you can do it any time?"

"You do it when you see the chance. I guess that's it," Moon said. "Married people are busy all day, so it's become the custom to do it at night."

"Custom," Kate said. "What's the custom among the Indians? I bet whenever they feel the urge, right? You ever do it outside?"

Moon pretended he had to think to recall and Kate said, "I want to do it outside when we get home."

"I built us a *bed*."

"We'll use the bed. But I want to do it different places. Try different other ways."

Moon looked at this girl lying next to him, amazed. "What other way is there?"

"I don't know if we can do them in the daylight, but I got some ideas." She smiled at him and said, "Being married is fun, you know it?"

Moon was getting dressed, buttoning his shirt and looking out the window, when he saw Brendan Early. He said, "Jesus Christ." Kate came over in her bloomers to look too.

There he was, Moon's best man, walking along the street in a file of jail prisoners carrying shovels and picks, the group dressed in washed-out denim uniforms—the letter "P" stenciled in white on the shirts and pants—being herded along by several armed men on horseback.

"Jesus Christ," Moon said again, with awe. "What's he done now?"

When Moon found them, the work detail was clearing a drainage ditch about two miles from town, up in the hills back of the mine works. Mounted, he circled and came down from above them to approach Bren Early working with a shovel, in his jail uniform, his new Stetson dirty and sweat-stained. There were four guards with shotguns. The one on the high side, dismounted and sitting about ten yards off in the shade of a cedar stand, heard Moon first and raised his shotgun as he got to his feet.

"Don't come no closer!"

Now Bren Early straightened and was looking this way, leaning on the high end of his shovel. He watched Moon nudging his buckskin down toward them—not knowing Moon's game, so not calling out or saying anything.

"I said don't come no closer!"

This man with the shotgun was the Cochise County Deputy Sheriff for Sweetmary. His name—Moon had learned in town—was R. J. Bruckner. Moon said it now, inquiringly.

"Mr. Bruckner?"

"What do you want?"

There did not appear to be any warmth or cordiality in the man.

He was heavy-set and mean-looking with a big nose and a florid complexion to go with his ugly disposition. Moon would try sounding patient and respectful and see what happened.

He said, "My, it's a hot day to be working, isn't it?"

"You got business with me, state it," Bruckner said, "or else get your nosey ass out of here."

My oh my, Moon thought, taking off his hat and resetting it low against the sun, giving himself a little time to adjust and remain calm. The plug of tobacco in his jaw felt dry and he sucked on it a little.

"I wonder if I could have a word with one of your prisoners."

"God Almighty," Bruckner said, "get the hell away from here."

"That good-looking fella there, name of Early. His mama's worried about him," Moon said, "and sent me out looking."

"Tell his mama she can visit him at Yuma. That boy's going away for twenty years."

"Can I ask what he's done?"

"Held up the Benson stage and was caught at it."

Bren Early, standing in the drainage ditch, was shaking his head slowly, meaning no, he didn't, or just weary of it all.

"Has he been tried already?"

"Hasn't come up yet."

"Then how do you know he's getting twenty years?"

"It's what I'll recommend to the Circuit Court in Tombstone."

"Oh," Moon nodded, showing how agreeable he was. "When is the trial going to be?"

"When I take him down there," Bruckner said.

"Pretty soon now?"

"When I decide," Bruckner said, irritated now. "Get the hell away from here 'fore I put you in the ditch with him."

R. J. Bruckner did not know at that moment—as Moon's hand went to his shirtfront but stopped before going inside the coat—how close he was to being shot.

Back at the Congress Hotel Moon said to his wife, "I have never had the urge like I did right then. It's not good, to be armed and feel like that."

"But understandable," Kate said. "What are we gonna do?"

"Stay here another night, if it's all right."

"Whatever you decide," his wife said. She loved this man very much, but sometimes his calmness frightened her. She watched him wash and change his shirt and slip on the shoulder holster that held the big Colt's revolver—hidden once his coat was on, but she knew it was there and she knew the man, seeing him again standing at the adobe wall in Sonora.

After supper Mr. and Mrs. Moon sat in rocking chairs on the porch of the Congress Hotel—Kate saying, "This is what you like to do, huh?"—until the Mexican boy came up to them and said in Spanish, "He left." Moon gave the boy two bits and walked down LaSalle Street to the building with the sign that said DEPUTY SHERIFF—COCHISE COUNTY.

Inside the office he told the assistant deputy on duty he was here to see a prisoner, one Brendan Early and, before the deputy could say anything, laid a five-dollar piece on the man's desk.

"Open your coat," the deputy said.

Moon handed the man his Colt's, then followed him through a locked door, down an aisle of cells and up a back stairway to a row of cells on the second floor. Moon had never seen a jail this size, able to hold thirty or more prisoners, in a dinky mining town.

"You know *why*," Bren Early said, talking to Moon through the bars—the deputy standing back a few paces watching them—"because the son of a bitch is making money off us. The mine company pays him fifty cents a day per man to work on roads and drainage and this horse fart Bruckner puts it in his pocket."

"You talk to a lawyer?"

"Shit no, not till I go to trial. Listen, there're rummies in here for drunk and disorderly been working *months*. He thinks I'm a road agent, I could be in here a *year* before I ever see a court-room. And then I got to face this other idiot who's gonna point to me and say I tried to rob the stage."

"Did you?"

"Jesus Christ, I'm telling you, I don't get out of here I'm gonna take my shovel and bust it over that horse fart's head."

"You're looking pretty good though," Moon said. "Better'n you did at the wedding trying to drink up all the whiskey."

Close to the bars Bren Early said, "You gonna get me out of here or I have to do it myself?"

"I have to take my wife home," Moon said. "Then, after that."

"After that, what? I'm not gonna last any time in this place. You know it, too."

"Don't get him mad at you," Moon said. "Say please and thank you or else keep your mouth shut till I get back."

"When—goddamn it."

"You might see it coming," Moon said, "but I doubt it."

This jail was hard time with no relief. Chop rocks and clear ditches or sweat to death in that second-floor, tin-roof cell. (The Fourth of July they sat up there listening to fools shooting their guns off in the street, expecting any moment bullets to come flying in the barred windows.) Bren Early could think of reports he'd read describing Confederate prisons, like Belle Isle in the James River and Libby's warehouse in Richmond, where Union soldiers rotted away and died by the thousands. Compared to those places the Sweetmary lockup was a resort hotel. But Bren would put R.J. Bruckner up with any of the sadistic guards he'd read about, including the infamous Captain Wirz of Andersonville.

One day after work Bruckner marched Bren Early down to the basement of the jail and took him into a room that was like a root cellar. Bren hoped for a moment he would be alone with Bruckner, but two other deputies stood by with pick handles while Bruckner questioned him about the stage holdup.

"One of your accomplices, now deceased, was named Pierson. What are the names of the other two?"

They stood with the lantern hanging behind them by the locked door.

"I wasn't part of it, so I don't know," Bren Early said.

Bruckner stepped forward and hooked a fist into Bren's stomach and Bren hit him hard in the face, jolting him; but that was his only punch before the two deputies stepped in, swinging their pick handles, and beat him to the dirt floor.

Bruckner said, "What's the names of your other two chums?"

Bren said, "I never saw 'em before."

"Once more," Bruckner said.

"I'll tell you one thing," Bren said.

"What is that?"

"When I get out I'm gonna tear your nose off, you ugly shitface son of a bitch."

As with J.A. McWilliams, killed in Florence a year before while calling Bren Early some other kind of son of a bitch, did he say it all or not? Bren did not quite finish before Bruckner hit him with his fists and the deputies waded in to beat him senseless with the pick handles. Dumb, wavy-haired know-it-all; they fixed him. And they'd see he never let up a minute out on the work detail . . . where Bren would look up at the high crests and at the brushy ravines and pray for Moon to appear as his redeemer.

"You might see it coming, but I doubt it," Moon had said.

Moon brought six Mimbre Apaches with him: the one named Red and five other stalkers who had chased wild horses with him, had served on the

Apache Police at San Carlos and had raised plenty of hell before that.

They scouted Bruckner's work detail for three days, studying the man's moves and habits. The man seemed reasonably alert, that was one consideration. The other: the ground was wide open on both sides of the drainage ditch where the twenty or more prisoners had been laboring these past few days. Clearing a ditch that went where? Moon wasn't sure, unless it diverted water from the mine shafts. A slit trench came down out of a wash from the bald crest of a ridge. There were patches of owl clover on the slope, brittlebush and stubby clumps of mesquite and greasewood, but no cover to speak of.

Moon and his Mimbres talked it over in their dry camp and decided there was only one way to do the job.

Seven A.M., the seventeenth morning of Bren Early's incarceration, found him trudging up the grade with his shovel, second man in the file of prisoners—herded by four mounted guards, Bruckner bringing up the rear—Bren's eyes open as usual to scan the bleak terrain, now reaching the section of ditch they would be working today, moving up alongside it until Bruckner would stick two fingers in his mouth and whistle them to stop, jump in and commence digging and clearing.

Bren didn't see Moon. He didn't see the Mimbre Apaches—not until he heard that sharp whistle, the signal, turned to the trench and saw movement, a bush it looked like, a *bush* and part of the ground coming up out of the ditch, Christ, with a face made of dirt in it, seeing for the first time something he had only heard about: what it was like to stand in open terrain and, Christ, there they were all around you right *there* as you stood where there wasn't a sign of anything living a moment before. The Mimbres came out of the drainage ditch with greasewood in their hair, naked bodies smeared with dirt, and took the four deputies off their horses and had them on the ground, pointing revolvers in their struck-dumb faces before they knew what had happened. There were yells from the prisoners dancing around. Some of them raised their shovels and picks to beat the life out of Bruckner and his guards. But Moon and his stubby shotgun—Moon coming out of the ditch a few yards up the grade—would have none of it. He was not here in behalf of their freedom or revenge. They yelled some more and began to plead—Take us with you; don't leave us here—then cursed in loud voices, with the guards lying face down in the sand, calling Moon obscene names. But Moon never said a word to them or to anyone. Bren Early wanted to go over to Bruckner, but when Moon motioned, he followed. They rode out of there on the deputies' horses and never looked back.

Bren Early went home with Moon, up past the white-washed agency buildings, up into the rugged east face of the Rincons. He saw Moon's stone house with its low adobe wall rimming the front of the property and its sweeping view of the San Pedro Valley. He saw Moon's wife in her light blue dress

and white apron—no longer the McKean girl—
saw the two cane chairs on the front porch and
smelled the beef roast cooking.

"Well, now you have it, what do you do?" Bren
said.

Moon looked at his wife and shrugged, not sure
how to answer. "I don't know," he said, "get up in
the morning and pull on my boots. How about you?"

"We'll see what happens," Bren said.

He rode out of there in borrowed clothes on a
borrowed horse, but with visions of returning in
relative splendor. Rich. At rest with himself. And
with a glint in his eye that would say to Moon,
"You *sure* you got what you want?"

4
Sweetmary: January, 1890

They were having their meeting in the stove-heated
company office halfway up the grade, a wind blowing winter through the mine works: Bren Early,
bearded, in his buffalo coat; Mr. Vandozen, looking like a banker in his velvet-lapeled Chesterfield
and pinch-nose glasses; a man named Ross Selkirk, the superintendent of the Sweetmary works,
who clenched a pipe in his jaw; and another company man, a geologist, by the name of Franklin
Hovey.

Mr. Vandozen stood at a high table holding his
glasses to his face as he looked over Bren Early's
registered claims and assay reports. He said once,
"There seems to be a question whether you're a
miner, Mr. Early, or a speculator."

It wasn't the question he was waiting for, so Bren didn't answer.

Mr. Vandozen tried again. "Have you actually mined any ore?"

"Some."

"This one, I'll bet," Mr. Vandozen said, holding up an assay report. "Test would indicate quite a promising concentrate, as high as forty ounces to the ton."

"Three thousand dollars an ore-wagon load," Bren said.

And Mr. Vandozen said, "Before it's milled. On the deficit side you have labor, machinery, supplies, shipping, payments on your note—" The LaSalle Mining vice president, who had come all the way from New Mexico to meet Bren Early, looked over at him. "What do you have left?"

Not a question that required an answer. Bren waited.

"What you have, at best, are pockets of dust," Mr. Vandozen said. "Fast calculations in your head, multiplying ounces times thirty-five, I can understand how it lights up men's eyes. But obviously you don't want to scratch for a few ounces, Mr. Early, or you wouldn't be here."

Bren waited.

"Our geological surveys of your claims are"— Mr. Vandozen shrugged—"interesting, but by no means conclusive enough to warrant sinking shafts and moving in equipment. Though I'm sure you feel you have a major strike."

"Gold fever, it's called," the geologist said. "The symptoms are your eyes popping out of your head." He laughed, but no one else did.

Mr. Vandozen waited longer than he had to, following the interruption. When the office was quiet and they could hear the stove hissing and the wind gusting outside, he said, "We could give you—you have five claims?—all right, five thousand dollars for the lot and a one half of one percent royalty on gold ore after so many tons are milled."

"How much on all the copper ore I've got?"

The shaggy-looking prospector in the buffalo coat stopped everyone cold with the magic word.

It brought Mr. Vandozen's face up from the reports and claim documents to look at this Mr. Early again in a new light.

"You're telling us you have copper?"

"If your geologist knows it, you know it."

"It was my understanding you were only interested in gold."

"I'm interested in all manner of things," Bren said. "What are you interested in, besides high-grade copper?"

Mr. Vandozen took off his pinch-nose glasses and inspected them before putting them away, somewhere beneath his Chesterfield.

"How much do you want?"

There, that was the question. Bren smiled in his beard.

"Ten thousand dollars for the five claims," Mr. Vandozen said. "A two percent royalty on all minerals."

Bren shook his head.

At the fifty-thousand-dollar offer he started for the door. At one-hundred thousand, plus royalties, plus a position with the company, the shaggy-looking miner-speculator stepped up to Mr. Vandozen and shook his hand. That part was done.

When the company superintendent, who was under Bren now in all matters except the actual operation of the mine, brought out a bottle of whiskey and said, "Mr. Early, I'll drink to your health but stay out of my way," Mr. Early looked at him and said:

"You run the works. There's only one area I plan to step into and I'm going to do it with both feet."

This shaggy-looking Bren Early entered the Gold Dollar with his buffalo coat draped over his left shoulder, covering his arm and hanging from shoulder to knee. He wore his Stetson, weathered now and shaped properly for all time, and his showy Merwin & Hulbert ivory-handled revolvers in worn-leather holsters. Business was humming for a cold and dismal afternoon, an hour before the day shift let out. The patrons, tending to their drinking and card playing, did not pay much attention to Bren at first. Not until he walked up behind the Sweetmary Deputy Sheriff who was hunched over the bar on his arms, and said to him:

"Mr. Bruckner?"

As the heavy-set man straightened and came around, Bren Early's right hand appeared from inside the buffalo coat with a pick handle, held short, and cracked it cleanly across the deputy sheriff's face.

Bruckner bellowed, fell sideways against the bar, came around with his great nose pouring blood and stopped dead, staring at Bren Early.

"Yes, you know me," Bren said, and swiped him again, hard, across the head.

Bruckner stumbled against the bar and this time came around with his right hand gripping his holstered Peacemaker. But caution stopped him in the nick of time from pulling it free. The left hand of this shaggy dude—standing like he was posing for a picture—was somewhere beneath that buffalo cape, and only the dude and God knew if he was holding a gun.

Bruckner said, "You're under arrest."

It was strange, Bren admired the remark. While the response from the Gold Dollar patrons was impromptu laughter, a short quick nervous fit of it, then silence. Bren was thinking, They don't know anything what it's like, do they?

He said to Bruckner then, "Wake up and listen to what I tell you. You're gonna pay me eight dollars and fifty cents for the seventeen days I spent on your work gang. You're gonna pay everyone else now working whatever they've earned. You will never again use prisoners to do company work. And as soon as I'm through talking you're gonna go across the street and get my Smith forty-fours and bring them to me in their U.S. Army holsters. If I see you come back in here holding them by the grips or carrying any other weapon, I'll understand your intention and kill you before you get through the door. Now if you doubt or misunderstand anything I've said, go ask Ross Selkirk who the new boss is around here and he'll set you straight."

Bruckner took several moments to say, "I'll be back."

Let him have that much, a small shred of self-respect. The son of a bitch.

As the batwings swung closed, Bren stepped to the bar, lifting his buffalo coat and laying it across the polished surface. The patrons behind him stared and nudged each other. Look—both his revolvers were holstered.

Brendan Early had come to Sweetmary.

⇌ 7 ⇌

1

A news reporter told how he had knocked on the door one evening and when Mrs. Pierson opened it he said, "Excuse me, is this a whorehouse?" The woman said, "No, it isn't," not fazed a bit, and closed the door.

Someone else said, "It may not be a house for whores, but she is little better than one."

"Or better than most," another news reporter at the Gold Dollar said, "or he wouldn't have set her up as he did. She is a doggone good-looking woman."

None of the reporters had known about Mrs. Pierson until Maurice Dumas turned the first stone and then the rest of them began to dig. Maurice Dumas himself, once he saw where the story was leading, backed off so as not to pry.

When the door of the house on Mill Street opened this time, the news reporter took off his hat and said, "Good afternoon, I'm William S. Wells, a journalist with the *St. Louis Globe-Democrat*. I'd like to ask you a few questions."

The good-looking dark-haired woman in the black dress stepped back to close the door. William S. Wells put his hand out, his foot already in place.

"Is it true Bren Early killed your son?"

Mrs. Pierson did not fight the door, though her hand remained on the knob. She looked at the journalist with little or no expression and said, "My son was killed while robbing the Benson stage by a passenger named Mr. DeLisle."

"If Bren Early did not kill your son," the journalist, Wells, said, "why did he buy this house for you?"

"He didn't buy this house for me."

"I understand he assumed the mortgage."

"Perhaps as an investment."

The journalist said, "Let's see now . . . the poor widow is running a boardinghouse, barely making ends meet following the death of her husband in a mill accident. Mr. Early comes along, pays off the note, gives you the deed to the house and you get rid of the boarders so you can live here alone . . . some of the time alone, huh?" The journalist produced a little smile. "And you want me to believe he bought it as an *invest*ment?"

Mrs. Pierson said, "Do you think I care what you believe?"

"Bren Early was on the stage your boy tried to hold up. The same Bren Early who owns this house."

"I rent from him," Mrs. Pierson said.

"Yet you're a widow with no means of support."

"I have money my husband left."

"Uh-huh. Well, you must keep it under your mattress since you don't have a bank account either."

The journalist put on his grin as he stared at Mrs. Pierson—yes, a very handsome lady with her dark hair parted in the middle and drawn back in a bun—knowing he had her in a corner; then stopped grinning as the door opened wider and he was looking at Brendan Early, the man moving toward him into the doorway. The journalist said, "Oh—" not knowing Bren was here. He backed away, went down the three front steps to the walk and said then, "I see an old friend of yours is in town."

Bren said nothing as he slammed the door closed.

"Why were you telling him all that?"

"What did I tell him? He seemed to know everything."

"You sounded like you were going to stand there and answer anything he asked."

The woman shrugged. "What difference does it make?" and watched Bren as he moved from the door to a front window in the parlor. "You said yourself, let them think what they want."

Holding the lace curtains apart, looking out at the street of frame houses, he said, "We can't stop them from thinking, but we don't have to answer their questions."

"They don't have to ask much," she said. "It's your house—the arrangement is fairly obvious. But as long as it isn't spoken of out loud then it isn't improper. Is that it?"

Bren wore a white shirt, a dark tie and vest; his suitcoat hung draped over the back of a chair where his holstered revolvers rested on the seat cushion. He had been preparing to go out this afternoon after spending last night and this morning with her: preparing, grooming himself, looking at himself in the mirror solemnly as if performing a ritual.

As he turned from the window now to look at her she waited, not knowing what he was going to say.

Then surprised her when he said, "Do I sound stuffy?"

She relaxed. "You sound grim, so serious."

"I'm not though. Not with you."

"No, the hard image you present to everyone else."

He came over to the chair where his coat was draped. "Maybe what I should do, put a notice in the paper. 'To Whom It May Concern . . . I'm the one wants to get married, she's the one wants to keep things as they are.' See what they ask you then."

"In other words," Janet Pierson said, "let them think what they want, as long as there's no doubt about your honor."

"I didn't mean it that way at all."

"But it's the way it is," the good-looking dark-haired woman said. "If you're going to spend your life standing on principle, you want to be sure everyone understands what the principle is."

He picked up his coat and pushed an arm into the sleeve. "You keep saying I worry about what people think of me, when I don't. All I said was, why tell that fella our personal business?"

"I'm sorry," she said. "You're right."

He pulled the coat down to fit smoothly as he turned to her. "I don't want you to say I'm *right*, I want to know what you're talking about."

"You get mad if I tell you what I feel."

He said, "Oh," and turned to the chair again to pick up his gunbelt and holsters.

"Are you coming back for supper?"

"I was planning on it. If we can have an evening without arguing."

"Are you pouting now?"

She shouldn't have said it—seeing his jaw tighten and hearing him say maybe he'd see her later, or maybe not—but sometimes she got tired of handling him so carefully, keeping him unruffled. Out in the street where he was going now, closing the door behind him, he was the legendary Bren Early who had shot and killed at least ten men who'd tested his nerve; a man whose posed photographs were displayed in the window of C.S. Fly's gallery on LaSalle Street and who was being written about by journalists from at least a dozen different newspapers. Bren Early: silent, deadly, absolutely true to his word.

But she could not help but think of a little boy playing guns.

He was a little boy sometimes when they were alone, unsure of himself.

He had come to her two and a half years ago, told her who he was and how he had met her son. He returned several times to visit, to sit in this parlor with her over coffee, and finally one day handed her the deed to the house—mortgage paid in full—asking nothing in return. Why?

He had not killed her son. A false rumor. He had, in fact, tried to prevent her son's death. But had failed and perhaps it was that simple: he felt responsible, owed her something because of his failure. He had said, "Don't ask questions. I like you, I want to do something for you." All right, and she liked him and it was easy enough to take the sign down and change the boardinghouse back to a residence. It seemed to happen naturally as they saw more of each other. He wanted a woman in town and she responded. Why not? She liked him enough.

Janet Pierson, at forty, was at least five years older than Bren. She was attractive, had maintained her slim figure, they enjoyed one another; so age was not a consideration. Until he said he wanted to marry her.

She asked why and felt early suspicions aroused. He said he wanted to marry her, that was why in itself; he loved her. Yes, he had said he loved her. And he had also said, many times, "You think too much," when she told him he really didn't want to marry her but felt an obligation or was afraid of what people thought. He had said over and over that people had nothing to do with it, goddamn it, *people* could think whatever they wanted; what *he* wanted was to be married to her. Then she had said the words that made him stare at her and then frown, perplexed, and finally get angry, the words he would never understand and she couldn't seem to explain.

She had said, "I think what you want to do is take the place of my son. You want to make up his loss."

And he had said, "You believe I think of you as my *mother*?"

Yes, but she would not admit that to him: the little boy who came in the house when he was finished playing his role on the street. She didn't understand it herself, she only felt it. So she referred to him being like a little boy without referring to herself as a mother or using the word.

There was risk involved, to tell the man who had been a cavalry officer and had stood his ground and shot ten men, that he was still, deep down, a little boy and wanted his own way. He would pound his fist down or storm out (See? she would say to herself), then calm down or come back in a little while and say, "How do you get ideas like that?"

And she would say, "I just know."

"Because you had a son? Listen, maybe what you're doing, you're still playing mama, Jesus Christ, and you're using *me*. I'm not doing it, *you* are."

Blaming her. Then saying he loved her and wanted to marry her and be with her always. Yet they very seldom went out of the house as a couple. Sitting together in a restaurant he was obviously self-conscious; as though being seen with her revealed a vulnerable, softer side of him. The only thing she was certain of: Bren Early didn't know what he wanted.

2

Maurice Dumas stood in the doorway of the Chinaman's place on Second Street. He had been waiting an hour and a half, watching toward Mill Street and, every once in a while, looking in at the empty restaurant wondering how the Chinaman stayed in business . . . then wondering if Mr.

Early had forgot or had changed his mind. Twice he'd run back to the corner of Second and LaSalle and looked across the street toward the Congress Hotel. The news reporters were still waiting on the porch.

When finally he saw Early coming this way from Mill Street, Maurice Dumas felt almost overwhelming relief. In the time it took Early to reach him—Early looking neat and fresh though it was quite warm this afternoon in May—Maurice Dumas had time to compose himself.

He nodded and said, "Mr. Early."

"He arrive?"

"Yes sir, on the noon shuttle from Benson."

"Alone?"

"I believe there was a Mexican gentleman with him."

It was something to stand close to this man and watch him in unguarded moments, watch him think and make decisions that would become news stories—like watching history being made.

"They went up to the mine office first and then to the hotel," Maurice said. "I guess where he's staying. Everybody thinks you're there, too, I guess. Or will come there. So they expect the hotel is where it'll happen—if it's gonna."

Bren Early thought a little more before saying, "Go see him. Tell him you spoke to me." He paused. "Tell him I'll be in this quiet place out of the sun if he wants to have a word with me."

It was the Mexican, Ruben Vega, who came to the Chinaman's place. He greeted Early, nodding and smiling as he joined him at a back table, away from the sun glare on the windows. They could have been two old friends meeting here in the empty restaurant, though Bren Early said nothing at first because he was surprised. He felt it strange that he was glad to see this man who was smiling warmly and telling him he had not changed one bit since that time at the wall in Sonora. It was strange, too, Bren felt, that he recognized the man immediately and could tell that the man had changed; he was older and looked older, with a beard now that was streaked with gray.

"Man," Ruben Vega said, "the most intelligent thing I ever did in my life, I didn't walk up to the wall with them . . . . You not drinking nothing?"

"Is he coming?" asked Bren.

"No, he's not coming. He sent me to tell you he isn't angry, it was too long ago." The Mexican looked around, saying then, "Don't they have nothing to drink in this place?"

They sent Maurice Dumas out to get a bottle of *mescal*, which the Mexican said he was thirsty for. Bren had beer, served by the Chinaman, and drank several glasses of it while they talked, allowing Maurice to sit with them but not paying any attention to him until he tried the *mescal* and made a terrible face and the Mexican said to Bren, "Your friend don't know what's good."

"If you like a drink that tastes like poison candy," Bren said, though he tried a short glass of it to see if it was still as bad as he remembered it was the first time he drank it in the sutler's store at Huachuca. "That could kill you," he said.

"No, but walking up to the wall where you and

the other one stood, that would have," Ruben Vega said.

"You might have made the difference," Bren said.

"Maybe I would have shot one of you, I don't know. But something told me it would be my last day on earth."

"How did you keep him alive?"

The Mexican shrugged. "Tied him to a horse. He kept himself alive to Morelos. Then in the infirmary they cleaned him, sewed him together. He has a hole here," Ruben Vega said, touching his cheek, "some teeth missing"—he grinned—"part of his ear. But he's no more ugly than he was before. See, the ugliness is inside him. I say to him, 'Man, what is it like to be you? To live inside your body?' He don't know what I'm talking about. I say to him, 'Why don't you be tranquil and enjoy life more instead of rubbing against it?' He still don't know what I'm talking about, so I leave him alone . . . Well, let me think. Why didn't he die? I don't know. From Morelos I took him to my old home at Bavispe, then down to Hermosillo . . . Guaymas, we looked at the sea and ate fish . . . a long way around to come back here, but only in the beginning he was anxious to go back and saying what he's going to do to you when he finds you."

"Others tried," Bren said.

"Yes, we hear that. Then time pass, he stop talking about it. We do some work in New Mexico for a mine company, bring them beef. Then do other work for them, make more money than before." The Mexican shrugged again. "He's not so ugly inside now."

"He must've paid you pretty well," Bren said. "You stay with him."

"I'll tell you the truth, I almost left him by the wall in Sonora, but I work for his family, his father before him. Yes, Sundeen always pay me pretty well as *segundo*. If I'm going to be in that business, stealing cows, running them across the border, I'm not very particular who I work with, uh? But he isn't so bad now. He doesn't talk so much as he use to."

Bren said, "How's he look at this job he's got?"

"Well, we just come here. He has some men coming the company hired. I guess we go up and drive those people off. What else?" He raised his *mescal* glass, then paused. "But we hear your friend is up there too, the other one from the wall. How is it you're here and he's up there, your friend?"

"It's the way it is, that's all," Bren said. "This land situation, who owns what, is none of my business."

"You don't care then," Ruben Vega said, "we go up there and run him off."

Maurice Dumas' gaze moved from the Mexican to Bren Early and waited for the answer.

"You say run him off and make it sound easy," Bren said. "It isn't a question of whether I care or not, have an interest, it's whether you can do it and come back in one piece. I'm like Maurice here and all the rest. Just a spectator."

3

It was after five o'clock when Ruben Vega returned to the Congress Hotel. The men who had been pointed out to him as journalists and not a part of a business convention were still on the front porch and in the lobby. They stopped talking when he came in, but no one called to him or said anything.

He mentioned it to Sundeen who stood at the full-length mirror in his room, bare to the waist, turning his head slowly, studying himself as he trimmed his beard.

"They know I come with you, but they don't ask me anything. You know why?"

"Why?" Sundeen said to himself in the mirror.

"Because they think I shine your shoes, run errands for you."

"You saw him?"

"Yes, I talk to him, tell him you're not mad no more."

"Wavy-haired son of a bitch. He look down his nose at you?"

"A little, holding back, not saying much. But he's all right. Maybe the same as you are."

Sundeen trimmed carefully with the scissors, using a comb to cover the deep scar in his left cheek where hair did not grow and was like an indentation made with a finger that remained when the finger was withdrawn, the skin around the hole tight and shiny.

"Instead of what you think," Sundeen said, "tell me what he had to say."

"He say it's none of his business. He's going to watch."

"You believe it?"

"Now you want to know what I think. Make up your mind."

Sundeen half-turned to the mirror to study his

profile, smoothing his beard with the back of his hand. "His partner's up there, but he's gonna keep his nose out of it, huh?"

Yes, they may be somewhat alike, Ruben Vega thought. He said, "The company pay him to work here, whatever he does, not to go up there and help his friend. So maybe he doesn't have the choice to make."

"What does he say about Moon?"

"Nothing. I ask, do you see him? No. I say, why don't they leave instead of causing this trouble? He say, ask them. I say well, he likes to live on a mountain—there plenty other mountains. He don't say anything. I say, what about the other people up there, they live with him? He say, you find out."

Sundeen looked at his body, sucking in his stomach, then picked up a shirt from the chair and put it on. "I think somebody's selling somebody a bill of goods. All we have to say to them is, look here, you people don't move out, this is what happens to you. Take one of 'em, stick a gun in his mouth and count three. They'll leave."

"Take which one?"

"It don't matter to me none. 'Cept it won't be Moon. Moon, I'm gonna settle with him. Early too. But I got time to think about that."

Ruben Vega was nodding. "Threaten them seriously—it look pretty easy, uh?"

"Not hard or easy but a fact of life," Sundeen said. "Nobody picks dying when there's a way not to."

Ruben Vega would agree to that. He could say to his boss, And it works both ways, for you as well as them. But why argue about it with a man who did not know how to get outside of himself to look at something? It had happened to him at the wall. It could happen to him again. Ruben Vega said, "Well, I hope you get enough men to do it."

Sundeen said, "Wait and see what's coming."

It was already arranged, since his meeting with Vandozen in Las Cruces, Vandozen asking how many men he'd need. Sundeen saying he'd wait and see. Vandozen then saying it was his custom to know things in advance, not wait and see. So he had already recruited some twenty men, among them several former Yuma prison guards, a few railroad bulls and a good number of strikebreakers from the coal fields of Pennsylvania: all hired at twenty dollars a week and looking forward to a tour of duty out in the fresh air and wide open spaces.

Today was Tuesday. A message waiting for Sundeen when he reported to the company stated his bunch would all arrive in Benson by rail on Friday. Fine. Let them get drunk and laid on Saturday, rest Sunday and they ride up into the mountains on Monday.

Sundeen said to the Mexican, "If that's all you got, you didn't learn much."

"He thought you were dead," Ruben Vega said. "I told him you should be, but you stayed alive and now you're much wiser."

Looking at him Sundeen said, "The fence-sitter. You gonna sit on the fence and watch this one too? Man, that time in Sonora—I swore I was gonna kill you after, if I hadn't been shot up."

"I save your life you feel you want to kill me," Ruben Vega said. "I think you still have something to learn."

4

Bren had not realized he was tense. Until walking back to the house on Mill Street he was aware of relief and was anxious to be with the woman again. He had not told her about Sundeen. He didn't like to argue with her or discuss serious matters. She was a woman and he wanted her to act like a woman, one he had selected. He did not expect continual expressions of gratitude; nor did he want her to wait on him or act as though her life was now dedicated solely to his pleasure. But she could make his life easier if she'd quit assuming she knew more about him than he did. Women were said to "know" and feel things men weren't able to because men were more blunt and practical. Bren believed that was a lot of horseshit. Women took advantage of men because they were all sitting on something men wanted. If they ever quit holding out or holding it over men's heads everybody would be a lot happier.

Not that Janet Pierson ever bargained with him that way. She seemed always willing and eager. He only wished she would quit thinking and analyzing why he did things and saying he wanted to be like a son to her.

Sometimes though he would bring it up, because it was on his mind, or to convince her she was wrong—as he did now, entering the front door and hearing her in the kitchen, coming up quietly behind her, pulling her into his arms, his hands moving over her body.

"I missed you," she said, resting against him.

"I missed you too. You think I'd do this to my mother?"

"I hope not."

"Unh-unh." Kissing her now, brushing her cheek and finding her ear with his mouth. "No . . . What you feel like to me is a young girl . . . soft and nice—"

She said, pressing against him, "That's what I feel. You make me aware of being a woman and it's a good feeling." This way acknowledging and appreciating him as a man, but knowing that what he needed now was to be comforted and held. Protected from something. The little boy come home—but not telling him this.

After they made love she would put her arms around him and hold him close to her in the silence and soon he would fall asleep. Then, as she would begin to ease her arm from beneath his shoulder, he would open his eyes for a moment, roll to his side and fall asleep again, freeing her. Though if she moved her hand over him, down over the taut muscles in his belly, they would make love again and after, this time, he would get out of bed as Bren Early: confident, the man who wore matched revolvers and loved her when it occurred to him to express it or when he felt the physical urge . . . not realizing the simple need to hold and be held and to believe in something other than himself.

Sometime soon she would talk to him and find out what he believed and what was important to him. And what was important to her also.

5

Was it luck or was it instinct? Maurice Dumas hoped the latter. There was always something going on when he set out to get a story: this time not at the White Tanks agency but several miles up the draw at Dana Moon's place.

The luck was running into the Apache at the agency office and letting him know through sign language—trying all kinds of motions before pointing to the office and then sticking his tongue in his cheek to resemble a wad of tobacco—that he was looking for the agent, Dana Moon.

They climbed switchbacks up a slope swept yellow-green with brittlebush and greasewood, through young saguaros that looked like a field of fence posts and on up into the wide, yawning trough of a barranca with steep walls of shale and wind-swept white oak and cedar. They climbed to open terrain, a bare crest against the sky but not the top, not yet. A little farther and there it was, finally, a wall . . . first the wall, and beyond it a low stone fortress of a house with a wooden porch and a yard full of people, horses and several wagons.

What was this, another Meat Day?

No, Maurice Dumas found out soon enough, it was a war council.

He felt strange riding in through the opening in the adobe wall with all eyes on him. Though there were not as many people as he originally thought—only about a dozen—they were certainly a colorful and unusual mixture: darkies, Mexicans and Indians, all standing around together and all, he observed now, armed to the teeth with revolvers, rifles and belts of cartridges. Specifically there were three hard-looking colored men; four Mexicans, one in a very large Chihuahua hat and bright yellow scarf; and the rest Apache Indians, including the one who brought him up here and who, Maurice Dumas found out, was named Red, an old compadre of Moon's.

"I hope I'm not interrupting anything," Maurice Dumas said, as Moon came down from the porch to greet him, "but there is something I think you better know about."

"Sundeen's arrival?" said Moon, who almost smiled then at the young reporter's look of surprise. "There are things we better know about if we intend to stay here. Have his men arrived yet?"

Maurice Dumas, again surprised, said, "What men?"

"You'd know if they had," Moon said. "So we still have some time. Step down and I'll introduce you to some of the main characters of the story you're gonna be writing."

The man seemed so aware and alert for someone who moved the way Moon did, hands in his pockets, in no hurry, big chew of tobacco in his jaw: just a plain country fellow among this colorful group of heavily armed neighbors.

First, Maurice Dumas met Mrs. Moon, Kate, and felt he must have appeared stupid when he looked up and saw a good-looking lady and not the washed-out, sodbuster woman he'd expected. When she learned where he was from, Mrs. Moon said, "Chicago, huh? I'll bet you're glad to get away from the stockyards and breathe fresh air for a change."

The news reporter said he didn't live near the yards, fortunately, and noticed Moon looking at his wife with an amused expression and then shaking his head; just a faint movement. The man seemed to get a kick out of her. He said, "What do you know about Chicago stockyards?" She answered him, "I visited there with my dad when I was little and have never felt the urge to go back." Strange, having a conversation like that in front of everyone.

Moon said, "Maurice, shake hands with a veteran of the War of the Rebellion and a cavalryman twenty-four years."

This was the young reporter's introduction to Bo Catlett, whom he had already heard about and who did not disappoint him in his appearance, with his high boots and felt campaign hat low over his eyes. Bo Catlett's expression was kindly, yet he was mean and hard-looking in that he seemed the type who would never hold his hat in his hand and stand aside or give an inch, certainly not give up his horse ranch. The other two colored men wore boots also, standing the way cavalrymen seem to pose, and appeared just as fit and ready as Bo Catlett. There were three more former members of the Tenth up with their families or tending the herds.

Red, the little Mimbre Apache, said something in Spanish to Moon and Moon said, "He thought, when you rode up and commenced making signs, you were asking him how old he was, how many moons, till you stuck your tongue in your cheek."

The Apaches sat along the edge of the porch, Maurice Dumas noticed, while all the others stood around. (Did it mean Indians were lazy by nature?, Maurice wondered. Or smart enough to squat when they got the chance?)

The news reporter wouldn't have minded sitting down himself in one of those cane rocking chairs. But first he had to meet Armando Duro—and his young son Eladio who was about eighteen—and this introduction turned into something he never expected.

Maurice had a feeling Moon had saved Armando until last out of deference, for he seemed especially polite and careful as he addressed him in Spanish, nodding toward Maurice as Maurice caught the words *Chicago Times*. Was the Mexican impressed?

The young news reporter was, for he had heard the name Armando Duro before, though he had not known this fiery champion of Mexican land rights was living in these mountains.

Here he was now rattling off Spanish a mile a minute, his son and his companions nodding in agreement while Moon listened intently at first, then seemed to get tired of hanging on and shifted his weight from one foot to the other as Armando went on and on. When there was a pause Maurice said quickly, "I'd like to interview Señor Duro if I could."

Moon said, "If you can get a word in." Armando's eyes darted from the news reporter to Moon. "And if you—*si puede hablar en Español*. Can you?"

"Doesn't he speak English?"

"When he wants to," Moon said. "It depends if he's in one of his royal pain-in-the-ass moods or not."

If the Mexican could understand him, how come Moon was saying this in front of him? Evidently because Moon had only so much patience with the man and had run out.

Following Moon's less than kind remark, Armando turned to the young news reporter and said in English, "Will you print the truth for a change if I give it to you?"

What kind of question was that? Maurice Dumas said the *Times* always printed the truth.

"The twisting of truth to fit your purpose," Armando said, "is the same as a lie."

Maurice didn't know what the man was talking about because the paper had hardly ever printed anything about Armando Duro or Mexican land rights to begin with. It was an old issue, settled in court, dead and buried. But since the man did represent the Mexican community here, some eighty or ninety people living on scattered farms and sheep pastures, Maurice decided he'd better pay attention.

He said, "Well, I suppose you see this present situation as an opportunity to air your complaints once again, bring them into the open." Maurice heard Moon groan and knew he had said the wrong thing.

Sure enough.

Armando started talking, taking them back to the time of Spanish land grants and plodding on through the war with Mexico and the Gadsden Purchase to explain why their acreage, their sheep graze, their golden fields of corn and bean patches belonged to them as if by divine succession and not to a mining company from a state named for a small island in the English Channel (which Maurice Dumas had not realized before this).

Bo Catlett and the colored troopers shuffled around or leaned against a wagon. Moon would continue to shift from one foot to another. His wife, what she did was shake her head and go into the house. Even Armando's son and the other Mexicans seemed ready to fall asleep. Only the Apaches, sitting along the edge of the porch, stared at Armando with rapt attention, not having any idea what he was talking about, even though Armando would lapse into fiery Spanish phrases every so often. He reminded the young news reporter of every politician he had ever heard speak, except that Armando talked in bigger circles that included God and kings.

"How am I going to write about all that?" Maurice said to Moon, after.

Moon said, "You picked your line of work, I didn't."

Armando got a rolled-up sheet of heavy paper from his wagon and came over to the news reporter opening it as you would a proclamation, which is what it was.

"Here," Armando said, handing it to Maurice, "show this to the mine company and print it in your newspaper so anyone who sees one of these will know it marks the boundary of our land."

The notice said, in large black letters:

WARNING
Anyone venturing onto
this land uninvited is

TRESPASSING

**on property granted by
Royal Decree and witnessed
before God. Trespassers
are not welcome and will
be fired on if they cross this boundary.**

**Armando Duro
and the
People of the Mountain**

Later on, just before Maurice Dumas left to go back down the switchback trail, he said to Moon, "Does that man know what he's doing?"

"It's his idea of the way to do it," Moon said.

"But that warning's not gonna do any good. You think?"

"Warning?" Moon said. "It reads more like an invitation."

"Can't you stop him, shut him up?"

"I suppose," Moon said, "but the sooner it starts, the sooner it's over, huh?"

6

Moon, Bo Catlett and Red, the leader of the Mimbres, packed up into the high reaches to shoot some game, drink whiskey, have a talk and get away from their women for a few days. Moon said that's all they would have, three days. On the piney shoulder of the mountain where they camped, they could hear the mine company survey crew exploding dynamite as they searched out new ore veins:

like artillery off to the west, an army gradually moving closer, having already wiped out several of the Mexican homesites.

Armando Duro had drawn the line and posted his trespass notices, giving himself a printed excuse to start shooting. But how did you tell a man like Armando he was a fool? Armando was not a listener, he was a talker.

Moon, in the high camp, took out a rough-sketch map he'd drawn and laid it on the pine needles for Bo Catlett and Red to look at, Moon pointing: little squares were homes and farms, though maybe he was missing some; the circles were graze. X's marked the areas where the survey crews had been working.

Here, scattered over the pastureland in the Western foothills, the Mexican homesteads. How would you defend them?

"No way to do it, considering they farmers," Bo Catlett said. "They ever see more than three coming they got to get out . . . Maybe try draw them up in the woods."

Moon shook his head. "Armando told them, don't leave your homes. Something about leaving your honor on the doorstep when you flee."

"I'm not talking about they should *flee*," Bo Catlett said. "But they start shooting from the house, that's where they gonna die. They don't have enough people in one place. Like you—" Bo Catlett looked at the map. "Where you at here?"

Moon pointed to the square on the Eastern slope, the closest one to the wavy line indicating the San Pedro River.

"You no better off'n they are," Bo Catlett said, "all by yourself there."

"I got open ground in front of me and high rock behind," Moon said, "with Red and some of his people right here, watching my back door. Nobody gets close without my knowing. So . . . around here, both sides of the crest, the Apache rancherías. Red, that's you right there. Coming south a bit, these circles are the horse pastures . . . Here's the canyon, Bo, where you got your settlement."

"Niggerville," Bo Catlett said. "Some day they put railroad tracks up there, you can bet money we be on the wrong side."

"Here's the box canyon," Moon continued, "where you gather your mustangs. I'm thinking we might do something with that blind alley. You follow me?"

"Invite 'em in," Bo Catlett said, "and close the door."

"It'd be a way, wouldn't it? If they come up to Niggerville and you pull back, draw 'em into the box."

"If they dumb enough, think I'm a black lead mare," Bo Catlett said.

"We'll find out," Moon said. "Red's gonna be our eyes, huh, Red? *Los ojos.*" And said in Spanish, "The eyes of the mountain people."

The Apache nodded and said, also in Spanish, "It's been a long time since we used them."

Moon said, "Him and a bunch were gonna summer up at Whiteriver, visit some of their people, but Red's staying now for the war. That's what they call it in town, the Rincon Mountains War."

Bo Catlett seemed to be thinking about the

name, trying it a few times in his mind. "We got any say in it?"

"We're still around when the smoke clears," Moon said, "I guess we can call it anything we want."

8

1

Phil Sundeen looked at the notice with the big word "WARNING" at the top like it was a birthday present he had always wanted. He read it slowly, came down to Armando's name at the bottom, said, "That's the one I want," and sent Ruben Vega out on a scout, see if the notices were "for true."

That Monday morning Ruben Vega rode a fifteen-mile loop through the west foothills, spotting the little adobes tucked away up on the slopes; seeing the planted fields, young corn not quite belly-high to his horse; seeing the notices stuck to saguaro and white oak and three times drawing rifle fire—Ruben Vega squinting up at the high rocks as the reports faded, then shaking his head and continuing on.

He made his way up through a mesquite thicket that followed the course of a draw to a point where he could study one of the videttes crouched high in the rocks, sky-lined for all to see, a young man in white with an old single-shot Springfield, defending his land. Ruben Vega, dismounted, circled behind the vidette to within forty feet and called out, *"Dígame!"*

The young man in white came around, saw the bearded man holding a revolver and fired his Springfield too quickly, without taking time to aim.

Ruben Vega raised his revolver. "Tell me where I can find Armando Duro."

Thirty dollars a week to frighten this young farmer and others like him. It was a pity. Ruben Vega said to the man, who was terrified but trying to act brave, he only wanted to speak to Armando Duro and needed directions to his house. That was all. He nodded, listening to the young farmer, holstered his gun and left.

Yes, he told Sundeen, the notices were "for real."

"They shoot at you?"

"They don't know what they're doing."

"I *know* that," Sundeen said. "I want to know if they're good for their word." When Ruben Vega told him yes, they had fired, though not to hit him, Sundeen said, "All right, let's go."

He paraded out his security force: his prison guards, railroad bulls and strikebreakers; most of whom wore city clothes and looked like workingmen on Sunday, not one under thirty years of age, Ruben Vega noticed. Very hard men with big fists, bellies full of beer and whiskey from their first weekend in town, armed with Winchester repeaters and revolvers stuck in their belts. Sixteen of them: two had quit by Monday saying it was too hot and dusty, the hell with it. One was dead of knife wounds and the one who had killed him was in jail. Ruben Vega knew he would never be their segundo, because these men would never do what a Mexican told them. But that was all right. They could take orders directly from Sundeen. Ruben Vega would scout for them, stay out of their way and draw his thirty dollars a week—the most he had ever made in his life—which would make these men even uglier if they knew the Mexican was being paid more than they were. But he didn't like this work. From the beginning he had not liked it at all.

He didn't like Sundeen waving off the few news reporters—one of them the young one who had been with Early—who had hired horses and wanted to follow. He didn't like it because it surprised him—Sundeen not wanting them along to write about him.

He asked, "Why not bring them?"

"Not this trip," Sundeen said. "Get up there and show us the way, partner."

Ruben Vega followed his orders and rode point, guiding Sundeen and his security force up into the hills where the WARNING notices were nailed to the saguaro and white oak. There. Now Sundeen could do what he wanted.

Looking over his crew of bulls and headbusters sweating in their Sunday suits, the crew squinting up at the high rock formations, Sundeen said, "Who wants to do the honors, chase their pickets off that high ground? I'd say there's no more'n likely two of 'em up there—couple of bean farmers couldn't hit shit if they stuck their weapons up their ass. How about you, you and you?" And said to the others, "Get ready now."

More than two, Ruben Vega thought, because they know we're coming to see Armando. Maybe all the guns they have are up there now. Guarding the pass to the man's house. Ruben Vega nudged his mount up next to Sundeen's.

"They'll have plenty guns up there," he said quietly.

Sundeen turned in his saddle to look at him and smiled as he spoke, as though he was talking about something else. "We don't know till we see, partner. Till we draw fire, huh?" Then to the three he had picked: "Go on up past the signs."

Another show to watch, Ruben Vega thought, seeing the three men moving their horses at a walk up through the ocotillo and yellow-flowering prickly pear, reaching the sign nailed to a saguaro . . . moving past the cactus . . . twenty feet perhaps, thirty, when the gunfire poured out of the rocks a hundred yards away: ten, a dozen rifles, Ruben Vega estimated, fired on the count, but the eruption of sound coming raggedly with puffs of smoke and followed by three single shots that chased the two riders still mounted, both of them bent low in their saddles and circling back. One man in his Sunday suit lay on the ground, out there alone now, his riderless horse running free. The one on the ground didn't move. Sundeen was yelling at his security force to commence firing. Then yelled at them to spread out as their horses began to shy and bump each other with the rifles going off close. "Spread out and rush 'em!" Sundeen yelled, pointing and then circling around to make sure they were all moving forward . . . Ruben Vega watching, wondering if Sundeen knew what he was doing . . . Sundeen pausing then as his men charged up the slope firing away . . . Ruben Vega impressed now that these dressed-up shitkickers would do what they were told and expose themselves to fire. Sundeen hung back, grinning as he looked over at Ruben Vega now sitting motionless in his saddle.

"Still riding the fence, huh?"

Ruben Vega said, "Well, you got a man killed."

"Three'd be better," Sundeen said, "but one's enough to inspire them."

It didn't take much to push the farmers out of the rocks. They reloaded and got off a volley, hitting nothing, then fell back from the steady fire of the Winchester repeaters, some of them running, others making their way back to Armando Duro's place where they would be forced to make a stand.

Sundeen and his people circled to high ground and found good cover in a fairly deep wash rimmed with brush. From here they looked down on Armando's house and yard: a whitewashed adobe with a roof of red clay tiles that had come from an old church in Tucson, a flower garden, a latticework covered with green vines, heavy shutters with round gunports over the windows. A snug cottage with thick walls up here in the lonesome.

Sundeen said, "Well, we can starve him out or maybe set the place on fire, but we'd never get home for supper, would we?" From a saddlebag he pulled out a towel with *Congress Hotel* printed on it and thew it to Ruben Vega, saying, "Hey, partner, make yourself useful."

Tied to a mesquite pole the towel was the truce flag Ruben Vega waved above the brush cover and held high in front of him as he walked down to the yard, unarmed, doing something for his thirty dollars a week.

He called to the house in Spanish, "Do I address Armando Duro? . . . Look, I have no gun. Will you come out, please, and talk like a gentleman? We have no fight with you. We come to talk and you begin shooting." He paused. "Before anyone else is injured please come talk to the man sent by the company. He has something important to explain."

"Say it now," a voice from the house said.

"I'm not the emissary of the company," Ruben Vega said. "Mr. Sundeen is the one. He wants to explain the company plan of making this a township . . . if you would honor us and agree to become the alcalde and administer the office."

"Where is he?" the voice asked.

"You come out and he'll come out," Ruben Vega said, beginning to feel relief now, knowing he was almost finished.

There was a long pause, silence, before the voice said again, "Where is he?"

"Up there," Ruben Vega said, pointing with his truce flag.

"He must come with no weapons. All of them must show themselves with no weapons," the voice said.

"Of course," Ruben Vega said, thinking, He's a child; you could offer him candy. As he saw the door open, Ruben Vega began to move away, turning to wave to Sundeen to come down, calling out, "All right . . . Come with your hands in the air, please!" Looking back at the house, still moving off to the side, he said in Spanish, "Your men come out too, please, everyone without weapons. We meet at this sign of truce and speak as gentlemen," thinking, Yes, isn't it a nice day and everybody's friends . . . Smile . . . but get your old ass out of the way as soon as you can, without hurrying, but move it.

2

Moon handed the glasses to Bo Catlett and picked up his Sharps rifle from the Y of the cliffrose branch in front of him.

"They all got *suits* on," Bo Catlett said, with the field glasses to his face. "Coming with their hands in the air. They sur*ren*dering?"

"You see the white flag?" Moon said.

"Man moving out of the way."

"I saw him do it once before," Moon said. "Something like this. What would you say's the range?"

From this position, where Moon and Bo Catlett, Red and three of his Mimbres crouched in the outcropping of rock and flowering cliffrose—high up on a slope of scrub pine—they had a long downview of the red-tile postage-stamp roof of the house and the tiny dark figures coming down to the yard, approaching the tiny figures in white coming out of the house.

Bo Catlett continued to study the scene through the field glasses, saying now, "You got . . . three hundred fifty yards 'tween us and them."

"Close," Moon said, "but more like four hundred," and sighted down the barrel of the Sharps. "It looks shorter aiming down." He lowered the big-bore rifle to adjust the rear sight and put it to his shoulder again to aim, both eyes open.

"Wearing suits," Bo Catlett was saying. "All dressed up to pay a visit, huh?"

Moon said something in slow Spanish, as though explaining carefully, and the Mimbres raised their Springfields and Spencers. He waited a moment and then said, "*Listo?*"

The Mimbres were ready. Bo Catlett continued to watch through the glasses.

"The one with the silver belt buckles," Moon said.

"His holster's empty," Bo Catlett said. "None of them appear armed."

"Come up here with their coats on," Moon said, "account of it's so cold. Only about ninety degrees out. Watch Sundeen, he'll do something. Take off his hat, something to give 'em a sign."

"Talking," Bo Catlett said. "Moving around some . . . Mexicans standing there listening to him, Armando, shit, look at him with his big hat on, arms folded, standing there . . . Sundeen looking up at the sky now, looking around . . . looking back at Armando . . . hey, yelling something . . . they drawing *guns*! He going for the Mexican!"

Moon fired.

The Mimbres fired.

The sounds hitting hard and flat in the stillness, echoing . . . the hard sounds hitting again, almost covering the popping sounds of pistol fire coming from the yard, where tiny dark figures and tiny white figures were left lying on the ground as the lines of figures began to come apart and scatter. The rifles echoed again, cracking the hot air hard, and in a moment the yard was empty but for the figures lying motionless: three dark figures, four white figures. A single white figure was being dragged, carried off by a crowd of dark figures.

Bo Catlett followed them through the glasses until they were out of sight, beyond a rise and a line of brush. He wasn't sure which one they'd dragged off until his gaze inched back to the yard, past the figures lying there, and saw the big Mexican hat on the ground.

"They got Armando," Bo Catlett said.

3

C.S. "Buck" Fly, who was a gentleman and had never been known to say an unkind word about anyone, paused and said, "I already shot that rooster."

"We went to very much trouble to get him," Ruben Vega said. "Rode all the way up there to talk to him."

"Is he coming here?" C.S. Fly asked, not wanting to give the Mexican a flat no, but not wanting to take the other Mexican's picture either. The other Mexican, Armando, was impatient and difficult to pose, because he thought he knew everything, including photography. C.S. Fly also had a lot on his mind. His wife was in Tombstone, where business was not too good; he had opened a gallery in Phoenix that wasn't doing much better; there was not much going on here in Sweetmary at the moment; and he was trying to make up his mind whether or not he should run for sheriff of Cochise County on the Republican ticket next year, as some of his friends were urging him to do. What did he want to take a picture of a pompous, officious Mexican land-granter for?

"You have to bring your picture machine to where he is. I'll show you," Ruben Vega said.

"Well, as I've mentioned, I already have Armando on file," Mr. Fly said. "One of him is plenty."

"But do you have him talking to Mr. Sundeen of the mine company, settling the difference between them, the two sides shaking hands in a picture you can sell to all the newspapers in the country?" Ruben Vega asked.

"No, I don't believe I have that one," C.S. Fly said. "Where is it they're meeting?"

Ruben Vega told him, a ranch out of town only a few miles, the J-L-Bar, owned by a man named Freels, a neutral ground between the mine and the mountains. Mr. Fly said all right, had his assistant load camera and equipment on a buckboard and they were on their way—heading out LaSalle Street, when the young news reporter Ruben Vega had met before rode up to join them, asking what was going on. Ruben Vega said come on, and asked where the other reporters were. (Sundeen had not said anything this time about keeping reporters away.) The young fellow from Chicago, Maurice Dumas, said they most always took a nap after their noon dinner and that's probably where they were. When he asked where they were going, Ruben Vega told him Mr. Fly was going to take a picture of an important occasion, a meeting between Sundeen and Armando.

Because his luck or intuition had been so keen lately, Maurice Dumas believed him, patting his pocket to make sure he had a pad and pencil. It looked like another *Chicago Times* exclusive coming up.

About three miles out of town, having come around a bend in the road that was banked close to a steep slope—with still a mile or so to go before reaching the J-L-Bar ranch—they saw something white hanging from a telegraph pole.

Was it a flag of some kind? There was no wind stirring it. As they approached, seeing it straight down the road now, maybe a hundred yards away, Maurice Dumas thought of a bag of laundry. Or, could it be a mail bag out by the Freels place? Something white—as they drew closer—tied to the pole about ten feet off the ground . . . No, not tied to the pole, hanging from a rope . . . Not a bag of laundry either. A man. Maurice Dumas heard the Mexican say something in Spanish. He heard C.S. Fly say, "Oh, my God."

It was Armando Duro, hung there by the neck, the rope reaching up and over the crossbar where the wires were attached and down to the base of the pole where the rope was lashed securely. Armando's head hung down, chin on his chest, his face so dark he looked like a Negro—which was why Maurice was not sure at first who it was. His hands were so much lighter in color, and his bare feet hanging there, toes pointing toward the ground. It looked as though someone had taken his boots.

Maurice heard Ruben Vega saying, "He told me, he said they'd bring him to the ranch," the Mexican not protesting but speaking very quietly. "He said they'd hold him there and take a picture, see, to prove he was being held and was unharmed."

C.S. Fly was busy setting up his camera in the

road, tilting the box upward, then getting down behind it to look, then adjusting it a little more. C.S. Fly didn't say a word.

"That's what he told me," Ruben Vega said. "They would hold him there and threaten to kill him, yes, if his people didn't move away somewhere else. But he never said he would do this. Never."

Was he telling them something or talking to himself? Maurice Dumas wondered.

Yes, it sounded more like he was trying to convince himself.

Was it an act, though, for their benefit?

No—listening to the Mexican's tone more than the actual words, Maurice Dumas believed the man was honestly surprised and telling the truth.

9

1

The news reporters hanging around the Congress Hotel and the Gold Dollar woke up in a hurry.

A man had been lynched in the middle of the afternoon and that goddamn kid from the *Chicago Times* had scooped them again. (The squirt was even wearing his cap cocked over more on the side of his head.)

Things were happening. C.S. Fly developed three pictures of Armando hanging from the pole like a sack of dirty laundry, made a "showing" of them in his gallery window, marched off to the telegraph office and wired Sheriff John Slaughter in Tombstone; notice, bypassing Deputy R.J. Bruckner.

Why? Because Bruckner was a company stooge and John Slaughter and C.S. Fly were friends, the newsmen speculated. Also to show the mine company that if he, Fly, ran for sheriff of Cochise County next year he was not going to place himself in the company's pocket.

Good stuff was developing. A lot of angles.

Item: Sweetmary was a company town. Without LaSalle Mining there would be no Sweetmary. Therefore the people of Sweetmary and its law enforcement agency would never testify against the company or do anything to put the company in legal jeopardy.

Item: John Slaughter wanted to serve out his term and return to ranching. It was said he was more than willing to use his political weight to help Fly get the Republican nomination. John Slaughter was not a company ass kisser, but he had been in office long enough to have become a realist. Since he was getting out anyway, what did he care what happened here in Sweetmary?

The reporters weren't finished writing that one when John Slaughter arrived in town with a gripsack full of warrants and subpoenas and informed the press that a circuit court judge and county attorney were on their way.

Theory: He was going through the motions to show his friend C.S. Fly the facts of life, liberty and the pursuit of justice in a mine company town.

Well, at least they were making a pretty good show of it.

Item: A warrant was issued for the arrest of Phil Sundeen (not even in town a week) and a Mexican by the name of Ruben Vega (Who?). Sundeen was served, arrested and escorted to jail without incident.

Vandozen, the company vice president, was seen in town for a few hours, then was gone—off in a closed carriage to Benson and the Southern Pacific Railroad depot. But a lawyer who had arrived from

Bisbee remained. That same day Sundeen posted a five-hundred-dollar bond and was released. The Mexican, Ruben Vega, could not be located.

Items:

C.S. Fly and the squirt from the *Chicago Times*, Maurice Dumas, were subpoenaed as witnesses.

Eladio Duro, Armando's son, appeared in town out of nowhere, riding a burro, and was taken into "protective custody" by John Slaughter.

Bruckner wandered around town and up to the mine works with sixteen John Doe warrants for the arrest of the members of Sundeen's security force. He returned with the same number of warrants saying they were nowhere to be found and that they had been discharged from the company payroll.

Bruckner did bring in four dead men, their Sunday suits tearing at the seams, their bodies were so swollen. Three had come from Armando's yard, another from not far away. But only two were identified from personal effects: a man named Wade Miller from Illinois and a man named Harry Shell from Kentucky. Holding his nose as he looked at the other two, Phil Sundeen said no, he did not know their names or was even sure now, because of their bloated condition, he had ever seen them before.

The reporters wanted to know: Well, why the hell didn't they ask Sundeen where the *rest* of his men were?

John Slaughter said he did, and Sundeen had answered: "Who, them? They did not like horseback riding and quit."

Well, did he try to get the truth out of Sundeen?

"You mean by the use of physical force?" John

Slaughter asked the reporters. "That is not allowed in the interrogation of suspects. At least not in this county."

But had he used force or not?

Maurice Dumas wrapped a five-dollar bill around a bottle of Green River and put it on R. J. Bruckner's desk as he sat down in the deputy's office. Bruckner did not leave it there more than a moment, getting it into a drawer as Maurice was saying, "Civil servants, I've found, work hard and get little appreciation for their efforts."

"What do you want?" asked Bruckner.

"Haven't you used force on Sundeen to make him talk?"

"Make him talk about what?"

"Where his men are."

"What men? Who saw him with any men?"

"I did," Maurice said.

"Who saw him or any men out where the Mex was found?"

"I saw them here in town."

"So what did you see? Nothing. Get your smart-aleck ass out of here, sonny."

"Who else have you got as a witness," Maurice said, showing his tenacity, "besides Armando's son. Any of the other Mexicans?"

"What Mexicans?"

"Armando's people—the ones that live up there."

"They're gone," Bruckner said, "disappeared. It's you and Fly and the Mex's kid . . . and the Indin agent, Moon."

This surprised Maurice. "You subpoenaed Moon? How come?"

"We believe he saw things."

"Sundeen told you that?"

"We know, that's all."

"Has he come to town?"

"He had better be here tomorrow for the hearing. He's not, I'll go and get him. I may be going for him later on anyway."

"Why? For what?"

"Get your smart-aleck ass out of here," Bruckner said. "Time's up."

Item: The circuit court hearing—to determine if a murder had been committed and if there was sufficient reason to believe Sundeen did it—would be held on the second floor of the city jail. The cells up there had not been occupied in several years. Sections of iron bars had been removed and transported to the mine works to be used, it was said, in the construction of a storage facility for high explosives and blasting equipment. Chairs and benches from the Masonic hall and a funeral parlor were now being placed in the second-floor courtroom for the comfort of spectators and visiting newsmen.

Judge Miller Hough of Tombstone was occupying the LaSalle Suite at the Congress Hotel. Prosecutor Stuart "Stu" Ison, who had practiced law in Sweetmary until winning the county position three years ago, was staying with friends.

The services of a young attorney by the name of Goldwater—said to be a nephew of the owner of the well-known Goldwater & Cateñeda General Store in Bisbee—had been retained to act as counsel for Phil Sundeen.

Color item: The mine and crushing mill continued to work two shifts, business as usual, as the town of Sweetmary bustled with activity in preparation for the hearing. The miners who came down the hill in their coarse work clothes seemed from another world. Many of them were, until recently, from Old World countries. Strange accents and foreign languages were not uncommon on the streets of this mining community.

The news reporters knew what their editors were going to say. Dandy . . . but, goddamn it, where was the Early-Moon confrontation stuff? The stage was set, the suspense built. Now a cattle rustler and ex-con by the name of Sundeen comes along and steals the spotlight. Did he lynch the Mexican or not? What did company-man Bren Early think about it? More important, what were Early and Moon up to during all this, squaring off or just looking at each other?

That was the trouble, they weren't doing anything. But how did you tell an editor Bren Early was holed up at Mrs. Pierson's, wouldn't answer the door, and Moon hadn't showed up yet? If, in fact, he ever would. The newsmen sent wires to their editors that said, in essence, "Big story to break soon," and had a few more drinks while they waited for something to happen.

2

The morning of the hearing the newsmen staying at the Congress came down to the dining room and there was Dana Moon and his wife having a breakfast of grits and ham. Moon did not understand what the newsmen were so excited about. Where had he *been*? Home. If they wanted to see him why didn't they come visit? They asked him why he had been subpoenaed and he said that's why they had come to town this morning, to find out.

Moon and his wife, news reporters trailing behind, stopped by the Fly Gallery to see the latest "showing" in the window: Armando hanging from the telegraph pole. Neither of them said anything as they continued down LaSalle Street to the jail and went upstairs to the hearing.

When the reporters who had been waiting outside Mrs. Pierson's house arrived, they said it didn't look like Bren Early was coming.

After all the excitement and suspense the hearing did not prove to be much of a show. (Which John Slaughter and others could have predicted from the beginning.) Though there was one surprise that stirred considerable interest.

Maurice Dumas, cap under his arm, took the witness stand and told the county attorney, yes, he had seen Mr. Sundeen ride out of Sweetmary with seventeen men. No, Mr. Sundeen would not let any of the reporters follow them. Five hours later he had joined Mr. C.S. Fly and a man in Mr. Sundeen's employ, one Ruben Vega, and accompanied them out to a place where they were to witness a meeting between Mr. Sundeen and Armando Duro. What they found instead was Armando hanging from a pole. Maurice Dumas began to tell about Ruben Vega being "genuinely astonished," but the county attorney, Stuart Ison, said that was all and for him to step down.

C.S. Fly supported the young newsman's testimony as to the purpose of their journey and what they found out on the road. He did not however—if he had witnessed it—mention Ruben Vega's stunned surprise.

Next, Eladio Duro took the stand. Answering the county attorney's questions he admitted, yes, his people had fired on Mr. Sundeen's group when they crossed the property line. (There were several objections by Mr. Goldwater, Sundeen's counsel, during Eladio's testimony, most of which were sustained by Judge Hough.) Eladio described men coming to their house and a Mexican convincing them it was safe to come out and speak to Mr. Sundeen. But as soon as they were outside, Sundeen's men drew pistols and began to shoot at them. Three people fell dead and another was wounded. Before his father could get back in the house Sundeen's men grabbed him and carried him off. Eladio was asked where his family and friends were now. He said they were hiding because they were afraid for their lives. (Objection: judgmental. Sustained.)

Mr. Goldwater, the defense attorney, cross-examined, asking Eladio if the Mexican who spoke to them first carried something in his hands. Yes, Eladio said, a flag of truce. He was asked if his people had fired weapons at Mr. Sundeen and his men. No. But weren't shots fired at Mr. Sundeen's men? No. From others not standing in the yard? Oh, yes; from Sundeen's men who were up on the slope above the house. But weren't three of Sundeen's men struck down by gunfire and killed? Yes, Eladio said. Shot by mistake, he assumed, by their own companions. Eladio was asked to think very carefully before answering the next question. Did the first shots come from the men in the yard or the men on the slope above the house? Eladio was silent and then said, they seemed to both come at the same time.

Mr. Goldwater then called Dana Moon to the stand and asked him if he had been present at Armando Duro's the morning of May the 19th.

"Not actually present," Moon said, already uncomfortable sitting here in this hot room full of people . . . picturing where the cells had been a few years before and where he had talked to Bren through the iron bars.

"But you observed what took place there?"

"Yes."

"You observed a man holding a white flag?"

"Yes."

"How far away were you?"

"About four hundred yards."

"Did you see any others, or another group of men, up on the slope above the house?"

"No."

"You observed the shooting?"

"Yes."

"Did you take part in the shooting?"

"Yes."

"Did you hit anyone?"

Moon hesitated. "I can't say for sure."

"Did you shoot to kill?"

"I fired to prevent Armando and his people, all of them unarmed, from being shot down in cold blood."

"Did you shoot to kill?"

"Yes."

Goldwater walked back to the table where Sundeen sat patiently listening before asking Moon, "Did anyone shoot at you?"

"I can't say."

"You mean you can't tell when someone is shooting at you?"

"If they did, they didn't come close."

"You were firing at . . . whom?"

Moon looked at Sundeen three strides away, closer than he had been the last time, in Sonora. Sundeen stared back at him as if ready to smile.

"Him," Moon said, "and his men. They were about . . . they were shooting at Armando's people."

"They were what?"

"I said they were shooting at Armando's people."

"But you fired at them first, didn't you?"

"They were drawing their weapons—at that distance . . . I would say they fired first or at the same time."

"You heard gunfire before you aimed and fired?"

Jesus Christ, Moon thought, feeling the perspiration under his shirt. He said, "I anticipated their fire. Their weapons were out. In a moment they were firing."

"You just said they were drawing their weapons."

"They were drawing—seeing it from that distance, weapons were out. In a moment they were firing."

"What does the distance have to do with it? You saw what you *thought* they intended to do and you reacted, didn't you? You began shooting."

"I knew what they were gonna do. What they *did*. They killed three of the Mexicans, didn't they?"

"I don't know," Mr. Goldwater said. "Did they? There was gunfire coming from two directions. Didn't you open fire first? . . ."

"No, they did."

"And they returned your fire?"

"That wasn't what happened."

"Well, from the facts we have, I would say there was either a grave misunderstanding—the two parties in the yard began to talk and you misinterpreted it, or . . . you deliberately fired at the yard, not caring who you hit, one group or the other. Or . . . and this is conjecture, though possibly worth investigating . . . you were purposely firing at the Mexican group—"

"Why would I do that?"

"You realize you admit you fired with intent to kill," the defense lawyer said. "That action is subject to interpretation, for I would dare to say the yard itself was a small target at four hundred yards, where the variance of a fraction of an inch could mean the difference in the taking of one man's life or another man's."

Moon looked at the county lawyer who was not objecting to any of these ideas the defense lawyer was planting. Moon said, "Sundeen was in the yard. Let's hear him tell what happened. It ought to be a pretty good story."

He saw Kate smile and heard sounds of approval from the audience.

But then the defense lawyer stepped in front of him, close, and said quietly, "I could ask who else was up there with you. Do you want to implicate others? Did they also shoot to kill?" The defense lawyer stared at him before adding, "Do you see where I can take this?" Moon felt relief when the dark-haired, well-dressed man from Bisbee turned to Judge Hough and said something and the judge asked Ison, the county lawyer, to approach the bench—the table next to which Moon sat in a straight chair.

Moon heard Goldwater say, "So far there is not one bit of evidence to support a murder charge against my client. No one here can place him with Armando at the scene of the hanging. However, your honor, if you are not reasonably convinced I'll put my client on the stand. He'll testify that he did, in fact, rescue Armando, not carry him off, and left him out there when he said he wanted to return to his people." The judge asked how could the court be certain that was what happened? The defense lawyer asked, who could dispute it?

Moon cleared his throat and almost said, "I can," at this point. He could tell them how he had watched from the high ground as the Mexicans put their dead over horses and rode out of there— maybe to somebody else's place or to hide in the timber—and Armando had not returned as long as they watched. But he couldn't tell them if they didn't ask, and it didn't look like that was going to happen. He tugged at the county lawyer's coat a couple of times, but Ison would not pay attention to him. Ison had his head stuck in there with the other two legal minds as they talked lawyer talk to each other and decided the outcome of these proceedings.

During the conference at the bench the people in the audience had begun to compare ideas and opinions and there was a buzz of noise in the low-ceilinged courtroom. It stopped when Judge Hough banged his gavel on the desk.

He said that based on a reasonable doubt because of a lack of substantial evidence the charge of suspicion of murder was hereby dismissed.

That was it. The judge left the courtroom and the news reporters converged on Moon and Sundeen: one group asking Moon if he had actually intended to kill Sundeen; another group asking Sundeen what he intended to do about it. Moon said, you heard my testimony. He was looking for the county lawyer, Ison, to tell the little ass-kisser a few things, but did not see him now. Moon felt himself being moved by the crowd clearing away from between them so that finally they stood facing each other.

Sundeen said, "Well, that's twice you have tried. Four hundred yards, huh?"

"Give or take a few," Moon said. "I see you got a hole in your face from the first time and a piece of ear missing."

The reporters were writing in their notepads now—the story unfolding before their eyes, better than they could have staged it, some of them not noticing Sundeen's hand going to his beard to stroke it gently as he stared at Moon.

"You hung a friend of mine and it doesn't look like the court is gonna do anything about it," Moon said.

Sundeen continued to stare at him. He said then, "Go on home. We'll get her done before too long."

"I suppose," Moon said.

One of the reporters said, "Get your guns and settle it now, why don't you? Out on the street."

Sundeen gave the man a hard stare and said, "For you, you little pissant? Who in the hell you think you are?"

Moon and Sundeen looked at each other again, each knowing something these reporters would never in their lives understand.

Maurice Dumas waited in front of the jail, watching the people coming out. When he saw Moon and his good-looking wife, Maurice had to push his way through the crowd to get close enough to hand Moon the folded piece of note paper. Moon looked at Maurice Dumas, nodded hello, then opened the note and read it while the reporters waited. Moon nodded to Maurice again and handed the note to his wife.

"From Bren," he said.

10

1

Janet Pierson felt left out. She was at ease with them, she liked them; but she didn't feel *with* them. Nor did she feel as close to Bren now. Bren and Dana Moon and his wife had shared something, had lived through an experience during another time that did not include her.

She was aware of the news reporters waiting outside the house, the crowd of them that had followed Moon and his wife here. She liked his wife, Kate; she felt she had known her a long time and the feeling surprised her. For some reason she could sympathize with her; though the young woman did not seem to need or want it. She could also sympathize with the news reporters and knew what they were feeling. She imagined—after Bren and Mr. and Mrs. Moon were gone—the reporters standing at the door asking her questions. What are they like? What did you talk about?

She imagined herself saying, Oh, they're very nice people. Polite, well-mannered.

But what did they talk about?

Nothing in particular. Old times mostly.

Did they get in a fight over the situation?

No, they're friends.

Come on, did they have words?

No. (Not exactly.)

Did they talk about any of the men they'd killed?

No, of course not.

Do you know how many those two have laid to rest?

They would get onto something like that and she would try to close the door.

Did Moon chew tobacco in the house?

Certainly not.

We hear his wife is a tough customer.

She's very nice.

Did she have anything to say?

Of course. She is not timid. She told me about their house.

Was there much tension between them, Early and Moon?

No, it was a very pleasant visit. Mr. Moon described his duties as an Indian agent. ("Through the office of Indian Affairs . . . handle all relations between the federal government and the Indians . . . direct the administration of tribal resources . . . supervise their 'trust' property . . . promote their health and physical welfare . . . guide their activities toward the attainment of economic self-sufficiency, self-government and the preservation of Indian cultural values." Bren said, "And what exactly does that mean?" And Moon said, "Try to keep them from doing what is most natural to them, raiding and making war.") While Mr. Early explained his responsibilities with the company. ("You get a big stockholder out here a thousand and some miles from home, what do you think is the first thing he wants to see?" "An Indian," Moon said. "That's the second thing," Bren said. "A whorehouse," Mrs. Moon said. "Correct," Bren said, and they had a good laugh over it.)

What else might be asked? Janet Pierson wondered if her name would appear in a newspaper or in *Harper's Weekly*. "In an interview with Mrs. Pierson, a close friend of the" . . . legendary, celebrated, renowned . . . famous . . . "the well-known figures who are playing important roles in the controversial land war . . ." What? "Mrs. Pierson stated they are very polite, well-mannered people."

She said, "I don't understand it at all. I don't. How can you sit there like it's just another day and completely ignore what's going on?"

Bren put on a concerned frown. "Honey, we're just visiting; catching up's what we're doing. You know it's been over three years?"

"Yes, I know it's been three years. You date everything you talk about," Janet Pierson said. "Sonora in eighty-seven. St. Helen's, some stagecoach station in eighty-nine. The wedding three years ago . . ."

There was a silence. They seemed content to let it go on, patient people, used to quiet; the Moons sitting together on the sofa could be on the porch Kate had described . . . Bren with a leg over the arm of his chair. Coffee cups on the end tables . . . News reporters outside dying of curiosity: Were they at each other's throats or plotting a way to kill Sundeen?

Bren said, you want some more coffee? The Moons said, no, thank you.

Janet Pierson, hands gripping the arms of her chair, said, "Would you like to hear about my past life, my marriage? How I came to live here? My husband, Paul, was a mining engineer. He designed and built the crushing mill up at the works that one day, when he wasn't feeling well and should have stayed in bed—I told him, in your condition you should *not* be walking around that machinery . . ."

Silence again.

Finally Kate Moon said, "Do you want them to talk about the situation? What do you want?"

"These *two*—" Janet Pierson began, almost angrily and had to calm herself. "These two, the heroic figures—some people must believe they're seven feet tall—what are they *doing*?"

"They're resting," Kate Moon said. "Ask them. Dana, what are you doing?"

"Wondering if we shouldn't be going."

"I'm sorry," Janet Pierson said. "I'm the one acting strange. I'm sincerely sorry."

Kate said, "Bren, what are you doing?"

"I don't know," Bren said. "Passing time? It does seem funny sitting here like this."

Moon looked at him. "What are you gonna do?"

Bren frowned again. "What do you mean, what am I gonna do?"

"Your man lynched my man."

"He isn't in any way *my* man."

"You both work for the same company."

"I don't work. I told you that. I draw money for my claims, that's all."

"All right, you're both paid by the same company."

"I don't have anything to do with this situation. What do you expect me to do, quit? You want me to walk out with them still owing me seventy thousand dollars?"

"I'm not your conscience," Moon said. "I'm not telling you what to do."

"You bet you're not."

There was a silence again.

Kate said to Janet Pierson, "You like it better now?"

"Please—I'm sorry," Janet Pierson said. She was; though she did not feel guilt or remorse. She had to hear what they thought, if she was going to understand them.

Bren rose from his chair. "I'm going to the latrine—if it ain't full of newspaper reporters."

"You still call it that?" Moon said.

Janet Pierson said she wanted to fix them something to eat and followed Bren out to the kitchen.

When they were alone, Moon said, "What are we doing here?"

"Be nice," Kate said.

"I am nice," he said. "That's all I'm doing, just sitting here being nice. I wonder what that son of a bitch Ison is doing. Probably having a drink and a good laugh with the judge and that other lawyer in his new suit."

"You knew what was gonna happen," Kate said. "Don't act so surprised."

He patted her hand. "I'm glad you're so sweet and understanding. I hope Ison and Hough run again next year so I can vote against them, the ass-kissers."

"Well, our old friend Sundeen would've got off anyway," Kate said. "What did they have to convict him with? Nothing."

"Let's go home."

"If she's fixing something, we should stay."

Moon looked toward the kitchen door. "Do you suppose he's living here with her?"

"It's his house," Kate said. "He either bought it for her, or so he can say he owns a bigger house than yours—"

"Jesus Christ," Moon said.

"I'm not sure which," Kate said. "But she's a nice person, so don't look down your nose at her."

"I'm not looking down my nose."

"I like her," Kate went on. "She's a feeling person, not afraid to tell you what she thinks."

"Or what other people think," Moon said. "You two should get along fine. You can tell us what's on our minds and save us the trouble of talking about it."

"She's worried about Bren; can't you see that?"

"Bren? Christ, nobody's shooting at Bren. He isn't even in it."

"That's what bothers her," Kate said. "He won't take sides." She looked up and smiled as Janet Pierson came into the sitting room. "We were just talking about you."

"I don't blame you," the woman said.

Kate made a tsk-tsk sound, overdoing it, shaking her head. "Why worry about what people think? You know what you're doing."

"Sometimes I guess I say too much."

"Sure, when you run out of patience," Kate said. "I know what you mean."

Moon's gaze moved from his wife to the woman, wondering what the hell they were talking about. Then looked toward the door at the sound of someone banging on it, three times. There was a pause. Janet Pierson didn't move. Then came three more loud banging sounds, the edge of somebody's fist pounding the wood panel hard enough to shake the door.

When Bren appeared again in the backyard, coming from the outhouse, the reporters on the other side of the fence in the vacant lot called to him, come on, just give us a minute or so. What were you talking about in there? . . . Debating the issues or what? . . . When's Moon going to meet Sundeen?

Then there was some kind of commotion. The reporters by the fence were looking away, moving off, then running from the vacant lot toward the front of the house. Bren went inside. There were onions and peppers on the wooden drain board in the kitchen, a pot of dry beans soaking. He heard the banging on the front door.

Janet Pierson was standing in the middle of the sitting room, saying, "They're not bashful at all, are they?"

Bren walked past her to the door, pulled it open and stopped, surprised, before he said, "What do you want?"

Deputy J.R. Bruckner stood at the door. Looking past Bren at Moon sitting on the sofa, Bruckner said, "Him. I got a warrant for the arrest of one

Dana Moon. He can come like a nice fella or kicking and screaming, but either way he's coming."

2

In Benson, Ruben Vega had to find the right church first, St. John the Apostle, then had to lie to the priest to get him to come from the priest house to the church to hear his Confession.

Kneeling at the small window in the darkness of the confessional, Ruben Vega said, "Bless me, father, for I have sinned. It has been . . . thirty-seven years since my last confession."

The old priest groaned, head lowered, pinching the bridge of his nose with his eyes closed.

"Since then I have fornicated with many women . . . maybe eight hundred. No, not that many, considering my work. Maybe six hundred only."

"Do you mean bad women or good women?" the priest asked.

"They are all good, Father," Ruben Vega said. "Let me think, I stole about . . . I don't know, twenty-thousand head of beeves, but only in that time maybe fifty horses." He paused for perhaps a full minute.

"Go on."

"I'm thinking."

"Have you committed murder?"

"No."

"All the stealing you've done—you've never killed anyone?"

"Yes, of course, but it was not to commit murder.

You understand the distinction? Not to *kill* some-one, to take a life; but only to save my own."

The priest was silent, perhaps deciding if he should go further into this question of murder. Finally he said, "Have you made restitution?"

"For what?"

"For all you've stolen. I can't give you absolution unless you make an attempt to repay those you've harmed or injured."

Jesus, Ruben Vega thought. He said, "Look, that's done. I don't steal no more. But I can't pay back twenty thousand cows. How in the name of Christ can I do that? Oh—" He paused. "And I told a lie. I'm not dying. But, listen, man, some-body is going to," Ruben Vega said, his face close to the screen that covered the little window, "if I don't get absolution for my sins."

He had forgotten how difficult they could make it when you wanted to unburden yourself. But now he was a new person, aware of his spurs making a clear, clean ching-ing sound as he walked out of the empty church—leaving thirty-seven years with the old man in the confessional—going to the depot now to buy a ticket on the El Paso & South-western, ride to Douglas, cross the border and go home.

He hung around the yards watching the freight cars being switched to different tracks, smelling the coal smoke, hearing the harsh sound of the cars banging together and the wail of the whistle as an eastbound train headed out for Ochoa and the climb through Dragoon Pass. He wanted to remain outside tonight in the fresh air rather than go to a hotel in Benson; so he camped by the river and watched the young boys laughing and splashing each other, trying to catch minnows. With dark, mosquitoes came. They drove him crazy. Then it began to rain, a light, steady drizzle, and Ruben Vega said to himself: What are you doing here? He bought a bottle of *mescal* and for ten of the sixty dollars in his pocket he spent the night in a whorehouse with a plump, dark-haired girl named Rosa who thought he was very witty and laughed at everything he said when he wasn't being serious. Though some of the wittiest things he said seriously and they passed over her. That was all right. He gave her a dollar tip. In the morning Ruben Vega cashed in his ticket for the El Paso & Southwestern, mounted his horse and rode back toward the Rincon Mountains standing cleanly defined in the sunlight.

3

R. J. Bruckner said, "Look. They give me a warrant signed by Judge Hough for the arrest of Dana Moon. I served it over all kinds of commotion and people trying to argue with me and those newspaper men getting in the way. It took me and four deputies to clear them out and put Moon in detention. Now you got a complaint, go see the judge or the county attorney, it's out of my hands."

"Are you gonna drink that whole bottle yourself?" Sundeen asked.

He reached behind him to close the door, giving them some privacy in the deputy's little office with its coal-oil lamp hanging above the desk.

"I was having a touch before supper," Bruckner said, getting another glass out of his desk and placing it before Sundeen. "Not that it's any of your business."

"I see they all went home," Sundeen said, "the judge, the prosecutor and John Slaughter, leaving you with a mess, haven't they?"

"I'm doing my job," Bruckner said, pouring a short drink for Sundeen and setting the bottle within easy reach. "I don't see there's any mess here."

Sundeen leaned close as if to pick up the glass and swept the desk clean with his hand and arm, sending bottle, glasses and papers flying against the side wall. It brought the deputy's head up with a jerk, eyes staring open at the bearded, bullet-marked face, the man leaning over the desk on his hands, staring back at him.

"Look again," Sundeen said. "Listen when I'm talking to you and keep your hands in sight, else I'll draw iron and lay it across your head."

It was the beginning of a long night for R.J. Bruckner. First this one coming in and saying he wanted Moon released from jail. What? How was he supposed to do that? You think he just set a person free when somebody asked? Sundeen said he was not asking, he was telling him. He wanted Moon, but he was not going to stick a gun through the bars to get him. He wanted Moon out on the street. Bruckner would send him out and he would take care of it from there.

Ah, now that didn't sound too bad.

Except that Bruckner was looking forward to having Moon stay with him awhile. He owed

Moon, the son of a bitch, at least a few lumps with a pick handle but had not gotten around to it yet.

Bruckner sat back thinking about it, saying, "Yeah, like he was shot down while trying to escape."

"Jesus, it doesn't take you long, does it?" Sundeen said.

Bruckner did not get that remark. He was thinking that he liked the idea of Moon being shot down even better than taking a pick handle to him . . . especially if it turned out he was the one pulled the trigger and not this company dude with the silver buckles.

"Yeah," he said, nodding, "let me think on it awhile."

Then was pulled up short again as Sundeen said, "You bag of shit, the thinking's been done. He walks out of here tonight at . . . let's say eleven o'clock, after you show him a release form."

"A release form? I don't have anything like that."

"Jesus, you show him *some*thing. A wire from the county clerk saying the charge's been dropped. Eleven o'clock, open the door for him to walk out and duck," Sundeen said. "You do anything else, like try and back-shoot him, you'll see fireworks go off in your face."

First Sundeen—

Then Bren Early walking into the office, looking at the mess on the floor where the bottle had knocked over the spittoon and the papers lying there were stained with tobacco juice and whiskey.

"Come to see your old partner?"

"In a minute," Early said, looking down at Bruckner from where Sundeen had stood a little while before. "You owe me a favor."

"For what?"

"Not killing you three years ago. That would be reason enough to do what I ask, but I'm gonna give you another one." Early brought paper scrip from his inside coat pocket and dropped it on the desk. "Being practical—why was he arrested in the first place?" Early watched Bruckner pick up the money and begin to count it. "Because he admitted in court trying to shoot somebody. But how're they gonna convict him if he stands mute at his trial? Moon being an agent of the federal government and all—"

"Five hundred," Bruckner said, looking up.

"Since he'd get off anyway—all you'd be doing is cutting a corner, wouldn't you?"

Bruckner folded the money into his shirt pocket and sat back, getting comfortable, big nose glistening in the coal-oil light. "I would need to do a little preparing, make it look real, you understand."

"I was thinking, in a few days when you take him to the county seat," Early said. "Out on the road someplace—"

"No, it's got to be tonight," Bruckner said.

"Why is that?"

"Because I'm on duty tonight and if I'm gonna do this I want to get it done, over with." Bruckner paused. He had to think, picture it, without taking too much time. If Sundeen and Early were both waiting outside . . . If they saw each other as Moon came out . . . If they went for each other, there'd be guns going off, wouldn't there, and he could maybe have a clear shot at Moon going out and then, what if he put the gun on Early, if Early was still standing up? . . . Shoot the accomplice . . . Jesus Christ, shoot Sundeen if he had to, if he saw the chance . . . Shoot all three of them during the confusion . . . Shoot those big names in the newspapers, God Almighty, gun them down, all three of them shot dead by Deputy Sheriff R. J. Bruckner . . . Oh yes, that's Bruckner, he's the one that gunned down Moon, Bren Early and Phil Sundeen, the Yuma terror, during a daring jailbreak . . . Wiped them out, all three of them. Jesus.

"What're you nervous about?" Early asked him.

Bruckner pulled out a handkerchief to wipe his forehead and down over his nose and mouth. "Goddamn dinky office is like a hotbox. I'm gonna get out of here pretty soon, run for the job in Tombstone next year. Shit, if I can't beat Fly, with my experience in law enforcement—"

"Let's get this done first," Early said.

Bruckner nodded, mind made up. "Tonight, eleven o'clock . . . No, five minutes before eleven. You come, leave a horse for him in front. Step inside and give me a nod. I'll go back and get your partner, lock myself up in his cell."

"Why not the back door?" Early said. "In the alley."

"That door don't open. It's bolted shut."

"All right, let me talk to him now."

"Tell him five minutes before eleven," Bruckner said.

This time it was Moon in the cell and Early looking through the bars.

He said, "I talked to John Slaughter before they moved their show out of here. John says they didn't have a choice, you shot three men in that yard. They'll hold your trial at the county seat. Now, considering everything, the company'll turn on the pressure to get a conviction. See if they can send you to Yuma."

"It's a lot of country from here to there," Moon said. "Kate visits tomorrow, I'll talk to her about it. You don't have to get involved in this."

"I already am," Early said. "Sundeen was here about a half-hour ago. The way I see it, he doesn't want you in here either. He's been keeping quiet, but that business in Sonora's still eating him."

"I know that," Moon said.

"I talked to Bruckner and he was already there waiting. Had the time set and everything."

"What'd you pay him?"

"Not much. He owes me a favor. But wouldn't it make his heart glad to shoot you going out the door and me standing there? Or Sundeen. He paid a visit—something's already been arranged here, I can feel it."

"I can smell it," Moon said. "But this isn't any of your business. If he's gonna open the door, I'll take my own chances."

"What was it you said the time I was in there and you were out here?" Early paused before reciting the words from three years ago. "'You might see it coming, but I doubt it.' Well, you'll probably hear me three blocks away."

"Drawing your sword and yelling, 'Charge,'" Moon said. "It should be something to watch."

4

The parlor was semi-dark with only one lamp lit, turned low. When Kate came down the stairs, Janet Pierson turned from the front window.

"Did you rest?"

"A little. I didn't sleep though."

Kate walked over to the hall tree and took down her husband's suitcoat and holstered revolver. (They had taken him out of the house in his shirt-sleeves, hurrying to get him past the throng of newsmen.)

Watching her, Janet said, "I envy you. I'm not sure why, but I do."

Kate draped the coat over the back of a chair. Holding the shoulder holster, she slipped the Colt's revolver in and out of the smooth leather groove, then drew the gun and looked at the loads in the chambers as she said, "You don't have to envy anyone. You can do whatever you want with your life."

"But you *know* what you want."

"This minute I do," Kate said. "I want my husband. If I have to shoot somebody to get him, I will. It's not something I have to think about and decide." She looked toward the kitchen, at the sound of the back door opening and closing, then at Janet again. "This doesn't mean anything to you personally. Why get mixed up in something just for the sake of taking sides?"

The question was left unanswered. Bren Early came in from the kitchen with saddlebags over one shoulder.

"I haven't seen a soul in front," Janet said to him.

"Tired of waiting around," Bren said. "They're in the saloon telling each other stories." He took the holstered revolver from Kate and slipped it into the saddlebag that hung in front of him. "I still think it'd be better if you waited here."

Kate shook her head. "I'll be out on the road. If you won't let me any closer—"

"You might hear shooting," Bren said. "This man wants to make it look real. Stay where you are till Moon gets there. But for some reason he doesn't—he gets delayed or has to ride out the other way, you come back here."

"What do you mean, gets delayed? I thought it was all arranged."

"It is. I'm talking about if something happens to change the plan . . . somebody comes along doesn't know about it. That's all."

"You're not telling me everything," Kate said. "What is it?"

"Believe me," Bren said, "Dana's gonna walk out. But you have to be patient and not spook if you hear a lot of noise. All right? Wait'll I'm gone a few minutes before you leave."

"I'll be out there before eleven," Kate said. "By the first bend."

Janet watched Bren pick up Moon's coat, then lean toward Kate and kiss her on the cheek. Turning he looked at Janet. "I'll be back in a little while." And went out through the kitchen.

The room was quiet again.

"I don't know what to say to him." Janet turned to the window to watch for him. He'd ride past the front of the house leading Moon's horse.

"Then don't say anything," Kate said, walking over to her, her gaze going out the window to the dark street.

"I feel—I don't feel part of him or what any of you are doing."

"Well, you can come up the mountain for a visit, except I don't think it's a very good time." Kate paused and put her hand on Janet's shoulder. "Why don't you just marry him and quit thinking about it?"

"You sound like Bren now."

"If you have to be absolutely sure before you make a move," Kate said, "then forget it. Else you're gonna be sitting here with cobwebs all over you."

5

LaSalle Street was quiet: first-shift miners in bed for the night, the second shift still up at the works where dots of lantern light marked the shaft scaffolding and company buildings; the crushing mill was dark, the ore tailings black humps running down the slope.

Sundeen, mounted, came down out of that darkness into the main street, holding his horse to a walk past the store fronts and evenly spaced young trees planted to grow along the sidewalk. The porch of the Congress Hotel was deserted. Lights showed in the lobby and in saloons and upstairs windows down the street. It was quarter to eleven. At the sound of gunfire they'd pour out of the saloons—most of them who were sober or not bet-

ting against a pot—the news reporters coming out
of their hangout, the Gold Dollar, which was on
the northeast corner of LaSalle and Fourth streets.
The jail was on the southwest corner, the cellblock
extending along Fourth toward Mill Street. On the
corner across Fourth from the jail was the Maricopa State Bank. On the corner across LaSalle—
where Sundeen now dropped his reins and stepped
down from his horse—was the I.S. Weiss Mercantile Store.

Sundeen, looking at the jail and its two lighted
windows—the one to the left of the door to Bruckner's office—did not see the dark figure sitting on
the steps of the bank, catty-corner from him.

When the figure got to its feet Sundeen caught
the movement and knew who it was: yes, crossing
Fourth Street toward the jail with something dark
draped over his shoulder and carrying a short club
or something in his left hand. No, not a club. The
object gave off a glint and took shape in the light
from the jail window and Sundeen saw it was a
stubby little shotgun.

Early stopped. He half turned to look across
toward the Mercantile Store.

"It isn't gonna be as easy as you thought."

"What is?" Sundeen said. Shit.

"Where's all your men at?"

"I didn't think I'd need them this evening."

"Well," Early said, "you better decide if you're
gonna be there when we come out."

"God damn Bruckner," Sundeen said. "I think
he has got cow shit for brains."

"No, he's not one to put your money on," Early
said. "Well, I'll see you if you're still gonna be

there." He moved past the jail window toward the front door.

There was nobody to trust, Bruckner had decided. Not a friend, not one of his four deputies. Not in something like this. The chance, if it came, would be there for him alone and he would have to do it himself if he wanted to reap the benefits. And, oh my Lord, the benefits. Both at hand and in the near future, with a saloon-full of news reporters across the street to begin the spread of his fame which would lead to his fortune. All he had to do, at the exact moment when he saw the chance, was pull the trigger three times—at least two times—and in the coming year he would be the Fighting Sheriff of Cochise County . . . working angles the mine company and the taxpayers never knew existed. Being ready was the key. Here is how he would do it:

Early sticks his head in the door, gives him the nod.

Unarmed, he goes back to the lockup, thanking the Lord he had put Moon in a cell by himself.

He steps in, Moon steps out, locks him in. As soon as Moon is through the door, into the front part of the jail . . .

He unlocks the cell with a spare key, goes through to the front, gets the loaded shotgun and Peacemaker from under the cabinet . . .

Runs to the door—maybe hearing Sundeen's gunfire about then—and opens up on them with the shotgun, close behind, while they're busy with Sundeen.

Then, as Sundeen comes across the street—and before anybody is out of the Gold Dollar—blow out Sundeen's lights.

If Sundeen's fire turns them back in the jail, which was possible, he'd bust them as they came through the door. Then step out and shoot Sundeen with the Peacemaker, saying later the man had fired at him after he'd told him to drop his gun, so he'd had no choice but to return fire. (He could hear himself telling it, saying something about being sworn to enforce the law, by God, no matter who the armed men were he had to face.) Killing the two should buy him the ticket to the county seat; but he would like to notch up Sundeen also, long as he was at it.

In case of an unexpected turn—if he somehow lost his weapons and found himself at close quarters, he had a two-shot bellygun under his vest, pressing into his vitals.

At a quarter to eleven Bruckner stopped pacing around the front room of the jail, moving from the railing that divided the room to the front window and back, went into his office and sat down, wishing he had just a couple swallows of that Green River drying on the floor.

At five to eleven he thought he heard voices outside. He turned to the window, but came around again as he heard the door open and close. Bren Early appeared in the doorway to his office wearing his .44's, saddlebags over his shoulder and carrying a sawed-off shotgun. At this moment Bruckner's plan began to go all to hell.

"O.K.," Bruckner said, getting up and coming out to the front room as Early stepped back. "You got his horse?"

Early nodded.

"I'll fetch him. Go on outside."

Early looked at Bruckner's empty holster, then over at the gun rack, locked with two vertical iron bars. "Where the keys?"

"Don't worry—go on outside." Bruckner took a ring of keys from the desk in the front room, walked to the metal-ribbed door leading to the cell block and unlocked it before looking back at Early.

"What're you waiting on?"

Early moved toward him, making a motion with the sawed-off shotgun.

Early coming back with him wasn't in the plan. But maybe it wouldn't hurt anything. It could even make it easier, having the two right together.

Bruckner glanced over his shoulder walking down the row of cells. He raised his hands as one of the prisoners, then another, saw them and pushed up from their bunks. A voice behind Early said, "Hey, partner, open this one. Let me out of this shit hole."

Moon stood at his cell door. He stepped aside as Bruckner entered, made a half-turn and came around to slam a fist into the side of Bruckner's face. The deputy hit the adobe wall and slid to the floor. Moon stood over him a moment, seeing blood coming out of the man's nose. He said, "Don't ever put your hands on me again," and gave him a parting boot in the ribs, drawing a sharp gasp from Bruckner.

Early held the lockup door open as Moon came through, then slammed it closed, cutting off the voices of the prisoners yelling to be let out.

"Sundeen was out in front. Just him I could see, but it doesn't mean he's alone," Early said.

From the saddlebags Moon took his folded-up coat and shoulder rig and slipped them on, saying, "How far you going in this?"

"See you get out of here, that's all. But Sundeen's a different matter. I mean if he wants to try." Early paused. "If he doesn't, maybe we should go find him, get the matter settled."

Moon was smoothing his coat, adjusting the fit of the holster beneath his left arm. He took the sawed-off from Early. "I ain't lost any sleep over him. Least I haven't yet."

"No, but he's gonna bother you now, he gets the chance. I'd just as soon finish it."

Moon seemed to study him, forming words in his mind. "Is it you've been sitting around too long, you're itchy? Or you just wanted to shoot somebody?"

"I can go home and leave it up to you," Early said, a cold edge there.

"Yes, you can. And I'd probably handle him one way or the other."

Early stared at Moon a moment, turned and walked toward the door.

Moon said, "You understand what I mean? I want to be sure about him."

Early pulled the door wide open and stepped aside. "Go on and find out then." Still with the cold edge.

Shit, Moon thought. He said, "Get over your touchiness. You sound like a woman." And walked out the door past him—the hell with it—out into the middle of the street, looking around, before he saw his horse over by the side of the bank. He didn't see any sign of Sundeen and didn't expect to;

the man wasn't going to shoot out of the dark and not get stand-up credit for his kill.

Early came out to the board sidewalk, pulling the door partly closed behind him. He said, "Go on home, sit on your porch. Kate's waiting up by the bend."

"Thanks," Moon said, glancing over, already moving toward Fourth Street.

"You don't have to thank me for anything," Early said. "We're even now, right? Don't owe each other a thing."

Jesus, Moon thought. He should hear himself.

He saw the light in the half-closed doorway behind Early widen. He saw a figure, Bruckner, and yelled, "Bren!" and had to drop the sawed-off with Bren in the way and the door too far; he had to drop it to pull the goddamn saddlebags off his shoulder and come out with the Colt's, seeing Early throwing himself out of the way as Bruckner's shotgun exploded and Moon's revolver kicked in his hand and he saw Bruckner punched off his feet as the .44 took him somewhere in the middle of his body. Bren was up then, yelling at him to go on, get out of here, waving his arm.

You better, Moon thought, picking up the sawed-off. He could see Bruckner's feet in the doorway, beyond Early. And sounds now from across the street, people starting to come out of the Gold Dollar, standing there, looking this way. Moon reached his horse and stepped up; he pointed toward Mill Street and was gone in the darkness.

⇌ 11 ⇌

1

Moon stopped at White Tanks on the way home "to put in an appearance," he told Kate, say hello to the reservation Apaches he hadn't seen in weeks and sort through his mail—any directives, bulletins or other bullshit he might have received from Washington.

Kate said she was glad she didn't have to read it. She would go home and light the fire. He watched her take off across the pasture toward the brushy slope and start up the switchback trail that climbed through the field of saguaro, watching her until she was a tiny speck, his little wife up there on the mountain, and said to himself, "You know how lucky you are?" He was anxious to get home to her. Maybe he'd look at the mail but check on the reservation people tomorrow.

He sat down at his desk though, to read the letter from the Bureau of Indian Affairs, Interior Department, Washington, D.C. It took him about a quarter of an hour to find out all the two and a half pages of official language actually said was, he was fired . . . would be relieved of his duties for disregarding such and such, as of a date three months from now. Fired because he hadn't brought his Indians down off the mountain, failing to comply with directive number . . . some long number. The fools. They could have said it in two words.

He'd go home and tell Kate and watch her eyes open—Kate poised there, not knowing whether to show relief or rail at the imbeciles in the bureau, pausing and then asking, "Well, how do you feel about it?"

How did he feel?

Relief, yes, able to wade out of the official muck, walk off. Or would he be walking *out*, leaving the reservation people when they needed him? Well, they may need *some*body, but he wasn't doing them a hell of a lot of good, was he? And what difference did it make now, since he didn't have a choice but to leave? Thinking about all that at once, blaming himself for not having thought of an answer sooner . . . and hearing the bootsteps on the porch, the ching-ing sound, without first hearing a horse approach—

The Mexican stood in the open doorway. The one from Sonora. The one from Duro's yard with the white flag. Hesitant. Raising his hands from his sides.

"You didn't walk here," Moon said.

"I didn't want to startle you. Maybe you come out shooting you hear me," Ruben Vega said. "Listen to me and believe it, all right? I don't work for Sundeen no more, but he's up on the mountain."

"Where?" Moon came out of his swivel chair.

"Going to your house."

"When was this?"

"Last night, very late."

Moon came around his desk and Ruben Vega had to get out of his way. He followed Moon out to the porch.

"Wait. I want to tell you something. I didn't *see* him up there, I heard it, where he's going."

Moon, at his horse gathering the reins, looked up at the Mexican. "Tell it quick."

"See, I quit him. I went to Benson. I was going to go home, but I decide after all the years, after all the bad things I done—"

Moon stepped up into his saddle.

"I came back here to do some good, be on the good side for a change—whether you believe me or not." He saw Moon's look. "Listen to me, all right? I came back, I stop by this place where I believe his men have been waiting, the J-L-Bar, an old, worn-out place. Yes, there they are. They say, where you been? Listen—"

Moon was reining, moving out.

"They say to me Sundeen comes tonight and we go up the mountain to get the man name Moon. You hear me?" Shouting it.

Ruben Vega ran to his horse ground-tied in the pasture. Maybe he would catch up to Moon already racing for the brush slope, maybe he wouldn't.

She'd say to him, "Come on to bed." He'd say, "It's daytime." She'd say, "I mean to *sleep*," after riding most the night—God, she had been glad to see him coming out the road with the lights of Sweetmary behind him. She wanted at least to hug and kiss him awhile, touch him, make sure he was here.

Kate built a fire in the stove and put on a pot of coffee before going outside again to tend Goldie. She led the palomino around the house to the corral that was made of upright mesquite poles wired together. This pen was attached to a timber and thatched-roof structure open at both ends that served as a horse barn. Kate heard the sound—a horse hoof on gravel . . . a soft whinny . . . then silence—as she was leading Goldie across the corral.

She looked through the barn to the back of the property where open graze reached to a brush thicket and a tumble of boulders. There the ground began to climb again. An Apache could be passing by. Even when Moon said they were close she rarely saw one, unless they were coming out and wanted to be seen. They kept to themselves. Red, the little bow-legged chief, was the only one she had ever spoken to; the women just grinned when she tried talking to them in Spanish learned from Moon. Yes, it could be an Apache going by. Her gaze raised to the escarpment of seamed rock standing against the sky. Or they might be up there watching over her.

But she had the feeling someone else was much closer. She turned to Goldie, patting her as she moved back to the saddlebags, raised the leather flap close to her face and drew the .38 double-action revolver Moon had given her that time in Sonora and had given to her again in the past month.

Someone was watching her. Not Apaches, someone else.

Kate led Goldie back to the mesquite-pole gate,

dragged it open enough to let them through. As she prepared to mount—looking over the saddle and through the open-ended barn again, she saw the four riders coming out of the brush thicket, walking their horses, looking right at her. Kate stepped into the saddle kicking, turned the corner to the front of the house and reined in, not knowing what to do, Goldie sidestepping, nervous, feeling Kate's heels and the reins and, between the two, Kate's indecision.

Sundeen sat his mount with two riders near. A bunch more were by the adobe wall and coming through the gate on foot, all of them holding rifles.

"Well, it's been a long time," Kate said, resigned.

"What?" Sundeen studied her, not knowing what she meant.

"You don't remember, do you?"

Sundeen, squinting now, shook his head.

"One time, I was twelve years old playing by the river," Kate said. "You come along, tried to pull my britches down and I smacked you with a rock."

"Jesus Christ," Sundeen said, "down Lanoria."

"You were grown then, too, you dirty pervert."

"Yeah, I believe I recall that—hit me with a big goddamn rock." He looked at one of his riders who was wearing a vest and derby hat. "Thing musta weighed five pounds. Hit me square on the forehead with it." Sundeen nudged his horse forward. "So you're the one, huh? You should've give in that time and seen the elephant at an early age." Still coming toward her. "Or I could give you another chance while we're waiting around." He pulled in then. "Hey now—but you better throw that gun down first."

Kate raised the .38 from her lap. "Or I could put a hole in the other side of your face, match the one you already got."

"Sweetheart," Sundeen said, "before you could aim that parlor gun I'd have sent you off to the angels. Now let it fall."

Of course, the man was thinking of his wife. Ruben Vega realized this. He should have realized also—knowing something about Moon—the man would control his emotion and not ride blindly up the ravine to be shot from his saddle. So Ruben Vega was able to catch up with the man once they were in the high rocks, somewhere north of the ravine, perhaps on an approach to the side or back of the house; Ruben Vega wasn't exactly sure where they were when he reached Moon. Or when the Apache appeared ahead of them, waiting in the trail. One moment the steep terrain ahead empty, the next moment the dark little half-naked man standing there with a carbine and a cartridge belt around his skirt. A headband of dark wool, as dark as his dark-leather face; he could be an old man, or any age.

The Apache, Red, motioned and went off through the towering outcropping of rocks, through a seam that became a trail when they dismounted and followed, winding, climbing through the rock and brush until the trail opened and the entire sky seemed to be close above them, a very clear soft blue. A beautiful day to feel good and be alive, the Mexican was thinking. Except for the situation, the man's wife—Moon and the Apache, and now three more Apaches who had appeared from nowhere, were looking down the wall of rock . . . as though from the top of a church steeple, the Mexican thought, seeing the stone side of the house below, the thatched roof of a barn, a corral, riders in the front yard . . . the glint of the woman's blonde hair in the sunlight close to Sundeen . . . Yes, it was Sundeen and two others . . . four more coming from the corral side of the house . . . the rest of them out by the adobe wall, watching the approach from the ravine.

A good day, the Mexican thought, feeling alive and yet calm inside. A day he would mark in his mind, whatever the date was. He would find it out later.

He said to Moon, "Is there a way down from here?"

Moon looked at him. The man could skip all the questions in his mind and trust him or not.

Moon said, "You go down . . . then what?"

The man was open. He had nothing to lose by listening.

"You stay behind me, out of sight," Ruben Vega said. "Come in close as you can when I talk to him."

"Tell him what?"

"I don't know. What comes in my mind. He'll be curious a few minutes—where have you been, partner? All that. Then you have to be close. I can talk to him some more, but it comes out the same in the end, uh? He isn't going to say to your wife, go on, stay out of the way. So—" the Mexican shrugged.

"Thirteen of them," Moon said.

"More than that last night at the J-L-Bar. He hired some more maybe he send someplace else, I

don't know." Moon was staring at him again and
Ruben Vega said, "I never done this before, but it's
a good day to begin. Now, how do you get down
from here?"

There were ten at the adobe wall now, dismounted.
One with a derby hat sat his horse in the middle of
the yard, a Winchester across his lap, squinting up
at the high rocks. One on the porch was holding
a coffee pot. Sundeen, still mounted, was gazing
about, looking up at the rocks trying to see something, nervous or not sure with that high ground
above him. Moon's wife was still on the palomino:
as though Sundeen hadn't made up his mind yet,
keep her here or take her somewhere, or trying to
think of a way to use her.

Good, Ruben Vega thought, approaching the
yard from the corral side of the house, almost to
the yard before they saw him. Very good.

"I think you need me," the Mexican said, "for
eyes. Man, I ride up, you don't even see me."

Sundeen gave him a patient look, shaking his
head. "Where the hell you been?"

"I went to Benson to go to church," Ruben Vega
said.

"Yeah, I know, piss all your money away and
come back for some more, haven't you? Well, make
yourself useful, partner. Ride on down a ways and
see if he's coming."

"I already did," Ruben Vega said. "He's coming
up pretty soon, over there," pointing to the wall
where the shooters were waiting with their rifles,
not wearing their suitcoats now, several of them
with straw hats pulled down low.

The one in the derby hat rode over that way and
Sundeen sat for some moments twisted around in
his saddle, looking toward the wall.

Now, the Mexican thought, right hand on his
thigh, inches from his revolver.

But he couldn't do it and the next moment it was
too late. Sundeen was turning back to him.

Ruben Vega looked away. He saw the revolver
on the ground next to the palomino. Moon's wife
sat still, though her eyes moved and she listened.
Of course, she listened. He wished he could tell her
something: Be ready. Be watching me.

"Alone?"

"What?" the Mexican said.

"Was he alone?"

"Yes. Maybe they can see him now," the Mexican said and looked toward the wall again.

But Sundeen didn't turn this time and the Mexican had a strange feeling of relief, not having to
decide in that moment to pull his gun . . . not wanting to shoot the man from a blind side, but not
wanting to die either. So how was he supposed to
do it? Thirty-seven years doing this, carrying a
gun since he was fourteen years old, not worrying
before about killing a man if he believed the man
might kill him first. Why was he thinking about it
now? Because he was getting old. Sundeen would
say to him, you're getting old; and he would say,
yes, because I'm still alive. It was a beautiful day
and if it was going to be the one he'd remember
he'd better do it now. Without thinking anymore.

But he thought of one more thing.

He said, "I'm taking the woman."

Alerting her with his words.

But alerting Sundeen also—seeing his expression only for a moment puzzled.

His hand going to his holster, to the hard grip of the .44, the Mexican saw Sundeen's hand moving, and knew he shouldn't have said anything and now was going to lose . . . But the woman was moving, kicking her palomino around . . . as Sundeen's revolver cleared and he was firing and firing again . . . and, Christ, it was like being punched hard, hearing himself grunt with the wind going out of him and the .44 in his hand, trying to put it on Sundeen . . . *ughhh*, grunting again in the noise of something hard socking him in the chest . . . firing as he saw the blue sky and felt himself going back, falling—

Sundeen had several thoughts in the next moments:

That was a good horse, Ruben's, not to have moved under all that commotion, the horse standing there, his old segundo gone crazy and now dead on the ground.

Everybody back there see it? It was time he showed them something.

Three snap shots dead center. Any *one* would have killed the crazy Mexican.

Three shots. Two left in his Peacemaker—that thought hitting him all at once as he saw the movement, as he saw the Apaches first, *Apaches*, a bunch of them off in the scrub, and Moon appearing at the corner of the house, Moon yelling his wife's name. Moon blocked out for a moment as the palomino shot past him—the woman's blonde hair in the horse's blonde mane. Sundeen extended his Peacemaker and fired, saw Moon again, there he was, and tried to concentrate his aim on Moon with one load left—and the heavy fire came all at once from the scrub. Sundeen fired at Moon suddenly moving—shit—yanked his reins to get out of there, yelling, "Get 'em, goddamn it . . . get 'em!"

Moon wanted him so bad, putting his Colt's gun on the man tight-reining, kicking his horse, at the same time, seeing the ones way over by the wall raising their rifles, opening fire, and thinking, *Kate*, looking to see where she was—there, past him, still low in her saddle and cutting through the scrub to come around by the corral behind him. In that moment of concern letting Sundeen get the jump he needed, Sundeen beating his mount toward the shooters by the wall. Moon aimed stiff-armed, ignoring the shooters, pulled the trigger five times, holding the sawed-off in his left hand and wishing he had the Sharps for just one, take his time and *right then*, blow out Sundeen's soul as his horse cleared the wall and there he was for a split moment against the sky. But not today.

Now it was Moon's turn to get out of there.

They withdrew to high ground, Moon, his wife and his Apaches, and took careful shots at the figures crouched on the other side of the wall now. The figures would return fire, shooting at puffs of smoke. Ruben Vega's body lay in the yard, his chestnut horse nuzzling him as though it were grazing.

"Keep 'em away from the house," Moon said.

Kate remembered the one on the porch with the coffee pot, the fresh coffee she'd made for her husband, and said there was one already in there.

After awhile heavy black smoke began to pour out of the stone chimney.

"He's burning the place," Kate said. "He's burning our home."

Moon waited in the high rocks with his Sharps rifle, seeing, from this angle, the side and back of the house, the clay-tile roof and most of the yard, but not the porch, the front of the house. The thick smoke billowed up from the chimney.

When the smoke began to seep out across the yard from the front, Moon judging it was coming out of the door and windows, he raised the Sharps and pressed his cheek to the smooth stock, the big curled hammer eased back in front of his eyes, the barrel pointing into the yard, and waited.

Finally Kate said, "There he is."

Moon saw the figure appear beyond his front sight, running for the wall. There was a faint sound, the men down there yelling, cheering him on. The figure reached the wall and bounded up to go over it in one motion. Moon paused, seeing the man stop and draw himself up to stand on the wall with hands on his hips and look around at his work . . . the smoke pouring out of the house.

Another fool, Moon thought. He shot the fool cleanly off the wall, the man dying as the heavy sound boomed out into the distance. It was not much satisfaction. After awhile Sundeen and his shooters pulled out.

Moon and Kate went down to their house, beat at the smoldering pockets of fire with blankets and dragged out the charred furniture that had been piled in the middle of the room. When this was done, Moon put the Mexican over his horse. They took him down to the White Tanks cemetery, buried him and recited a prayer over his grave. If they ever learned his name they would put up a marker.

2

R. J. Bruckner showed the news reporters and anyone interested the little derringer that had saved his life. The gun, lying on the deputy's desk, looked like it had been hit with a hammer. Patting his belly, Bruckner said he kept the little pea-shooter right here, see, exactly where Moon's bullet had caught him. The bullet struck the derringer and embedded parts of it into his flesh the doctor had to pull out with tweezers.

Where had Moon got a gun to shoot with? the newsmen wanted to know.

When his wife had visited, Bruckner said. He had taken Mrs. Moon's word she had no weapons on her person, so had not searched her.

Maurice Dumas, who was present, asked himself when Moon's wife had visited him in the eight hours Moon was in jail. Maurice thought about it and shook his head. She hadn't.

Bruckner said Moon had pulled the gun and locked him in the cell, not knowing—Bruckner patting his pocket now—he always carried a spare key. He had then grabbed his six-shooter, run out to the street and would have shot Moon dead had not Bren Early gotten in the way, Early having come just then to visit Moon.

The news reporters gave Bruckner narrow looks while some of them laughed out loud, which was a mistake. It shut off Bruckner's trust of them and willingness to talk. After that it was like pulling teeth to get information from him.

Grimly he stuck to his story that it was Moon's wife who'd given him the gun and had brought the horse some of the newsmen had actually seen running down Fourth Street toward Mill with Moon aboard. Yes, in fact Moon had sneered at him and actually *told* him, when he was being locked in the cell, that it was his wife had brought it. Also, he knew for a fact Moon's wife had left Mrs. Pierson's house about the time of Moon's escape. She was no longer in town, was she? "Now get your asses out of my office." Bruckner didn't have any need for these grinning, smart-aleck out-of-towners. He had work to do. First thing, post the wanted dodger on Dana Moon. It showed Moon's face, taken from a C.S. Fly photo, and said:

$5,000
REWARD

(Dead or Alive)

for information leading to
the arrest or seizure of

DANA MOON
Escaped Fugitive

37 years of age, dark hair, dark-complected. Former United States Government Indian Agent at White Tanks Sub-agency. Approach with caution. If whereabouts known, notify Deputy Sheriff R.J. Bruckner, Sweetmary, Arizona Territory.

Brucker hung the dodger outside the jail on a bulletin board for all to see. On the same board were:

A LaSalle Mining Company notice warning hunters and prospectors to avoid posted areas where survey crews were working with dynamite.

And, a recruiting poster—"HIGH PAY— INTERESTING WORK"—calling for individuals who were experienced in the handling of firearms and owned their own horse to apply for a position with the LaSalle Mining Security Division. "$20 A WEEK TO START. SEE P. SUNDEEN."

Maurice Dumas looked at the board for several minutes, the thought striking him, wasn't it strange the company posters were right there with the Moon "wanted" dodger? Like the company was footing the bill for all three enterprises. They surely looked alike in appearance. He could write an article about that, posing the question: Was the company paying for Dana Moon's arrest . . . or death? (Bruckner had refused to answer that directly, saying it was county business.)

But first, locate Early, if possible, and see if he was willing to chat about things in general. Maurice Dumas was still feeling intuitive as well as pretty lucky.

Was it because he had not yet been pushy, but had politely given his name and said he was sorry to have disturbed her? Maurice couldn't believe it when she said come in. Look at that. The first news reporter to be invited into the house of the mysterious Mrs. Pierson. He entered hesitantly, cap in hand, looking around with an expression of awe, for this place could some day be of historical interest.

She did not invite him to sit down, but immediately said, "You're the one he talks to, aren't you?"

"Well, we have spoken privately several times, yes," Maurice said. "I mean he's told me things he hasn't told the other journalists, that I know of."

"Like what?"

"Well . . . how he feels about things."

"He does? He tells you that, how he feels?"

"I don't mean to imply I have his complete confidence, no, ma'am." He didn't realize until now that she was upset. Judging from her tone, more than a little angry.

"Well, the next time you see him," Janet Pierson said, "tell him to quit acting like a spoiled brat and grow up."

"Mr. *Early*?"

"Like he got out of bed on the wrong side every morning. Tell him to make up his mind what he's mad at. If it's me, if I'm to blame, I'll gladly move out. Ask him if that's what he wants. Because I'm not taking any more of his pouting."

"Bren *Early*?"

"Or his silence. All day he sat here, he didn't say a word. 'Can I get you something? . . . Would you like your dinner now?' Like walking on eggs, being so careful not to bother him too much. He'd grunt something. Did that mean yes or no? He'd grunt something else. Finally I said, 'Well, if you're gonna act as if I'm not here, one of us might as well leave.' No answer. Can you imagine living with someone like that?"

She did not seem too mysterious now.

"Bren Early?" Maurice said, puzzled. "No, I can't imagine him like that. He's so . . . calm. Are you sure he wasn't just being calm?"

"God," Janet Pierson said, "you *don't* know him, do you? You believe the one in the photograph with the revolvers is the real person."

"Well, what I do know about him is certainly real and impressive enough to me," Maurice said.

"It is, huh?" Mrs. Pierson said something then that Maurice thought about for a long time after. She said, "That C.S. Fly, he should take all pictures of famous people in their underwear, and when they're not looking."

He found Bren Early where he should have looked first, the Chinaman's: Early sitting in the quiet room, though near the front this time, by one of the windows. He was sipping whiskey. On the table in front of him was a handwritten menu, in ink, and one of the Dana Moon "wanted" dodgers, Moon's face in the photo looking up at Bren Early.

Maurice Dumas left his cap on and pulled up a chair. "The Chicago Kid," some of the others were calling him now. Or "Lucky Maurice." Lucky, hell, it was sensing a story and digging for it, letting nothing discourage or deter. Go after it.

"Moon's wife didn't bring him the gun," Maurice said. He was going to add, flatly, "You did," but softened it at the last second. "I have a feeling it might have been you."

Bren Early was looking at the menu. He said, "Did you know this place is called the Oriental?"

"No, I didn't think it had a name."

"The Oriental," Early said.

Maurice waited a moment. "I also believe the company put up the five-thousand reward. Because I don't think the county would spend that kind of money on something that's—when you get right down to it—company business. Am I right or wrong?"

Early said, "Are you gonna have something to eat?"

"No, I don't think so."

"Well, if you aren't gonna eat, why don't you leave?"

Maurice felt a chill go up the back of his neck. He managed to say, "I just thought we might talk."

"There's nothing to talk about," Early said.

"Well, maybe I will have something to eat, if it's all right."

Maurice ate some kind of pork dish, sitting there self-conscious, feeling he should have left and tried the man at a better time. Though Early did say one thing as he sipped his whiskey and then picked up the Moon "wanted" poster. He said, "A man who likes his front porch hasn't any business on one of these."

"No," Maurice said, to agree.

"Sometimes they put the wrong people on these things."

Early didn't say anything after that. He finished his whiskey and walked out, leaving the young reporter sitting there with his pork dish.

⇒ 12 ⇒

1

Sundeen appeared in Sweetmary, picked up fresh mounts and supplies and went out again with twenty men, some eager new ones along. He'd hinted he was close to running Moon to ground, but would not give details. This time Maurice Dumas and several news reporters trailed after him, keeping well behind his dust.

There were saddle bums and gunnysackers who came up from around Charleston and Fairbank with Moon's "wanted" dodger folded in their pockets.

These men would study the pictures of Moon in Fly's gallery a long time, pretending to have keen looks in their eyes. They would drink whiskey in the saloons—all these ragtag chuck-line riders turned manhunters—talking in loud voices how they packed their .45–70's for distance or how an old Ballard could outshoot a Henry. They would go out to their campsites along the Benson road, stare up at the Rincons and talk about dogging the man's sign clear to hell for that kind of reward money, come back here and buy a saloon with a whorehouse upstairs.

Best chance, everyone agreed, squat down in a blind and wait for the shot. Moon was bound to appear somewhere, though not likely to be snared and taken alive. Yes, it was up to chance; but some lucky bird would get the shot, come back with Moon wrapped in canvas and collect the $5,000; more money than could be made in ten years of herding and fence riding.

The saddle bums and gunnysackers straggled out in pairs and small groups, those who had soldiered saying they were going on an extended campaign and would forage, live off the country. Most of them came dragging back in four or five days, hungry and thirsty, saying shit, Moon wasn't up there—like they had expected to find him sitting on a stump waiting. Wasn't anybody up there far as they could see.

How about Sundeen?

Him either.

The news reporters who had trailed out after Sundeen came back with sore legs and behinds— all of them except the Chicago Kid—to say Phil Sundeen had not found anything either. All he was doing was pushing his men up one draw and down another, finding some empty huts but not a sign of the mountain people.

Days went by. What seemed to be the last of the manhunters came limping in with the same story— nothing up there but wind and dry washes—and looked around for old chums who had gone out in other parties. A rough tally indicated some had not returned. Were they still hunting? Not likely, unless they were living on mesquite beans. Were they dead? Or had they gone home by way of Benson?

Ask Moon that one.

Ask him if you could ever find him. Or if he was still up there. Maybe he had left here for safer climes.

Like hell, said a man by the name of Asa Bailey from Contention. He had seen Moon, close enough to touch the tobacco wad in the man's jaw.

The news reporters sat him down at a table in the Gold Dollar with a full bottle, got out their note pads and said, O.K., go ahead.

Asa Bailey told them there had been three of them in the party and gave the names Wesley and Urban as the other two—last seen headed southeast, having sworn off manhunting forever.

They had come across Sundeen and his bunch at the Moon place and Sundeen had run them off, telling them to keep their nose out of company business. They had stayed close enough to watch, though, and observed Sundeen riding off with most of his men, leaving two or three at the burntout house. Yes, Sundeen had set a torch to the place, though the roof and walls seemed in good shape.

Asa Bailey said he had been a contract guide out of Camp Grant some years before and knew Moon and his Apaches surely weren't going to stand around nor leave directions where they went. Moon would use his Apaches as his eyes and pull tricks to decoy Sundeen out of his boots: let him see a wisp of smoke up in the high reaches and Sundeen would take half a day getting up there to a cold fire set by some Apache woman or little kid. Let them wear themselves out and go home hungry, was Moon's game, all the time watching Sundeen.

"So we would play it too," Asa Bailey said, "pretend we was Moon and hang back off Sundeen's flank and sooner or later cross Moon's sign. Sundeen'd camp, we'd camp, rigging triplines, and making a circle around us with loose rocks we'd hear if somebody tried to approach.

"We were the stalkers, huh? Like hell. Imagine you're sitting all night in what you believe is an ambush. Dawn, you're asleep as Wesley and Urban are over a ways gathering the horses. You feel something—not hear it, *feel* it. And open your eyes in the cold gray light and not dare to even grunt. The man's hunched over you with the barrel tip of his six-gun sticking in your mouth. There he was with the kindly eyes and the tobacco wad you see in the pictures."

There wasn't a sound at that table until one of the newsmen said, "Well, what did he say?"

"What did he *say*? Nothing."

"Nothing at all?"

Asa Bailey reached across an angle of the table, grabbed the newsman by the shirtfront, drew his revolver and stuck it in the man's bug-eyed face, saying, "You want me to explain things to you or do you get the picture?"

2

Franklin Hovey, the company geologist, came in with a survey crew and two ore wagons of camp gear and equipment. Noticeably shaken, he said he would quit his job before going out with another survey party. "You don't *see* them," he said, "but there they are, like they rose out of the ground."

The news reporters finally got hold of him coming out of the telegraph office and practically bums-rushed him to the Gold Dollar. "Here, Franklin, something for your nerves." The reporters having a glass also since they were here.

"Whom did you telegraph?" they asked him.

"Mr. Vandozen. He must be apprised of what's happened."

The reporters raised their eyebrows and asked, "Well, what did happen out there?"

Franklin Hovey said his crew of eight had been working across a southwest section of the range at about seven thousand feet. One morning, three days ago, a tall nigger had appeared at their camp, came walking his horse in as they were sitting at the map table having breakfast. He gave them a polite good morning, said his name was Catlett and asked if they planned to blast hereabouts.

"I told him yes, and pointed to an outcropping of ledge along the south face that looked promising. I can't give you his exact words as the darkie said them, but he took off his old hat, scratched his wooly head and said, 'If you disturbs that rock, boss, it gwine come down in de canyon where de tanks at. Is you sure you wants to do that?'"

A couple of the reporters looked at each other with helpless expressions of pain, but no one interrupted the geologist. Franklin Hovey said, "See, there was a natural water tank in the canyon where they grazed a herd of horses. I told the darkie,

'That might be; but since the canyon is part of the company lease, we can blow it clear to hell if it strikes our fancy.' The darkie said something like, 'Strike yo fancy, huh?', not understanding the figure of speech. He said, 'Boss, we sees that rock come down in there, we-uns gwine strike yo fancy clean off this mountain.' I said, 'And who is the we-uns gwine do sech a thing as that?'"

Franklin sat back, beginning to relax with some liquor in him, glancing around the table to see if everyone appreciated his dialect. There were a couple of chuckles.

"The darkie himself smiled, knowing it was meant only as good-natured parody, and said, 'If y'all be so kind, jes don't mess the graze and the water. Awright, boss?'

"Now one of our powdermen went over to the wagon where we kept the explosives, got a stick of Number One and pointed it at the darkie, saying— this was *not* good-natured, though I'll admit it was funny at the time. The powderman pointed the stick and said, 'How'd you like it if we tie this to your tail, Mr. Nig, with a lit fuse and see how fast it can send you home?' The darkie, Catlett, said, 'Yeah, boss, that would send a body home, I expects so.' He smiled again. But this time there was something different about his smile."

There was a silence. Those around the table could see by Franklin Hovey's expression he was thinking about that time again, that moment, as though realizing now it should have warned him, at least told him something.

"Did you blow the ledge?" a reporter asked.

"Yes, we did. Though we set off a small warning

charge first to indicate our intention. I insisted we do that."

The reporters waited, seeing the next part coming, remembering the story Asa Bailey, the former contract guide, had told only a few days before.

"Our party was well armed," Franklin Hovey continued, "and we set a watch that night around the perimeter of the camp. As I've said, we were at about seven thousand feet on bare, open ground. With night guards on four sides and enough moonlight to see by, we were positive no one could sneak up to that camp."

"They hit you at dawn," a reporter said.

Others told him to shut up as Franklin Hovey shook his head.

"No, we arose, folded our cots, ate breakfast . . . dis*cussed* the darkie's threat while we were eating and, I remember, laughed about it, some of the others imitating him, saying, 'Yessuh, boss, ah's gwine strike yo fancy,' things like that. After breakfast we went over to the dynamite wagon to get what we'd need for the day—you might've seen it, a big ore wagon with a heavy canvas top to keep the explosives dry and out of the weather. One of the men opened the back end"—Franklin paused—"and they came out. They came out of the wagon that was in the middle of our camp, in the *middle*, our tents and the two other wagons surrounding it. They came *out* of it . . . the same colored man and another one and two Indians." Franklin shook his head, awed by the memory of it. "I don't even see how there was room in there with the fifty-pound cases, much less how they got in to begin with . . . Well, they held guns on us, took ours and threw them into the canyon . . . tied our hands in front of us and then tied the eight of us together in a line, arm to arm . . . while the one named Catlett took a dynamite cartridge, primed it with a Number Six detonator and crimped onto that about ten feet of fuse, knowing exactly how to set the blasting cap in there and gather the end of the cartridge paper around it tight and bind it up good with twine. This man, I realized, knew how to shoot dynamite. I said, 'Now wait a minute, boy, we are only doing our job here, following orders.' The darkie said, 'Thas all ah'm doing too, boss. Gwine send y'all home.' I said to him again, 'Now wait a minute,' and the other members of the crew began to get edgy and speak up, saying we were only working men out here doing a job. The darkie said, 'Y'all doing a job awright, on our houses.'"

"Was Moon there?" a reporter asked.

"I told you," Franklin Hovey said, "it was the two colored men and two Apache Indians which, I forgot to mention, had streaks of yellowish-brown paint on their faces.

"The other colored man also began to prime sticks with blasting caps; so that between the two of them they soon had eight sticks of dynamite ready to fire, though not yet with the fuses attached. The one named Catlett approached me and poked a stick down into the front of my pants. Again, as you can imagine, I began to reason with him. He shook his head, pulled the stick out and walked around the line of us tied shoulder to shoulder and now placed the dynamite stick in my back pocket, saying, 'Yeah, tha's the place.'"

Many of the reporters were grinning and had to

quickly put on a serious, interested expression as Franklin Hovey looked around the table.

"Well, they were behind us for several minutes, so we couldn't see what they were doing. Then they placed a stick of Number One, which will shatter solid rock into small fragments—they placed a stick in every man's back pocket or down into his pants if he didn't have a pocket. Then came around in front of us again and began drawing the fuses out between our legs, laying each one on the ground in about a ten-foot length.

"I forgot to mention they had found a box of cigars in somebody's gear and all four of them were puffing away on big stogies, blowing out the smoke as they stood about with their weapons, watching us. But not laughing or carrying on, as you might expect. No, they appeared serious and very calm in their manner.

"The tall colored man, Catlett, said something and the four of them began lighting the ends of the fuses with their cigars.

"Well, we began to pull and push against each other. We tried to reason—or maybe I should say plead with them by this time—seeing those fuses burning at eighteen seconds a foot, which seems slow, huh? Well, I'll tell you, those sputtering, smoking fuse ends were racing, not crawling, right there coming toward our legs. 'Stomp 'em out!' somebody yelled and all of us began dancing and stomping the ground before the burning ends were even close. The two colored men and the Apaches had moved back a ways. Now they raised their rifles, pointed 'em right at us and Catlett said, 'Stand still. You move, we'll shoot you dead.'"

Franklin Hovey waited, letting his listeners think about it.

"Which would you prefer, to be shot or blown up?" he said. "If you chose the former, I'd probably agree. But you would *not* choose it, I guarantee, looking into the muzzles of their guns. I promise you you'd let that fuse burn through between your feet at its pace and by then try not to move a muscle while being overcome by pure fear and terrible anguish. There was a feeling of us pressing against each other, rooted there, but not one of us stomped on a fuse. It burned between our feet and was out of sight behind us, though we could hear it and smell the powder and yarn burning. With maybe a half minute left to live, I closed my eyes. I waited. I waited some more. There was an awful silence."

And silence at the table in the Gold Dollar.

"I could not hear the fuse burning. Nothing. I opened my eyes. The four with the guns stood watching us, motionless. It was like the moment had passed and we knew it, but still not one of us moved."

Franklin Hovey let the reporters and listeners around the table wait while he finished the whiskey in his glass and passed the back of his hand over his mouth.

"The fuses," he said then, "had not been connected to the dynamite sticks, but burned to the ends a few feet behind us. It was a warning, to give us a glimpse of eternity: The tall one, Catlett, approached and said if they ever saw us again, well, we'd just better not come back. They hitched a team to the dynamite wagon and drove off with close to a thousand pounds of high explosives."

"That's it, huh?" a reporter said. "What was it the nigger said to you?"

"I told you, he gave us a warning."

"Just said, don't come back?"

Franklin Hovey seemed about to explain, elaborate, then noticed that two of the girls who worked in the Gold Dollar were in the crowd of listeners.

"He said something, well, that wasn't very nice."

"We see you again, we crimp the fuse on, stick the dynamite stick up your ass and shoot you to the moon . . . boy," were Bo Catlett's exact words.

3

A man by the name of Gean was brought down in a two-wheel Mexican cart lying cramped in the box with his new straw hat on his chest, both legs shattered below the knees by a single .50-caliber bullet. He said he felt it, like a scythe had swiped off his legs, before he even heard the report; that's how far away the shooter was. He said he should never have left the railroad. If he ever went back he would be some yard bull, hobbling after tramps on his crutches, if the company doctor was able to save his legs.

The one who had guided the cart down out of the mountains was Maurice Dumas. The Chicago Kid was tired, dirty and irritable and did not say much that first day. He took Gean to the infirmary where there were all manner of crushed bones from mine and mill accidents, some healing, some turning black, lying there in a row of cots. It smelled terrible in the infirmary and the reporters who came to interview Gean handed him a bottle and asked only a few questions.

Had Sundeen found Moon?

Shit, no. It was the other way around.

Moon was carrying the fight now?

Teasing, pecking at Sundeen's flanks.

Was it Moon who shot him?

Get busted from five hundred yards, who's to say? But it's what he would tell his grandchildren. Yes, I was shot by Dana Moon himself back in the summer of '93 and lived to tell about it. Maybe.

How many men did Moon have?

A ghost band. Try and count them.

What about the Mexicans?

They'd come across women and children, ask them, Where they at? No savvy, mister. We'd burn the crops and move on.

And the colored?

The niggers? Same thing. Few Indin women and little wooly-headed breeds. Where's your old man at? Him gone. Him gone where? Me no know, be home by-'m-by. Shit, let's go. But it was at a nigger place the sniping had begun . . . riding off from the house after loading up with chuck and leading a steer . . . ba-*wang*, this rifle shot rang out, coming from, I believe, California, and we broke for cover. When we looked back, there was one of ours laying in the weeds. After it happened two times Sundeen had a fit, men getting picked off and all you could see up in the rocks was puffs of smoke. But he took care of that situation.

How did he do that?

Well, he took hostages so they wouldn't fire at us. I was walking up a grade toward a line shack,

smoke wisping out the chimney, I got cut down
and lay there looking at sky till one of your people
found me and saved my life. Though I won't pay
him a dime for that bed-wagon ride back here; I
been sick ever since.

What else—how about Indians?

Shit, the only Indians he'd ever seen in his life
was fort Indins and diggers. The ones rode for
Moon were slick articles or wore invisible war-
paint, for they had not laid eyes on a one.

The company doctor took off Gean's right leg.
Gean said he could have done it back home under
an El Paso & Southwestern freight car and saved
the fare from New Mexico.

4

My, that Gean has the stuff, doesn't he? Tough old
bird.

Maurice Dumas said to Bill Wells of the *St.
Louis Globe-Democrat*, "Everybody was so taken
with his spunk, or anxious to get out of there, they
didn't ask the right question."

"About what?"

"The hostages. He said they took hostages, then
started talking about how I found him and put him
in the cart."

"What about the hostages?"

"They shot them," Maurice said.

He wasn't sure he was going to tell this until he
did, sitting with Bill Wells in the New Alliance. Like
one reporter confiding in another. What should I
do? Should I reveal what happened or not?

Why not?, was the question, Bill Wells said. "Are you afraid of Sundeen?"

"Of course I am," Maurice said.

"We have power, all of us together, that even the company wouldn't dare to buck," Bill Wells said. It was a fact, though at the moment Bill Wells was glad they had come to this miners' saloon rather than mix with the crowd at the Gold Dollar. "Tell me what happened."

Maybe Sundeen thought it would be an easy trip: march up there with his hooligans and run the people off their land, burn their homes and crops, scatter the herds—like Sherman marching to the sea. Sundeen did have an air about him at first, as though he knew what he was doing.

But there were not that many mountain people to run off. And how did you burn adobe except to blacken it up some? Tear down a house, the people would straggle back and build another. The thing Sundeen had to do was track down the leaders and deal with them face to face.

But how did you find people who did not leave a trail? Even the cold camps they did find were there to misdirect and throw them off the track. Sundeen's men began to spit and growl and Sundeen himself became more abusive in his speech, less confident in his air.

They had burned a field of new corn when one of Sundeen's tail-end riders was shot out of his saddle. The next day it happened again. One rifle shot, one dead.

Sundeen came to a Mexican goat farm early in the morning, tore through the house and barn, flushed

assorted women and kids, ah!, and three grown
men that brought a squinty light to Sundeen's eyes.
He tried to question them in his Sonora-whorehouse
Spanish—no doubt missing his old segundo—and
even hit them some with leather gloves on, drawing
blood. Where's Moon? No answer. *Smack*, he'd
throw a fist into that impassive dark face and the
man would be knocked to the ground. The women
and children cried and carried on, but the three
men never said a word. Sundeen tied their hands
behind them and loaded them into that two-wheel
cart with a mule to pull it and had them lead his
column when he moved on.

But then, you see, he didn't draw any sniper
fire and that seemed to aggravate him more than
having his men picked off.

Soon after taking the hostages they woke up in
the morning to find half their horses gone, disappeared from the picket rope. Sundeen sent riders
to Sweetmary for a new string. They came back to
report the story of the survey crew being hit.

It was in a high meadow facing a timbered slope
and a little shack perched up in the rocks above
that Sundeen, all of a sudden, reached the end of
his skimpy patience. It was no doubt seeing the
smoke coming out of the stovepipe. Somebody was
up there, a quarter of a mile away. And he was sure
they were in the timber also, in the deep pine shadows. There was not a sound when he began to yell.

"Moon! Come on out! . . . You and your boogers,
Moon! . . . Let's get it done!"

His words echoed out there and faded to nothing.

Sundeen pulled the three Mexicans from the
cart and told them to move out in the meadow,

keep going, then yelled for them to stop when they were about forty yards off. They stood in the sun bareheaded, looking up at the timber and turning to look back at Sundeen who brought all his riders up along the edge of the meadow, spread out in a line.

He yelled now, "You see it, Moon? . . . Show yourself or we'll blow out their lights!"

Nothing moved in the pines. The only sound, a low moan of wind coming off the escarpment above.

The three men, bareheaded and in white, hands tied behind them, didn't know which way to face, to look at the silent trees or at the rifles pointed at them now.

"I've given him enough warning," Sundeen said. "He's heard it, isn't that right? If he's got ears he heard it." If he's up there, somebody said. "He's up there, I know he is," Sundeen said. "Man's been watching us ten days, scared to come out. All right, I give him a chance, haven't I?" He looked up and yelled out once more, "Moon?" Waited a moment and said, "Shit . . . go ahead, fire."

"And they killed them?"

Maurice nodded.

"But if he knew you were a witness—"

"He'd forgotten I was along by then, other things on his mind."

Bill Wells was thoughtful, then asked, "Was Moon up there, in the trees?"

"Somebody was. Shots were fired and Sundeen divided his men to come at the timber from two sides. That was when Gean was shot."

"And you were considering you might keep it a secret?"

"I wasn't sure how I felt. I mean I've never handled anything like this before," Maurice said. "Though I know we're sworn to print the truth, letting the chips fall where they may."

"Or stack the chips against the company's hand," Bill Wells said, the idea bringing a smile. "Yes, I can see Vandozen squirming and sweating now."

— 13 —

1

There was a framed slate in the Gold Dollar, back of the bar, that gave the betting odds on a Sundeen-Moon showdown:

    2–1 one week
    5–1 four days
    10–1 two days

It meant you could bet one dollar to win two if you thought Sundeen would track down Moon and bring him in dead or alive within one week. The house was betting against it ever happening. When a week passed and Sundeen hadn't returned, you lost your dollar. For shorter periods you could bet the higher odds that were posted.

When Sundeen returned a few days ago with four men face-down over their saddles and the rest of his troop worn raw and ugly, they erased the old odds and wrote on the slate:

    4–1 one week
    10–1 four days

20–1 two days
100–1 one day

A miner at the bar, who had not seen the new odds before, said, "I'd hide that thing I was you. Case he comes in here."

"Who, Mr. Sundeen?" said Ed O'Day, who ran the Gold Dollar and sometimes served behind the bar. "He wants to bet on himself we'd be glad to cover it. Or, he wants to bet against himself I'm sure there some takers. Making a wager isn't anything personal. The man is not gonna bet against himself and take a dive, is he? No, not in this kinda contest. So, he thinks he's gonna come out the victor, let him put up his money."

Ed O'Day was a known high-roller; he ran faro, monte and poker tables in the back of his place and would bet either side of an issue depending on the odds.

Bren Early stepped toward them, moving his elbow along the polished edge of the bar. He said, "You're betting against him finding Moon is all you're doing."

"Mr. Early, how are you? Sorry I didn't see you there. The usual?"

Bren nodded. The slight—not being noticed immediately—was as much an insult to him as the odds board: putting Sundeen against Moon and ignoring him completely. Bren had a hard knot inside his stomach. He wanted to cut this barkeeper down, level him with a quiet remark that had an eternal ring. (Something to do with, serving these miners and tourists, "What would you know about put-

ting your life on the line?" Or, ". . . What would
you know about facing death?") But he couldn't
think of the words when he was on edge like this.
Goddamn it.

Pouring him a whiskey, Ed O'Day said, "Finding Moon is ninety percent of it, yes. If that ever
happens it would be a different story."

"How would you set the odds then?" Bren
asked, satisfied that his tone did not show the
edge.

"Well, I'm inclined to believe they would favor
Mr. Sundeen. I don't mean as a shooting contest. I
mean if he runs him down the game's over."

"How do you come to that?" Bren asked the
know-it-all, feeling the knot tighten.

Ed O'Day looked both ways along the bar and
leaned closer as he said, "You take a person raised
on sour milk and make him look dumb in front of
his fellow man—You see what I mean? He ever sets
eyes on Moon he's gonna kill him."

"You know that as fact," Bren said.

"No, but I'd bet on it."

"You heard right now that Sundeen had located
him—you'd put your money on Sundeen?"

"I'd say it would be the safer bet."

"Turn the same odds around?"

Ed O'Day hesitated. "You said if he locates
him—"

"Gets Moon to stand still and fight."

"Just Sundeen, or his men too?"

"His men, anybody he wants to bring along."

The miner standing next to Bren said, "Anybody
or everybody? The way he's signing up people, he's

gonna be taking an army next time—saying up at the works the next time's the last time. Though I don't want to mess up your bet none."

"That's talk," Ed O'Day said, but looked at Bren Early to get his reaction.

"No, it's fact," the miner said. "Sundeen sent to Benson, St. David, Fairbank—twenty a week, grub and quarters. Most the miners want to quit and join up; but Selkirk told him no, he couldn't hire no miners. See, he's gonna take all the men he can find and not come back till it's done."

The miner's heavy mustache, showing fine traces of gray, reminded Bren of Moon. He wondered what Moon was doing this minute. Squinting at heat waves for signs of dust. Or tending his guns, wiping down Old Certain Death with an oil rag. Damn.

"I don't care how many people he raises," Bren said, "I want to know what odds you're giving if both sides stand to shoot and you want Sundeen . . . ten to one?"

"*Ten* to one?" Ed O'Day said. "Talking about if the two sides ever meet."

"No bet less they do."

"Doesn't matter how many men Sundeen has?"

"He can hire the U.S. Army," Bren said.

"Ten to one," Ed O'Day said and thought about it some more. "Well, it's interesting if we're talking about real money."

"Give me a Maricopa bank check," Bren said.

Ed O'Day went over to the cash register and came back with the check, an ink pot and a pen.

Bren leaned over the bar and scratched away for a minute, picked up the check, to blow on it, wave it in the air, and laid it on the polished surface again.

"Seven thousand Sundeen goes out and never comes back."

Ed O'Day, who wore the same expression drawing a pair of aces he did picking his teeth, said, "Is this the bet we been talking about all along?"

"I'm cutting out the only-if's and what-if's," Bren said. "Sundeen comes back for any reason after he leaves—if it's just to go to the toilet, this check is yours. But when he doesn't, and you learn he's dead, you pay off ten to one. Which is what?"

"Comes to seventy thousand," Ed O'Day answered, like it was no more than a day's take.

"This man here is our witness," Bren said. "Have him write his name on the check somewhere."

The miner looked from Bren to Ed O'Day with his mouth partly open. "You're paying him seventy thousand dollars if Sundeen gets killed?"

"No different'n writing life insurance," Ed O'Day said and winked at Bren—

Who felt good now and didn't mind at all the man's cocksure coyness.

"I'll even pay double if he gets struck by lightning," Ed O'Day said.

Bren let an easy grin form, as if in appreciation, though there was more grin inside him than out.

He said, "You never can tell."

2

"All the people," a reporter sitting on the Congress front porch said. You would think the circus was in town. It is, another reporter said; featuring Phil Sundeen and his wild animal show. Christ, look at them. Bunch of range bums and bushwackers trying to pass as Quantrill's guerrillas.

Bren found Maurice Dumas sitting in the lobby staring at nothing. When he asked what was the matter, Maurice said he was thinking of going home; watching innocent people get shot was not his idea of covering a war. Bren said, no, when men fought without honor it was a sorry business.

"But we're gonna teach them a lesson, partner, and I sure hope you're here to see it."

Maurice perked up. "You're getting into it?"

Bren nodded.

"When?"

"I'll tell you," Bren said, "this looks like it's gonna be my busy night. If you could help me out some I guarantee you'll be in the front row when the fireworks go off."

"Get what things done?"

"Find Sundeen first. Tell him I'll meet him at the Chinaman's, the Oriental in about an hour."

"You mean—"

"Unh-unh," Bren said, "that's what I don't want to happen by mistake, ahead of time. Tell him I got something important to say. No guns. You'll inspect him and he can have somebody inspect me if he wants. Tell him it's the answer to how to end this deal and that he's gonna like it."

"I don't know if I can stand to speak to him," Maurice said.

"Listen, you write this story they'll make you the editor. Don't let personal feelings get in your way. The other thing—" Bren paused, looking around the lobby. He said, "Come on," and led Maurice to the back hall where the first-floor rooms were located. The light from the wall fixtures was dim, but it was quiet here, private. Bren took a thick envelope from his pocket and handed it to Maurice.

"List of some things I'm gonna need and the money to buy 'em with. Open it."

Maurice did.

"Put the money in your pocket."

"Looks like a lot."

"Two hundred dollars is all."

Maurice unfolded a sheet of paper. It was Moon's "wanted" dodger.

"You'll see the notes on there I've written."

"Yeah?" Maurice read them, then gave Bren a funny look, frowning. "You serious? You want this printed?"

"Trust me and don't ask questions, it's part of the scheme," Bren said. "You'll see where to get everything; it's all on the list. The case of whiskey, buy something good. The pack animal and cross-buck, I wouldn't pay more than fifty dollars. What else? It's going on seven o'clock, how about we meet at the livery stable eleven thirty, quarter of twelve. Sound good?"

"I don't know if I can have everything by then." Maurice looked worried now.

But not Bren. He said, "Hey, are you kidding me? Anybody rises as early as you is a natural-born go-getter."

3

Vandozen, seated in the middle of the settee, seemed to blend with the room, belong: formal but relaxed in his light-gray business suit and wing collar; pinch-nose glasses hanging from a black ribbon, resting on his vest.

Janet Pierson said, "Mr. Vandozen is here." Saying it as Bren came through the kitchen and the two men were already face to face. "He's been waiting for you. I asked him if he'd like some coffee—"

"How about cognac?" Bren said.

Vandozen nodded. "A small one. Mrs. Pierson was kind enough to let me wait."

"I didn't know you were in town." Bren glanced at Janet.

Vandozen watched her go out to the kitchen as he said, "I built a place near Lordsburg, to be close to our New Mexico operations, some good ones just getting started." His gaze returned to Bren who was seated now in an easy chair, his hat off, coat open. "I can be here overnight on the Southern Pacific, but I hadn't planned on coming as often as I have."

"No, this kind of business," Bren said, "you don't plan its twists and turns, do you?"

"We're going to end it," Vandozen said. "I want you to go out, talk to this Moon. Tell him we'll make a deal with him."

"What kind of deal?" Bren said, taken by surprise. Jesus Christ, he didn't want any *deal*. Not now. He stared at Vandozen sitting on that velvet settee like it was his throne.

"You're going to arrange a meeting between this Moon and myself." Vandozen paused, his gaze moving as Janet came in with a decanter and two brandy snifters, and watched her as she served them, saying, "Very nice. Thank you."

Bren remained silent, edgy now. Damn. Seeing his plan coming apart. He said, "It's dark in here. Why don't you turn up the lamps?"

"It's fine," Vandozen said. "Though you can close that front window if you don't mind."

There were occasional sounds from outside, men's voices in the street: first-shift miners returning to their quarters, some of them a little drunk.

Jesus Christ, whose house was it? Bren said, "What do you want to talk for? Your man's going out again; he'll get it done."

"He's *not* getting it done," Vandozen said, with emphasis but more quietly than Bren had spoken. "This business should have been handled quickly with a show of force. Offer one choice, leave, that's all. What does he do, stumbles around, can't even find them. When he does, he ties up three Mexicans and shoots them with a newspaperman as a witness. Which is going to take some countering, not to mention money."

"It's gonna be over soon," Bren said.

"I know it is. You bring this Moon to me and we'll make a deal."

"His name's Dana . . . Dana Moon," Bren said.

"That's fine. Go get him. Tell him we'll meet at his office or mine, I don't care. Criminal charges against him will be dropped. We'll pay for—no, we'll work out some plan of assistance for anyone whose home or crops were damaged. Tell him any future survey work will be done in isolated areas."

Bren said, "Ah, now we're getting to it. You haven't found the copper you thought you would, huh?"

"I can say test samples have been misleading,

promising more than the locations would ever yield," Vandozen said. "But that's beside the point. I made an error in judgment, this business going on; allowed it to take on far more prominence— considerably more of my time than it's worth. So you and I are going to bring it to a halt."

"I don't believe it's part of my job," Bren said, "since I'm not a messenger boy."

Vandozen looked at him for what seemed a long time, though perhaps only ten seconds. "What *is* your job?" he asked.

"I don't know. Tell me."

"Isn't this Moon a friend of yours?"

"*Dana* Moon."

"You two, I understand, used to be close friends?"

"What's that got to do with it?"

"Don't you want to help him?"

"Dana can handle it himself."

"For God's sake—" Janet Pierson said.

The two men looked at her seated in the straight chair, away from them.

"I'm sorry," she said. "I didn't mean to interrupt."

"Mrs. Pierson understands," Vandozen said. "Or, I should say, she doesn't understand why you don't want to help your friend." Still with the quiet tone.

"I didn't say I wouldn't help him."

"Or why you don't want to help the company. You're a stockholder . . . making, what?, ten thousand dollars a year. Why would you knowingly act in violation of your contract?"

"Knowing what?"

"Well, doing anything that's not in the company's best interest. That's standard in any employee contract."

"The fine print, huh?"

"You don't recall reading that?"

Bren didn't answer. He sat with his cognac, looking at Vandozen, a question in his mind, but afraid Vandozen's answer would destroy his plan completely. Still he had to ask it.

"What about Sundeen? You call him off?"

"Not yet."

Bren let his breath out slowly. "When you gonna see him?"

"He's to see me first thing in the morning."

"So he doesn't know about this yet."

"He'll be fired five minutes after he walks in the office."

Bren sat in the deep chair another moment, comfortable, beginning to feel pretty good, yes, confident again. He finished his cognac and pulled himself out of the chair.

"Well, I might as well get going. You'll know something tomorrow."

Janet Pierson said, "Do you mind? It's stuffy in here."

Vandozen watched her raise the window and stand looking out, her back to him.

"Why does he have to go tonight?"

"Because he's childish," Vandozen said. "He has to go out and kick rocks, or run his horse till it lathers." He reached over to place his glass on the end table and sat back again.

"He is like a little boy," Janet said.

"Yes, he is . . . Why don't you come over here?"

Vandozen watched her turn from the window. "Come on . . . sit here."

When she was next to him, on the edge of the settee, he put his hand on her shoulder and brought her gently back against the cushion. His hand remained as he said, "Tell him you're leaving."

She looked at his face that was lined but not weathered, the skin on his neck loose, crepe-like, in the starched white collar.

"I admired you when you admitted you'd made a mistake."

"Not a mistake, a misjudgment. Come to Lordsburg with me."

"Don't you have a wife?"

"In New Jersey. Not in New Mexico, Colorado or Arizona."

"I admired the way you never raised your voice, even when you said things with feeling."

"Yes," Vandozen said, drawing her against his shoulder, "in certain areas I have firm convictions and feelings."

4

Bren sat at a corner table in the Oriental. He let Sundeen take his time and look around. When Sundeen finally came over he pulled out the chair across from Bren and sat down.

"Now then," Sundeen said, "where were we?"

"They're trying to call the game." Bren sat with his hands flat on the table. "Vandozen says he's had enough of your monkeyshines. He's gonna fire you tomorrow, and all those hoboes you got riding for you."

Sundeen nodded, not surprised. "You would think he had something personal to do with this." He sat back in his Douglas chair saying, "Shit."

"There's hope," Bren said, "if you can get your misfits out of town before morning. He can't find you, he can't fire you, can he?"

"I don't know—don't many of 'em snap to as they should," Sundeen said. "There's some mean Turks, but most of 'em ain't worth cow shit."

"How many you need? . . . How many does Moon have?"

"Who in the hell knows? All I seen was women and little kids."

"Some Mexicans with their hands tied, I understand."

"And their eyes open. They knew what they were doing. I cut the ropes, let 'em hold their old cap-n-balls, they'd still be dead, wouldn't they? I lost men blown to hell from a distance. Are we talking about rules of some kind or what?"

"We're getting off track," Bren said.

"You're the one called this," Sundeen said, his snarly, ugly nature peeking through. "We can settle up right now, you want, and quit talking about it."

"You got spirit," Bren said, "but save it and let's do this show with a little style. You don't want to meet in some back alley; you got a reputation to think of—as poor as it is."

"Jesus," Sundeen said, on the edge now, hands gripping the arms of his chair.

Like working a wild stallion, hold him on the line, but don't let him break his neck. Bren said, "If you're big enough to handle your men, gather 'em and head up to White Tanks. I'll get Moon, whatever people he's got . . . You come up the draw and we'll meet at his place."

Sundeen said, "Through that steep-sided chute? You must believe I'm dumb."

"Scout it. Turn all the rocks over, you want. I'm talking about we meet at the top, have a stand-up battle like we had in Sonora. Quit this tracking around and do the thing right." Bren paused. Sundeen remained silent. "Unless you lack the gristle."

Sundeen said, "You don't need to prod, if that's what you're doing. I'm thinking." And said then, "Why don't we meet at White Tanks?"

"Moon won't do it, I'll tell you that right now. He'll fight for his home, but not for any government layout. He doesn't look at this the way you and I do."

Sundeen was thoughtful again. "It would make some noise, wouldn't it?"

"Hear it clear across the country," Bren said. "Get your name in the history book."

Sundeen grinned then, tickled. "Jesus Christ, is this the way it's done?"

"Why not? Better than maybe we meet sometime maybe we don't."

"Well . . . Moon's place then. I guess it's as good as another."

As Sundeen got up, Bren said, "Whatever happened to that old segundo of yours?"

"Ruben Vega," Sundeen said. "He tried to change sides and didn't make it."

"That's too bad. He seemed a good one for his age."

"Yeah, he was quicker than most," Sundeen said, "but in this game there ain't any second prize, is there?"

5

The sound jolted Bruckner awake: something dropped on his desk. Somebody standing there.

Maurice said, "The printer over at the paper asked me to give these to you."

"What?" Bruckner said. "The hell you want?"

Maurice stepped back from the man's stale whiskey odor. "You're supposed to post them around right away. Printer said it was ordered from the county."

Bruckner rubbed a hand over his face, opened his eyes and the squirt reporter was gone. He looked at his watch: twenty past twelve; heard horses outside and turned to his window.

Three horses out there . . . the squirt news reporter mounting and another fella already up, leading a packhorse with gear and a wood crate lashed to the cross-buck. Bruckner watched them head down LaSalle Street into darkness.

When he turned to his desk again he frowned and said out loud, "What in the hell—" Bren Early's photo was looking at him from a stack of "wanted" dodgers that said:

$5,000
REWARD
(Dead or Alive)

for information leading to
the arrest or seizure of

CAPT. BRENDAN EARLY

wanted for the killing of
P. Sundeen (and probably others)
Approach with utmost caution!!!

— 14 —

1

Kate said to Moon, "What do you need all those enemies for when you got a friend like Bren Early?"

Moon said, "How long you want to live in a line-camp and cook outside in the weather? It's a way to get it done and move back in our home."

"If you win," she said.

Moon said, "I don't worry about that part till I'm there."

"Do you think it makes sense?"

Moon had taken his wife aside for this chat, away from the others sitting around the tents and brush wickiups of the camp, one of the high-up Apache rancherías.

He said to Kate, "Don't look at it as a sensible person would. Try to see it through Bren's eyes first, the chance to do battle and win some medals."

"Who gives him the medals?"

"You know what I mean—add to his stature. He missed the war and he's been moaning about it ever since. Now he sees a chance to win fame and get his picture in the paper, big."

"At whose expense?" Kate said.

"You got to look at it another way too," Moon said. "Sundeen is gonna dog us till we put an end to him. I'd rather meet him across the wall than keep looking over my shoulder . . . worrying about you at home the times I'm gone."

"Now you make it sound like a just cause," Kate said, "but I believe the idea tickles you as much as Bren."

"No, not that much," Moon said, feeling itchy, excited, but trying not to show it. "Come on."

They walked back through the pines to the ranchería, past the children and the squat Mimbre women at the cookfires, to where Bren was sitting on his bedroll, Maurice Dumas next to him. The Apaches had sighted them early this morning and brought them up to the camp. The case of whiskey had been opened and a bottle passed around as they discussed this business of meeting Sundeen. The whiskey was good after nearly a month of sour corn-beer. The talk was good. The idea seemed good, too. But did it make sense? Or didn't it have it?

Bo Catlett was here and another former 10th cavalryman by the name of Thomas Jefferson. Eladio Duro, the son of Armando, was here with a heavily armed farmer named Alfonso who wore three belts of bullets. Red was here—it was his camp—with seven Mimbre Apache males who remained silent and let Red speak for them—as he was doing now in halting Spanish.

When he finished Bo Catlett said, "It seem that way," and looked at Bren Early. "Captain, Red say, do these people want to die? Or is it us want to die?"

"Tell him," Bren said, "these people will never stop hunting him as long as they live, or we let them live."

"He knows all about that," Bo Catlett said. "He wants to know, what is this standing and waiting for your enemy to come at you?"

"Tell him it's the way white men face each other with honor. I mean civilized people," Bren said to Bo. "It's the way we've always done it."

"Tell him *that*?" Bo Catlett said, glancing at Moon and back to Bren. "You gonna have to explain it to *me* first. Lest you plan to bushwack him in the draw. We got seven hundred pounds of dynamite could help."

"Artillery," Bren said, and was thoughtful a moment. "I told him he could bring his men up. Gave him my word on that."

Bo Catlett translated into Spanish and Moon watched Red and his Mimbres as they looked at one another.

"They think you must be drunk," Moon said to Bren. "Let me make a speech for a minute."

He spoke in Spanish, for the benefit of the Apaches and the Mexican farmers, though Bo Catlett's people were included. Moon said that some of this business with Sundeen was personal and he didn't expect anyone to fight because of something that happened a long time ago in Sonora. But Sundeen and his people also represented the company and the company wanted this land.

"Tell them it's a question of honor," Bren said. "Oh-*nohr*."

"It's a question of how you want to live," Moon said in Spanish. "My business isn't to hide and shoot at them the rest of my life. I have other things I want to do." He looked at Kate. "But I can't do them until I finish this. Can we win? I believe so. I believe the company will look at us and decide it isn't worth all the time and money and they'll go somewhere else for their copper." Moon's gaze moved to Bren. "In fact, I'm surprised the company hasn't sent somebody to talk to us—"

Bren didn't move; then shrugged; then tried to think of something to say.

"—but I believe the company will when they see we're determined to stay."

"That's it," Bren said. "This is the company's final show of strength. And when they see it fail, they'll cave in."

Moon seemed to accept this. He said, "Will some of us die?" And looked at Eladio and Alfonso. "Some of us already have. But I would rather face them now than risk being shot in the back planting corn. Maybe you don't like to fight this way. I don't blame you. But this is the way it is."

When Moon appeared finished, Bren said, "Did you mention honor? It didn't sound very inspiring."

Moon said, "It's their lives. It's up to them."

Following the trail down from the ranchería, Moon close to Kate, he wanted to talk to her, be near her. But Bren rode a length behind and told how Sooy Smith had entered Okolona and captured a big bunch of Rebel officers and men on furlough, February 17, 1864—Bren full of war again—February 20, 3:00 P.M., reached a point south of Prairie Station with two brigades and learned that Nathan Bedford Forrest was facing him with a force of 7,000. You know what Sooy did?

"What?" Moon said, interested.

"God—" Kate said.

Maurice Dumas watched and listened, fascinated.

Later in the morning the mountain people began to arrive at the stone house with the charred furniture in the yard:

Bo Catlett, Thomas Jefferson and two more in "US" braces and worn cavalry boots. Bo said they had flipped coins and the ones who lost had to stay home with the families and the herds. They had a talk with Moon and Bren Early, got Bren to agree to an idea and the 10th Cavalry veterans went down into the barranca with two fifty-pound cases of dynamite.

Young Eladio Duro, Alfonso with his cartridge belts, and six farmers carrying old Ballards and Remingtons represented their families. (Others were scattered and could not be notified.) Eladio wore a green sash, a sword and a caplock Dragoon pistol his grandfather had carried at Resaca de la Palma. Everyone full of war.

Red and his seven Mimbres squatted in the yard with a clay pot of ochre paint; with bowls of *atole*, the flour gruel they would eat as their last meal before battle; with small leather sacks of *hod-dentin*, the magic powder that would protect them from bullets; with cigars and tulapai, the corn-beer, and chants that reminded them they were the *Shis-Inday*, the invincible Apache . . . the chosen ones. Those not chosen for this—another twenty in Red's band—were in the thicket behind the house, up on the escarpment and watching the back trails. (Sundeen would have to come straight at them up the barranca, and not pull any sneaky tricks.)

Bren unloaded and reloaded his .44 Russians and his fancy Merwin & Hulberts and shoved a seven-cartridge tube into the stock of his polished Spencer . . . ready for war, brimming over with it, telling Moon how Sooy Smith had dug in to make a stand at Ivey's Farm against Barteau who had taken over for Tyree Bell, see, when Tyree Bell had become sick . . . confusing but, to Moon, a good sound; it matched the excitement he felt.

Maurice Dumas spent some time inside the smoke-blackened house with Kate, helping her as she baked about a dozen loaves of bread, but most of the time looking out the window at the Apaches and the Mexican farmers, at Moon and Early out by the adobe wall.

It was exciting and it was scary, too. Maurice wondered if he was the only one who felt it. Everyone else seemed so calm, or resigned. He said to Kate, "The thing is, they don't *have* to do this."

"Yes, they do," Kate said. "They believe they do, which is the same thing."

"Twenty-two," Maurice said, "against however many Sundeen brings. Probably twice as many."

"Twenty-three," Kate said, finished with the bread, loading a Henry now with .44's.

"*You're* gonna take part in this?"

"It's my house too," Kate said.

In a little while Moon sent Maurice Dumas down to White Tanks to tell Sundeen he could come any time he wanted.

2

Someone had brought the Capt. Brendan Early dodger, ". . . wanted for the killing of P. Sundeen," and showed it around. Sundeen read it and shook his head, pretending to be amused, but did not think it was funny. The news reporters at White Tanks quoted him as saying, "I hope there is money on that son of a————'s head, for I am sure as—— going to collect it."

Yes, the news reporters had finally come to the field, brought by the message Maurice Dumas had left displayed in the hotel lobby: *Come to White Tanks for final showdown, Rincon Mountains War. Scheduled to begin around noon today!* Bren Early's idea. ("Why do you want all them?" Maurice had asked him. Bren's answer: "The more people there are who sympathize with our fight against the giant company, the more likely the company is to back off." Now it was *our* fight.)

When Maurice came down the mountain to White Tanks and saw the crowd, he couldn't believe it. Riders, wagons, buggies, Indians, a few women, little kids playing on the fence around the stock pen—there must have been two hundred people or more. When he reached the agency buildings and began sorting everybody out, Maurice found that maybe half were spectators, gawkers, and the rest were in the pay of Sundeen . . . something like a hundred armed men!

Had Bren Early counted on that many opposing

them? Not by half, Maurice recalled. Perhaps forty men at the most.

But one *hundred*—all hard-eyed cutthroats in a variety of getups: derbies, straws, sombreros, dusty business suits and batwing chaps . . . shotguns, rifles, six-shooters, all were armed with at least two guns; they stood about talking, drinking whiskey, checking and fooling with their weapons . . . talking in loud, confident voices and finding, it seemed, a great deal to laugh about.

My God.

C.S. Fly was not present. Maurice learned the famed photographer had declined the invitation, saying he had pictures enough for a fools' gallery as is. However there were others—among them A. Frank Randall of Willcox and someone representing Beuhman & Hartwell of Tucson—busy taking pictures of Sundeen, groups of his cutthroats holding rifles and revolvers, and some of the White Tanks reservation Indians who posed, not having any idea what was going on.

Maurice had to push through a crowd on the porch of the agency office to get to Sundeen inside, sitting with his boots propped up on Moon's desk and telling the news reporters his riders would "bite shallow" else they would eat those people up in two minutes. Maurice waited for Sundeen to notice him, then said, "They're ready for you."

Sundeen eyed him. "How many people's he got?"

"I'm not at liberty to say."

"At *liberty*," Sundeen said, drawing up out of the swivel chair. "You little squirt, I'll free your soul for you."

"About twenty," Maurice said.

He turned and walked out. Should he have told? Did he have a choice?

The least he could do was ride back up there and tell how many Sundeen had. God—and watch their faces drop.

The photographer from Beuhman & Hartwell caught him outside on the steps and said, "If you're going back up, I'm going with you." Then Bill Wells of the St. Louis paper and several other reporters said they were going too. Then a man Maurice had never seen before came up and said, "Maurice, I've been looking for you. I'll be in your debt if you'll present me to Dana Moon and Captain Early."

Maurice was certain he had never seen the man before this. For how could he have forgotten him? The gleaming store teeth and waxed guardsman mustache twirled to dagger points—

"Colonel Billy Washington, at your service, Maurice."

—the pure-white Stetson, the tailored buckskin coat with white fringe, the black polished boots with gold tassels in front—

"You've heard of me, have you?"

"Yes sir, I certainly have," Maurice said. God, all this happening at once. "I just have never seen you in person before."

"Well, you see me now," Colonel Washington said.

3

Bo Catlett rode up out of the barranca and crossed the open ground to the wall. He said to the people standing behind it, "They on the way."

"How many?" asked Bren.

"Say a hundred, give or take." Bo Catlett rode into the yard before stepping down, pulled his carbine from the boot and slapped his mount toward the smell of feed and water over in the corral.

"Five to one," Bren said, sounding pleased.

Kate looked at him, her Henry resting on the wall. Moon gazed down the slope, past the open ground to the trough of the barranca. He could see figures now, a line of tiny dark specks coming up the switchback trail, through the field of saguaro.

Bren raised the field glasses hanging from his neck and studied the enemy approaching. "Straggling . . . close it up there!"

Moon looked at his Apaches. They looked at him, faces painted now with streaks of ochre. He turned to look at the Mexicans lining the wall: Eladio with his sword and green sash among the farmers in white cotton.

"Tell 'em to get ready," Bren said, field glasses at his face.

"You don't have to stay," Moon said in Spanish. "No one is asked to fight one hundred men."

The Indians and the Mexicans remained at the wall, looking from Moon to the slope. They saw another of the colored men now, Thomas Jefferson, coming across the open ground and through the gate space in the wall.

"They dismounting, like to come as skirmishers."

Bren lowered his glasses and called out, "Come on! Take your medicine like little men! . . . Christ, what're they fooling around down there for?"

Moon said to Bo Catlett, "They'd do better to stay mounted and run at us."

"Man never soldiered," Bo said. "Can see he don't know doodly shit what he's doing."

The sound of firing came from down the slope now . . . the tiny figures spreading out, moving up slowly, dropping down to fire, waiting, moving up again.

"Christ, it'll take 'em till tomorrow," Bren said. The Mexican farmers were raising their rifles. "Not yet," Moon said in Spanish. "If you shoot now I think they won't come close enough. We want them up there on the open ground."

"We get them up," Bo said.

"What's your signal?" Moon asked him.

"Three quick ones. My boys'll light the fuses and get."

Moon held his hand out. In a moment Bren noticed and handed him the glasses. Moon studied the figures coming up through the brush and fencepost saguaros. He raised his gaze to a high point on one side of the barranca, then moved across to the other side where the barranca narrowed and Bo Catlett's powdermen had planted the charges. The tiny figures dotting the slope were coming up through the narrowing of the trough and spreading out again, more of them firing now, the closest nearing two hundred yards. They could blow the charges now and wipe out about a quarter of Sundeen's men and send the rest running. But that wasn't the plan. No, Bren had promised Sundeen safe passage—one general to another. That was all right. Because the plan was to get them all up on high ground, in the open, then blow the narrows and cut off their retreat, prevent them from falling back to cover. Get them milling around in the

open and shoot the spirit right out of them, blow
Sundeen to his reward and close the book. That
was the plan.

The first skirmishers were approaching a hundred and fifty yards now, snapping shots and moving up, feeling the excitement of it probably, feeling
braver and with no one shooting back. Moon
moved his glasses over them to pick out Sundeen.
Not in the first bunch . . . there he was with his
funneled hat and silver buckles, crossed gunbelts
and a six-shooter in each hand, waving his men to
come on, goddamn it, get up there.

Moon set the glasses on the wall and raised his
Big-Fifty Sharps.

"Don't you do it," Bren said.

Moon said, "I'm just seeing how easy it would be."

"Let him come up all the way."

Pretty soon now.

The skirmishers were firing from a hundred
yards and the tail end of Sundeen's men was moving through the narrows. The firing increased.
Sundeen positioned a line of shooters behind
cover, just across the open ground—about twenty
of them—gave a signal and they all fired at once.

Seeing this about to happen, the people behind
the wall ducked down or went to one knee. All
except Bren Early. After the second fusillade he
said, "At Fredericksburg, where Doubleday's Iron
Brigade stood up to the Rebel guns, D.H. Hill sent
a flag of truce over with his compliments to General Doubleday—"

Another volley ripped out from the brush slope.
Bren tried not to hunch his shoulders.

"—saying he had never in his experience seen

infantry stand and suffer casualties under artillery fire more bravely."

Moon said, "You have got something in your head about having to die to win glory. If that's the deal, I pass . . . Bo, let's close the back door. Give your troopers the signal."

Bren, standing, said, "Hold there," and picked up the glasses from the wall. "Some more are coming up behind."

Kate had said to Moon, "I'm not staying in the house; you know that." He said no, he guessed not. "But if you worry out there about me instead of yourself, you'll get shot. So think of me as another hand, not as a woman or your loved one." Moon had agreed because there was no fighting her. Though he had said, "If something happens to you, your old dad will kill me."

At the wall now Kate was alert, aware of being in the middle of men's business and would pick out little things that surprised or impressed her. The stoic look of the Apaches. Were they afraid? Was Eladio afraid? Yes, he looked it; but didn't leave when given the chance. Was Bren afraid, standing up to their rifle fire? Or was he beyond fear, playing his hero role? Bo Catlett and the other cavalryman—she thought of them as professional soldiers who would stand because that's what you did. Moon. Moon had good sense, he *must* be afraid. But his look was the same, his gaze, his unhurried moves, the hunk of tobacco in his jaw. She did not think of herself until the concentrated fire came from the slope and she crouched close to the adobe, feeling the pistol in the waistband of her skirt digging into her, clutching the Henry tightly and seeing her knuckles, close to her face, standing out white and hard. There was a feeling of terrible pressure. She could die on this spot . . . hearing Moon say if that was the deal he'd pass, saying it so calmly . . . all of them appearing calm as the rifle fire cracked and sang through the air. Determined, not resigned, but quiet about it. You'd better be, huh? Was it that simple? Run and they'd shoot you in the back. It was fascinating, even with the feeling of pressure. The ultimate, a life or death situation. Bren said, "Hold there . . ." The firing stopped. They began to raise up from the wall.

"They're riding through Sundeen's people," Bren said. "They're not his. Some other bunch."

"That's your friend," Moon said. "What's his name."

"Maurice. Christ Almighty, one of 'em's leading a pack animal."

Kate could see the shooters who had been down in the scrub and rocks standing now, looking around, as this parade of single-file riders came through them led by Maurice Dumas . . . nine, *ten* of them, the packhorse carrying something covered with canvas, poles sticking out, bringing up the rear. They came across the open ground and now the second rider, wearing a tall white hat, drew even with Maurice in his cap. As Kate got a good look at the man she said, "My God," and turned to Moon who was staring at them and showing the first expression of pure surprise she had ever seen on his face.

The man in the white Stetson and fringed buckskin dismounted in the yard. Maurice, still mounted, was saying something as the others rode into the yard behind him. The man in the white hat raised his hand to stop Maurice. "No need," he said, and walked over to Moon and Bren Early.

"Gentlemen, I would know you anywhere. Even if I had not seen your renowned C.S. Fly photographs I would know you are the famous scout, Dana Moon . . . and you, sir, Captain Brendan Early." He was taking something out of his fringed coat now—his false teeth and waxed handlebars agleam, something that looked like picture postcards in vivid colors, and said, "Gentlemen, may I present myself . . . Colonel Billy Washington, here to extend a personal invitation to both of you to join the world-famous Billy Washington All-American Wild West Show as star attractions and performers . . . *if*, of course, you get out of this jackpot you're in alive. What do you say, gents?"

Moon looked at Kate. Kate looked at Moon.

Bren was saying, "What—"

The man from Beuhman & Hartwell and his assistant were setting up their camera, both of them glancing up at the sun. The news reporters were looking around at the scenery and down the slope toward the skirmishers standing in the scrub, judging the distance with keen gaze, beginning to make notes . . . the Mimbres, the Mexican farmers, the two black cavalrymen looking at the reporters and the bill-show man in the white hat and buckskins, staring at them. Where did they come from?

Bren was saying now, "Will you all kindly move out of the way? Go inside the house. Go on." Shooing them, going over to the photographer who was beneath his black cloth now. "Mister, will you move out of the way—"

Kate kept looking at Moon. She said, "What are we doing here?"

Moon didn't say anything; but his eyes held hers until they heard the voice call out from the slope.

"What in the hell's going on!"

Sundeen stood with several of his men at the edge of a brush thicket, looking up at the wall, at the people they could see close beyond the wall and through the gate opening. Now he yelled, "Get those people out of there!" and waved his arm.

"Jesus Christ," he said to the man in the derby hat next to him, who had been with Sundeen since the beginning of this company business, "you believe it?"

The man didn't say anything; he was squinting in the glare, frowning. The man didn't seem to know what to think.

"Goddamn it," Sundeen said, "give 'em a round."

When the man in the derby hat didn't move or raise his Winchester, Sundeen took the rifle from him, levered as he jerked it eye-level, fired, levered, fired . . . seeing them scatter now . . . levered and fired again, sending his shots singing off the adobe wall where some of them had been standing, then yelled, "We're coming up!"

He half turned and began waving to his men to come on. Not one of them moved. Sundeen pulled his hat off, stared, put his hat on again close over his eyes, pushed the rifle at the man in the derby hat, placed his hands on his hips and looked all around him at his mean Turks. They stood in the hot dusty scrub and shale watching him or looking up the slope.

Very slowly, Sundeen said, "What is going on?"

Before the man in the derby hat could answer— if he was going to—a voice from the yard yelled, "Hold your fire, I'm coming out!"

Sundeen watched the picture-taker and his assistant appear with their camera and heavy tripod, coming out of the yard and moving to a rise off to the side where they began to set up the equipment. Sundeen stared, pulling his funneled hat brim lower. As the picture-takers were getting ready, the man in the bill-show cowboy outfit appeared at the wall and called out, "Mr. Sundeen!—"

Sundeen let go, yelling now as loud as he could, "Get that fancy son of a bitch out of there!" Said, "Jesus," in his breath and started up the slope by himself.

Kate saw him first. She had begun to feel a letdown, a tired after-feeling; but now the pressure of fear returned. Looking around, she said, "Dana?"

No one was facing this way.

Only the young newsman, Maurice. Moon was over by the others, moving them toward the house. Kate thought, You have to hurry. They have to hurry. This is what they were waiting for. Bren was walking Billy Washington across the yard, the wildwest show impresario holding onto Bren's arm with one hand, gesturing with the other as he spoke, waving his arm in a wide arc to take in the world.

"Dana!"

Moon came around, alert to his wife's tone. He

looked out toward the wall, his gaze holding as he came back toward the gate opening. He stood there, as if to greet Sundeen coming across the open ground.

Kate said, "Dana?"

He didn't look at her now. Kate turned to the wall where the Henry rifle rested on the flat surface, pointing out. She stood some fifteen feet from her husband.

Maurice stood between them, but several feet back from the wall. He didn't know if he should stay here. No one had said anything to him. Sundeen had reached the flat piece of ground beyond the wall. He was about fifty feet away now. Beyond Moon—and the group of Apaches and Mexican farmers spaced farther down the wall—on the rise off to the side, the photographer was fooling with his camera, the assistant holding open the black cloth for him to duck underneath. From Beuhman & Hartwell, Tucson. Maurice remembered that. He wasn't sure of the spelling though. Or how to spell the colored man's name—the two colored soldiers in their army braces and boots, off beyond Moon's wife. Sundeen's belt buckles glinted in the direct sunlight. Sundeen with a revolver on each hip, bullet belts crossed in an old-time desperado style . . . My God, was Moon armed? . . . Yes, the shoulder rig. He was in his shirtsleeves and wore braces and there seemed to be all manner of straps over his shoulders and around his back. Moon with a shoulder holster. Sundeen with his gun butts almost touching his hands hanging at his sides.

Did he say something? Mention Sonora?

Maurice could see all the hired manhunters

waiting down there at the edge of the scrub. There was sky behind Sundeen's head and shoulders.

He said, "You first, Moon, then your friend. Where is he at?"

"He doesn't come right now," Moon said, "you'll never see him again."

This took place in moments, right before Maurice's eyes. Bren Early was somewhere behind him in the yard. Maurice wanted to turn around, but couldn't take his eyes off Sundeen . . . or Moon, he could see by shifting his eyes a little. He wanted to call out Bren Early's name, get him over here. But at this moment there was an awful silence. Two armed men facing each other. Was there a signal? Men shot each other from a distance or sneaked up or came into a place shooting if one wanted to kill another. Did this happen? Maybe it did, for it was certainly happening now, Maurice thinking: Before your very eyes.

Sundeen said, "Your move."

Maurice saw Moon's right hand cross his body.

He saw Sundeen's right hand with a revolver in it. Like that. He saw the glint of sunlight on gun metal.

He heard an explosion, a heavy, hard report and a quick cocking lever action in the echo . . . to his left, where Kate Moon stood holding the big Henry rifle at her shoulder . . . and Sundeen was stumbling back, firing with a shocked look on his face, firing wildly again as Moon extended his revolver and fired and Kate fired the Henry, the two of them hammering Sundeen with .44's and that was the end of him. There was a silence. Sundeen lay on his back with his arms and legs spread out.

Maurice heard voices, someone in the yard calling out, running this way. He saw Kate lower the Henry and look at her husband, first with concern, then beginning to smile faintly. Moon looked over at his wife, not smiling but with a calm expression. Moon shook his head then. Maurice turned to see Bren Early coming with a matched .44 Russian in each hand.

Bren saying, "You got him? . . . You *got* him!" At the wall now, pointing a revolver down the slope and yelling at his men, his Apaches and Mexicans and pair of old cavalrymen, "Now! Pour it into 'em, boys!"

Moon turned away. Bren looked at him, a dumb, bewildered expression.

"We got to finish it!" All excited.

Moon shook his head. "You're too late for your glory." He looked at his wife. "When did it happen?"

Kate said, "I think it was over before it started."

"I guess so." Moon said then, "You shoot good for a little girl."

She said, "I wasn't gonna see you die for no reason."

Bren looked at them, from Moon to Kate and back. His gaze moved to Sundeen stretched face up on the bare ground and beyond him to the men standing in the scrub, Bren full of desperate energy brought to a halt.

"His people are still there . . . *look*."

But with little conviction in his tone. A last, too-late call to battle.

Remember it, Maurice thought. All of it:

Bo Catlett sitting on the wall, lighting a cigar.

The other cavalry veteran leaning against it, his back to the scene of battle.

The Mimbre Apaches—gone. Where? Just gone. The Mexican farmers and the young one with the sword, moving away, walking off past the newsmen and the bill-show dude standing on the porch.

Moon gazing in that direction—

He said, "Well, we've paid up and lived to tell about it."

The bill-show man in buckskins was coming out toward them now, getting important-looking papers out of his pocket.

Moon watched him. He said to Bren, "It wouldn't hurt to travel, see the sights, would it?"

Kate shook her head, resigned or admiring or both. She said to Moon, "You're the sights. You and your partner."

Maurice Dumas got out his notebook and started writing it all down as fast as he could.

FORTY LASHES
LESS ONE

⊷ 1 ⊷

The train was late and didn't get into Yuma until after dark. Then the ticket agent at the depot had to telephone the prison and tell them they had better get some transportation down here. He had three people waiting on a ride up the hill: a man he had never seen before who said he was the new prison superintendent, and another man he knew was a deputy sheriff from Pima County and he had a prisoner with him, handcuffed, a big colored boy.

Whoever it was on the phone up at the prison said they had sent a man two hours ago and if the train had been on time he would have met them. The ticket agent said well, they were here now and somebody better hurry with the transportation, because the Southern Pacific didn't care for convicts hanging around the depot, even if the boy was handcuffed.

The Pima deputy said hell, it wasn't anything new; every time he delivered a man he had to sit and wait on the prison people to get off their ass. He asked the big colored boy if he minded waiting, sitting in a nice warm train depot, or would he rather be up there in one of them carved-out cells with the wind whistling in across the river? The Pima deputy said something about sweating all day and freezing at night; but the colored boy, whose name was Harold Jackson, didn't seem to be listening.

The new prison superintendent—the new, temporary superintendent—Mr. Everett Manly, heard him. He nodded, and adjusted his gold-frame glasses. He said yes, he was certainly familiar with Arizona winters, having spent seven years at the Chiricahua Apache Mission School. Mr. Manly heard himself speak and it sounded all right. It sounded natural.

On the train Mr. Manly had exchanged a few words with the deputy, but had not spoken to the colored boy. He could have asked him his name and where he was from; he could have asked him about his sentence and told him that if he behaved himself he would be treated fairly. He could have asked him if he wanted to pray. But with the Pima deputy sitting next to the colored boy—all afternoon and evening on the wicker seats, bumping and swaying, looking out at the sun haze on the desert and the distant, dark brown mountains—Mr. Manly had not been able to get the first words out, to start a conversation. He was not afraid of the colored boy, who could have been a cold-blooded killer for all he knew. It was the idea of the deputy sitting there listening that bothered him.

He thought about starting a friendly conversation with the ticket agent: ask him if he ever got up to the prison, or if he knew the superintendent, Mr. Rynning, who was in Florence at the present time seeing to the construction of the new penitentiary. He could say, "Well, it won't be long now, there won't be any more Yuma Territorial Prison," and kidding, add, "I suppose you'll be sorry to see it closed." Except maybe he wasn't supposed to talk about it in idle conversation. It had been mentioned in newspapers—"Hell-Hole on the Bluff to Open Its Doors Forever by the Spring of 1909"— pretty clever, saying *opening* its doors instead of closing them. And no doubt the station agent knew all about it. Living here he would have to. But a harmless conversation could start false rumors and speculation, and before you knew it somebody from the Bureau would write and ask how come he was going around telling everybody about official government business.

If the ticket agent brought up the subject that would be different. He could be noncommittal. "You heard the old prison's closing, huh? Well, after thirty-three years I imagine you won't be too sorry to see it happen." But the ticket agent didn't bring up the subject.

A little while later they heard the noise outside. The ticket agent looked at them through his barred window and said, "There's a motor conveyance pulling into the yard I reckon is for you people."

Mr. Manly had never ridden in an automobile before. He asked the driver what kind it was and the driver told him it was a twenty-horsepower Ford Touring Car, powerful and speedy, belonged to the superintendent, Mr. Rynning. It was comfortable, Mr. Manly said, but kind of noisy, wasn't it? He wanted to ask how much a motor rig like this cost, but there was the prison above him: the walls and the guard towers against the night sky, the towers, like little houses with pointed roofs; dark houses, nobody home. When the gravel road turned and climbed close along the south wall, Mr. Manly had to look almost straight up, and he said to the guard driving the car, "I didn't picture the walls so high." And the guard answered, "Eighteen feet up and eight feet thick. A man can't jump it and he can't bore through neither."

"My last trip up this goddamn rock pile," the Pima deputy said, sitting in the back seat with his prisoner. "I'm going to the railroad hotel and get me a bottle of whiskey and in the morning I'm taking the train home and ain't never coming back here again."

The rest of the way up the hill Mr. Manly said nothing. He would remember this night and the strange feeling of riding in a car up Prison Hill, up close to this great silent mound of adobe and granite. Yuma Territorial Prison, that he had heard stories about for years—that he could almost reach out and touch. But was it like a prison? More like a tomb of an ancient king, Mr. Manly was thinking. A pyramid. A ghostly monument. Or, if it was a prison, then one that was already deserted. Inside the walls there were more than a hundred men. Maybe a hundred and fifty counting the guards. But there was no sound or sign of life, only this motor car putt-putting up the hill, taking forever to reach the top.

What if it did take forever, Mr. Manly thought. What if they kept going and going and never reached the prison gate, but kept moving up into stoney darkness for all eternity—until the four of them realized this was God's judgment upon them. (He could hear the Pima deputy cursing and saying, "Now, wait a minute, I'm just here to deliver a prisoner!") It could happen this way, Mr. Manly thought. Who said you had to die first? Or, how did a person know when he was dead? Maybe he had died on the train. He had dozed off and opened his eyes as they were pulling into the depot—

A man sixty years old could die in his sleep. But—and here was the question—if he was dead and this was happening, why would he be condemned to darkness? What had he done wrong in his life?

Not even thinking about it very hard, he answered at once, though quietly: What have you done right? Sixty years of life, Mr. Manly thought. Thirty years as a preacher of the Holy Word, seven years as a missionary among pagan Indians. Half his life spent in God's service, and he was not sure he had converted even one soul to the Light of Truth.

They reached the top of the bluff at the west end of the prison and, coming around the corner, Mr. Manly saw the buildings that were set back from the main gate, dim shapes and cold yellow lights that framed windows and reflected on the hard-packed yard. He was aware of the buildings and thought briefly of an army post, single- and two-story structures with peaked roofs and neatly painted verandas. He heard the driver point out the guard's mess and recreation hall, the arsenal, the stable, the storehouses; he heard him say, "If you're staying in the sup'rintendent's cottage, it's over yonder by the trees."

Mr. Manly was familiar with government buildings in cleanswept areas. He had seen them at the San Carlos reservation and at Fort Huachuca and at the Indian School. He was staring at the prison wall where a single light showed the main gate as an oval cavern in the pale stone, a dark tunnel entrance crisscrossed with strips of iron.

The driver looked at Mr. Manly. After a moment he said, "The sally port. It's the only way in and, I guarantee, the only way out."

Bob Fisher, the turnkey, stood waiting back of the inner gate with two of his guards. He seemed either patient or half asleep, a solemn-looking man with a heavy, drooping mustache. He didn't have them open the iron lattice door until Mr. Manly and the Pima deputy and his prisoner were within the dark enclosure of the sally port and the outer gate was bolted and locked behind them. Then he gave a sign to open up and waited for them to step into the yard light.

The Pima deputy was pulling a folded sheaf of papers out of his coat pocket, dragging along his handcuffed prisoner. "I got a boy name of Harold Jackson wants to live with you the next fifteen years." He handed the papers to the turnkey and fished in his pants pocket for the keys to the handcuffs.

Bob Fisher unfolded the papers close to his stomach and glanced at the first sheet. "We'll take care of him," he said, and folded the papers again.

Mr. Manly stood by waiting, holding his suitcase.

"I'll tell you what," the Pima deputy said. "I'll let you buy me a cup of coffee 'fore I head back."

"We'll see if we got any," Fisher said.

The Pima deputy had removed the handcuffs from the prisoner and was slipping them into his coat pocket. "I don't want to put you to any trouble," he said. "Jesus, a nice friendly person like you."

"You won't put us to any trouble," Fisher answered. His voice was low, and he seemed to put no effort or feeling into his words.

Mr. Manly kept waiting for the turnkey to notice him and greet him and have one of the guards take his suitcase; but the man stood at the edge of the yard light and didn't seem to look at any of them directly, though maybe he was looking at the prisoner, telling him with the sound of his voice that he didn't kid with anybody. What does he look like, Mr. Manly was thinking. He lowered his suitcase to the ground.

A streetcar motorman, that was it. With his gray guard uniform and gray uniform hat, the black shiny peak straight over his eyes. A tough old motorman with a sour stomach and a sour outlook from living within the confinement of a prison too many years. A man who never spoke if he didn't have to and only smiled about twice a year. The way the man's big mustache covered the sides of his mouth it would be hard to tell if he ever smiled at all.

Bob Fisher told one of the guards to take the Pima deputy over to the mess hall, then changed his mind and said no, take him outside to the guard's mess. The Pima deputy shrugged; he didn't care where he got his coffee. He took time to look at Mr. Manly and say, "Good luck, mister." As Mr. Manly said, "Good luck to you too," not looking at the turnkey now but feeling him there, the Pima deputy turned his back on them; he waited to get through the double gates and was gone.

"My name is Everett Manly," Mr. Manly said. "I expect—"

But Fisher wasn't ready for him yet. He motioned to the guards and watched as they led the prisoner off toward a low, one-room adobe. Mr. Manly waited, also watching them. He could see the shapes of buildings in the darkness of the yard, here and there a light fixed above a doorway. Past the corner of a two-story building, out across the yard, was the massive outline of a long, windowless adobe with a light above its crisscrossed iron door. Probably the main cellblock. But in the darkness he couldn't tell about the other buildings, or make any sense of the prison's layout. He had the feeling again that the place was deserted except for the turnkey and the two guards.

"I understand you've come here to take charge."

All the waiting and the man had surprised him. But all was forgiven, because the man was looking at him now, acknowledging his presence.

"I'm Everett Manly. I expect Mr. Rynning wrote you I was coming. You're—"

"Bob Fisher, turnkey."

Mr. Manly smiled. "I guess you would be the man in charge of the keys." Showing him he had a sense of humor.

"I've been in charge of the whole place since Mr. Rynning's been gone."

"Well, I'm anxious to see everything and get to work." Mr. Manly was being sincere now, and humble. "I'm going to admit though, I haven't had much experience."

In his flat tone, Fisher said, "I understand you haven't had any."

Mr. Manly wished they weren't standing here alone. "No *prison* experience, that's true. But I've dealt with people all my life, Mr. Fisher, and nobody's told me yet convicts aren't people." He smiled again, still humble and willing to learn.

"Nobody will have to tell you," Fisher said. "You'll find out yourself."

He turned and walked off toward the one-room adobe. Mr. Manly had no choice but to pick up his suitcase and follow—Lord, with the awful feeling again and wishing he hadn't put so many books in with his clothes; the suitcase weighed a ton and he probably looked like an idiot walking with quick little steps and the thing banging against his leg. And then he was grateful and felt good again, because Bob Fisher was holding the door open for him and let him go inside first, into the lighted room where the colored boy was jackknifed over a table without any clothes on and the two guards were standing on either side of him.

One of the guards pulled him up and turned him around by the arm as Fisher closed the door. "He's clean," the guard said. "Nothing hid away down him or up him."

"He needs a hosing is all," the other guard said.

Fisher came across the plank floor, his eyes on the prisoner. "He ain't worked up a sweat yet."

"Jesus," the first guard said, "don't get close to him. He stinks to high heaven."

Mr. Manly put down his suitcase. "That's a long dusty train ride, my friend." Then, smiling a little, he added, "I wouldn't mind a bath myself."

The two guards looked over at him, then at Fisher, who was still facing the prisoner. "That's your new boss," Fisher said, "come to take Mr. Rynning's place while he's gone. See he gets all the bath water he wants. This boy here washes tomorrow with the others, after he's put in a day's work."

Mr. Manly said, "I didn't intend that to sound like I'm interfering with your customs or regulations—"

Fisher looked over at him now, waiting.

"I only meant it was sooty and dirty aboard the train."

Fisher waited until he was sure Mr. Manly had nothing more to say. Then he turned his attention to the prisoner again. One of the guards was handing the man a folded uniform and a broad-brimmed sweat-stained hat. Fisher watched him as he put the clothes on the table, shook open the pants and stepped into them: faded, striped gray and white convict pants that were short and barely reached to the man's high-top shoes. While he was buttoning up, Fisher opened the sheaf of papers the Pima deputy had given him, his gaze holding on the first sheet. "It says here you're Harold Jackson."

"Yes-suh, captain."

The Negro came to attention as Fisher looked up, a hint of surprise in his solemn expression. He seemed to study the prisoner more closely now and took his time before saying, "You ain't ever been here before, but you been somewhere. Where was it you served time, boy?"

"Fort Leavenworth, captain."

"You were in the army?"

"Yes-suh, captain."

"I never knew a nigger that was in the army. How long were you in it?"

"Over in Cuba eight months, captain. At Leavenworth four years hard labor."

"Well, they learned you some manners," Fisher said, "but they didn't learn you how to stay out of prison, did they? These papers say you killed a man. Is that right?"

"Yes-suh, captain."

"What'd you kill him with?"

"I hit him with a piece of pipe, captain."

"You robbing him?"

"No-suh, captain, we jes' fighting."

Mr. Manly cleared his throat. The pause held, and he said quickly, "Coming here he never gave the deputy any trouble, not once."

Fisher took his time as he looked around. He said, "I generally talk to a new man and find out who he is or who he believes he is, and we get a few things straightened out at the start." He paused. "If it's all right with you."

"Please go ahead," Mr. Manly said. "I just wanted to say he never acted smart on the trip, or was abusive. I doubt he said more than a couple words."

"That's fine." Fisher nodded patiently before looking at Harold Jackson again. "You're our last nigger," he said to him. "You're the only one we got now, and we want you to be a good boy and work hard and do whatever you're told. Show you we mean it, we're going to help you out at first, give you something to keep you out of trouble."

There was a wooden box underneath the table. Mr. Manly didn't notice it until one of the guards stooped down and, with the rattling sound of chains, brought out a pair of leg-irons and a ball-peen hammer.

Mr. Manly couldn't hold back. "But he hasn't done anything yet!"

"No, sir," Bob Fisher said, "and he ain't about to with chains on his legs." He came over to Mr. Manly and, surprising him, picked up his suitcase and moved him through the door, closing it firmly behind them.

Outside, Fisher paused. "I'll get somebody to tote your bag over to Mr. Rynning's cottage. I expect you'll be most comfortable there."

"I appreciate it."

"Take your bath if you want one, have something to eat and a night's sleep—there's no sense in showing you around now—all right?"

"What are you going to do to the colored boy?"

"We're going to put him in a cell, if that's all right."

"But the leg-irons."

"He'll wear them a week. See what they feel like."

"I guess I'm just not used to your ways," Mr. Manly said. "I mean prison ways." He could feel the silence again among the darkened stone buildings and high walls. The turnkey walked off toward the empty, lighted area by the main gate. Mr. Manly had to step quickly to catch up with him. "I mean I believe a man should have a chance to prove himself first," he said, "before he's judged."

"They're judged before they get here."

"But putting leg-irons on them—"

"Not all of them. Just the ones I think need them, so they'll know what irons feel like."

Mr. Manly knew what he wanted to say, but he didn't have the right words. "I mean, don't they hurt terrible?"

"I sure hope so," Fisher answered.

As they came to the lighted area, a guard leaning against the iron grill of the gate straightened and adjusted his hat. Fisher let the guard know he had seen him, then stopped and put down the suitcase.

"This Harold Jackson," Fisher said. "Maybe you didn't hear him. He killed a man. He didn't miss Sunday school. He beat a man to death with an iron pipe."

"I know—I heard him."

"That's the kind of people we get here. Lot of them. They come in, we don't know what's on their minds. We don't know if they're going to behave or cause trouble or try and run or try and kill somebody else."

"I understand that part all right."

"Some of them we got to show right away who's running this place."

Mr. Manly was frowning. "But this boy Harold Jackson, he seemed all right. He was polite, said yes-sir to you. Why'd you put leg-irons on him?"

Now it was Fisher's turn to look puzzled. "You saw him same as I did."

"I don't know what you mean."

"I mean he's a nigger, ain't he?"

Looking up at the turnkey, Mr. Manly's gold-frame spectacles glistened in the overhead light. "You're saying that's the only reason you put leg-irons on him?"

"If I could tell all the bad ones," Bob Fisher said, "as easy as I can tell a nigger, I believe I'd be sup'rintendent."

Jesus Christ, the man was even dumber than he looked. He could have told him a few more things: sixteen years at Yuma, nine years as turnkey, and he hadn't seen a nigger yet who didn't need to wear irons or spend some time in the snake den. It was the way they were, either lazy or crazy; you had to beat 'em to make 'em work, or chain 'em to keep 'em in line. He would like to see just one good nigger. Or one good, hard-working Indian for that matter. Or a Mexican you could trust. Or a preacher who knew enough to keep his nose in church and out of other people's business.

Bob Fisher had been told two weeks earlier, in a letter from Mr. Rynning, that an acting superintendent would soon be coming to Yuma.

Mr. Rynning's letter had said: "Not an experienced penal administrator, by the way, but, of all things, a preacher, an ordained minister of the Holy Word Church who has been wrestling with devils in Indian schools for several years and evidently feels qualified to match his strength against convicts. This is not my doing. Mr. Manly's name came to me through the Bureau as someone who, if not eminently qualified, is at least conveniently located and willing to take the job on a temporary basis. (The poor fellow must be desperate. Or, perhaps misplaced and the Bureau doesn't know what else to do with him but send him to prison, out of harm's way.) He has had some administrative experience and, having worked on an Apache reservation, must know something about inventory control and logistics. The bureau insists on an active administrator at Yuma while, in the same breath, they strongly suggest I remain in Florence during the new prison's final stage of preparation. Hence, you will be meeting your new superintendent in the very near future. Knowing you will oblige him with your utmost cooperation I remain . . ."

Mr. Rynning remained in Florence while Bob Fisher remained in Yuma with a Holy Word Pentacostal preacher looking over his shoulder.

The clock on the wall of the superintendent's office said ten after nine. Fisher, behind the big mahogany desk, folded Mr. Rynning's letter and put it in his breast pocket. After seeing Mr. Manly through the gate, he had come up here to pick up his personal file. No sense in leaving anything here if the preacher was going to occupy the office. The little four-eyed son of a bitch, maybe a few days here would scare hell out of him and run him back to Sunday school. Turning in the swivel chair, Fisher could see the reflection of the room in the darkened window glass and could see himself sitting at the desk; with a thumb and first finger he smoothed his mustache and continued to fool with it as he looked at the clock again.

Still ten after nine. He was off duty; had been since six. Had waited two hours for the preacher.

It was too early to go home: his old lady would still be up and he'd have to look at her and listen to her talk for an hour or more. Too early to go home, and too late to watch the two women convicts take their bath in the cook shack. They always finished and were gone by eight-thirty, quarter to nine. He

had been looking forward to watching them tonight, especially Norma Davis. Jesus, she had big
ones, and a nice round white fanny. The Mexican
girl was smaller, like all the Mexican girls he had
ever seen; she was all right, though; especially with
the soapy water on her brown skin. It was a shame;
he hadn't watched them in about four nights. If
the train had been on time he could have met the
preacher and still got over to the cook shack before
eight-thirty. It was like the little son of a bitch's
train to be late. There was something about him,
something that told Fisher the man couldn't do
anything right, and would mess up anything he
took part in.

Tomorrow he'd show him around and answer
all his dumb questions.

Tonight—he could stare at the clock for an hour
and go home.

He could stare out at the empty yard and hope
for something to happen. He could pull a surprise
inspection of the guard posts, maybe catch somebody sleeping.

He could stop at a saloon on the way home. Or
go down to Frank Shelby's cell, No. 14, and buy a
pint of tequila off him.

What Bob Fisher did, he pulled out the papers
on the new prisoner, Harold Jackson, and started
reading about him.

One of the guards asked Harold Jackson if he'd
ever worn leg-irons before. Sitting tired, hunch-
shouldered on the floor, he said yeah. They looked
down at him and he looked up at them, coming
full awake but not showing it, and said yes-suh, he

believed it was two times. That's all, if the captain didn't count the prison farm. He'd wore irons there because they liked everybody working outside the jail to wear irons. It wasn't on account he had done anything.

The guard said all right, that was enough. They gave him a blanket and took him shuffling across the dark yard to the main cell block, then through the iron-cage gate where bare overhead lights showed the stone passageway and the cell doors on both sides. The guards didn't say anything to him. They stopped at Cell No. 8, unlocked the door, pushed him inside, and clanged the ironwork shut behind him.

As their steps faded in the passageway, Harold Jackson could make out two tiers of bunks and feel the closeness of the walls and was aware of a man breathing in his sleep. He wasn't sure how many were in this cell. He let his eyes get used to the darkness before he took a step, then another, the leg chains clinking in the silence. The back wall wasn't three steps away. The bunks, three decks high on both sides of him, were close enough to touch. Which would make this a six-man room, he figured, about eight feet by nine feet. Blanket-covered shapes lay close to him in the middle bunks. He couldn't make out the top ones and didn't want to feel around; but he could see the bottom racks were empty. Harold Jackson squatted on the floor and ducked into the right-side bunk.

The three-tiered bunks and the smell of the place reminded him of the troopship, though it had been awful hot down in the hold. Ten days sweating down in that dark hold while the ship was tied up at Tampa and they wouldn't let any of the Negro troops go ashore, not even to walk the dock and stretch their legs. He never did learn the name of that ship, and he didn't care. When they landed at Siboney, Harold Jackson walked off through the jungle and up into the hills. For two weeks he stayed with a Cuban family and ate sugar cane and got a kick out of how they couldn't speak any English, though they were Negro, same as he was. When he had rested and felt good he returned to the base and they threw him in the stockade. They said he was a deserter. He said he came back, didn't he? They said he was still a deserter.

He had never been in a cell that was this cold. Not even at Leavenworth. Up there in the Kansas winter the cold times were in the exercise yard, stamping your feet and moving to keep warm; the cell was all right, maybe a little cold sometimes. That was a funny thing, most of the jails he remembered as being hot: the prison farm wagon that was like a circus cage and the city jails and the army stockade in Cuba. He'd be sitting on a bench sweating or laying in the rack sweating, slapping mosquitoes, scratching, or watching the cockroaches fooling around and running nowhere. Cockroaches never looked like they knew where they were going. No, the heat was all right. The heat, the bugs were like part of being in jail. The cold was something he would have to get used to. Pretend it was hot. Pretend he was in Cuba. If he had to pick a jail to be in, out of all the places—if somebody said, "You got to go to jail for ten years, but we let you pick the place"—he'd pick the stockade at Siboney. Not because it was a good jail, but because it was in

Cuba, and Cuba was a nice-looking place, with the ocean and the trees and plenty of shade. That's a long way away, Harold Jackson said to himself. You ain't going to see it again.

There wasn't any wind. The cold just lay over him and didn't go away. His body was all right; it was his feet and his hands. Harold Jackson rolled to his side to reach down below the leg-irons that dug hard into his ankles and work his shoes off, then put his hands, palms together like he was praying, between the warmth of his legs. There was no use worrying about where he was. He would think of Cuba and go to sleep.

In the morning, in the moments before opening his eyes, he wasn't sure where he was. He was confused because a minute ago he'd have sworn he'd been holding a piece of sugar cane, the purple peeled back in knife strips and he was sucking, chewing the pulp to draw out the sweet juice. But he wasn't holding any cane now, and he wasn't in Cuba.

The bunk jiggled, strained, and moved back in place as somebody got down from above him. There were sounds of movement in the small cell, at least two men.

"You don't believe it, take a look."

"Jesus Christ," another voice said, a younger voice. "What's he doing in here?"

Both of them white voices. Harold Jackson could feel them standing between the bunks. He opened his eyes a little bit at a time until he was looking at prison-striped legs. It wasn't much lighter in the cell than before, when he'd gone to sleep, but he could see the stripes all right and he knew that outside it was morning.

A pair of legs swung down from the opposite bunk and hung there, wool socks and yellow toenails poking out of holes. "What're you looking at?" this one said, his voice low and heavy with sleep.

"We got a coon in here with us," the younger voice said.

The legs came down and the space was filled with faded, dirty convict stripes. Harold Jackson turned his head a little and raised his eyes. His gaze met theirs as they hunched over to look at him, studying him as if he was something they had never seen before. There was a heavy-boned, beard-stubbled face; a blond baby-boy face; and a skinny, slick-haired face with a big cavalry mustache that drooped over the corners of the man's mouth.

"Somebody made a mistake," the big man said. "In the dark."

"Joe Dean seen him right away."

"I smelled him," the one with the cavalry mustache said.

"Jesus," the younger one said now, "wait till Shelby finds out."

Harold Jackson came out of the bunk, rising slowly, uncoiling and bringing up his shoulders to stand eye to eye with the biggest of the three. He stared at the man's dead-looking deep-set eyes and at the hairs sticking out of a nose that was scarred and one time had been broken. "You gentlemen excuse me," Harold Jackson said, moving past the young boy and the one who was called Joe Dean. He stood with his back to them and aimed at the slop bucket against the wall.

They didn't say anything at first; just stared at him. But as Harold Jackson started to go the younger one murmured, "Jesus Christ—" as if awed, or saying a prayer. He stared at Harold as long as he could, then broke for the door and began yelling through the ironwork, "Guard! Guard! Goddamn it, there's a nigger in here pissing in our toilet!"

⇒ 2 ⇒

Raymond San Carlos heard the sound of Junior's voice before he made out the words: somebody yelling—for a guard. Somebody gone crazy, or afraid of something. Something happening in one of the cells close by. He heard quick footsteps now, going past, and turned his head enough to look from his bunk to the door.

It was morning. The electric lights were off in the cell block and it was dark now, the way a barn with its doors open is dark. He could hear other voices now and footsteps and, getting louder, the metal-ringing sound of the guards banging crowbars on the cell doors—good morning, get up and go to the toilet and put your shoes on and fold your blankets—the iron clanging coming closer, until it was almost to them and the convict above Raymond San Carlos yelled, "All right, we hear you! God Almighty—" The other convict in the cell, across from him in an upper bunk, said, "I'd like to wake them sons of bitches up some time." The man above Raymond said, "Break their goddamn eardrums." The other man said, "No, I'd empty slop pails on 'em." And the crowbar clanged against the door and was past them, banging, clanging down the passageway.

Another guard came along in a few minutes and unlocked each cell. Raymond was ready by the time he got to them, standing by the door to be first out. One of the convicts in the cell poked Raymond in the back and, when he turned around, pointed to the bucket.

"It ain't my turn," Raymond said.

"If I want you to empty it," the convict said, his partner close behind him, looking over his shoulder, "then it's your turn."

Raymond shrugged and they stood aside to let him edge past them. He could argue with them and they could pound his head against the stone wall and say he fell out of his bunk. He could pick up the slop bucket and say, "Hey," and when they turned around he could throw it at them. Thinking about it afterward would be good, but the getting beat up and pounded against the wall wouldn't be good. Or they might stick his face in a bucket. God, he'd get sick, and every time he thought of it after he'd get sick.

He had learned to hold onto himself and think ahead, looking at the good results and the bad results, and decide quickly if doing something was worth it. One time he hadn't held onto himself—the time he worked for the Sedona cattle people up on Oak Creek—and it was the reason he was here.

He had held on at first, for about a year while the other riders—some of them—kidded him about having a fancy name like Raymond San Carlos when he was Apache Indian down to the soles of his feet. Chiricahua Apache, they said. Maybe a little taller than most, but look at them black beady eyes and the flat nose. Pure Indin.

The Sedona hands got tired of it after a while; all except two boys who wouldn't leave him alone: a boy named Buzz Moore and another one they called Eljay. They kept at him every day. One of them would say, "What's that in his hair?" and pretend to pick something out, holding it between two fingers and studying it closely. "Why, it's some fuzz off a turkey feather, must have got stuck there from his headdress." Sometimes when it was hot and dry one of these two would look up at the sky and say, "Hey, chief, commence dancing and see if you can get us some rain down here." They asked him if he ever thought about white women, which he would never in his life ever get to have. They'd drink whiskey in front of him and not give him any, saying it was against the law to give an Indian firewater. Things like that.

At first it hadn't been too hard to hold on and go along with the kidding. Riding for Sedona was a good job, and worth it. Raymond would usually grin and say nothing. A couple of times he tried to tell them he was American and only his name was Mexican. He had made up what he thought was a pretty good story.

"See, my father's name was Armando de San Carlos y Zamora. He was born in Mexico, I don't know where, but I know he come up here to find work and that's when he met my mother who's an American, Maria Ramirez, and they got married. So when I'm born here, I'm American too."

He remembered Buzz Moore saying, "Maria Ramirez? What kind of American name is that?"

The other one, Eljay, who never let him alone, said, "So are Apache Indins American if you want to call everybody who's born in this country American. But anybody knows Indins ain't citizens. And if you ain't a citizen, you ain't American." He said to Raymond, "You ever vote?"

"I ain't never been where there was anything to vote about," Raymond answered.

"You go to school?"

"A couple of years."

"Then you don't know anything about what is a U.S. citizen. Can you read and write?"

Raymond shook his head.

"There you are," Eljay said.

Buzz Moore said then, "His daddy could have been Indin. They got Indins in Mexico like anywhere else. Why old Geronimo himself lived down there and could have sired a whole tribe of little Indins."

And Eljay said, "You want to know the simple truth? He's Chiricahua Apache, born and reared on the San Carlos Indin reservation, and that's how he got his fancy name. Made it up so people wouldn't think he was Indin."

"Well," Buzz Moore said, "he could be some part Mexican."

"If that's so," Eljay said, "what we got here is a red greaser."

They got a kick out of that and called him the red greaser through the winter and into April—until the day up in the high meadows they were gathering spring calves and their mammas and chasing them down to the valley graze. They were using revolvers and shotguns part of the time to scare the stock out of the brush stands and box canyons and keep them moving. Raymond remembered the feel of the 12-gauge Remington, holding it pointed up with the stock tight against his thigh. He would fire it this way when he was chasing stock—aiming straight up—and would feel the Remington kick against his leg. He kept off by himself most of the day, enjoying the good feeling of being alone in high country. He remembered the day vividly: the clean line of the peaks towering against the sky, the shadowed canyons and the slopes spotted yellow with arrowroot blossoms. He liked the silence; he liked being here alone and not having to think about anything or talk to anybody.

It wasn't until the end of the day he realized how sore his leg was from the shotgun butt punching it. Raymond swung down off the sorrel he'd been riding and limped noticeably as he walked toward the cook fire. Eljay was standing there. Eljay took one look and said, "Hey, greaser, is that some kind of one-legged Indin dance you're doing?" Raymond stopped. He raised the Remington and shot Eljay square in the chest with both loads.

On this morning in February, 1909, as he picked up the slop bucket and followed his two cellmates out into the passageway. Raymond had served almost four years of a life sentence for second-degree murder.

The guard, R.E. Baylis, didn't lay his crowbar against No. 14, the last door at the east end of the cellblock. He opened the door and stepped inside and waited for Frank Shelby to look up from his bunk.

"You need to be on the supply detail today?" R.E. Baylis asked.

"What's today?"

"Tuesday."

"Tomorrow," Shelby said. "What's it like out?"

"Bright and fair, going to be warm."

"Put me on an outside detail."

"We got a party building a wall over by the cemetery."

"Hauling the bricks?"

"Bricks already there."

"That'll be all right," Shelby said. He sat up, swinging his legs over the side of the bunk. He was alone in the cell, in the upper of a double bunk. The triple bunk opposite him was stacked with cardboard boxes and a wooden crate and a few canvas sacks. A shelf and mirror hung from the back wall. There was also a chair by the wall with a hole cut out of the seat and a bucket underneath. A roll of toilet paper rested on one of the arms. The convicts called the chair Shelby's throne. "Get somebody to empty the bucket, will you?" Looking at the guard again, Shelby said, "You need anything?"

R.E. Baylis touched his breast pocket. "Well, I guess I could use some chew."

"Box right by your head," Shelby said. "I got Mail Pouch and Red Man. Or I got some Copenhagen if you want."

R.E. Baylis fished a hand in the box. "I might as well take a couple—case I don't see you again today."

"You know where to find me." Shelby dropped to the floor, pulled on half-boots, hopping a couple of times to keep his balance, then ran a hand through his dark hair as he straightened up, standing now in his boots and long underwear. "I believe I was supposed to get a clean outfit today."

"Washing machine broke down yesterday."

"Tomorrow then for sure, uh?" Shelby had an easy, unhurried way of talking. It was known that he never raised his voice or got excited. They said the way you told if he was mad or irritated, he would fool with his mustache; he would keep smoothing it down with two fingers until he decided what had to be done and either did it himself or had somebody else do it. Frank Shelby was serving forty-five years for armed robbery and second-degree murder and had brought three of his men with him to Yuma, each of them found guilty on the same counts and serving thirty years apiece.

Junior was one of them. He banged through the cell door as Shelby was getting into his prison stripes, buttoning his coat. "You got your mean go-to-hell look on this morning," Shelby said. "Was that you yelling just now?"

"They stuck a nigger in our cell last night while we was asleep." Junior turned to nail the guard with his look, putting the blame on him.

"It wasn't me," R.E. Baylis said. "I just come on duty."

"You don't throw his black ass out, we will," Junior said. By Jesus, this was Worley Lewis, Jr. talking, nineteen-year-old convict going on forty-nine before he would ever see the outside of a penitentiary, but he was one of Frank Shelby's own and that said he could stand up to a guard and mouth him if he had a good enough reason. "I'm telling you, Soonzy'll kill the son of a bitch."

"I'll find out why—" the guard began.

"It was a mistake," Shelby said. "Put him in the wrong cell is all."

"He's in there now, great big buck. Joe Dean seen him first, woke me up, and I swear I couldn't believe my eyes."

Shelby went over to the mirror and picked up a comb from the shelf. "It's nothing to get upset about," he said, making a part and slanting the dark hair carefully across his forehead. "Tonight they'll put him someplace else."

"Well, if we can," the guard said.

Shelby was watching him in the mirror: the gray-looking man in the gray guard uniform, R.E. Baylis, who might have been a town constable or a deputy sheriff twenty years ago. "What's the trouble?" Shelby asked.

"I mean he might have been ordered put there, I don't know."

"Ordered by who?"

"Bob Fisher. I say I don't know for sure."

Shelby turned from the mirror. "Bob don't want any trouble."

"Course not."

"Then why would he want to put Sambo in with my boys?"

"I say, I don't know."

Shelby came toward him now, noticing the activity out in the passageway, the convicts standing around and talking, moving slowly as the guards began to form them into two rows. Shelby put a hand on the guard's shoulder. "Mr. Baylis," he said, "don't worry about it. You don't want to ask Bob Fisher; we'll get Sambo out of there ourselves."

"We don't want nobody hurt or anything."

The guard kept looking at him, but Shelby was finished. As far as he was concerned, it was done. He said to Junior, "Give Soonzy the tobacco. You take the soap and stuff."

"It's my turn to keep the tally."

"Don't give me that look, boy."

Junior dropped his tone. "I lugged a box yesterday."

"All right, you handle the tally, Joe Dean carries the soap and stuff." Shelby paused, as if he was going to say something else, then looked at the guard. "Why don't you have the colored boy empty my throne bucket?"

"It don't matter to me," the guard said.

So he pulled Harold Jackson out of line and told him to get down to No. 14—as Joe Dean, Soonzy, and Junior moved along the double row of convicts in the dim passageway and sold them tobacco and cigarette paper, four kinds of plug and scrap, and little tins of snuff, matches, sugar cubes, stick candy, soap bars, sewing needles and thread, playing cards, red bandana handkerchiefs, shoelaces, and combs. They didn't take money; it would waste too much time and they only had ten minutes to go down the double line of eighty-seven men. Junior put the purchase amount in the tally book and the customer had one week to pay. If he didn't pay in a week, he couldn't buy any more stuff until he did. If he didn't pay in two weeks Junior and Soonzy would get him in a cell alone and hit him a few times or stomp the man's ribs and kidneys. If a customer wanted tequila or mescal, or corn whiskey when they had it, he'd come around to No. 14 after supper, before the doors were shut for the night, and pay a dollar a half-pint, put up in medicine bottles from the sick ward that occupied the second floor of the cell block. Shelby only sold alcohol in the morning to three or four of the convicts who needed it first thing or would never get through the day. What most of them wanted was just a day's worth of tobacco and some paper to roll it in.

When the figure appeared outside the iron lattice Shelby said, "Come on in," and watched the big colored boy's reaction as he entered: his gaze shifting twice to take in the double bunk and the boxes and the throne, knowing right away this was a one-man cell.

"I'm Mr. Shelby."

"I'm Mr. Jackson," Harold said.

Frank Shelby touched his mustache. He smoothed it to the sides once, then let his hand drop to the edge of his bunk. His eyes remained on the impassive dark face that did not move now and was looking directly at him.

"Where you from, Mr. Jackson?"

"From Leavenworth."

That was it. Big time con in a desert prison hole. "This place doesn't look like much after the federal pen, uh?"

"I been to some was worse, some better."

"What'd you get sent here for?"

"I killed a man was bothering me."

"You get life?"

"Fifteen years."

"Then you didn't kill a man. You must've killed another colored boy." Shelby waited.

Harold Jackson said nothing. He could wait too.

"I'm right, ain't I?" Shelby said.

"The man said for me to come in here."

"He told you, but it was me said for you to come in."

Harold Jackson waited again. "You saying you the man here?"

"Ask any of them out there," Shelby said. "The guards, anybody."

"You bring me in to tell me about yourself?"

"No, I brought you in to empty my slop bucket."

"Who did it before I come?"

"Anybody I told."

"If you got people willing, you better call one of them." Harold turned and had a hand on the door when Shelby stopped him.

"Hey, Sambo—"

Harold came around enough to look at him. "How'd you know that was my name?"

"Boy, you are sure starting off wrong," Shelby said. "I believe you need to be by yourself a while and think it over."

Harold didn't have anything to say to that. He turned to the door again and left the man standing there playing with his mustache.

As he fell in at the end of the prisoner line, a guard named R.E. Baylis gave him a funny look and came over.

"Where's Shelby's bucket at?"

"I guess it's still in there, captain."

"How come he didn't have you take it?"

Harold Jackson stood at attention, looking past the man's face to the stone wall of the passageway. "You'll have to ask him about that, captain."

"Here they come," Bob Fisher said. "Look over there."

Mr. Manly moved quickly from the side of the desk to the window to watch the double file of convicts coming this way. He was anxious to see everything this morning, especially the convicts.

"Is that all of them?"

"In the main cell block. About ninety."

"I thought there'd be more." Mr. Manly studied the double file closely but wasn't able to single out Harold Jackson. All the convicts looked alike. No, that was wrong; they didn't all look alike.

"Since we're shutting down we haven't been getting as many."

"They're all different, aren't they?"

"How's that?" Bob Fisher said.

Mr. Manly didn't answer, or didn't hear him. He stood at the window of the superintendent's office—the largest of a row of offices over the mess hall—and watched the convicts as they came across the yard, passed beyond the end of a low adobe, and came into view again almost directly below the window. The line reached the door of the mess hall and came to a stop.

Their uniforms looked the same, all of them wearing prison stripes, all faded gray and white. It was the hats that were different, light-colored felt hats and a few straw hats, almost identical hats, but all worn at a different angle: straight, low over the eyes, to the side, cocked like a dandy would wear his hat, the brim funneled, the brim up in front, the brim down all around. The hats were as different as the men must be different. He should make a note of that. See if anything had been written on the subject: determining a man's character

by the way he wore his hat. But there wasn't a note
pad or any paper on the desk and he didn't want to
ask Fisher for it right at the moment.

He was looking down at all the hats. He couldn't
see any of their faces clearly, and wouldn't unless a
man looked up. Nobody was looking up.

They were all looking back toward the yard.
Most of them turning now so they wouldn't have
to strain their necks. All those men suddenly interested in something and turning to look.

"The women convicts," Bob Fisher said.

Mr. Manly saw them then. My God—two women.

Fisher pressed closer to him at the window.
Mr. Manly could smell tobacco on the man's
breath. "They just come out of the latrine, that
adobe there," Fisher said. "Now watch them boys
eyeing them."

The two women walked down the line of convicts, keeping about ten feet away, seeming at ease
and not in any hurry, but not looking at the men
either.

"Taking their time and giving the boys sweet
hell, aren't they? Don't hear a sound, they're so
busy licking their lips."

Mr. Manly glanced quickly at the convicts. The
way they were looking, it was more likely their
mouths were hanging open. It gave him a funny
feeling, the men dead serious and no one making
a sound.

"My," Fisher said, "how they'd like to reach out
and grab a handful of what them girls have got."

"Women—" Mr. Manly said almost as a question. Nobody had told him there were women at
Yuma.

A light-brown-haired one and a dark-haired one that looked to be Mexican. Lord God, two good-looking women walking past those men like they were strolling in the park. Mr. Manly couldn't believe they were convicts. They were *women*. The little dark-haired one wore a striped dress— smaller stripes than the men's outfits—that could be a dress she'd bought anywhere. The brown-haired one, taller and a little older, though she couldn't be thirty yet, wore a striped blouse with the top buttons undone, a white canvas belt and a gray skirt that clung to the movement of her hips as she walked and flared out as it reached to her ankles.

"Tacha Reyes," Fisher said

"Pardon me?"

"The little chilipicker. She's been here six months of a ten-year sentence. I doubt she'll serve it all though. She behaves herself pretty good."

"What did she do? I mean to be here."

"Killed a man with a knife, she claimed was trying to make her do dirty things."

"Did the other one—kill somebody?"

"Norma Davis? Hell, no. Norma likes to do dirty things. She was a whore till she took up armed robbery and got caught holding up the Citizens' Bank of Prescott, Arizona. Man with her, her partner, was shot dead."

"A woman," Mr. Manly said. "I can't believe a woman would do that."

"With a Colt forty-four," Fisher said. "She shot a policeman during the hold-up but didn't kill him. Listen, you want to keep a pretty picture of women in your head don't get close to Norma. She's serving ten years for armed robbery and attempted murder."

The women were inside the mess hall now. Mr. Manly wanted to ask more questions about them, but he was afraid of sounding too interested and Fisher might get the wrong idea. "I notice some of the men are carrying buckets," he said.

"The latrine detail." Fisher pointed to the low adobe. "They'll go in there and empty them. That's the toilet and wash house, everything sewered clear out to the river. There—now the men are going into mess. They got fifteen minutes to eat, then ten minutes to go to the toilet before the work details form out in the exercise yard."

"Do you give them exercises to do?"

"We give them enough work they don't need any exercise," Fisher answered.

Mr. Manly raised his eyes to look out at the empty yard and was surprised to see a lone convict coming across from the cellblock.

"Why isn't that one with the others?"

Bob Fisher didn't answer right way. Finally he said, "That's Frank Shelby."

"Is he a trusty?"

"Not exactly. He's got some special jobs he does around here."

Mr. Manly let it go. There were too many other things he wanted to know about. Like all the adobe buildings scattered around, a whole row of them over to the left, at the far end of the mess hall. He wondered where the women lived, but didn't ask that.

Well, there was the cook shack over there and the tailor shop, where they made the uniforms.

Bob Fisher pointed out the small one-story adobes. Some equipment sheds, a storehouse, the reception hut they were in last night. The mattress factory and the wagon works had been shut down six months ago. Over the main cellblock was the hospital, but the doctor had gone to Florence to set up a sick ward at the new prison. Anybody broke a leg now or crushed his hand working the rocks, they sent for a town doctor.

And the chaplain, Mr. Manly asked casually. Was he still here?

No, there wasn't any chaplain. The last one retired and they decided to wait till after the move to get another. There wasn't many of the convicts prayed anyway.

How would you know that? Mr. Manly wanted to ask him. But he said, "What are those doors way down there?"

At the far end of the yard he could make out several iron-grill doors, black oval shapes, doorways carved into the solid rock. The doors didn't lead outside, he could tell that, because the top of the east wall and two of the guard towers were still a good piece beyond.

"Starting over back of the main cellblock, you can't see it from here," Bob Fisher said, "a gate leads into the TB cellblock and exercise yard."

"You've got consumptives here?"

"Like any place else. I believe four right now." Fisher hurried on before Mr. Manly could interrupt again. "The doors you can see—one's the crazy hole. Anybody gets mean loco they go in there till they calm down. The next one they call the snake den's a punishment cell."

"Why is it called—"

"I don't know, I guess a snake come in through the air shaft one time. The last door there on the right goes into the women's cellblock. You seen them. We just got the two right now."

There, he could ask about them again and it would sound natural. "The one you said, Norma something, has she been here long?"

"Norma Davis. I believe about a year and a half."

"Do the men ever—I mean I guess you have to sort of watch over the women."

"Mister, we have to watch over everybody."

"But being women—don't they have to have their own, you know, facilities and bath?"

Fisher looked right at Mr. Manly now. "They take a bath in the cook shack three, four times a week."

"In the cook shack." Mr. Manly nodded, surprised. "After the cooks are gone, of course."

"At night," Fisher said. He studied Mr. Manly's profile—the soft pinkish face and gold-frame glasses pressed close to the windowpane—little Bible teacher looking out over his prison and still thinking about Norma Davis, asking harmless sounding questions about the women.

Fisher said quietly, "You want to see them?"

Mr. Manly straightened, looking at Fisher now with a startled expression. "What do you mean?"

"I wondered if you wanted to go downstairs and have another look at Norma and Tacha."

"I want to see everything," Mr. Manly said. "Everything you have here to show me."

3

When Frank Shelby entered the mess hall he stepped in line ahead of Junior. In front of him, Soonzy and Joe Dean looked around.

"You take care of it?" Junior asked him.

"He needs some time in the snake den," Shelby said.

Soonzy was looking back down the line. "Where's he at?"

"Last one coming in."

"I'll handle him," Junior said.

Shelby shook his head. "I want somebody else to start it. You and Soonzy break it up and get in some licks."

"No problem," Junior said. "The spook's already got leg-irons on."

They picked up tin plates and cups and passed in front of the serving tables for their beans, salt-dried beef, bread, and coffee. Soonzy and Joe Dean waited, letting Shelby go ahead of them. He paused a moment, holding his food, looking out over the long twelve-man tables and benches that were not yet half filled. Joe Dean moved up next to him. "I see plenty of people that owe us money."

"No, I see the one I want. The Indin," Shelby said, and started for his table.

Raymond San Carlos was pushing his spoon into the beans that were pretty good but would be a lot better with some ketchup. He looked up as Frank Shelby and Junior put their plates down across from him. He hurried and took the spoonful of beans, then took another one more slowly. He knew they had picked him for something. He was sure of it when Soonzy sat down on one side of him and Joe Dean stepped in on the other. Joe Dean acted surprised at seeing him. "Well, Raymond San Carlos," he said, "how are you today?"

"I'm pretty good, I guess."

Junior said, "What're you pretty good at, Raymond?"

"I don't know—some things, I guess."

"You fight pretty good?"

It's coming, Raymond said to himself, and told himself to be very calm and not look away from this little boy son-of-a-bitch friend of Frank Shelby's. He said, "I fight sometimes. Why, you want to fight me?"

"Jesus," Junior said. "Listen to him."

Raymond smiled. "I thought that's what you meant." He picked up his coffee and took a sip.

"Don't drink it," Shelby said.

Raymond looked directly at him for the first time. "My coffee?"

"You see that colored boy? He's picking up his plate." As Raymond looked over Shelby said, "After he sits down I want you to go over and dump your coffee right on his woolly head."

He was at the serving table now, big shoulders and narrow hips. Some of the others from the latrine had come in behind him. He was not the biggest man in the line, but he was the tallest and seemed to have the longest arms.

"You want me to fight him?"

"I said I want you to pour your coffee on his head," Shelby answered. "That's all I said to do. You understand that, or you want me to tell you in sign language?"

Harold Jackson took a place at the end of a table. There were two men at the other end. Shifting his gaze past them as he took a bite of bread, he could see Frank Shelby and the mouthy kid and, opposite them, the big one you would have to hit with a pipe or a pick handle to knock down, and the skinny one, Joe Dean, with the beard that looked like ass fur off a sick dog. The dark-skinned man with them, who was getting up now, he hadn't seen before.

There were five guards in the room. No windows. One door. A stairway—at the end of the room behind the serving tables—where the turnkey and the little man from the train were coming down the stairs now: little man who said he was going to be in charge, looking all around—my, what a fine big mess hall—looking and following the turnkey, who never changed his face, looking at the grub now, nodding, smiling—yes, that would sure stick to their ribs—taking a cup of coffee the turnkey offered him and tasting it. Two of the guards walked over and now the little man was shaking hands with them.

That was when Harold felt somebody behind

him brush him, and the hot coffee hitting his head was like a shock, coming into his eyes and feeling as if it was all over him.

Behind him, Raymond said, "What'd you hit my arm for?"

Harold wiped a hand down over his face, twisting around and looking up to see the dark-skinned man who had been with Shelby, an Indian-looking man standing, waiting for him. He knew Shelby was watching, Shelby and anybody else who had seen it happen.

"What's the matter with you?" Harold said.

Raymond didn't move. "I want to know why you hit my arm."

"I'll hit your mouth, boy, you want. But I ain't going to do it here."

Raymond let him have the tin plate, backhanding the edge of it across his eyes, and Harold was off the bench, grabbing Raymond's wrist as Raymond hit him in the face with the coffee cup. Harold didn't get to swing. A fist cracked against his cheekbone from the blind side. He was hit again on the other side of the face, kicked in the small of the back, and grabbed by both arms and around his neck and arched backward until he was looking at the ceiling. There were faces looking at him, the dark-skinned boy looking at him calmly, people pressing in close, then a guard's hat and another, and the turnkey's face with the mustache and the expression that didn't change.

"Like he went crazy," Junior said. "Just reared up and hit this boy."

"I was going past," Raymond said.

Junior was nodding. "That's right. Frank seen

it first, we look over and this spook has got Raymond by the neck. Frank says help him, and me and Soonzy grabbed the spook quick as we could."

The turnkey reached out, but Harold didn't feel his hand. He was looking past him.

"Let him up," Fisher said.

Somebody kicked him again as they jerked him to his feet and let go of his arms. Harold felt his nose throbbing and felt something wet in his eyes. When he wiped at his eyes he saw the red blood on his fingers and could feel it running down his face now. The turnkey's face was raised; he was looking off somewhere.

Fisher said, "You saw it, Frank?"

Shelby was still sitting at his table. He nodded slowly. "Same as Junior told you. That colored boy started it. Raymond hit him to get free, but he wouldn't let go till Junior and Soonzy got over there and pinned him."

"That's all?"

"That's all," Shelby said.

"Anybody else see it start?" Fisher looked around. The convicts met his gaze as it passed over them. They waited as Fisher took his time, letting the silence in the room lengthen. When he looked at Harold Jackson again there was a moment when he seemed about to say something to him. The moment passed. He turned away and walked back to the food tables where Mr. Manly was waiting, his hands folded in front of him, his eyes wide open behind the gold-frame glasses.

"You want to see the snake den," Bob Fisher said. "Come on, we got somebody else wants to see it too."

After breakfast, as the work details were forming in the yard, the turnkey and the new superintendent and two guards marched Harold Jackson past the groups all the way to the snake den at the back of the yard.

Raymond San Carlos looked at the colored boy as he went by. He had never seen him before this morning. Nobody would see him now for about a week. It didn't matter. Dumb nigger had done something to Shelby and would have to learn, that's all.

While Raymond was still watching them—going one at a time into the cell now—one of the guards, R.E. Baylis, pulled him out of the stone quarry gang and took him over to another detail. Raymond couldn't figure it out until he saw Shelby in the group and knew Shelby had arranged it. A reward for pouring coffee on a man. He was out of that man-breaking quarry and on Shelby's detail because he'd done what he was told. Why not?

As a guard with a Winchester marched them out the main gate Raymond was thinking: Why not do it the easy way? Maybe things were going to be better and this was the beginning of it: get in with Shelby, work for him; have all the cigarettes he wanted, some tequila at night to put him to sleep, no hard-labor details. He could be out of here maybe in twenty years if he never did nothing to wear leg-irons or get put in the snake den. Twenty years, he would be almost fifty years old. He couldn't change that. Or he could do whatever he felt like doing and not smile at people like Frank Shelby and Junior and the two convicts in his cell. He could get his head pounded against the stone wall and spend the rest of his life here. It was a lot to think about, but it made the most sense to get in with Shelby. He would be as dumb as the nigger if he didn't.

Outside the walls, the eight-man detail was marched past the water cistern—their gaze going up the mound of earth past the stonework to the guard tower that looked like a bandstand sitting up there, a nice shady pavilion where a rapid-fire weapon was trained on the main gate—then down the grade to a path that took them along the bluff overlooking the river. They followed it until they reached the cemetery.

Beyond the rows of headstones an adobe wall, low, and uneven, under construction, stood two to three feet high on the riverside of the cemetery.

Junior said, "What do they want a wall for? Them boys don't have to be kept in."

"They want a wall," Shelby said, "because it's a good place for a wall and there ain't nothing else for us to do."

Raymond agreed four year's worth to that. The work was to keep them busy. Everybody knew they would be moving out of here soon, but every day they pounded rocks into gravel for the roads and made adobe bricks and built and repaired walls and levees and cleared brush along the riverbank. It was a wide river with a current—down the slope and across the flat stretch of mud beach to the water— maybe a hundred yards across. There was nothing on the other side—no houses, only a low bank and what looked to be heavy brush. The land over there could be a swamp or a desert; nobody had ever said what it was like, only that it was California.

All morning they laid the big adobe bricks in place, gradually raising the level string higher as they worked on a section of wall at a time. It was dirty, muddy work, and hot out in the open. Raymond couldn't figure out why Shelby was on this detail, unless he felt he needed sunshine and exercise. He laid about half as many bricks as anybody else, and didn't talk to anybody except his three friends. It surprised Raymond when Shelby began working on the other side of the wall from him and told him he had done all right in the mess hall this morning. Raymond nodded; he didn't know what to say. A few minutes went by before Shelby spoke again.

"You want to join us?"

Raymond looked at him. "You mean work for you?"

"I mean go with us," Shelby said. He tapped a brick in place with the handle of his trowel and sliced off the mortar oozing out from under the brick. "Don't look around. Say yes or no."

"I don't know where you're going."

"I know you don't. You say yes or no before I tell you."

"All right," Raymond said. "Yes."

"Can you swim?"

"You mean the river?"

"It's the only thing I see around here to swim," Shelby said. "I'm not going to explain it all now."

"I don't know—"

"Yes, you do, Raymond. You're going to run for the river when I tell you. You're going to swim straight across and find a boat hidden in the brush, put there for us, and you're going to row back fast as you can and meet us swimming over."

"If we're all swimming what do you want the boat for?"

"In case anybody can't make it all the way."

"I'm not sure I can, even."

"You're going to find out," Shelby said.

"How wide is it here?"

"Three hundred fifty feet. That's not so far."

The river had looked cool and inviting before; not to swim across, but to sit in and splash around and get clean after sweating all morning in the adobe mud.

"There's a current—"

"Don't think about it. Just swim."

"But the guard—what about him?"

"We'll take care of the guard."

"I don't understand how we going to do it." He was frowning in the sunlight trying to figure it out.

"Raymond, I say run, you run. All right?"

"You don't give me any time to think about it."

"That's right," Shelby said. "When I leave here you come over the wall and start working on this side." He got up and moved down the wall about ten or twelve feet to where Soonzy and Junior were working.

Raymond stepped over the three-foot section of wall with his mortar bucket and continued working, facing the guard now who was about thirty feet away, sitting on a rise of ground with the Winchester across his lap and smoking a cigarette. Beyond him, a hundred yards or so up the slope, the prison wall and the guard tower at the northwest corner stood against the sky. The guard up there could be looking this way or he could be looking inside, into the yard of the TB cellblock. Make

a run for the river with two guns within range.
Maybe three, counting the main tower. There was
some brush, though, a little cover before he got to
the mud flat. But once they saw him, the whistle
would blow and they'd be out here like they came
up out of the ground, some of them shooting and
some of them getting the boat, wherever the boat
was kept. He didn't have to stay with Shelby, he
could go up to the high country this spring and
live by himself. Maybe through the summer. Then
go some place nobody knew him and get work.
Maybe Mexico.

Joe Dean came along with a wheelbarrow and
scooped mortar into Raymond's bucket. "If we're
not worried," Joe Dean said, leaning on the wall,
"what're you nervous about?"

Raymond didn't look up at him. He didn't like
to look at the man's mouth and tobacco-stained
teeth showing in his beard. He didn't like having
anything to do with the man. He didn't like having
anything to do with Junior or Soonzy either. Or
with Frank Shelby when he thought about it honestly and didn't get it mixed up with cigarettes and
tequila. But he would work with them and swim
the river with them to get out of this place. He said
to Joe Dean, "I'm ready any time you are."

Joe Dean squinted up at the sun, then let his
gaze come down to the guard. "It won't be long,"
he said, and moved off with his wheelbarrow.

The way they worked it, Shelby kept his eye on
the guard. He waited until the man started looking
for the chow wagon that would be coming around
the corner from the main gate any time now. He

waited until the guard was finally half-turned, looking up the slope, then gave a nod to Junior.

Junior jabbed his trowel into the foot of the man working next to him.

The man let out a scream and the guard was on his feet at once, coming down from the rise.

Shelby waited until the guard was hunched over the man, trying to get a look at the foot. The other convicts were crowding in for a look too and the man was holding his ankle, rocking back and forth and moaning. The guard told him goddamn-it, sit still and let him see it.

Shelby looked over at Raymond San Carlos, who was standing now, the wall in front of him as high as his hips. Shelby nodded and turned to the group around the injured man. As he pushed Joe Dean aside he glanced around again to see the wall empty where Raymond had been standing. "What time is it?" he said.

Joe Dean took out his pocket watch. "Eleven-fifty about."

"Exactly."

"Eleven-fifty-two."

Shelby took the watch from Joe Dean as he leaned in to see the clean tear in the toe of the man's shoe and the blood starting to come out. He waited a moment before moving over next to the wall. The guard was asking what happened and Junior was trying to explain how he'd tripped over the goddamn mortar bucket and, throwing his hand out as he fell, his trowel had hit the man's shoe. His foot, the guard said—you stabbed him. Well, he hadn't meant to, Junior told the guard.

Jesus, if he'd meant to, he wouldn't have stabbed him in the foot, would he?

From the wall Shelby watched Raymond moving quickly through the brush clumps and not looking back—very good—not hesitating until he was at the edge of the mud flats, a tiny figure way down there, something striped, hunched over in the bushes and looking around now. Go on, Shelby said, looking at the watch. What're you waiting for? It was eleven fifty-three.

The guard was telling the man to take his shoes off, he wasn't going to do it for him; and goddamn-it, get back and give him some air.

When Shelby looked down the slope again Raymond was in the water knee-deep, sliding into it; in a moment only his head was showing. Like he knew what he was doing, Shelby thought.

Between moans the injured man said Oh God, he believed his toes were cut off. Junior said maybe one or two; no trowel was going to take off all a man's toes, 'less you come down hard with the edge; maybe that would do it.

Twenty yards out. Raymond wasn't too good a swimmer, about average. Well, that was all right. If he was average then the watch would show an average time. He sure seemed to be moving slow though. Swimming was slow work.

When the chow wagon comes, the guard said, we'll take him up in it. Two of you men go with him.

It's coming now, somebody said.

There it was, poking along close to the wall, a driver and a helper on the seat, one of the trust-ies. The guard stood up and yelled for them to get down here. Shelby took time to watch the injured man as he ground his teeth together and eased his shoe off. He wasn't wearing any socks. His toes were a mess of blood, but at least they all seemed to be there. He was lucky.

Raymond was more than halfway across now. The guard was motioning to the wagon, trying to hurry it. So Shelby watched Raymond: just a speck out there, you'd have to know where to look to find him. Wouldn't that be something if he made it? God Almighty, dumb Indin probably could if he knew what to do once he got across. Or if he had some help waiting. But he'd look for the boat that wasn't there and run off through the brush and see all that empty land stretching nowhere.

Eleven fifty-six. He'd be splashing around out there another minute easy before he reached the bank.

Shelby walked past the group around the injured man and called out to the guard who had gone partway up the slope, "Hey, mister!" When the guard looked around Shelby said, "I think there's somebody out there in the water."

The guard hesitated, but not more than a moment before he got over to the wall. He must have had a trained eye, because he spotted Raymond right away and fired the Winchester in the air. Three times in rapid succession.

Joe Dean looked up as Shelby handed him his pocket watch. "He make it?" Joe Dean asked.

"Just about."

"How many minutes?"

"Figure five anyway, as a good average."

Junior said to Shelby, "What do you think?"

"Well, it's a slow way out of here," Shelby answered. "But least we know how long it takes now and we can think on it."

Mr. Manly jumped in his chair and swiveled around to the window when the whistle went off, a high, shrieking sound that ripped through the stillness of the office and seemed to be coming from directly overhead. The first thing he thought of, immediately, was, *somebody's trying to escape*! His first day here . . .

Only there wasn't a soul outside. No convicts, no guards running across the yard with guns.

Of course—they were all off on work details.

When he pressed close to the window Mr. Manly saw the woman, Norma Davis, standing in the door of the tailor shop. Way down at the end of the mess hall. He knew it was Norma, and not the other one. Standing with her hands on her hips, as if she was listening—Lord, as the awful piercing whistle kept blowing. After a few moments she turned and went inside again. Not too concerned about it.

Maybe it wasn't an escape. Maybe it was something else. Mr. Manly went down the hall and opened the doors, looking into empty offices, some that hadn't been used in months. He turned back and, as he reached the end of the hall and the door leading to the outside stairway, the whistle stopped. He waited, then cautiously opened the door and went outside. He could see the front gate from here: both barred doors closed and the inside and outside guards at their posts. He could call to the inside guard, ask him what was going on.

And what if the man looked up at him on the

stairs and said it was the noon dinner whistle? It was just about twelve.

Or what if it was an exercise he was supposed to know about? Or a fire drill. Or anything for that matter that a prison superintendent should be aware of. The guard would tell him, "That's the whistle to stop work for dinner, sir," and not say anything else, but his look would be enough.

Mr. Manly didn't know where else he might go, or where he might find the turnkey. So he went back to his office and continued reading the history file on Harold Jackson.

Born Fort Valley, Georgia, September 11, 1879.

Mr. Manly had already read that part. Field hand. No formal education. Arrested in Georgia and Florida several times for disorderly conduct, resisting arrest, striking an officer of the law. Served eighteen months on a Florida prison farm for assault. Inducted into the army April 22, 1898. Assigned to the 24th Infantry Regiment in Tampa, Florida, June 5. Shipped to Cuba.

He was going to read that part over again about Harold Jackson deserting and being court-martialed.

But Bob Fisher, the turnkey, walked in. He didn't knock, he walked in. He looked at Mr. Manly and nodded, then gazed about the room. "If there's something you don't like about this office, we got some others down the hall.

"Caught one of them trying to swim the river, just about the other side when we spotted him." Fisher stopped as Mr. Manly held up his hand and rose from the desk.

"Not right now," Mr. Manly said. "I'm going

to go have my dinner. You can give me a written report this afternoon."

Walking past Fisher wasn't as hard as he thought it would be. Out in the hall Mr. Manly paused and looked back in the office. "I assume you've put the man in the snake den."

Fisher nodded.

"Bring me his file along with your report, Bob." Mr. Manly turned and was gone.

4

Harold Jackson recognized the man in the few moments the door was open and the guards were shoving him inside. As the man turned to brace himself Harold saw his face against the outside sunlight, the dark-skinned face, the one in the mess hall. The door slammed closed and they were in darkness. Harold's eyes were used to it after half a day in here. He could see the man feeling his way along the wall until he was on the other side of the ten-by-ten-foot stone cell. It had been almost pitch dark all morning. Now, at midday, a faint light came through the air hole that was about as big around as a stovepipe and tunneled down through the domed ceiling. He could see the man's legs good, then part of his body as he sat down on the bare dirt floor. Harold drew up his legs and stretched them out again so the leg-iron chains would clink and rattle—in case the man didn't know he was here.

Raymond knew. Coming in, he had seen the figure sitting against the wall and had seen his eyes open and close as the sunlight hit his face, black against blackness, a striped animal in his burrow hole. Raymond knew. He had hit the man a good lick across the eyes with his tin plate, and if the man wanted to do something about it, now it was up to him. Raymond would wait, ready for him—while he pictured again Frank Shelby standing by the wall and tried to read Shelby's face.

The guards had brought him back in the skiff, making him row with his arms dead-tired, and dragged him wet and muddy all the way up the hill to the cemetery. Frank Shelby was still there. All of them were, and a man sitting on the ground, his foot bloody. Raymond had wanted to tell Shelby there wasn't any boat over there, and he wanted Shelby to tell him, somehow, what had gone wrong. He remembered Shelby staring at him, but not saying anything with his eyes or his expression. Just staring. Maybe he wasn't picturing Shelby's face clearly now, or maybe he had missed a certain look or gesture from him. He would have time to think about it. Thirty days in here. No mattress, no blanket, no slop bucket, use the corner, or piss on the nigger if he tried something. If the nigger hadn't done something to Shelby he wouldn't be here and you wouldn't be here, Raymond thought. Bread and water for thirty days, but they would take the nigger out before that and he would be alone. There were men they took from here to the crazy hole after being alone in the darkness too long. It can happen if you think about being here and nothing else, Raymond said to himself. So don't think about it. Go over and hit the nigger hard in the face and get it over with. God, if he wasn't so tired.

Kick him in the face to start, Harold was thinking, as he picked at the dried blood crusted on the bridge of his nose. Two and a half steps and aim it for his cheekbone, either side. That would be the way, if he didn't have on the irons and eighteen inches of chain links. He try kicking the man, he'd land flat on his back and the man would be on top of him. He try sneaking up, the man would hear the chain. 'Less the man was asleep and he worked over and got the chain around the man's neck and crossed his legs and stretched and kicked hard. Then they come in and say what happen? And he say I don't know, captain, the man must have choked on his bread. They say yeah, bread can kill a man all right; you stay in here with the bread the rest of your life. So the best thing would be to stand up and let the man stand up and hit him straightaway and beat him enough but not too much. Beat him just right.

He said, "Hey, boy, you ready?"

"Any time," Raymond answered.

"Get up then."

Raymond moved stiffly, bringing up his knees to rise.

"What's the matter with you?"

"I'll tell you something," Raymond said. "If you're any good, maybe you won't get beat too bad. But after I sleep and rest my arms and legs I'll break your jaw."

"What's the matter with your arms and legs?"

"From swimming the river."

Harold Jackson stared at him, interested. He hadn't thought of why the man had been put in here. Now he remembered the whistle. "You saying you tried to bust out?"

"I got across."

"How many of you?"

Raymond hesitated. "I went alone."

"And they over there waiting."

"Nobody was waiting. They come in a boat."

"Broad daylight—man, you must be one dumb Indin fella."

Raymond's legs cramped as he started to rise, and he had to ease down again, slowly.

"We got time," Harold Jackson said. "Don't be in a hurry to get yourself injured."

"Tomorrow," Raymond said, "when the sun's over the hole and I can see your black nigger face in here."

Harold saw the chain around the man's neck and his legs straining to pull it tight. "Indin, you're going to need plenty medicine before I'm through with you."

"The only thing I'm worried about is catching you," Raymond said. "I hear a nigger would rather run than fight."

"Any running I do, red brother, is going to be right at your head."

"I got to see that."

"Keep your eyes open, Indin. You won't see nothing once I get to you."

There was a silence before Raymond said, "I'll tell you something. It don't matter, but I want you to know it anyway. I'm no Indian. I'm Mexican born in the United States, in the territory of Arizona."

"Yeah," Harold Jackson said. "Well, I'm Filipina born in Fort Valley, Georgia."

"Field nigger is what you are."

"Digger Indin talking, eats rats and weed roots."

"I got to listen to a goddamn field hand."

"I've worked some fields," Harold said. "I've plowed and picked cotton, I've skinned mules and dug privies and I've busted rock. But I ain't never followed behind another convict and emptied his bucket for him. White or black. *Nobody.*"

Raymond's tone was lower. "You saw me carrying a bucket this morning?"

"Man, I don't have to see you, I know you carry one every morning. Frank Shelby says dive into it, you dive."

"Who says I work for Frank Shelby?"

"He say scratch my ass, you scratch it. He say go pour your coffee on that nigger's head, you jump up and do it. Man, if I'm a field nigger you ain't no better than a house nigger." Harold Jackson laughed out loud. "Red nigger, that's all you are, boy. A different color but the same thing."

The pain in Raymond's thighs couldn't hold him this time. He lunged for the dark figure across the cell to drive into him and slam his black skull against the wall. But he went in high. Harold got under him and dumped him and rolled to his feet. They met in the middle of the cell, in the dim shaft of light from the air hole, and beat each other with fists until they grappled and kneed and strained against each other and finally went down.

When the guard came in with their bread and water, they were fighting on the hard-packed floor. He yelled to another guard who came fast with a wheelbarrow, pushing it through the door and the short passageway into the cell. They shoveled sand at Harold and Raymond, throwing it stinging hard

into their faces until they broke apart and lay gasping on the floor. A little while later another guard
came in with irons and chained them to ring bolts
on opposite sides of the cell. The door slammed
closed and again they were in darkness.

Bob Fisher came through the main gate at eight-
fifteen that evening, not letting on he was in a
hurry as he crossed the lighted area toward the
convicts' mess hall.

He'd wanted to get back by eight—about the
time they'd be bringing the two women out of their
cellblock and over to the cook shack. But his wife
had started in again about staying here and not
wanting to move to Florence. She said after sixteen
years in this house it was their *home*. She said a
rolling stone gathered no moss, and that it wasn't
good to be moving all the time. He reminded her
they had moved twice in twenty-seven years, counting the move from Missouri. She said then it was
about time they settled; a family should stay put,
once it planted roots. What family? he asked her.
Me and you? His wife said she didn't know anybody in Florence and wasn't sure she wanted to. She
didn't even know if there was a Baptist church in
Florence. What if there wasn't? What was she supposed to do then? Bob Fisher said that maybe she
would keep her fat ass home for a change and do
some cooking and baking, instead of sitting with
them other fatties all day making patchwork quilts
and bad-mouthing everybody in town who wasn't a
paid-up member of the church. He didn't honestly
care where she spent her time, or whether she baked
pies and cakes or not. It was something to throw

at her when she started in nagging about staying
in Yuma. She said how could anybody cook for a
person who came home at all hours with whiskey
stinking up his breath? Yes, he had stopped and had
a drink at the railroad hotel, because he'd had to
talk to the express agent about moving equipment
to Florence. Florence, his wife said. She wished she
had never heard the name—the same name as her
cousin who was still living in Sedalia, but now she
didn't even like to think of her cousin any more and
they had grown up together as little girls. Bob Fisher
couldn't picture his wife as a little girl. No, that tub
of fat couldn't have ever been a little girl. He didn't
tell her that. He told her he had to get back to the
prison, and left without finishing his coffee.

Fisher walked past the outside stairway and
turned the corner of the mess hall. There were lights
across the way in the main cellblock. He moved out
into the yard enough to look up at the second floor
of the mess hall and saw a light on in the superintendent's office. The little Sunday school teacher
was still there, or had come back after supper. Before going home Fisher had brought in his written
report of the escape and the file on Raymond San
Carlos. The Sunday school teacher had been putting his books away, taking them out of a suitcase
and lining them up evenly on the shelf. He'd said
just lay the report on the desk and turned back to
his books. What would he be doing now? Probably
reading his Bible.

Past the latrine adobe Fisher walked over to the
mess hall and tried the door. Locked for the night.
Now he moved down the length of the building,
keeping close to the shadowed wall though moving

at a leisurely pace—just out for a stroll, checking around, if anybody was curious. At the end of the building he stopped and looked both ways before crossing over into the narrow darkness between the cook-shack adobe and the tailor shop.

Now all he had to do was find the right brick to get a free show. About chin-high it was, on the right side of the cook-shack chimney that stuck out from the wall about a foot and would partly hide him as he pressed in close. Fisher worked a finger in on both sides of the brick that had been chipped loose some months before, and pulled it out as slowly as he could. He didn't look inside right away; no, he always put the brick on the ground first and set himself, his feet wide apart and his shoulders hunched a little so the opening would be exactly at eye level. They would be just past the black iron range, this side of the work table where they always placed the washtub, with the bare electric light on right above them.

Fisher looked in. Goddamn Almighty, just in time.

Just as Norma Davis was taking off her striped shirt, already unbuttoned, slipping it off her shoulders to let loose those round white ninnies that were like nothing he had ever seen before. Beauties, and she knew it, too, the way she stuck them out, standing with her hands on her hips and her belly a round little mound curving down into her skirt. What was she waiting for? Come on, Fisher said, take the skirt off and get in the tub. He didn't like it when they only washed from the waist up. With all the rock dust in the air and bugs from the mat-

tresses and sweating under those heavy skirts, a
lick-and-a-promise, armpits-and-neck wash wasn't
any good. They had to wash theirselves all over to
be clean and healthy.

Maybe he could write it into the regulations:
Women convicts must take a full bath every other
day. Or maybe every day.

The Mexican girl, Tacha Reyes, appeared from
the left, coming from the end of the stove with a
big pan of steaming water, and poured it into the
washtub. Tacha was still dressed. Fisher could tell
by her hair she hadn't bathed yet. She had to wait
on Norma first, looking at Norma now as she felt
the water. Tacha had a nice face; she was just a
little skinny. Maybe give her more to eat—

Norma was taking off her skirt. Yes, *sir,* and that
was all she had. No underwear on. Bare-ass naked
with black stockings that come up over her knees.
Norma turned, leaning against the work table to
pull the stockings off, and Bob Fisher was looking
at the whole show. He watched her lay her stockings on the table. He watched her pull her hair back
with both hands and look down at her ninnies as
she twisted the hair around so it would stay. He
watched her step over to the tub, scratching under
one of her arms, and say, "If it's too hot I'll put
you in it."

"It should be all right," Tacha said.

Another voice, not in the room but out behind
him, a voice he knew, said, "Guard, what's the
matter? Are you sick?"

Twisting around, Bob Fisher hit the peak of his
hat on the chimney edge and was straightening it,

his back to the wall, as Mr. Manly came into the space between the buildings.

"It's me," Fisher said.

"Oh, I didn't know who it was."

"Making the rounds. I generally check all the buildings before I go to bed."

Mr. Manly nodded. "I thought somebody was sick, the way you were leaning against the wall."

"No, I feel fine. Hardly ever been sick."

"It was the way you were standing, like you were throwing up."

"No, I was just taking a look in here. Dark places you got to check good." He couldn't see Mr. Manly's eyes, but he knew the little son of a bitch was looking right at him, staring at him, or past him, where part of the brick opening might be showing and he could see light coming through. "You ready to go," Fisher said, "I'll walk you over to the gate."

He came out from the wall to close in on Mr. Manly and block his view; but he was too late.

"What's that hole?" Mr. Manly said.

"A hole?"

"Behind you, I can see something—"

Bob Fisher turned to look at the opening, then at Mr. Manly again. "Keep your voice down."

"Why? What is it?"

"I wasn't going to say anything. I mean it's something I generally check on myself. But," Fisher said, "if you want to take a look, help yourself."

Mr. Manly frowned. He felt funny now standing here in the darkness. He said in a hushed tone, "Who's in there?"

"Go ahead, take a look."

Through the slit of the opening something moved,

somebody in the room. Mr. Manly stepped close to the wall and peered in.

The light glinted momentarily on his glasses as his head came around, his eyes wide open.

"She doesn't have any clothes on!"

"Shhhh." Fisher pressed a finger to his heavy mustache. "Look and see what they're doing."

"She's bare-naked, washing herself."

"We want to be sure that's all," Fisher said.

"What?"

"Go on, see what she's doing."

Mr. Manly leaned against the wall, showing he was calm and not in any hurry. He peered in again, as though looking around a corner. Gradually his head turned until his full face was pressed against the opening.

What Norma was doing, she was sliding a bar of yellow soap over her belly and down her thighs, moving her legs apart, and coming back up with the soap almost to her breasts before she slid it down again in a slow circular motion. Mr. Manly couldn't take his eyes off her. He watched the Mexican girl bring a kettle and pour water over Norma's shoulders, and watched the suds run down between her breasts, Lord Jesus, through the valley and over the fertile plain and to the dark forest. He could feel his heart beating and feel Bob Fisher close behind him. He had to quit looking now; Lord, it was long enough. It was too long. He wanted to clear his throat. She was turning around and he got a glimpse of her behind as he pulled his face from the opening and stepped away.

"Washing herself," Mr. Manly said. "That's all I could see she was doing."

Bob Fisher nodded. "I hoped that was all." He stooped to pick up the brick and paused with it at the opening. "You want to look at Tacha?"

"I think I've seen enough to know what they're doing," Mr. Manly answered. He walked out to the open yard and waited there for Fisher to replace the brick and follow him out.

"What I want to know is what you're doing spying on them."

"Spying? I was checking, like I told you, to see they're not doing anything wrong."

"What do you mean, wrong?"

"Anything that ain't natural, then. You know what I mean. Two women together without any clothes on—I want to know there ain't any funny business going on."

"She was washing herself."

"Yes, sir," Fisher said, "that's all I saw too. The thing is, you never know when they might start."

Mr. Manly could still see her, the bar of yellow soap moving over her body. "I've never heard of anything like that. They're both *women*."

"I'll agree with you there," Fisher said, "but in a prison you never know. We got men with no women, and women with no men, and I'll tell you we got to keep our eyes open if we don't want any funny business."

"I've heard tell of men," Mr. Manly said—the sudsy water running down between her breasts—"but *women*. What do you suppose they do?"

"I hope I never find out," Fisher said. He meant it, too.

He got Mr. Manly out of there before the women came out and saw them standing in the yard; he walked Mr. Manly over to the main gate and asked him if he had read the report on the escape attempt.

Mr. Manly said yes, and that he thought it showed the guards to be very alert. He wondered, though, wasn't this Raymond San Carlos the same one the Negro has assaulted in the mess hall? The very same, Fisher said. Then wasn't it dangerous to put them both in the same cell? Dangerous to who? Fisher asked. To *them*, they were liable to start fighting again and try and kill each other. They already tried, Fisher said. They were chained to the floor now out of each other's reach. Mr. Manly asked how long they would leave them like that, and Fisher said until they made up their minds to be good and kind to each other. Mr. Manly said that could be never if there was a grudge between them. Fisher said it didn't matter to him, it was up to the two boys.

Fisher waited in the lighted area as Mr. Manly passed through the double gates of the sally port and walked off toward the superintendent's cottage. He was pretty sure Mr. Manly had believed his story, that he was checking on the women to see they didn't do queer things. He'd also bet a dollar the little Sunday school teacher wouldn't make him chink the hole up either.

That was dumb, taking all his books over to the office. Mr. Manly sat in the living room of the superintendent's cottage, in his robe and slippers, and didn't have a thing to read. His Bible was on the night table in the bedroom. Yes, and he'd made a note to look up what St. Paul said about being in prison, something about all he'd gone through and

how one had to have perseverance. He saw Norma
Davis rubbing the bar of soap over her body, sliding
it up and down. No—what he wished he'd brought
were the file records of the two boys in the snake
den. He would have to talk to them when they got
out. Say to them, look, boys, fighting never solved
anything. Now forget your differences and shake
hands.

They were different all right, a Negro and an
Indian. But they were alike too.

Both here for murder. Both born the same year.
Both had served time. Both had sketchy back-
grounds and no living relatives anybody knew of.
The deserter and the deserted.

A man raised on a share-crop farm in Georgia;
joined the army and, four months later, was listed
as a deserter. Court-martialed, sentenced to hard
labor.

A man raised on the San Carlos Indian reservation; deserted by his Apache renegade father before he was born. Father believed killed in Mexico;
mother's whereabouts unknown.

Both of them in the snake den now, a little room
carved out of stone, with no light and hardly any
air. Waiting to get at each other.

Maybe the sooner he talked to them the better.
Bring them both out in ten days—no matter what
Bob Fisher thought about it. Ten days was long
enough. They needed spiritual guidance as much
as they needed corporal punishment. He'd tell
Fisher in the morning.

As soon as Mr. Manly got into bed he started
thinking of Norma Davis again, seeing her clearly
with the bare light right over her and her body

gleaming with soap and water. He saw her in the room then, her body still slippery-looking in the moonlight that was coming through the window. Before she could reach the bed, Mr. Manly switched on the night-table lamp, grabbed hold of his Bible and leafed as fast as he could to St. Paul's letters to the Corinthians.

For nine days neither of them spoke. They sat facing each other, their leg-irons chained to ring bolts that were cemented in the floor. Harold would stand and stretch and lean against the wall and Raymond would watch him. Later on Raymond would get up for a while and Harold would watch. They never stood up at the same time or looked at each other directly. There was silence except for the sound of the chains when they moved. Each pretended to be alone in the darkness of the cell, though each was intently aware of the other's presence. Every day about noon a guard brought them hardtack and water. The guard was not allowed to speak to them, and neither of them spoke to him. It was funny their not talking, he told the other guards. It was spooky. He had never known a man in the snake den not to talk a storm when he was brought his bread and water. But these two sat there as if they had been hypnotized.

The morning of the tenth day Raymond said, "They going to let you out today." The sound of his voice was strange, like someone else's voice. He wanted to clear his throat, but wouldn't let himself do it with the other man watching him. He said, "Don't go anywhere, because when I get out of here I'm going to come looking for you."

"I be waiting," was all Harold Jackson said.

At midday the sun appeared in the air shaft and gradually faded. Nobody brought their bread and water. They had been hungry for the first few days but were not hungry now. They waited and it was early evening when the guard came in with a hammer and pounded the ring bolts open, both of them, Raymond watching him curiously but not saying anything. Another guard came in with shovels and a bucket of sand and told them to clean up their mess.

Bob Fisher was waiting outside. He watched them come out blinking and squinting in the daylight, both of them filthy stinking dirty, the Negro with a growth of beard and the Indian's bony face hollowed and sick-looking. He watched their gaze creep over the yard toward the main cellblock where the convicts were standing around and sitting by the wall, most of them looking this way.

"You can be good children," Fisher said, "or you can go back in there, I don't care which. I catch you fighting, twenty days. I catch you looking mean, twenty days." He looked directly at Raymond. "I catch you swimming again, thirty days and leg-irons a year. You understand me?"

For supper they had fried mush and syrup, all they wanted. After, they were marched over to the main cellblock. Raymond looked for Frank Shelby in the groups standing around outside, but didn't see him. He saw Junior and nodded. Junior gave him a deadpan look. The guard, R.E. Baylis, told them to get their blankets and any gear they wanted to bring along.

"You putting us in another cell?" Raymond

asked him. "How about make it different cells? Ten days, I'll smell him the rest of my life."

"Come on," Baylis said. He marched them down the passageway and through the rear gate of the cellblock.

"Wait a minute," Raymond said. "Where we going?"

The guard looked around at him. "Didn't nobody tell you? You two boys are going to live in the TB yard."

5

A work detail was making adobe bricks over by the south wall, inside the yard. They mixed mud and water and straw, stirred it into a heavy wet paste and poured it into wooden forms. There were bricks drying all along the base of the wall and scrap lumber from the forms and stacks of finished bricks, ready to be used here or sold in town.

Harold Jackson and Raymond San Carlos had to come across the yard with their wheelbarrows to pick up bricks and haul them back to the TB cellblock that was like a prison within a prison: a walled-off area with its own exercise yard. There were eight cells here, in a row facing the yard, half of them empty. The four tubercular convicts stayed in their cells most of the time or sat in the shade and watched Harold and Raymond work, giving them advice and telling them when a line of bricks wasn't straight. They were working on the face wall of the empty cells, tearing out the weathered, crumbling adobe and putting in new bricks; repairing cells that would probably never again be occupied. This was their main job. They worked at it side by side without saying a word to each other.

They also had to bring the tubercular convicts their meals, and sometimes get cough medicine from the sick ward. A guard gave them white cotton doctor masks they could put on over their nose and mouth for whenever they went into the TB cells; but the masks were hot and hard to breathe through, so they didn't wear them after the first day. They used the masks, and a few rags they found, to pad the leg-irons where the metal dug into their ankles.

The third day out of the snake den Raymond began talking to the convicts on the brick detail. He recognized Joe Dean in the group, but didn't speak to him directly. He said, man alive, it was good to breathe fresh air again and feel the sun. He took off his hat and looked up at the sky. All the convicts except Joe Dean went on working. Raymond said, even being over with the lungers was better than the snake den. He said somebody must have made a mistake, he was supposed to be in thirty days for trying to escape, but they let him out after ten. Raymond smiled; he said he wasn't going to mention it to them, though.

Joe Dean was watching him, leaning on his shovel. "You take care of him yet?"

"Take care of who?" Raymond asked him.

"The nigger boy. I hear he stomped you."

"Nobody stomped me. Where'd you hear that?"

"Had to chain him up."

"They chained us both."

"Looks like you're partners now," Joe Dean said.

"I'm not partners with him. They make us work together, that's all."

"You going to fight him?"

"Sure, when I get a chance."

"He don't look too anxious," another convict said. "That nigger's a big old boy."

"I got to wait for the right time," Raymond said. "That's all."

He came back later for another wheelbarrow load of bricks and stood watching them as they worked the mud and mixed in straw. Finally he asked if anybody had seen Frank around.

"Frank who you talking about?" Joe Dean asked.

"Frank Shelby."

"Listen to him," Joe Dean said. "He wants to know has anybody seen Frank."

"I got to talk to him," Raymond said. "See if he can get me out of there."

"Scared of TB, huh?"

"I mean being with the black boy. I got enough of him."

"I thought you wanted to fight him."

"I don't know," Joe Dean said. "It sounds to me like you're scared to start it."

"I don't want no more of the snake den. That's the only thing stopping me."

"You want to see Frank Shelby," one of the other convicts said, "there he is." The man nodded and Raymond looked around.

Shelby must have just come out of the mess hall. He stood by the end-gate of a freight wagon that Junior and Soonzy and a couple of other convicts were unloading. There was no guard with them, unless he was inside. Raymond looked up at the guard on the south wall.

"I'll tell you something," Joe Dean said. "You can forget about Frank helping you."

Raymond was watching the guard. "You know, uh? You know him so good he's got you working in this adobe slop."

"Sometimes we take bricks to town," Joe Dean said. "You think on it if you don't understand what I mean."

"I got other things to think on."

As the guard on the south wall turned and started for the tower at the far end of the yard, Raymond picked up his wheelbarrow and headed for the mess hall.

Shelby didn't look up right away. He was studying a bill of lading attached to a clipboard, checking things off. He said to Junior, "The case right by your foot, that should be one of ours."

"Says twenty-four jars of Louisiana cane syrup."

"It's corn whiskey." Shelby still didn't look up, but he said then, "What do you want?"

"They let me out of the snake den," Raymond said. "I was suppose to be in thirty days, they let me out."

Shelby looked at him now. "Yeah?"

"I wondered if you fixed it."

"Not me."

"I thought sure." He waited as Shelby looked in the wagon and at the clipboard again. "Say, what happened at the river? I thought you were going to come right behind me."

"It didn't work out that way."

"Man, I thought I had made it. But I couldn't find no boat over there."

"I guess you didn't look in the right place," Shelby said.

"I looked where you told me. Man, it was work.

I don't like swimming so much." He watched
Shelby studying the clipboard. "I was wondering—
you know I'm over in a TB cell now."

Shelby didn't say anything.

"I was wondering if you could fix it, get me out
of there."

"Why?"

"I got to be with that nigger all the time."

"He's got to be with you," Shelby said, "so
you're even."

Raymond grinned. "I never thought of it that
way." He waited again. "What do you think?"

"About what?"

"About getting me back with everybody."

Shelby started fooling with his mustache,
smoothing it with his fingers. "Why do you think
anybody wants you back?"

Raymond didn't grin this time. "I did what you
told me," he said seriously. "Listen, I'll work for
you any time you want."

"I'm not hiring today."

"Well, what about getting me out of the TB
yard?"

Shelby looked at him. He said, "Boy, why would
I do that? I'm the one had you put there. Now you
say one more word Soonzy is going to come down
off the wagon and break both your arms."

Shelby watched Raymond pick up his wheelbarrow and walk away. "Goddamn Indin is no better
than a nigger," he said to Junior. "You treat them
nice one time and you got them hanging around
the rest of your life."

When Raymond got back to the brick detail Joe
Dean said, "Well, what did he say?"

"He's going to see what he can do," Raymond answered. He didn't feel like talking any more, and was busy loading bricks when Harold Jackson came across the yard with his wheelbarrow. Harold wore his hat pointed low over his eyes. He didn't have a shirt on and, holding the wheelbarrow handles, his shoulders and arm muscles were bunched and hard-looking. One of the convicts saw him first and said to Raymond, "Here comes your buddy." The other convicts working the adobe mud looked up and stood leaning on their shovels and hoes as Harold Jackson approached.

Raymond didn't look at him. He stacked another brick in the wheelbarrow and got set to pick up the handles. He heard one of the convicts say, "This here Indian says you won't fight him. Says you're scared. Is that right?"

"I fight him any time he wants."

Raymond had to look up then. Harold was staring at him.

"Well, I don't know," the convict said. "You and him talk about fighting, but nobody's raised a hand yet."

"It must be they're both scared," Joe Dean said. "Or it's because they're buddies. All alone in that snake den they got to liking each other. Guard comes in thinks they're rassling on the floor—man, they're not fighting, they're buggering each other."

The other convicts grinned and laughed, and one of them said, "Jesus Christ, what they are, they're sweethearts."

Raymond saw Harold Jackson take one step and hit the man in the face as hard as he could. Raymond wanted to say no, don't do it. It was a strange thing and happened quickly as the man spun toward him and Raymond put up his hands. One moment he was going to catch the man, keep him from falling against him. The next moment he balled up a fist and drove it into the man's face, right out in the open yard, the dumbest thing he had ever done, but doing it now and not stopping or thinking, going for Joe Dean now and busting him hard in the mouth as he tried to bring up his shovel. God, it felt good, a wild hot feeling, letting go and stepping into them and swinging hard at all the faces he had been wanting to smash and pound against a wall.

Harold Jackson held back a moment, staring at the crazy Indian, until somebody was coming at him with a shovel and he had to grab the handle and twist and chop it across the man's head. If he could get room and swing the shovel—but there were too many of them too close, seven men in the brick detail and a couple more, Junior and Soonzy, who came running over from the supply detail and grabbed hunks of lumber and started clubbing at the two wild men.

By the time the guard on the south wall fired his Winchester in the air and a guard came running over from the mess hall, Harold lay stunned in the adobe muck; Raymond was sprawled next to him and neither of them moved.

"Lord," Junior said, "we had to take sticks this time to get them apart."

Soonzy shook his head. "I busted mine on that nigger, he went right on fighting."

"They're a scrappy pair," Junior said, "but they sure are dumb, ain't they?"

Bob Fisher told the guard to hose them off and throw them in the snake den. He told Soonzy and Junior and the men on the brick detail to get back to work. Chained? the guard wanted to know. Chained, Fisher said, and walked off toward the stairs at the end of the mess hall, noticing the convicts who had come out of the adobe huts and equipment sheds, brought out by the guard's rifle fire, all of them looking toward the two men lying in the mud. He noticed Frank Shelby and some convicts by the freight wagon. He noticed the cooks in their white aprons, and the two women, Norma and Tacha, over by the tailor shop.

Fisher went up the stairs and down the hall to the superintendent's office. As he walked in, Mr. Manly turned from the window.

"The same two," Fisher said.

"It looked like they were all fighting." Mr. Manly glanced at the window again.

"You want a written report?"

"I'd like to know what happened."

"Those two start fighting. The other boys try to pull them apart and the two start swinging at everybody. Got to hit 'em with shovels to put 'em down."

"I didn't see them fighting each other."

"Then you must have missed that part." Past Mr. Manly's thoughtful expression—through the window and down in the yard—he saw a convict walking toward the tailor shop with a bundle under his arm. Frank Shelby. This far away he knew it was Shelby. Norma Davis stood in the door waiting for him.

"Soon as I heard the shots," Mr. Manly said, "I

looked out. They were separated, like two groups fighting. They didn't look close enough to have been fighting each other."

Bob Fisher waited. "You want a written report?"

"What're you going to do to them?"

"I told them before, they start fighting they go back in the snake den. Twenty days. They know it, so it won't be any surprise."

"Twenty days in there seems like a long time."

"I hope to tell you it is," Fisher said.

"I was going to talk to them when they got out the other day. I meant to—I don't know, I put it off and then I guess some other things came up."

Fisher could see Shelby at the tailor shop now, close to the woman, talking to her. She turned and they both went inside.

"I'm not saying I could have prevented their fighting, but you never know, do you? Maybe if I *had* spoken to them, got them to shake hands— you understand what I mean, Bob?"

Fisher pulled his gaze away from the tailor shop to the little man by the window. "Well, I don't know about that."

"It could have made a difference."

"I never seen talking work much on anybody."

"But twenty days in there," Mr. Manly said, "and it could be my fault, because I didn't talk to them." He paused. "Don't you think, Bob, in this case, you ought to give them no more than ten days? You said yourself ten days was a long time. Then soon as they come out I'll talk to them."

"That Indian was supposed to be in thirty days," Fisher said, "and you changed it to ten. Now I've already told them twenty and you want to cut it down again. I tell a convict one thing and you say something else and we begin to have problems."

"I'm only asking," Mr. Manly said, "because if I could have done something, if I'm the one to blame, then it wouldn't be fair to those two boys."

"Mister, they're convicts. They do what we tell them. Anything."

Mr. Manly agreed, nodding. "That's true, we give the orders and they have to obey. But we still have to be fair, no matter who we're dealing with."

Bob Fisher wondered what the hell he was doing here arguing with this little four-eyed squirt. He said, "They don't know anything about this. They don't know you meant to talk to them."

"But I know it," Mr. Manly said, "and the more I think about it the more I know I got to talk to them." He paused. "Soon."

Fisher saw it coming, happening right before his eyes, the little squirt's mind working behind his gold-frame glasses.

"Yes, maybe you ought to bring them in tomorrow."

"Just a minute ago you said ten days—"

"Do you have any children, Bob?"

The question stopped Fisher. He shook his head slowly, watching Mr. Manly.

"Well, I'm sure you know anyway you got to have patience with children. Sure, you got to punish them sometimes, but first you got to teach them right from wrong and be certain they understand it."

"I guess my wife's got something wrong with her. She never had any kids."

"That's God's will, Bob. What I'm getting at,

these two boys here, Harold and Raymond, they're just like children." Mr. Manly held up his hand. "I know what you're going to say, these boys wasn't caught stealing candy, they took a life. And I say that's true. But still they're like little children. They're grown in body but not in mind. They got the appetites and temptations of grown men. They fight and carry on and, Lord knows, they have committed murder, for which they are now paying the price. But we don't want no more murders around here, do we, Bob? No, sir. Nor do we want to punish anybody for something that isn't their fault. We got two murderers wanting to kill each other. Two mean-looking boys we chain up in a dungeon. But Bob, tell me something. Has anybody ever spoke kindly to them? I mean has anybody ever helped them overcome the hold the devil's got on them? Has anybody ever showed them the path of righteousness, or explained to them Almighty God's justice and the meaning of everlasting salvation?"

Jesus Christ, Bob Fisher said—not to Mr. Manly, to himself. He had to get out of here; he didn't need any sermons today. He nodded thoughtfully and said to Mr. Manly, "I'll bring them in here whenever you want."

When Junior and Soonzy came back from clubbing the Indian and the colored boy, Frank Shelby told them to get finished with the unloading. He told them to leave a bottle of whiskey in the wagon for the freight driver and take the rest of it to his cell. Soonzy said Jesus, that nigger had a hard head, and showed everybody around how the hunk of wood was splintered. Junior said my, but they were dumb to start a fight out in the yard. This old boy over there called them sweethearts and that had started them swinging. If they wanted to fight, they should have it out in a cell some night. A convict standing there said, boy, he'd like to see that. It would be a good fight.

Shelby was looking at Norma Davis outside the tailor shop. He knew she was waiting for him, but what the convict said caught in his mind and he looked at the man.

"Which one would you bet on?"

"I think I'd have to pick the nigger," the convict said. "The way he's built."

Shelby looked around at Soonzy. "Who'd you pick?"

"I don't think neither of them look like much."

"I said who'd you pick."

"I don't know. I guess the nigger."

"How about in the mess hall," Shelby said. "The Indin showed he's got nerve. Pretty quick, too, the way he laid that plate across the boy's eyes."

"He's quick," Junior said.

"Quick and stronger than he looks," Shelby said. "You saw him swimming against the river current."

"Well, he's big for an Indin," Junior said. "Big and quick and, as Frank says, he's got some nerve. Another thing, you don't see no marks on him from their fighting in the snake den. He might be more'n the nigger can handle."

"I'd say you could bet either way on that fight," Shelby said. He told Junior to hand him the bundle for the tailor shop—a bolt of prison cloth wrapped in brown paper—and walked off with it.

Most of them, Shelby was thinking, would bet on the nigger. Get enough cons to bet on the Indin and it could be a pretty good pot. If he organized the betting, handled the whole thing, he could take about ten percent for the house. Offer some long-shot side bets and cover those himself. First, though, he'd have to present the idea to Bob Fisher. A prize fight. Fisher would ask what for and he'd say two reasons. Entertain the cons and settle the problem of the two boys fighting. Decide a winner and the matter would be ended. Once he worked out the side bets and the odds.

"Bringing me a present?" Norma asked him.

Shelby reached the shade of the building and looked up at her in the doorway. "I got a present for you, but it ain't in this bundle."

"I bet I know what it is."

"I bet you ought to. Who's inside?"

"Just Tacha and the old man."

"Well, you better invite me in," Shelby said, "before I start stripping you right here."

"Little anxious today?"

"I believe it's been over a week."

"Almost two weeks," Norma said. "Is there somebody else?"

"Two times I was on my way here," Shelby said, "Fisher stopped me and sent me on a work detail."

"I thought you got along with him."

"It's the first time he's pulled anything like that."

"You think he knows about us?"

"I imagine he does."

"He watches me and Tacha take a bath."

"He comes in?"

"No, there's a loose brick in the wall he pulls

out. One time, after I was through, I peeked out the door and saw him sneaking off."

Shelby grinned. "Dirty old bastard."

"Maybe he doesn't feel so old."

"I bet he'd like to have some at that." Shelby nodded slowly. "I just bet he would."

Norma was watching him. "Now what are you thinking?"

"But he wouldn't want anybody to know about it. That's why he don't come in when you're taking a bath. Tacha's there."

Norma smiled. "I can see your evil mind working. If Tacha wasn't there—"

"Yes, sir, then he'd come in."

"Ask if I wanted him to soap my back."

"Front and back. I can see him," Shelby said. "One thing leads to another. After the first time, he don't soap you. No, sir, he gets right to it."

"Then one night you come in"—Norma giggled—"and catch the head guard molesting a woman convict."

Shelby shook his head, grinning.

"He's trying to pull his pants on in a hurry and you say, 'Good evening, Mr. Fisher. How are tricks?'"

"God *damn*," Shelby said. "that's good."

"He's trying to button his pants and stick his shirt in and thinking as hard as he can for something to say." Norma kept giggling and trying not to. "He says, uh—"

"What does he say?"

"He says, 'I just come in for some coffee. Can I get you a cup, Mr. Shelby?' And you say, 'No, thank you. I was just on my way to see the superintendent.' He says, 'About what, Mr. Shelby?' And you say, 'About how some of the guards have been messing with the women convicts.'"

"It's an idea," Shelby said, "but I don't know of anything he can do for me except open the gate and he ain't going to do that, no matter what I get on him. No, I was wondering—if you and him got to be good friends—what he might tell you if you were to ask him."

Norma raised her arm and used the sleeve to wipe the wetness from her eyes. "What might he tell me?"

"Like what day we're supposed to move out of here. If we're going by train. If we're all going at once, or in groups." Shelby spoke quietly and watched her begin to nod her head as she thought about it. "Once we know when we're moving we can begin to make plans. I can talk to my brother Virgil, when he comes to visit, get him working on the outside. But we got to know *when*."

Norma was picturing herself in the cook shack with Fisher. "It would have to be the way I asked him. So he wouldn't suspect anything."

"Honey, you'd know better than I could tell you."

"I suppose once I got him comfortable with me."

"You won't have any trouble at all."

"It'll probably be a few times before he relaxes."

"Get him to think you like him. A man will believe anything when he's got his pants off."

"We might be having a cup of coffee after and I'll make a little face and look around the kitchen and say, 'Gee, honey, I wish there was some place else we could go.'"

"Ask him about the new prison."

"That's what I'm leading to," Norma said. "I'll tell him I hope we'll have a better place than this. Then I'll say, like I just thought of it, 'By the way, honey, when are we going to this new prison?'"

"Ask him if he's ever done it on a train?"

"I'll think of a way. I bet he's a horny old bastard."

"So much the better. He's probably never got it off a good-looking woman before in his life."

"Thank you."

"You're welcome."

"The only thing is what to do about Tacha."

"I'll have to think on that," Shelby said.

"Maybe he'd like both of us."

"Honey, he don't even have dreams like that anymore."

Tacha Reyes looked up from her sewing machine as they came into the shop and Shelby dropped the bundle on the work table. The old man, who had been a tailor here for twenty-six years since murdering his wife, continued working. He sat hunched over with his legs crossed, sewing a button to a striped convict coat.

Norma didn't say anything to them. She followed Shelby into the back room where the supplies and bolts of material were kept. The first few times they went back there together she said they were going to inventory the material or look over the thread supply or count buttons. Now she didn't bother. They went into the room and closed the door.

Tacha sat quietly, not moving. She told herself

she shouldn't listen, but she always did. Sometimes she heard Norma, the faint sound of her laughing in there; she never heard Frank Shelby. He was always quiet.

Like the man who owned the café in St. David. He would come up behind her when she was working in the kitchen and almost before she heard him he would be touching her, putting his hands on her hips and bringing them up under her arms, pretending to be counting her ribs and asking how come she was so skinny, how come, huh, didn't she like the cooking here? And when she twisted away from him—what was the matter, didn't she like working here?

"How can he come in," Tacha said, "do whatever he wants?"

The tailor glanced over at the stock-room door. He didn't look at Tacha. "Norma isn't complaining."

"She's as bad as he is."

"I wouldn't know about that."

"She does whatever he wants. But he's a convict, like any of them."

"I'll agree he's a convict," the tailor said.

"You're afraid to even talk about him."

"I'll agree to that too," the tailor said.

"Some people can do whatever they want. Other people have to let them." Tacha was silent again. What good was talking about it?

The owner of the café in St. David thought he could do whatever he wanted because he paid her seven dollars a week and said she didn't have to stay if she didn't want to. He would kiss her and she would have to close her eyes hard and hold her breath and feel his hand coming up over her breast.

Her sister had said so what, he touches you a little. Where else are you going to make seven dollars a week? But I don't want him to, Tacha had said. I don't love him. And her sister had told her she was crazy. You don't have to love a man even to marry him. This man was providing for her and she should look at it that way. He gave her something, she should give him something.

She gave him the blade of a butcher knife late one afternoon when no one was in the café and the cook had gone to the outhouse. She jabbed the knife into him because he was hurting her, forcing her back over the kitchen table, smothering her with his weight and not giving her a chance to speak, to tell him she wanted to quit. Her fingers touched the knife on the table and, in that little moment of panic, as his hand went under her skirt and up between her legs, she pushed the knife into his stomach. She would remember his funny, surprised expression and remember him pushing away from her again with his weight, and looking down at the knife handle, touching it gently with both hands then, standing still, as if afraid to move, and looking down at the knife. She remembered saying, "I didn't mean to—" and thinking, Take it out, you can do whatever you want to me, I didn't mean to do this.

"Some people lead," the tailor said, "some follow."

Tacha looked over at him, hunched over his sewing. "Why can Frank Shelby do whatever he wants?"

"Not everything, he can't."

"Why can he go in there with her?"

"Ask him when he's through."

"Do you know something?" Tacha said. "You never answer a question."

"I've been here—" the tailor began, and stopped as the outside door opened.

Bob Fisher stepped inside. He closed the door quietly behind him, his gaze going to the stock room, then to Tacha and past her to the tailor.

"Where's Norma at?"

Tacha waited. When she knew the tailor wasn't going to answer she said, "Don't you know where she is?"

Fisher's dull expression returned to Tacha. "I ask a question, I don't need a question back."

"She's in there," Tacha said.

"I thought I saw a convict come in here."

"He's in there with her."

"Doing what?"

"Doing *it*," Tacha said. "What do you think?"

Bob Fisher took time to give her a look before he walked over to the stock room. Then he didn't hesitate: he pushed the door and let it bang wide open and stood looking at them on the flat bolts of striped prison material they had spread on the floor, at the two of them lying close and pulling apart, at their upturned faces that were momentarily startled.

"You through?" Fisher said.

Shelby started to grin and shake his head. "I guess you caught us, boss."

Tacha could see Norma's skirt pulled up and her bare thighs. She saw Shelby, behind Fisher, getting to his feet. He was buttoning the top of his pants now. Norma was sitting up, slowly buttoning her blouse, then touching her hair, brushing it away from her face.

Tacha and the tailor began working again as Fisher looked around at them. He motioned Norma to get up. "You go on to your cell till I'm ready for you."

Shelby waited, while Norma gave Fisher a look and a shrug and walked out. He said then, "Were me and her doing something wrong? Against regulations?"

"You come with me," Fisher said.

Once outside, they moved off across the yard, toward the far end of the mess hall. Fisher held his set expression as his gaze moved about the yard. Shelby couldn't figure him out.

"Where we going?"

"I want to tell the new superintendent what you were doing."

"I didn't know of any law against it."

Fisher kept walking.

"What's going on?" Shelby said. Christ, the man was actually taking him in. Before they got to the latrine adobe Shelby said, "Well, I wanted to talk to him anyway." He paused. "About this guard that watches the girls take their bath. Pulls loose a brick and peeks in at them."

Fisher took six strides before saying, "She know who this guard is?"

"You bet," Shelby said.

"Then tell the sup'rintendent."

Son of a bitch. He was bluffing. Shelby glanced at him, but couldn't tell a thing from the man's expression.

Just past the latrine Shelby said, "I imagine this

guard has got a real eyeful, oh man, but looking ain't near anything like doing, I'll tell you, 'cause I've done both. That Norma has got a natural-born instinct for pleasing a man. You know what she does?"

Fisher didn't answer.

Shelby waited, but not too long. "She knows secret things I bet there ain't ten women in the world can do. I been to Memphis, I been to Tulsa, to Nogales, I know what I'm talking about. You feel her mouth brushing your face and whispering dirty things in your ear—you know something? Once a man's had some of that woman—I mean somebody outside—he'd allow himself to be locked up in this place the rest of his life if he thought he could get some every other night. Get her right after she comes out of the bath."

Shelby paused to let Fisher think about it. As they were nearing the outside stairs he said, "Man, I tell you, anybody seen her bare-ass naked knows that's got to be a woman built for pleasure."

"Upstairs," Fisher said.

Shelby went up two steps and paused, looking around over his shoulder. "The thing is, though. She don't give it out to nobody but me. 'Less I say it's all right." Shelby looked right at his eyes. "You understand me, boss?"

Mr. Manly heard them coming down the hall. He swiveled around from the window and moved the two file folders to one side of the desk, covering the Bible. He picked up a pencil. On his note pad were written the names *Harold Jackson* and *Raymond San Carlos*, both underlined, and the notations: *Ten days will be Feb. 23, 1909. Talk to both at same time. Ref. to St. Paul to the Corinthians 11:19–33 and 12:1–9.*

When the knock came he said, "Come in" at once, but didn't look up until he knew they were in the room, close to the desk, and he had written on the note paper: *See Ephesians 4:1–6.*

Bob Fisher came right out with it. "He wants to tell you something."

In that moment Shelby had no idea what he would say; because Fisher wasn't bluffing and wasn't afraid of him; because Fisher stood up and was a tough son of a bitch and wasn't going to lie and lose face in front of any con. Maybe Fisher would deny the accusation, say prove it. Shelby didn't know what Fisher would do. He needed time to think. The next moment Mr. Manly was smiling up at him.

"I'm sorry I don't know everybody's name yet."

"This is Frank Shelby," Fisher said. "He wants to tell you something."

Shelby watched the little man rise and offer his hand and say, "I'm Everett Manly, your new superintendent." He watched Mr. Manly sit down again and look off somewhere.

"Frank Shelby . . . Shelby . . . forty-five years for armed robbery. Is that right?"

Shelby nodded.

"Forty-five years," Mr. Manly said. "That's a long time. Are you working to get some time off for good behavior?"

"I sure am," Shelby said. He didn't know if the man was serious or not, but he said it.

"How long have you been here at Yuma?"

"Little over a year."

"Have you got a good record here? Keep out of fights and trouble?"

"Yes, *sir*."

"Ever been in the snake den?"

"No, sir."

"Got two boys in there now for fighting, you know."

Shelby smiled a little and shook his head. "It's funny you should mention them," he said. "Those two boys are what I wanted to talk to you about."

Bob Fisher turned to look at him but didn't say a word.

"I was wondering," Shelby went on, "what you'd think of us staging a prize fight between those two boys?"

"A prize fight?" Mr. Manly frowned. "Don't you think they've done enough fighting? Lord, it seems all they like to do is fight."

"They keep fighting," Shelby said, "because they never get it settled. But, I figure, once they have it out there'll be peace between them. You see what I mean?"

Mr. Manly began to nod, slowly. "Maybe."

"We could get them some boxing gloves in town. I don't mean the prison pay for them. We could take us up a collection among the convicts."

"I sure never thought of fighting as a way to achieve peace. Bob, have you?"

Fisher said quietly, "No, I haven't."

Shelby shrugged. "Well, peace always seems to follow a war."

"You got a point there, Frank."

"I know the convicts would enjoy it. I mean it

would keep their minds occupied a while. They don't get much entertainment here."

"That's another good point," Mr. Manly said.

Shelby waited as Mr. Manly nodded, looking as if he was falling asleep. "Well, that's all I had to say. I sure hope you give it some thought, if just for the sake of those two boys. So they can get it settled."

"I promise you I will," Mr. Manly said. "Bob, what do you think about it? Off-hand."

"I been in prison work a long time," Fisher said. "I never heard of anything like this."

"I'll tell you what, boys. Let me think on it." Mr. Manly got up out of the chair, extending a hand to Shelby. "It's nice meeting you, Frank. You keep up the good work and you'll be out of here before you know it."

"Sir," Shelby said, "I surely hope so."

Bob Fisher didn't say a word until they were down the stairs and Shelby was heading off along the side of the building, in the shade.

"Where you going?"

Shelby turned, a few steps away. "See about some chow."

"You can lose your privileges," Fisher said. "All of them inside one minute."

Go easy, Shelby thought, and said, "It's up to you."

"I can give it all to somebody else. The stuff you sell, the booze, the soft jobs. I pick somebody, the tough boys will side with him and once it's done he's the man inside and you're another con on the rock pile."

"I'm not arguing with you," Shelby said. "I used

my head and put together what I got. You allow it because I keep the cons in line and it makes your job easier. You didn't give me a thing when I started."

"Maybe not, but I can sure take it all away from you."

"I know that."

"I will, 'less you stay clear of Norma Davis."

Shelby started to smile—he couldn't help it—even with Fisher's grim, serious face staring at him.

"Watch yourself," Fisher said. "You say the wrong thing, it's done. I'm telling you to keep away from the women. You don't, you lose everything you got."

That was all Bob Fisher had to say. He turned and went back up the stairs. Shelby watched him, feeling better than he'd felt in days. He sure would keep away from the women. He'd give Norma all the room she needed. The state Bob Fisher was in, Norma would have his pants off him before the week was out.

6

"Boys, I tell you the Lord loves us all as His children; but you cross Him and He can be mean as a roaring lion. Not mean because he hates you boys, no-sir; mean because he hates sin and evil so much. You don't believe me, read your Psalms, fifty, twenty-two, where it says, 'Now consider this, ye that forget God, lest I tear you in pieces'—you hear that?—'tear you in *pieces* and there be none to deliver. . . .' None to deliver means there ain't nothing left of you."

Mr. Manly couldn't tell a thing from their expressions. Sometimes they were looking at him, sometimes they weren't. Their heads didn't move much. Their eyes did. Raymond's eyes would go to the window and stay there a while. Harold would stare at the wall or the bookcase, and look as if he was asleep with his eyes open.

Mr. Manly flipped back a few pages in his Bible. When he looked up again his glasses gleamed in the overhead light. He had brought the two boys out of the snake den after only three days this time. Bob Fisher hadn't said a word. He'd marched them over, got them fed and cleaned up, and here they were. Here, but somewhere else in their minds. Standing across the desk fifteen, twenty minutes now, and Mr. Manly wondered if either of them had listened to a word he'd said.

"Again in the Psalms, boys, chapter eleven, sixth verse, it says, 'Upon the wicked shall rain snares, fire and brimstone and a horrible tempest'—that's like a storm—'and this shall be the portion of their cup.'

"Raymond, look at me. 'He that keepeth the commandments keepeth his own soul'—Proverbs, chapter nineteen, verse sixteen—'but he that despiseth His way shall die.'

"Harold Jackson of Fort Valley, Georgia, 'There shall be no reward for the evil man.' That's Proverbs again, twenty-four, twenty. 'The candle of the wicked shall be put out.' Harold, you understand that?"

"Yes-suh, captain."

"What does it mean?"

"It mean they put out your candle."

"It means God will put *you* out. You're the candle, Harold. If you're evil you get no reward and the Lord God will snuff out your life. You want that to happen?"

"No-suh, captain."

"Raymond, you want to have your life snuffed out?"

"No, sir, I don't want no part of that."

"It will happen as sure as it is written in the Book. Harold, you believe in the Book?"

"What book is that, captain?"

"The Holy Bible."

"Yes-suh, I believe it."

"Raymond, you believe it?"

"What is that again?"

"Do you believe in the Holy Bible as being the inspired word of Almighty God as told by Him directly into the ears of the boys that wrote it?"

"I guess so," Raymond said.

"Raymond, you don't guess about your salvation. You believe in Holy Scripture and its truths, or you don't."

"I believe it," Raymond said.

"Have you ever been to church?"

"I think so. When I was little."

"Harold, you ever attend services?"

"You mean was I in the arm service, captain?"

"I mean have you ever been to church."

"Yes, I been there, captain."

"When was the last time?"

"Let's see," Harold said. "I think I went in Cuba one time."

"You *think* you went to church?"

"They talk in this language I don't know what they saying, captain."

"That was ten years ago," Mr. Manly said, "and you don't know if it was a church service or not."

"I think it was."

"Raymond, what about you?"

"Yes, sir, when I was little, all the time."

"What do you remember?"

"About Jesus and all. You know, how they nail him to this cross."

"Do you know the Ten Commandments?"

"I think I know some of them," Raymond said. "Thou shall not steal. Thou shall not commit adultery."

"Thou shalt not kill," Mr. Manly prompted.

"Thou shall not kill. That's one of them."

"The one that sent you here. Both of you. And now you're disobeying that commandment again by fighting. Did you know that? When you fight you break the Lord's commandment against killing?"

"What if you only hit him?" Raymond asked. "Beat him up good, but he don't die."

"It's the same thing. Look, when you hit somebody you hurt him a little bit or you hurt him a lot. When you kill somebody you hurt him for good. So hitting is the same as killing without going all the way. You understand that, Harold?"

"What was that, captain?"

Mr. Manly swiveled around slowly to look out the window, toward the convicts standing by the main cellblock. Close to a hundred men here, and only a handful of them, at the most, understood the Divine Word. Mr. Manly was sixty years old and knew he would never have time to teach them all. He only had a few months here before the place was closed. Then what? He had to do what he could, that's all. He had to begin somewhere, even if his work was never finished.

He came around again to face them and said, "Boys, the Lord has put it on the line to us. He says you got to keep His commandments. He says you don't keep them, you die. That doesn't mean you die and they put in a grave—no-sir. It means you die and go straight down to hell to suffer the fires of the damned. Raymond, you ever burn yourself?"

"Yes, sir, my hand one time."

"Boys, imagine getting burned all over for the

rest of your life by the hottest fire you ever saw, hotter'n a blast furnace."

"You'd die," Raymond said.

"Only it doesn't kill you," Mr. Manly said quickly. "See, it's a special kind of fire that hurts terrible but never burns you up."

They looked at him, or seemed to be looking at him; he wasn't sure.

He tried again. "Like just your head is sticking out of the fire. You understand? So it don't suffocate you. But, boy, these flames are licking at your body and it's so hot you're a-screaming your lungs out, 'Water, water, somebody give me just a drop of water—please!' But it's too late, because far as you're concerned the Lord is fresh out of mercy."

Raymond was looking at the window again and Harold was studying the wall.

"Hell—" Mr. Manly began. He was silent for a while before he said, "It's a terrible place to be and I'm glad you boys are determined not to go there."

Harold said, "Where's that, captain?"

After they were gone Mr. Manly could still see them standing there. He got up and walked around them, picturing them from the back now, seeing the Negro's heavy, sloping shoulders, the Indian standing with a slight cock to his hip, hands loose at his sides. He'd like to stick a pin in them to see if they jumped. He'd like to holler in their ears. What's the matter with you? Don't you understand plain English? Are you too ignorant, or are you too full of evil? Answer me!

If they didn't understand the Holy Word, how was he ever going to preach it to them? He raised his eyes to the high ceiling and said, "Lord, if You're going to send me sinners, send me some with schooling, will you, please?"

He hadn't meant to say it out loud. In the silence that followed he hurried around the desk to sit down again.

Maybe that was the answer, though, and saying it out loud was the sign. Save somebody else, somebody who'd understand him, instead of two boys who couldn't even read and write. Sixty years old, he didn't have time to start saving illiterates. Somebody like Frank Shelby. Save him.

No, Frank was already trying. It was pretty clear he'd seen the error of his past life and was trying to correct it.

Norma Davis.

Get Norma in here and ask her if she was ready to accept the Lord Jesus Christ as her saviour. If she hadn't already.

No, something told Mr. Manly she hadn't yet. She was in for robbery, had shot a man, and had been arrested for prostitution in Wichita, Kansas. It wasn't likely she'd had time to be saved. She looked smart though.

Sit her down there, Mr. Manly thought.

He wasn't sure how he'd begin, but he'd get around to picking some whores out of the Bible to tell her about—like that woman at the well. Jesus knew she was a whore, but He was still friendly and talked to her. See, He wasn't uppity about whores, they were just sinners to him like any other sinners. Take the time they're stoning the whore and He stops them, saying, Wait, only whoever of ye is without sin may cast a stone. And they had to quit doing it. See, Norma, we are all of us sinners in one way or another.

He kept looking at the way her top buttons were undone and the blouse was pulled open so he could see part of the valley between her breasts.

Where the soap had run down and over her belly.

She was sitting there trying to tempt him. Sure, she'd try to tempt him, try to show him up as a hypocrite.

She would undo a couple more buttons and he'd watch her calmly. He would say quietly, shaking his head slowly, "Norma, Norma."

She'd pull that blouse wide open and her eyes and her breasts would be staring right smack at him.

Sit back in the swivel chair then; show her he was at ease. Keep the expression very calm. And kindly.

She'd get up and lean over the desk then so they'd hang down. Great big round things with big reddish-brown tips. Then she'd jiggle them a little and he'd say in his quiet voice, "Norma, what are you doing that for? Don't you feel silly?"

Maybe he wouldn't ask her if she felt silly, but he'd say something.

She'd see she wasn't getting him, so then she'd take off her belt and slowly undo her skirt, watching him all the time, and let it fall. She'd back off a little bit and put her hands on her hips so he could see her good.

"Norma, child, cover your nakedness."

No, sir, that wasn't going to stop her. She was coming around the desk now. She'd stepped out of the skirt and was taking off the blouse, all the way off, coming toward him now without a stitch on.

He had better stand up, or it would be hard to talk to her.

Mr. Manly rose from the chair. He reached out to place his hands on Norma's bare shoulders and, smiling gently, said, "Child, 'If ye live after the flesh ye shall die'—Romans, eight, thirteen—'but if ye mortify the deeds of the body, ye shall live.'"

From the doorway Bob Fisher said, "Excuse me."

Mr. Manly came around, seeing the open door that had been left open when the two went out; he dropped his hands awkwardly to the edge of the desk.

Bob Fisher kept staring at him.

"I was just seeing if I could remember a particular verse from Romans," Mr. Manly said.

"How'd you do with Harold and Raymond?"

"It's too early to tell. I want to see them again in the morning."

"They got work to do."

"In the morning," Mr. Manly said.

Bob Fisher thought it over, then nodded and left the office. Walking down the hall, he was thinking that the little preacher may have been trying to remember a verse, but he sure looked like a man about to get laid.

Lord, give me these two, Mr. Manly said to the window and to the yard below. Give me a sign that they understand and are willing to receive the Lord Jesus Christ into their hearts.

He didn't mean a tongue of fire had to appear over the two boys' heads, or they had to get knocked to the ground the way St. Paul did. All they had to do was show some interest, a willingness to accept their salvation.

Lord, I need these two to prove my worthiness and devotion as a preacher of your Holy Writ. I need them to show for thirty years service in your ministry. Lord, I need them for my record, and I expect You know it.

Sit them down this time. Maybe that would help. Mr. Manly turned from the window and told them to take chairs. "Over there," he said. "Bring them up close to the desk."

They hesitated, looking around. It seemed to take them forever to carry the chairs over, their leg chains clinking on the wooden floor. He waited until they were settled, both of them looking past him, seeing what there was to see at this lower angle than yesterday.

"I'm going to tell you something. I know you both had humble beginnings. You were poor, you've been hungry, you've experienced all kinds of hardships and you've spent time in jail. Well, I never been to jail before I got sent here by the Bureau"—Mr. Manly paused as he grinned; neither of them noticing it—"I'll tell you though, I'll bet you I didn't begin any better off than you boys did. I was born in Clayburn County, Tennessee—either of you been there?"

Raymond shook his head. Harold said nothing.

"Well, it's in the mountains. I didn't visit Knoxville till I was fifteen years old, and it wasn't forty miles from home. I could've stayed there and farmed, or I could have run off and got into trouble. But you know what I did? I joined the Holy Word Pentacostal Youth Crusade and pledged myself to the service of the Lord Jesus. I preached over twenty years in Tennessee and Kentucky before coming out here to devote the rest of my life to mission work—the rest of it, five years, ten years. You know when your time is up and the Lord's going to call you?"

Harold Jackson's eyes were closed.

"Harold"—the eyes came open—"you don't know when you're going to die, do you?"

"No-suh, captain."

"Are you ready to die?"

"No-suh, captain. I don't think I ever be ready."

"St. Paul was ready."

"Yes-suh."

"Not at first he wasn't. Not until the Lord knocked him smack off his horse with a bolt of lightning and said, 'Saul, Saul, why do you persecuteth me?' Paul was a Jew-boy at that time and he was persecuting the Christians. Did you know that, Raymond?"

"No, I never knew that."

"Yes, sir, before he became Paul he was a Jew-boy name of Saul, used to put Christians to death, kill them in terrible ways. But once he become a Christian himself he made up for all the bad things he'd done by his own suffering. Raymond, you ever been stoned?"

"Like with rocks?"

"Hit with big rocks."

"I don't think so."

"Harold, you ever been shipwrecked?"

"I don't recall, captain."

Mr. Manly opened his Bible. "You boys think

you've experienced hardships, listen, I'm going to read you something. From two Corinthians. 'Brethren, gladly you put up with fools, because you are wise . . .' Let me skip down. 'But whereas any man is bold . . . Are they ministers of Christ?' Here it is '. . . in many more labors, in lashes above measure, often exposed to death. From the Jews'— listen to this—'five times I received forty lashes less one. Thrice I was scourged, once I was stoned, thrice I suffered shipwreck, a night and a day I was adrift on the sea; on journeyings often, in perils from floods, in perils from robbers, in perils from my own nation . . . in labor and hardships, in many sleepless nights, in hunger and thirst, in fastings often, in cold and nakedness.'"

Mr. Manly looked up. "Here's the thing, boys. St. Paul asked God three times to let him up from all these hardships. And you know what God said to him?" Mr. Manly's gaze dropped to the book. "He said, 'My grace is sufficient for thee, for strength is made perfect in weakness.'"

Now Mr. Manly sat back, just barely smiling, looking expectantly from Raymond to Harold, waiting for one of them to speak. Either one, he didn't care.

He didn't even care what they said, as long as one of them spoke.

Raymond was looking down at his hands, fooling with one of his fingernails. Harold was looking down too, his head bent low, and his eyes could have been open or closed.

"Strength—did you hear that, boys?—is made perfect in weakness."

He waited.

He could ask them what it meant.

He began thinking about the words. If you're weak the Lord helps you. Or strength stands out more in a weak person. Like it's more perfect, more complete, when a weak person gets strong.

No, that wasn't what it meant.

It meant no matter how weak you were you could get strong if you wanted.

Maybe. Or else it was the part just before which was the important part. God saying My grace is sufficient for thee. That's right, no matter what the temptaion was.

Norma Davis could come in here and show herself and do all kinds of terrible things—God's grace would be sufficient. That was good to know.

It wasn't helping those two boys any, though. He had to watch that, thinking of himself more than them. They were the ones had to be saved. They had wandered from the truth and it was up to him to bring them back. For . . . "whoever brings back a sinner from the error of his ways will save his own soul from death"—James, five-something—"and it will cover a multitude of sins."

That was the whole thing. If he could save these two boys he'd have nothing to worry about the rest of his life. He could maybe even slip once in a while—give in to temptation—without fear of his soul getting sent to hell. He wouldn't give in on purpose. You couldn't do that. But if somebody dragged you in and you went in scrapping, that was different.

"Boys," Mr. Manly said, "whoever brings back a sinner saves his own soul from death and it will cover a multitude of sins. Now do you want your souls to be saved, or don't you?"

Mr. Manly spent two days reading and studying before he called Raymond and Harold into the office again.

While they were standing by the desk he asked them how they were getting along. Neither of them wanted to answer that. He asked if there had been any trouble between them since the last time they were here. They both said no, sir. He asked if there had been any mean words between them. They said no, sir. Then it looked like they were getting somewhere, Mr. Manly said, and told them to bring the chairs over and sit down.

"'We know,'" he said to Raymond, "'that we have passed from death unto life because we love the brethren. He that loveth not his brethren abideth in death.'" Mr. Manly looked at Harold Jackson. "'Whoever hateth his brother is a murderer, and ye know that no murderer hath eternal life abiding in him.' James, chapter three, the fourteenth and fifteenth verses."

They were looking at him. That was good. They weren't squinting or frowning, as if they were trying to figure out the words, or nodding agreement; but by golly they were looking at him and not out the window.

"Brethren means brother," he said. "You know that. It doesn't mean just your real brother, if you happen to have any brothers. It means everybody's your brethren. You two are brethren and I'm your brethren, everybody here at Yuma and everybody in the whole world, we are all brethren of Jesus

Christ and sons of Almighty God. Even women. What I'm talking about, even women are your brethren, but we don't have to get into that. I'm saying we are all related by blood and I'll tell you why. You listening?"

Raymond's gaze came away from the window, his eyes opening wide with interest.

Harold said, "Yes-suh, captain."

"We are all related," Mr. Manly said, watching them, "because we all come from the first two people in the world, old Adam and Eve, who started the human race. They had children and their children had children and the children's children had some more, and it kept going that way until the whole world become populated."

Harold Jackson said, "Who did the children marry?"

"They married each other."

"I mean children in the same family."

Mr. Manly nodded. "Each other. They married among theirselves."

"You mean a boy did it with his sister?"

"Oh," Mr. Manly said. "Yes, but it was different then. God said it was all right because it was the only way to get the earth populated. See, in just a few generations you got so many people they're marrying cousins now, and second cousins, and a couple hundred years it's not even like they're kin any more."

Mr. Manly decided not to tell them about Adam living to be nine hundred and thirty and Seth and Enoch and Kenan and Methuselah, all of them getting up past nine hundred years old before they died. He had to leave out details or it might con-fuse them. It was enough to tell them how the population multiplied and the people gradually spread all over the world.

"If we all come from the same people," Raymond said, "where do niggers come from?"

So Mr. Manly had to tell them about Noah and his three sons, Shem, Ham, and Japheth, and how Ham made some dirty remark on seeing his daddy sleeping naked after drinking too much wine. For that Noah banished Ham and made his son a "slave of slaves." Ham and his family had most likely gone on down to Africa and that was where niggers came from, descendents of Ham.

Harold Jackson said, "Where does it say Indins come from?"

Mr. Manly shook his head. "It don't say and it don't matter. People moved all over the world, and those living in a certain place got to look alike on account of the climate. So now you got your white race, your yellow race, and your black race."

"What's an Indin?" Harold said. "What race?"

"They're not sure," Mr. Manly answered. "Probably somewhere in between. Like yellow with a little nigger thrown in. You can call it the Indian race if you want. The colored race is the only one mentioned in the Bible, on account of the story of Noah and Ham."

Harold said, "How do they know everybody was white before that?"

Mr. Manly frowned. What kind of a question was that? "They just know it. I guess because Adam and Eve was white." He said then, "There's nothing wrong with being a nigger. God made you a nigger for a reason. I mean some people have to be niggers and some have to be Indians. Some have to be white. But we are all still brethren."

Harold's eyes remained on Mr. Manly. "It say in the Bible this man went to Africa?"

"It wasn't called Africa then, but they're pretty sure that's where he went. His people multiplied and before you know it they're living all over Africa and that's how you got your different tribes. Your Zulus. Your Pygmies. You got your—oh, all different ones with those African names."

"Zulus," Harold Jackson said. "I heard something about Zulus one time."

Mr. Manly leaned forward on the edge of the desk. "What did you hear about them?"

"I don't know. I remember somebody talking about Zulus. Somebody saying the word."

"Harold, you know something? For all you know you might be a Zulu yourself."

Harold gave him a funny look. "I was born in Fort Valley, Georgia."

"Where was your mama and daddy born?"

"Fort Valley."

"Where was your granddaddy born?"

"I don't know."

"Or your great-granddaddy. You know, he might have been born in Africa and brought over here as a slave. Maybe not him, but somebody before him, a kin of yours, was brought over. All your kin before him lived in Africa, and if they lived in a certain part of Africa then, by golly, they were Zulus."

Mr. Manly had a book about Africa in his collection. He remembered a drawing of a Zulu warrior, a tall Negro standing with a spear and a slender black and white cowhide shield.

He said, "Harold, your people are fine hunters and warriors. Oh, they're heathen, they paint theirselves up red and yellow and wear beads made out of lion's claws; but, Harold, they got to kill the lion first, with spears, and you don't go out and kill a lion unless you got plenty of nerve."

"With a spear, huh?" Harold said.

"Long spear they use, and this shield made out of cowhide. Some of them grow little beards and cut holes in the lobes of their ears and stick in these big hunks of dried sugar cane, if I remember correctly."

"They have sugar cane?"

"That's what it said in the book."

"They had a lot of sugar cane in Cuba. I never see anybody put it in their ear."

"Like earrings," Mr. Manly said. "I imagine they use all kinds of things. Gold, silver, if they got it."

"What do they wear?"

"Oh, just a little skimpy outfit. Some kind of cloth or animal skin around their middle. Nothing up here. Wait a second," Mr. Manly said. He went over to his bookcase. He found the book right away, but had to skim through it twice before he found the picture and laid the book open in front of Harold. "There. That's your Zulu warrior."

Harold hunched over the book. As he studied the picture Mr. Manly said, "Something else I remember. It says in there these Zulus can run. I mean *run*. The boys training to be warriors, they'd run twenty miles, take a little rest and run some more. Run thirty-forty miles a day isn't anything for a Zulu. Then go out and kill a lion. Or a elephant."

Mr. Manly noticed Raymond San Carlos glancing over at the book and he said quickly, "Same with your Indians; especially your desert tribes, like the Apaches. They can run all day long, I understand, and not take a drink of water till sundown. They know where to find water, too, way out in the middle of the desert. Man told me once, when Apaches are going where they know there isn't any water they take a horse's intestine and fill it full of water and wrap it around their bodies. He said he'd match an Apache Indian against a camel for traveling across the desert without any water."

"There's plenty of water," Raymond said, "if you know where to look."

"That's what I understand."

"Some of the older men at San Carlos, they'd take us boys and make us go up in the mountains and stay there two, three days without food or water."

"You did that?"

"Plenty of times."

"You'd find water?"

"Sure, and something to eat. Not much, but enough to hold us."

"Say, I just read in the paper," Mr. Manly said. "You know who died the other day? Geronimo."

"Is that right?"

"Fort Sill, Oklahoma. Died of pneumonia."

"That's too bad," Raymond said. "I mean I think he would rather have got killed fighting."

"You ever seen him? No, you would have been too young."

"Sure, I seen him. Listen, I'll tell you something I never told anybody. My father was in his band. Geronimo's."

"Is that a fact?"

"He was killed in Mexico when the soldiers went down there."

"My goodness," Mr. Manly said, "we're talking about warriors, you're the son of an Apache warrior."

"I never told anybody that."

"Why not? I'd think you'd be proud to tell it."

"It doesn't do me any good."

"But if it's true—"

"You think I'm lying?"

"I mean since it's a fact, why not tell it?"

"It don't make any difference to me. I could be Apache, I could be Mexican, I'm in Yuma the rest of my life."

"But you're living that life," Mr. Manly said. "If a person's an Indian then he should look at himself as an Indian. Like I told Harold, God made him a nigger for a reason. All right, God made you an Indian. There's nothing wrong with being an Indian. Why, do you know that about half our states have Indian names? Mississippi. The state I come from, Tennessee. Arizona. The Colorado River out yonder. Yuma."

"I don't know," Harold said, "that spear looks like it could break easy."

Mr. Manly looked over at him and at the book. "They know how to make 'em."

"They fight other people?"

"Sure they did. Beat 'em, too. What I understand, your Zulus owned most of the southern part of Africa, took it from other tribes and ruled over them."

"Never got beat, uh?"

"Not that I ever heard of. No, sir, they're the greatest warriors in Africa."

"Nobody ever beat the Apache," Raymond said, "till the U.S. Army come with all their goddamn guns."

"Raymond, don't ever take the Lord's name in vain like that."

"Apaches beat the Pimas, the Papagos, Maricopas—took anything we wanted from them."

"Well, I don't hold with raiding and killing," Mr. Manly said, "but I'll tell you there is something noble about your uneducated savage that you don't see in a lot of white men. I mean just the way your warrior stands, up straight with his shoulders back and never says too much, doesn't talk just to hear himself, like a lot of white people I know. I'll tell you something else, boys. Savage warriors have never been known to lie or go back on their word, and that's a fact. Man up at the reservation told me that Indians don't even have a word in their language for lie. Same thing with your Zulus. I reckon if a boy can run all day long and kill lions with a spear, he don't ever *have* to lie."

"I never heard of Apaches with spears," Raymond said.

"Oh, yes, they had them. And bows and arrows."

Harold was waiting. "I expect the Zulus got guns now, don't they?"

"I don't know about that," Mr. Manly answered. "Maybe they don't need guns. Figure spears are good enough." A smile touched his mouth as he looked across the desk at Raymond and Harold. "The thing that tickles me," he said, "I'm liable to have a couple of real honest-to-goodness Apache and Zulu warriors sitting right here in my office and I didn't even know it."

That evening, when Bob Fisher got back after supper, the guard at the sally port told him Mr. Manly wanted to see him right away. Fisher asked him what for, and the guard said how was he supposed to know. Fisher told the man to watch his mouth, and headed across the compound to see what the little squirt wanted.

Fisher paused by the stairs and looked over toward the cook shack. The women would be starting their bath about now.

Mr. Manly was writing something, but put it aside as Fisher came in. He said, "Pull up a chair," and seemed anxious to talk.

"There's a couple of things I got to do yet tonight."

"I wanted to talk to you about our Apache and our Zulu."

"How's that?"

"Raymond and Harold. I've been thinking about Frank Shelby's idea—he seems like a pretty sensible young man, doesn't he?"

Jesus Christ, Bob Fisher thought. He said, "I guess he's smart enough."

Mr. Manly smiled. "Though not smart enough to stay out of jail. Well, I've been thinking about this boxing-match idea. I want you to know I've given it a lot of thought."

Fisher waited.

"I want Frank Shelby to understand it too—you might mention it to him if you see him before I do."

"I'll tell him," Fisher said. He started to go.

"Hey, I haven't told you what I decided."

Fisher turned to the desk again.

"I've been thinking—a boxing match wouldn't be too good. We want them to stop fighting and we tell them to go ahead and fight. That doesn't sound right, does it?"

"I'll tell him that."

"You're sure in a hurry this evening, Bob."

"It's time I made the rounds is all."

"Well, I could walk around with you if you want and we could talk."

"That's all right," Fisher said, "go ahead."

"Well, as I said, we won't have the boxing match. You know what we're going to have instead?"

"What?"

"We're going to have a race. I mean Harold and Raymond are going to have a race."

"A race," Fisher said.

"A foot race. The faster man wins and gets some kind of a prize, but I haven't figured that part of it out yet."

"They're going to run a race," Fisher said.

"Out in the exercise yard. Down to the far end and back, maybe a couple of times."

"When do you want this race held?"

"Tomorrow I guess, during free time."

"You figure it'll stop them fighting, uh?"

"We don't have anything to lose," Mr. Manly said. "A good race might just do the trick."

Get out of here, Bob Fisher thought. He said, "Well, I'll tell them."

"I've already done that."

"I'll tell Frank Shelby then." Fisher edged toward the door and got his hand on the knob.

"You know what it is?" Mr. Manly was leaning back in his chair with a peaceful, thoughtful expression. "It's sort of a race of races," he said. "You know what I mean? The Negro against the Indian, black man against red man. I don't mean to prove that one's better than the other. I mean as a way to stir up their pride and get them interested in doing something with theirselves. You know what I mean?"

Bob Fisher stared at him.

"See, the way I figure them—" Mr. Manly motioned to the chair again. "Sit down, Bob, I'll tell you how I see these two boys, and why I believe we can help them."

By the time Fisher got down to the yard, the women had taken their bath. They were back in their cellblock and he had to find R.E. Baylis for the keys.

"I already locked everybody in," the guard said.

"I know you did. That's why I need the keys."

"Is there something wrong somewhere?"

Bob Fisher had never wanted to look at that woman as bad as he did this evening. God, he felt like he *had* to look at her, but everybody was getting in his way, wasting time. His wife at supper nagging at him again about moving to Florence. The little squirt preacher who believed he could save a couple of bad convicts. Now a slow-witted guard asking him questions.

"Just give me the keys," Fisher said.

He didn't go over there directly. He walked past the TB cellblock first and looked in at the empty yard, at the lantern light showing in most of the cells and the dark ovals of the cells that were not occupied. The nigger and the Indian were in separate cells. They were doing a fair job on the wall; but, Jesus, they'd get it done a lot sooner if the little squirt would let them work instead of wasting time preaching to them. Now foot races. God Almighty.

Once you were through the gate of the women's cellblock, the area was more like a room than a yard—a little closed-in courtyard and two cells carved into the granite wall.

There was lantern light in both cells. Fisher looked in at Tacha first and asked her what she was doing. Tacha was sitting on a stool in the smoky dimness of the cell. She said, "I'm reading," and looked down at the book again. Bob Fisher told himself to take it easy now and not to be impatient. He looked in Tacha's cell almost a minute longer before moving on to Norma's.

She was stretched out in her bunk, staring right at him when he looked through the iron strips of the door. A blanket covered her, but one bare arm and shoulder were out of the blanket and, Jesus, it didn't look like she had any clothes on. His gaze moved around the cell to show he wasn't too interested in her.

"Everything all right?"

"That's a funny thing to ask," Norma said. "Like this is a hotel."

"I haven't looked in here in a while."

"I know you haven't."

"You need another blanket or anything?"

"What's anything?"

"I mean like kerosene for the lantern."

"I think there's enough. The light's awful low though."

"Turn it up."

"I can't. I think the wick's stuck. Or else it's burned down."

"You want me to take a look at it?"

"Would you? I'd appreciate it."

Bob Fisher brought the ring of keys out of his coat pocket with the key to Norma's cell in his hand. As he opened the door and came in, Norma raised up on one elbow, holding the blanket in front of her. He didn't look at her; he went right to the lamp and peered in through the smoky glass. As he turned the wick up slowly, the light grew brighter, then dimmed again as he turned it down.

"It seems all right now." Fisher glanced at her, twisted bare back. He tried the lantern a few more times, twisting the wick up and down and knowing her bare back—and that meant her bare front too—wasn't four feet away from him. "It must've been stuck," he said.

"I guess it was. Will you turn it down now? Just so there's a nice glow."

"How's that?"

"That's perfect."

"I think you got enough wick in there."

"I think so. Do you want to get in bed with me?"

"Jesus Christ," Bob Fisher said.

"Well, do you?"

"You're a nervy thing, aren't you?"

Norma twisted around a little more and let the blanket fall. "I can't help it."

"You can't help what?"

"If I want you to do it to me."

"Jesus," Bob Fisher said. He looked at the cell

door and then at Norma again, cleared his throat
and said in a lower tone, "I never heard a girl asking for it before."

"Well," Norma said, throwing the blanket aside
as she got up from the bunk and moved toward
him, "you're hearing it now, daddy."

"Listen, Tacha's right next door."

"She can't see us."

"She can hear."

"Then we'll whisper." Norma began unbutton-
ing his coat.

"We can't do nothing here."

"Why not?"

"One of the guards might come by."

"Now you're teasing me. Nobody's allowed in
here at night, and you know it."

"Boy, you got big ones."

"There, now slip your coat off."

"I can't stay here more'n a few minutes."

"Then quit talking," Norma said.

7

Frank Shelby said, "A race, what do you mean, a race?"

"I mean a foot race," Fisher told him. "The nigger and the Indin are going to run a race from one end of the yard to the other and back again, and you and every convict in this place are going to be out here to watch it."

"A race," Shelby said again. "Nobody cares about any foot race."

"You don't have to care," Fisher said. "I'm not asking you to care. I'm telling you to close your store and get everybody's ass out of the cellblock. They can stand here or over along the south wall. Ten minutes, I want everybody out."

"This is supposed to be our free time."

"I'll tell you when you get free time."

"What if we want to make some bets?"

"I don't care, long as you keep it quiet. I don't want any arguments, or have to hit anybody over the head."

"Ten minutes, it doesn't give us much time to figure out how to bet."

"You don't know who's going to win," Fisher said. "What's the difference?"

About half the convicts were already in the yard. Fisher waited for the rest of them to file out: the card players and the convicts who could afford Frank Shelby's whiskey and the ones who were always in their bunks between working and eating. They came out of the cellblock and stood around waiting for something to happen. The guards up on the wall came out of the towers and looked around too, as if they didn't know what was going on. Bob Fisher hadn't told any of them about the race. It wouldn't take more than a couple of minutes. He told the convicts to keep the middle area of the yard clear. They started asking him what was going on, but he walked away from them toward the mess hall. It was good that he did. When Mr. Manly appeared on the stairway at the end of the building Fisher was able to get to him before he reached the yard.

"You better stay up on the stairs."

Mr. Manly looked surprised. "I was going over there with the convicts."

"It's happened a sup'rintendent's been grabbed and a knife put at his throat till the gate was opened."

"You go among the convicts; all the guards do."

"But if any of us are grabbed the gate stays closed. They know that. They don't know about you."

"I just wanted to mingle a little," Mr. Manly said. He looked out toward the yard. "Are they ready?"

"Soon as they get their leg-irons off."

A few minutes later, Raymond and Harold were brought down the length of the yard. The convicts watched them, and a few called out to them. Mr. Manly didn't hear what they said, but he noticed neither Raymond nor Harold looked over that way. When they reached the stairs he said, "Well, boys, are you ready?"

"You want us to run," Raymond said. "You wasn't kidding, uh?"

"Course I wasn't."

"I don't know. We just got the irons off. My legs feel funny."

"You want to warm up first?"

Harold Jackson said, "I'm ready any time he is."

Raymond shrugged. "Let's run the race."

Mr. Manly made sure they understood—down to the end of the yard, touch the wall between the snake den and the women's cellblock, and come back past the stairs, a distance Mr. Manly figured to be about a hundred and twenty yards or so. He and Mr. Fisher would be at the top of the stairs in the judge's stand. Mr. Fisher would fire off a revolver as the starting signal. "So," Mr. Manly said, "if you boys are ready—"

There was some noise from the convicts as Raymond and Harold took off as the shot was fired and passed the main cellblock in a dead heat. Raymond hit the far wall and came off in one motion. Harold stumbled and dug hard on the way back but was five or six yards behind Raymond going across the finish.

They stood with their hands on their hips breathing in and out while Mr. Manly leaned over the rail of the stair landing, smiling down at them.

He said, "Hey, boys, you sure gave it the old try. Rest a few minutes and we'll run it again."

Raymond looked over at Harold. They got down again and went off with the sound of the revolver, Raymond letting Harold set the pace this time, staying with him and not kicking out ahead until they were almost to the finish line. This time he took it by two strides, with the convicts yelling at them to *run*.

Raymond could feel his chest burning now. He walked around breathing with his mouth open, looking up at the sky that was fading to gray with the sun below the west wall, walking around in little circles and seeing Mr. Manly up there now. As Raymond turned away he heard Harold say, "Let's do it again," and he had to go along.

Harold dug all the way this time; he felt his thighs knotting and pushed it some more, down and back and, with the convicts yelling, came in a good seven strides ahead of the Indian. Right away Harold said, "Let's do it again."

In the fourth race he was again six or seven strides faster than Raymond.

In the fifth race, neither of them looked as if he was going to make it back to the finish. They ran pumping their arms and gasping for air, and Harold might have been ahead by a half-stride past the stairs; but Raymond stumbled and fell forward trying to catch himself, and it was hard to tell who won. There wasn't a sound from the convicts this time. Some of them weren't even looking this way. They were milling around, smoking cigarettes, talking among themselves.

Mr. Manly wasn't watching the convicts. He was

leaning over the railing looking down at his two boys: at Raymond lying stretched out on his back and at Harold sitting, leaning back on his hands with his face raised to the sky.

"Hey, boys," Mr. Manly called, "you know what I want you to do now? First I want you to get up. Come on, boys, get up on your feet. Raymond, you hear me?"

"He looks like he's out," Fisher said.

"No, he's all right. See?"

Mr. Manly leaned closer over the rail. "Now I want you two to walk up to each other. Go on, do as I say. It won't hurt you. Now I want you both to reach out and shake hands . . .

"Don't look up here. Look at each other and shake hands."

Mr. Manly started to grin and, by golly, he really felt good. "Bob, look at that."

"I see it," Fisher said.

Mr. Manly called out now, "Boys, by the time you get done running together you're going to be good friends. You wait and see."

The next day, while they were working on the face wall in the TB cellblock, Raymond was squatting down mixing mortar in a bucket and groaned as he got to his feet. "Goddamn legs," he said.

"I know what you mean," Harold said. He was laying a brick, tapping it into place with the handle of his trowel, and hesitated as he heard his own voice and realized he had spoken to Raymond. He didn't look over at him; he picked up another brick and laid it in place. It was quiet in the yard. The tubercular convicts were in their cells, out of the heat and the sun. Harold could hear a switch-engine working, way down the hill in the Southern Pacific yard; he could hear the freight cars banging together as they were coupled.

After a minute or so Raymond said, "I can't hardly walk today."

"From running," Harold said.

"They don't put the leg-irons back on, uh?"

"I wondered if they forgot to."

"I think so. They wouldn't leave them off unless they forgot."

There was silence again until Harold said, "They can leave them off, it's all right with me."

"Sure," Raymond said, "I don't care they leave them off."

"Place in Florida, this prison farm, you got to wear them all the time."

"Yeah? I hope I never get sent there."

"You ever been to Cuba?"

"No, I never have."

"That's a fine place. I believe I like to go back there sometime."

"Live there?"

"Maybe. I don't know."

"Look like we need some more bricks," Raymond said.

The convicts mixing the adobe mud straightened up with their shovels in front of them as Raymond and Harold came across the yard pushing their wheelbarrows. Joe Dean stepped around to the other side of the mud so he could keep an eye on the south-wall tower guard. He waited until the two boys were close, heading for the brick pile.

"Well, now," Joe Dean said, "I believe it's the two sweethearts."

"If they come back for some more," another convict said, "I'm going to cut somebody this time."

Joe Dean watched them begin loading the wheelbarrows. "See, what they do," he said. "they start a ruckus so they'll get sent to the snake den. Sure, they get in there, just the two of them. Man, they hug and kiss, do all kinds of things to each other."

"That is Mr. Joe Dean talking," Harold said. "I believe he wants to get hit in the mouth with a 'dobe brick."

"I want to see you try that," Joe Dean said.

"Sometime when the guard ain't looking," Harold said. "Maybe when you ain't looking either."

They finished loading their wheelbarrows and left.

In the mess hall at supper they sat across one end of a table. No one else sat with them. Raymond looked around at the convicts hunched over eating. No one seemed aware of them. They were all talking or concentrating on their food. He said to Harold, "Goddamn beans, they always got to burn them."

"I've had worse beans," Harold said. "Worse everything. What I like is some chicken, that's what I miss. Chicken's good."

"I like a beefsteak. With peppers and catsup."

"Beefsteak's good too. You like fried fish?"

"I never had it."

"You never had fish?"

"I don't think so."

"Man, where you been you never had fish?"

"I don't know, I never had it."

"We got a big river right outside."

"I never seen anybody fishing."

"How long it take you to swim across?"

"Maybe five minutes."

"That's a long time to swim."

"Too long. They get a boat out quick."

"Anybody try to dig out of here?"

"I never heard of it," Raymond said. "The ones that go they always run from a work detail, outside."

"Anybody make it?"

"Not since I been here."

"Man start running he got to know where he's going. He got to have a place to go to." Harold looked up from his plate. "How long you here for?"

"Life."

"That's a long time, ain't it?"

They were back at work on the cell wall the next day when a guard came and got them. It was about midafternoon. Neither of them asked where they were going; they figured they were going to hear another sermon from the man. They marched in front of the guard down the length of the yard and past the brick detail. When they got near the mess hall they veered a little toward the stairway and the guard said, "Keep going, straight ahead."

Raymond and Harold couldn't believe it. The guard marched them through the gates of the sally port and right up to Mr. Rynning's twenty-horsepower Ford Touring Car.

"Let me try to explain it to you again," Mr. Manly said to Bob Fisher. "I believe these boys have got to develop some pride in theirselves. I don't mean they're supposed to get uppity with us. I mean they got to look at theirselves as man in the sight of men, and children in the eyes of God."

"Well, I don't know anything about that part," Bob Fisher said. "To me they are a couple of bad cons, and if you want my advice based on years of dealing with these people, we put their leg-irons back on."

"They can't run in leg-irons."

"I know they can't. They need to work and they need to get knocked down a few times. A convict stands up to you, you better knock him down quick."

"Have they stood up to you, Bob?"

"One of them served time in Leavenworth, the other one tried to swim the river and they're both trying to kill one another. I call that standing up to me."

"You say they're hard cases, Bob, and I say they're like little children, because they're just now beginning to learn about living with their fellow-man, which to them means living with white men and getting along with white men."

"Long as they're here," Fisher said, "they damn well better. We only got one set of rules."

Mr. Manly shook his head. "I don't mean to change the rules for them." It was harder to explain than he thought it would be. He couldn't look right at Fisher; the man's solemn expression, across the desk, distracted him. He would glance at Fisher and then look down at the sheet of paper that was partly covered with oval shapes that were like shields, and long thin lines that curved awkwardly into spearheads. "I don't mean to treat them as privileged characters either. But we're not going to turn them into white men, are we?"

"We sure aren't."

"We're not going to tell them they're just as good as white men, are we?"

"I don't see how we could do that," Fisher said.

"So we tell them what an Indian is good at and what a nigger is good at."

"Niggers lie and Indians steal."

"Bob, we tell them what they're good at as members of their race. We already got it started. We tell them Indians and niggers are the best runners in the world."

"I guess if they're scared enough."

"We train them hard and, by golly, they begin to believe it."

"Yeah?"

"Once they begin to believe in something, they begin to believe in themselves."

"Yeah?"

"That's all there is to it."

"Well, maybe you ought to get some white boys to run against them."

"Bob, I'm not interested in them running *races*. This has got to do with distance and endurance. Being able to do something no one else in this prison can do. That race out in the yard was all wrong, more I think about it."

"Frank Shelby said he figured the men wouldn't mind seeing different kinds of races instead of just back and forth. He said run them all over and have them jump things—like climb up the wall on ropes, see who can get to the top first. He said he thought the men would get a kick out of that."

"Bob, this is a show. It doesn't prove nothing. I'm talking about these boys running *miles*."

"Miles, uh?"

"Like their granddaddies used to do."

"How's that?"

"Like Harold Jackson's people back in Africa. Bob, they kill lions with *spears*."

"Harold killed a man with a lead pipe."

"There," Mr. Manly said. "That's the difference. That's what he's become because he's forgot what it's like to be a Zulu nigger warrior."

Jesus Christ, Bob Fisher said to himself. The little squirt shouldn't be sitting behind the desk, he should be over in the goddamn crazy hole. He said, "You want them to run miles, uh?"

"Start them out a few miles a day. Work up to ten miles, twenty miles. We'll see how they do."

"Well, it will be something to see, all right, them running back and forth across the yard. I imagine the convicts will make a few remarks to them. The two boys get riled up and lose their temper, they're back in the snake den and I don't see you've made any progress at all."

"I've already thought of that," Mr. Manly said. "They're not going to run in the yard. They're going to run outside."

The convicts putting up the adobe wall out at the cemetery were the first ones to see them. A man raised up to stretch the kinks out of his back and said, "Look-it up there!"

They heard the Ford Touring Car as they looked around and saw it up on the slope, moving along the north wall with the two boys running behind it. Nobody could figure it out. Somebody asked what were they chasing the car for. Another convict said they weren't chasing the car, they were being taken somewhere. See, there was a guard in the back seat with a rifle. They could see him good against the pale wall of the prison. Nobody had ever seen convicts taken somewhere like that. Any time the car went out it went down to Yuma, but no convicts were ever in the car or behind it or anywhere near it. One of the convicts asked the work-detail guard where he supposed they were going. The guard said it beat him. That motor car belonged to Mr. Rynning and was only used for official business.

It was the stone-quarry gang that saw them next. They looked squinting up through the white dust and saw the Ford Touring Car and the two boys running to keep up with it, about twenty feet behind the car and just barely visible in all the dust the car was raising. The stone-quarry gang watched until the car was past the open rim and the only thing left to see was the dust hanging in the sunlight. Somebody said they certainly had it ass-backwards; the car was supposed to be chasing the cons. They tried to figure it out, but nobody had an answer that made much sense.

Two guards and two convicts, including Joe Dean, coming back in the wagon from delivering a load of adobe bricks in town, saw them next— saw them pass right by on the road—and Joe Dean and the other convict and the two guards turned around and watched them until the car crossed the railroad tracks and passed behind some depot sheds. Joe Dean said he could understand why the guards didn't want the spook and the Indian riding with them, but he still had never seen anything like it in all the time he'd been here. The guards said they had never seen anything like it either. There was funny things going on. Those two had raced each other, maybe they were racing the car now. Joe Dean said Goddamn, this was the craziest prison he had ever been in.

That first day, the best they could run in one stretch was a little over a mile. They did that once: down prison hill and along the railroad tracks and out back of town, out into the country. Most of the time, in the three hours they were out, they would run as far as they could, seldom more than a quarter of a mile—then have to quit and walk for a while, breathing hard with their mouths open and their lungs on fire. They would drop thirty to forty feet back of the car and the guard with the Winchester would yell at them to come on, get the lead out of their feet.

Harold said to Raymond, "I had any lead in my feet I'd take and hit that man in the mouth with it."

"We tell him we got to rest," Raymond said.

They did that twice, sat down at the side of the road in the meadow grass and watched the guard coming with the rifle and the car backing up through its own dust. The first time the guard pointed the rifle and yelled for them to get on their feet. Harold told him they couldn't move and asked him if he was going to shoot them for being tired.

"Captain, we *want* to run, but our legs won't mind what we tell them."

So the guard gave them five minutes and they sat back in the grass to let their muscles relax and stared at the distant mountains while the guards sat in the car smoking their cigarettes.

Harold said to Raymond, "What are we doing this for?"

Raymond gave him a funny look. "Because we're tired, what do you think?"

"I mean running. What are we running for?"

"They say to run, we run."

"It's that little preacher."

"Sure it is. What do you think, these guards thought of it?"

"That little man's crazy, ain't he?"

"I don't know," Raymond said. "Most of the time I don't understand him. He's got something in his head about running."

"Running's all right if you in a hurry and you know where you going."

"That road don't go anywhere."

"What's up ahead?"

"The desert," Raymond said. "Maybe after a while you come to a town."

"You know how to drive that thing?"

"A car? I never even been in one."

Harold was chewing on a weed stem, looking at the car. "It would be nice to have a ride home, wouldn't it?"

"It might be worth the running," Raymond said.

The guard got them up and they ran some more. They ran and walked and ran again for almost another mile, and this time when they went down they stretched out full length: Harold on his stomach, head down and his arms propping him up; Raymond on his back with his chest rising and falling.

After ten minutes the guard said all right, they were starting back now. Neither of them moved as the car turned around and rolled past them. The guard asked if they heard him. He said goddamn-it, they better get up quick. Harold said captain, their legs hurt so bad it didn't look like they could make it. The guard levered a cartridge into the chamber of the Winchester and said their legs would hurt one hell of a lot more with a .44 slug shot through them. They got up and fell in behind the car. Once they tried to run and had to stop within a dozen yards. It wasn't any use, Harold said. The legs wouldn't do what they was told. They could walk though. All right, the guard said, then walk. But god*damn*, they were so slow, poking along, he had to keep yelling at them to come on. After a while, still not in sight of the railroad tracks, the guard driving said to the other guard, if they didn't hurry they were going to miss supper call. The guard with the Winchester said well, what was he supposed to do about it? The guard driving said it looked like there was only one thing they *could* do.

Raymond liked it when the car stopped and the guard with the rifle, looking like he wanted to kill them, said all right, goddamn-it, get in.

Harold liked it when they drove past the cemetery work detail filing back to prison. The convicts had moved off the road and were looking back, waiting for the car. As they went by Harold raised one hand and waved. He said to Raymond, "Look at them poor boys. I believe they convicts."

8

"You know why they won't try to escape?" Mr. Manly said.

Bob Fisher stood at the desk and didn't say anything, because the answer was going to come from the little preacher anyway.

"Because they see the good in this. They realize this is their chance to become something."

"Running across a pasture field."

"You know what I mean."

"Take a man outside enough times," Fisher said, "he'll run for the hills."

"Not these two boys."

"Any two. They been outside every day for a week and they're smelling fresh air."

"Two weeks, and they can run three miles without stopping," Mr. Manly said. "Another couple of weeks I want to see them running five miles, maybe six."

"They'll run as long as it's easier than working."

Mr. Manly smiled a little. "I see you don't know them very well."

"I have known them all my life," Bob Fisher said. "When running becomes harder than working, they'll figure a way to get out of it. They'll break each other's legs if they have to."

"All right, then I'll talk to them again. You can be present, Bob, and I'll prove to you you're wrong."

"I understand you write a weekly report to Mr. Rynning," Fisher said. "Have you told him what you're doing?"

"As a matter of fact, I have."

"You told him you got them running outside?"

"I told him I'm trying something out on two boys considered incorrigible, a program that combines spiritual teaching and physical exercise. He's made no mention to me what he thinks. But if you want to write to him, Bob, go right ahead."

"If it's all the same to you," Fisher said, "I want it on the record I didn't have nothing to do with this in any way at all."

Three miles wasn't so bad and it was easier to breathe at the end of the stretch. It didn't feel as if their lungs were burning any more. They would walk for a few minutes and run another mile and then walk again. Maybe they could do it again, run another mile before resting. But why do it if they didn't have to, if the guards didn't expect it? They would run a little way and when Raymond or Harold would call out they had to rest the car and would stop and wait for them.

"I think we could do it," Raymond said.

"Sure we could."

"Maybe run four, five miles at the start."

"We could do that too," Harold said, "but why would we want to?"

"I mean to see if we could do it."

"Man, we could run five miles right now if we wanted."

"I don't know."

"If we had something to run for. All I see it doing is getting us tired."

"It's better than laying adobes, or working on the rock pile."

"I believe you're right there," Harold said.

"Well," Raymond said, "we can try four miles, five miles at any time we want. What's the hurry?"

"What's the hurry," Harold said. "I wish that son of a bitch would give us a cigarette. Look at him sucking on it and blowing the smoke out. Man."

They were getting along all right with the guards, because the guards were finding out this was pretty good duty, driving around the countryside in a Ford Touring Car. Ride around for a few hours. Smoke any time they wanted. Put the canvas top up if it got too hot in the sun. The guards weren't dumb, though. They stayed away from trees and the riverbank, keeping to open range country once they had followed the railroad tracks out beyond town.

The idea of a train going by interested Harold. He pictured them running along the road where it was close to the tracks and the train coming up behind them out of the depot, not moving too fast. As the guards watched the train, Harold saw himself and Raymond break through the weeds to the gravel roadbed, run with the train and swing up on one of those iron-rung ladders they had on boxcars. Then the good part. The guards are watching the train and all of a sudden the guards see them on the boxcar—*waving to them.*

"Waving good-bye," Harold said to Raymond when they were resting one time and he told him about it.

Raymond was grinning. "They see the train going away, they don't know what to do."

"Oh, they take a couple of shots," Harold said. "But they so excited, man, they can't even hit the train."

"We're waving bye-bye."

"Yeah, while they shooting at us."

"It would be something, all right." Raymond had to wipe his eyes.

After a minute Harold said, "Where does the train go to?"

"I don't know. I guess different places."

"That's the trouble," Harold said. "You got to know where you going. You can't stay on the train. Sooner or later you got to get off and start running again."

"You think we could run five miles, uh?"

"If we wanted to," Harold said.

It was about a week later that Mr. Manly woke up in the middle of the night and said out loud in the bedroom, "All right, if you're going to keep worrying about it, why don't you see for yourself what they're doing?"

That's what he did the next day: hopped in the front seat of the Ford Touring Car and went along to watch the two boys do their road work.

It didn't bother the guard driving too much. He had less to say was all. But the guard with the Winchester yelled at Raymond and Harold more than he ever did before to come on, pick 'em up, keep closer to the car. Mr. Manly said the dust was probably bothering them. The guard said it was bothering him too, because he had to see them before he could watch them. He said you get a con outside you watch him every second.

Raymond and Harold ran three miles and saw Mr. Manly looking at his watch. Later on, when they were resting, he came over and squatted down in the grass with them.

"Three miles in twenty-five minutes," he said. "That's pretty good. You reckon you could cover five miles in an hour?"

"I don't think so," Raymond said. "It's not us, we want to do it. It's our legs."

"Well, wanting something is half of getting it," Mr. Manly said. "I mean if you want something bad enough."

"Sure, we want to do it."

"Why?"

"Why? Well, I guess because we got to do it."

"You just said you wanted to."

"Yeah, we like to run."

"And I'm asking you why." Mr. Manly waited a moment. "Somebody told me all you fellas want to do is get out of work."

"Who tole you that?"

"It doesn't matter who it was. You know what I told him? I told him he didn't know you boys very well. I told him you were working harder now, running, than you ever worked in your life."

"That's right," Raymond said.

"Because you see a chance of doing something nobody else in the prison can do. Run twenty miles in a day."

Raymond said, "You want us to run twenty miles?"

"*You* want to run twenty miles. You're an Apache Indian, aren't you? And Harold's a Zulu. Well, by golly, an Apache Indian and a Zulu can run twenty miles, thirty miles a day, and there ain't a white man in this territory can say that."

"You want us to run twenty miles?" Raymond said again.

"I want you to start thinking of who you are, that's what I want. I want you to start thinking like warriors for a change instead of like convicts."

Raymond was watching him, nodding as he listened. He said, "Do these waryers think different than other people?"

"They think of who they are." An angry little edge came into Mr. Manly's tone. "They got pride in their tribe and their job, and everything they do is to make them better warriors—the way they live, the way they dress, the way they train to harden theirselves, the way they go without food or water to show their bodies their willpower is in charge here and, by golly, their bodies better do what they're told. Raymond, you say you're Apache Indian?"

"Yes, sir, that's right."

"Harold, you believe you're a Zulu?"

"Yes-suh, captain, a Zulu."

"Then prove it to me, both of you. Let me see how good you are."

As Mr. Manly got to his feet he glanced over at the guards, feeling a little funny now in the silence and wondering if they had been listening. Well, so what if they had? He was superintendent, wasn't he? And he answered right back, You're darn right.

"You boys get ready for some real training," he said now. "I'm taking you at your word."

Raymond waited until he walked away and had reached the car. "Who do you think tole him we're doing this to get out of work?"

"I don't know," Harold said. "Who do you think?"

"I think that son of a bitch Frank Shelby."

"Yeah," Harold said, "he'd do it, wouldn't he?"

On Visiting Day the mess-hall tables were placed in a single line, dividing the room down the middle. The visitors remained on one side and the convicts on the other. Friends and relatives could sit down facing each other if they found a place at the tables; but they couldn't touch, not even hands, and a visitor was not allowed to pass anything to a convict.

Frank Shelby always got a place at the tables and his visitor was always his brother, a slightly older and heavier brother, but used to taking orders from Frank.

Virgil Shelby said, "By May for sure."

"I don't want a month," Frank said. "I want a day."

"I'm telling you what I know. They're done building the place, they're doing something inside the walls now and they won't let anybody in."

"You can talk to a workman."

"I talked to plenty of workmen. They don't know anything."

"What about the railroad?"

"Same thing. Old boys in the saloon talk about moving the convicts, but they don't know when."

"Somebody knows."

"Maybe they don't. Frank, what are you worried about? Whatever the day is we're going to be ready. I've been over and across that rail line eight times—nine times now—and I know just where I'm going to take you off that train."

"You're talking too loud."

Virgil took time to look down the table both ways, at the convicts hunched over the tables shoulder to shoulder and their visitors crowded in on this side, everyone trying to talk naturally without being overheard. When Virgil looked at his brother again, he said, "What I want to know is how many?"

"Me. Junior, Soonzy, Joe Dean. Norma." Frank Shelby paused. "No, we don't need to take Norma."

"It's up to you."

"No, we don't need her."

"That's four. I want to know you're together, all in the same place, because once we hit that train there's going to be striped suits running all over the countryside."

"That might be all right."

"It could be. Give them some people to chase after. But it could mess things up too."

"Well, right now all I hear is you wondering what's going to happen. You come with more than that, or I live the next forty years in Florence, Arizona."

"I'm going to stay in Yuma a while, see what I can find out about the train. You need any money?" Virgil asked.

"If I have to buy some guards. I don't know, get me three, four hundred."

"I'll send it in with the stores. Anything else?"

"A good idea, buddy."

"Don't worry, Frank, we're going to get you out. I'll swear to it."

"Yeah, well, I'll see you."

"Next month," Virgil said. He turned to swing a leg over the bench, then looked at his brother again. "Something funny I seen coming here—these two convicts running behind a Ford automobile. What do you suppose they was doing, Frank?"

Shelby had to tear his pants nearly off to see Norma again. He ripped them down the in-seam from crotch to ankle and told the warehouse guard he'd caught them on some bailing wire and, man, it had almost fixed him good. The guard said to get another pair out of stores. Shelby said all right, and he'd leave his ripped pants at the tailor's on the way back. The guard knew what Shelby was up to; he accepted the sack of Bull Durham Shelby offered and played the game with him. It wasn't hurting anybody.

So he got his new pants and headed for the tailor shop. As soon as he was inside, Norma Davis came off the work table, where she was sitting smoking a cigarette, and went into the stock room. Shelby threw the ripped pants at the tailor, told Tacha to watch out the window for Bob Fisher, and followed Norma into the back room, closing the door behind him.

"He's not as sure of himself as he used to be," Tacha said. "He's worried."

The tailor was studying the ripped seam closely. Tacha was looking out the window, at the colorless tone of the yard in sunlight: adobe and granite and black shadow lines in the glare. The brick detail was at work across the yard, but she couldn't hear them. She listened for sounds, out in the yard and in the room behind her, but there were none.

"They're quiet in there, uh?"

The tailor said nothing.

"You expect them to make sounds like animals, those two. That old turnkey makes sounds. God, like he's dying. Like somebody stuck a knife—" Tacha stopped.

"I don't know what you're talking about," the tailor said.

"I'm talking about Mr. Fisher, the turnkey, the sounds he makes when he's in her cell."

"And I don't want to know." The tailor kept his head low over his sewing machine.

"He sneaks in at night—"

"I said I don't want to hear about it."

"He hasn't been coming very long. Just the past few weeks. Not every night either. He makes some excuse to go in there, like to fix the lantern or search the place for I don't know what. One time she say, 'Oh, I think there is a tarantula in here,' and the turnkey hurries in there to kill it. I want to say to him, knowing he's taking off his pants then, 'Hey, mister, that's a funny thing to kill a tarantula with.'"

"I'm not listening to you," the tailor said. "Not a word."

In the closeness of the stock room Shelby stepped back to rest his arm on one of the shelves. Watching Norma, he loosened his hat, setting it lightly

on his forehead. "Goodness," he said, "I didn't
even take off my hat, did I?"

Norma let her skirt fall. She smoothed it over
her hips and began buttoning her blouse. "I feel
like a mare, standing like that."

"Honey, you don't look like a mare. I believe
you are about the trickiest thing I ever met."

"I know a few more ways."

"I bet you do, for a fact."

"That old man, he breathes through his nose
right in your ear. Real loud, like he's having heart
failure."

Shelby grinned. "That would be something. He
has a stroke while he's in there with you."

"I'll tell you, he isn't any fun at all."

"You ain't loving him for the pleasure, sweetheart. You're supposed to be finding out things."

"He doesn't know yet when we're going."

"You asked him?"

"I said to him, 'I will sure be glad to get out
of this place.' He said it wouldn't be much longer
and I said, 'Oh, when are we leaving here?' He said
he didn't know for sure, probably in a couple of
months."

"We got to know the day," Shelby said.

"Well, if he don't know it he can't hardly tell me,
can he?"

"Maybe he can find it out."

"From who?"

"I don't know. The superintendent, somebody."

"That little fella, he walks around, he looks like
he's lost, can't find his mama."

"Well, mama, maybe you should talk to him."

"Get him to come to my cell."

"Jesus, you'd eat him up."

Norma giggled. "You say terrible things."

"I mean by the time you're through there wouldn't be nothing left of him."

"If *you're* through, you better get out of here."

"I talked to Virgil. He doesn't know anything either."

"Don't worry," Norma said. "One of us'll find out. I just want to be sure you take me along when the time comes."

Shelby gave her a nice little sad smile and shook his head slowly. "Sweetheart," he said, "how could I go anywhere without you?"

Good timing, Norma Davis believed, was one of the most important things in life. You had to think of the other person. You had to know his moods and reactions and know the right moment to spring little surprises. You didn't want the person getting too excited and ruining everything before it was time.

That's why she brought Bob Fisher along for almost two months before she told him her secret.

It was strange; like instinct. One night, as she heard the key turning in the iron door of the cellblock, she knew it was Bob and, for some reason, she also knew she was going to tell him tonight. Though not right away.

First he had to go through his act. He had to look in at Tacha and ask her what was she doing, reading? Then he had to come over and see Norma in the bunk and look around the cell for a minute and ask if everything was all right. Norma was ready. She told him she had a terrible sore ankle and would he look at it and see if it was sprained or anything. She got him in there and then had to slow down and be patient while he actually, honest to God, looked at her ankle and said in a loud voice it looked all right to him. He whispered after that, getting out of his coat and into the bunk with her, but raising up every once in a while to look at the cell door.

Norma said, "What's the matter?"

"Tacha, she can hear everything."

"If she bothers you, why don't you put her some place else?"

"This is the women's block. There isn't any place else."

Norma got her hand inside his shirt and started fooling with the hair on his chest. "How does Tacha look to you?"

"Cut it out, it tickles," Fisher said. "What do you mean, how does she look?"

"I don't know, I don' think she looks so good. I hear her coughing at night."

"Listen, I only got a few minutes."

Norma handled the next part of it, making him believe he was driving her wild, and as he lay on the edge of the bunk breathing out of his nose, she told him her secret.

She said, "Guess what? I know somebody who's planning to escape."

That got him up and leaning over her again.

"Who?"

"I heard once," Norma said, "if you help the authorities here they'll help you."

"Who is it?"

"I heard of convicts who helped stop men trying to escape and got pardoned. Is that right?"

"It's happened."

"They were freed?"

"That's right."

"You think it might happen again?"

"It could. Who's going out?"

"Not out of here. From the train. You think if I found out all about it and told you I'd get a pardon?"

"I think you might," Fisher said. "I can't promise, but you'd have a good chance."

"It's Frank Shelby."

"That's what I thought."

"His brother Virgil's going to help him."

"Where do they jump the train?"

"Frank doesn't know yet, but soon as I find out I'll tell you."

"You promise?"

"Cross my heart."

"You're a sweet girl, Norma. You know that?"

She smiled at him in the dim glow of the lantern and said, "I try to be."

Another week passed before Bob Fisher thought of something else Norma had said.

He was in the tailor shop that day, just checking, not for any special reason. Tacha looked up at him and said, "Norma's not here."

"I can see that."

"She's at the toilet—if you're looking for her."

"I'm not looking for her," Fisher said.

He wasn't sure if Tacha was smiling then or not—like telling him she knew all about him. Little Mexican bitch, she had better not try to get smart with him.

It was then he thought of what Norma had said. About Tacha not looking so good. Coughing at night.

Hell, yes, Bob Fisher said to himself and wondered why he hadn't thought of it before. There was only one place around here to put anybody who was coughing sick. Over in the TB cellblock.

⚔ 9 ⚔

The guard, R.E. Baylis, was instructed to move
the Mexican girl to the TB area after work, right
before supper. It sounded easy enough.

But when he told Tacha she held back and didn't
want to go. What for? Look at her. Did she look
like she had TB? She wasn't even sick. R.E. Baylis told her to get her things, she was going over
there and that's all there was to it. She asked him
if Mr. Fisher had given the order, and when he
said sure, Tacha said she thought so; she should
have known he would do something like this.
Goddamn-it, R.E. Baylis thought, he didn't have
to explain anything to her. He did though. He said
it must be they were sending her over there to help
out—bring the lungers their food, get them their
medicine. He said there were two boys in there
supposed to be looking after the lungers, but nobody had seen much of them the past couple of
months or so, what with all the running they were
doing. They would go out early in the morning, just
about the time it was getting light, and generally
not get back until the afternoon. He said some of
the guards were talking about them, how they had

changed; but he hadn't seen them in a while. Tacha only half listened to him. She wasn't interested in the two convicts, she was thinking about the TB cellblock and wondering what it would be like to live there. She remembered the two he was talking about; she knew them by sight. Though when she walked into the TB yard and saw them again, she did not recognize them immediately as the same two men.

R.E. Baylis got a close look at them and went to find Bob Fisher.

"She give you any trouble?" Fisher asked.

He sat at a table in the empty mess hall with a cup of coffee in front of him. The cooks were bringing in the serving pans and setting up for supper.

"No trouble once I got her there," R.E. Baylis said. "What I want to know is what the Indin and the nigger are doing?"

"I don't know anything about them and don't want to know. They're Mr. Manly's private convicts." Fisher held his cup close to his face and would lean in to sip at it.

"Haven't you seen them lately?"

"I see them go by once in a while, going out the gate."

"But you haven't been over there? You haven't seen them close?"

"Whatever he's got them doing isn't any of my business. I told him I don't want no part of it."

"You don't care what they're doing?"

"I got an inventory of equipment and stores have to be tallied before we ship out of here and that ain't very long away."

"You don't care if they made spears," R.E. Baylis said, "and they're throwing them at a board stuck in the ground?"

Bob Fisher started coughing and spilled some of his coffee down the front of his uniform.

Mr. Manly said, "Yes, I know they got spears. Made of bamboo fishing poles and brick-laying trowels stuck into one end for the point. If a man can use a trowel to work with all day, why can't he use one for exercise?"

"Because a spear is a weapon," Fisher said. "You can kill a man with it."

"Bob, you got some kind of stain there on your uniform."

"What I mean is you don't let convicts make *spears*."

"Why not, if they're for a good purpose?"

No, Bob Fisher said to himself—with R.E. Baylis standing next to him, listening to it all—this time, goddamn-it, don't let him mix you up. He said, "Mr. Manly, for some reason I seem to have trouble understanding you."

"What is it you don't understand, Bob?"

"Every time I come up here, it's like you and me are talking about two different things. I come in, I know what the rules are here and I know what I want to say. Then you begin talking and it's like we get onto something else."

"We look at a question from different points of view," Mr. Manly said. "That's all it is."

"All right, R.E. Baylis here says they got spears. I haven't been over to see for myself. We was downstairs—I don't know, something told me I should see you about it first."

"I'm glad you did."

"How long have they had 'em?"

"About two weeks. Bob, they run fourteen miles yesterday. Only stopped three times to rest."

"I don't see what that's got to do with the spears."

"Well, you said you wanted it to show in the record you're not having anything to do with this business. Isn't that right?"

"I want it to show I'm against their being taken outside."

"I haven't told you anything what's going on, have I?"

"I haven't asked neither."

"That's right. This is the first time you've mentioned those boys in over two months. You don't know what I'm teaching them, but you come in here and tell me they can't have spears."

"It's in the rules."

"It says in the rules they can't have spears for any purpose whatsoever?"

"It say a man found with a weapon is to be put under maximum security for no less than ten days."

"You mean put in the snake den."

"I sure do."

"You believe those two boys have been found with weapons?"

"When you make a spear out of a trowel, it becomes a weapon."

"But what if I was the one told them to make the spears?"

"I was afraid you might say that."

"As a matter of fact, I got them the fishing poles myself. Bought them in town."

"Bought them in town," Bob Fisher said. His

head seemed to nod a little as he stared at Mr. Manly. "This here is what I meant before about not understanding some things. I would sure like to know why you want them to have spears?"

"Bob," Mr. Manly said, "that's the only way to learn, isn't it? Ask questions." He looked up past Fisher then, at the wall clock. "Say, it's about supper time already."

"Mr. Manly, I'll wait on supper if you'll explain them spears to me."

"I'll do better than that," Mr. Manly said, "I'll show you. First though we got to get us a pitcher of ice water."

"I'll even pass on that," Fisher said. "I'm not thirsty *or* hungry."

Mr. Manly gave him a patient, understanding grin. "The ice water isn't for us, Bob."

"No sir," Fisher said. He was nodding again, very slowly, solemnly. "I should've known better, shouldn't I?"

Tacha remembered them from months before wearing leg-irons and pushing the wheelbarrows. She remembered the Negro working without a shirt on and remembered thinking the other one tall for an Indian. She had never spoken to them or watched them for a definite reason. She had probably not been closer than fifty feet to either of them. But she was aware now of the striking change in their appearance and at first it gave her a strange, tense feeling. She was afraid of them.

The guard had looked as if he was afraid of them too, and maybe that was part of the strange feeling. He didn't tell her which cell was to be hers.

He stared at the Indian and the Negro, who were across the sixty-foot yard by the wall, and then hurried away, leaving her here.

As soon as he was gone the tubercular convicts began talking to her. One of them asked if she had come to live with them. When she nodded he said she could bunk with him if she wanted. They laughed and another one said no, come on in his cell, he would show her a fine old time. She didn't like the way they stared at her. They sat in front of their cells on stools and a wooden bunk frame and looked as if they had been there a long time and seldom shaved or washed themselves.

She wasn't sure if the Indian and the Negro were watching her. The Indian was holding something that looked like a fishing pole. The Negro was standing by an upright board that was as tall as he was and seemed to be nailed to a post. Another of the poles was sticking out of the board. Neither of them was wearing a shirt; that was the first thing she noticed about them from across the yard.

They came over when she turned to look at the cells and one of the tubercular convicts told her again to come on, put her blanket and stuff in with his. Now, when she looked around, not knowing what to do, she saw them approaching.

She saw the Indian's hair, how long it was, covering his ears, and the striped red and black cloth he wore as a headband. She saw the Negro's mustache that curved around his mouth into a short beard and the cuts on his face, like knife scars, that slanted down from both of his cheekbones. This was when she was afraid of them, as they walked up to her.

"The cell on the end," Raymond said. "Why don't you take that one?"

She made herself hold his gaze. "Who else is in there, you?"

"Nobody else."

Harold said, "You got the TB?"

"I don't have it yet."

"You do something to Frank Shelby?"

"Maybe I did," she said, "I don't know."

"If you don't have the TB," Harold said, "you did something to somebody."

She began to feel less afraid already, talking to them, and yet she knew there was something different about their faces and the way they looked at her. "I think the turnkey, Mr. Fisher, did it," Tacha said, "so I wouldn't see him going in with Norma."

"I guess there are all kinds of things going on," Harold said. "They put you in here, it's not so bad. It was cold at night when we first come, colder than the big cellblock, but now it's all right." He glanced toward the tubercular convicts. "Don't worry about the scarecrows. They won't hurt you."

"They lock everybody in at night," Raymond said. "During the day one of them tries something, you can run."

That was a strange thing too: being afraid of them at first because of the way they looked, then hearing them say not to worry and feeling at ease with them, believing them.

Raymond said, "We fixed up that cell for you. It's like a new one."

She was inside unrolling her bedding when the guard returned with the superintendent and the turnkey, Mr. Fisher. She heard one of them say,

"Harold, come out here," and she looked up to see them through the open doorway: the little man in the dark suit and two in guard uniforms, one of them, R.E. Baylis, holding a dented tin pitcher. The Indian was still in the yard, not far from them, but she didn't see the Negro. The superintendent was looking toward her cell now, squinting into the dim interior.

Mr. Manly wanted to keep an eye on Bob Fisher and watch his reactions, but seeing the woman distracted him.

"Who's that in there, Norma Davis?"

"The other one," Fisher said, "the Mexican."

"I didn't see any report on her being sick."

"She's working here. Your two boys run off, there's nobody to fetch things for the lungers."

Mr. Manly didn't like to look at the tubercular convicts; they gave him a creepy feeling, the way they sat there all day like lizards and never seemed to move. He gave them a glance and called again, "Harold, come on out here."

The Negro was buttoning a prison shirt as he appeared in the doorway. "You want me, captain?"

"Come over here, will you?"

Mr. Manly was watching Fisher now. The man's flat open-eyed expression tickled him: old Bob Fisher staring at Harold, then looking over at Raymond, then back at Harold again, trying to figure out the change that had come over them. The change was something more than just their appearance. It was something Mr. Manly felt, and he was pretty sure now Bob Fisher was feeling it too.

"What's the matter, Bob, ain't you ever seen an Apache or a Zulu before?"

"I seen Apaches."

"Then what're you staring at?"

Fisher looked over at Harold again. "What're them cuts on his face?"

"Tell him, Harold."

"They tribal marks, captain."

Fisher said, "What the hell tribe's a field nigger belong to?"

Harold touched his face, feeling the welts of scar tissue that were not yet completely healed. He said, "My tribe, captain."

"He cut his own face like that?"

Fisher kept staring at the Negro as Mr. Manly said, "He saw it in an Africa book I got—picture of a native with these marks like tattoos on his face. I didn't tell him to do it, you understand. He just figured it would be all right, I guess. Isn't that so, Harold?"

"Yes-suh, captain."

"Same with Raymond. He figured if he's a full-blooded Apache Indian then he should let his hair grow and wear one of them bands."

"We come over here to look at spears," Fisher said.

Mr. Manly frowned, shaking his head. "Don't you see the connection yet? A spear is part of a warrior's get-up, like a tool is to a working man. Listen, I told you, didn't I, these boys can run fifteen miles in a day now and only stop a couple of times to rest."

"I thought it was fourteen miles," Fisher said.

"Fourteen, fifteen—here's the thing. They can run that far *and* go from morning to supper time without a drink of water, any time they want."

"A man will do that in the snake den if I make him." Bob Fisher wasn't backing off this time.

Mr. Manly wasn't letting go. "Inside," he said, "is different than running out in the hot sun. Listen, they each pour theirselves a cup of water in the morning and you know what they do? They see who can go all day without taking a drink or more than a couple of sips." He held his hand out to R.E. Baylis and said, "Let me have the pitcher." Then he looked at Raymond and Harold again. "Which of you won today?"

"I did," Raymond said.

"Let's see your cups."

Raymond went into his cell and was back in a moment with a tin cup in each hand. "He drank his. See, I got some left."

"Then you get the pitcher of ice water," Mr. Manly said. "And, Harold, you get to watch him drink it."

Raymond raised the pitcher and drank out of the side of it, not taking very much before lowering it again and holding it in front of him.

"See that?" Mr. Manly said. "He knows better than to gulp it down. One day Raymond wins, the next day Harold gets the ice water. I mean they can both do it any time they want."

"I would sure like to see them spears," Fisher said.

Mr. Manly asked Harold where they were and he said, "Over yonder by the wall, captain."

Tacha watched them cross the yard. The Negro waited for the Indian to put the pitcher on the ground and she noticed they gave each other a look as they fell in behind the little man in the dark suit and the two guards. They were over by the wall a few minutes talking while Mr. Fisher hefted one of the bamboo spears and felt the point of it with his finger. Then the superintendent took the spear from him and gave it to the Indian. The Negro picked up the other spear from against the wall and they came back this way, toward the cells, at least a dozen paces before turning around. Beyond them, the group moved away from the upright board. The Indian and the Negro faced the target for a moment, then stepped back several more feet, noticing Tacha now in the doorway of her cell.

She said, "You're going to hit that, way down there?"

"Not today," Raymond answered.

Everyone in the yard was watching them now. They raised the spears shoulder high, took aim with their outstretched left arms pointing, and threw them hard in a low arc, almost at the same moment. Both spears fell short and skidded along the ground past the board to stop at the base of the wall.

Raymond and Harold waited. In the group across the yard Mr. Manly seemed to be doing the talking, gesturing with his hands. He was facing Bob Fisher and did not look over this way. After a few minutes they left the yard, and now Mr. Manly, as he went through the gate last, looked over and waved.

"Well," Raymond said—he stooped to pick up the tin pitcher—"who wants some ice water?"

Within a few days Tacha realized that, since moving to the TB cellblock, she felt better—whether it made sense or not. Maybe part of the feeling was being outside most of the day and not bent over a sewing machine listening to Norma or trying to talk to the old man. Already that seemed like a long time ago. She was happier now. She even enjoyed being with the tubercular convicts and didn't mind the way they talked to her sometimes, saying she was a pretty good nurse though they would sure rather have her be something else. They needed to talk like men so she smiled and didn't take anything they said as an offense.

In the afternoon the Apache and the Zulu would come in through the gate, walking slowly, carrying their shirts. One of the tubercular convicts would yell over, asking how far they had run and one or the other would tell them twelve, fifteen, sixteen miles. They would drink the water in their cups. One of the convicts would fill the cups again from the bucket they kept in the shade. After drinking the second cup they would decide who the winner would be that day and pour just a little more water into his cup, leaving the other one empty. The TB convicts got a kick out of this and always laughed. Every day it was the same. They drank the water and then went into the cell to lie on their bunks. In less than an hour the TB convicts would be yelling for them to come out and start throwing their spears. They would get out their money or rolled cigarettes when the Apache and the Zulu appeared and, after letting them warm up a few minutes, at least two of the convicts would bet on every throw. Later on, after the work crews were in for the day, there would be convicts over from the main yard watching through the gate. None of them ever came into the TB yard. They were betting too and would yell at the Apache and the Zulu—calling them by those names—to hit the board, cut the son of a bitch dead center. Frank Shelby appeared at the gate only once. After that the convicts had to pay to watch and make bets. Soonzy, Junior, and Joe Dean were at the grillwork every day during free time.

Harold Jackson, the Zulu, walked over to the gate one time. He said, "How come we do all the work, you make all the money?"

Junior told him to get back over there and start throwing his goddamn spear or whatever it was.

Harold let the convicts get a good look at his face scars before he walked away. After the next throw, when he and Raymond were pulling their spears out of the board, Harold said, "Somebody always telling you what to do, huh?"

"Every place you go," Raymond said.

They were good with the spears. Though when the convicts from the outside yard were at the gate watching they never threw from farther than thirty-five feet away, or tried to place the spears in a particular part of the board. If they wanted to, they could hit the board high or low at the same time.

It was Tacha who noticed their work shoes coming apart from the running and made moccasins for them, sewing them by hand—calf-high Apache moccasins she fashioned out of old leather water bags and feed sacks.

And it was Tacha who told Raymond he should put war paint on his face. He wasn't scary enough looking.

"Where do you get war paint?" Raymond asked her. "At the store?"

"I think from berries."

"Well, I don't see no berries around here."

The next day she got iodine and a can of white enamel from the sick ward and, after supper, sat Raymond on a stool and painted a white streak across the bridge of his nose from cheekbone to cheekbone, and orange-red iodine stripes along the jawline to his chin.

Harold Jackson liked it, so Tacha painted a white stripe across his forehead and another one down between his eyes to the tip of his nose.

"Hey, we waryers now," Raymond said.

They looked at themselves in Tacha's hand mirror and both of them grinned. They were pretty mean-looking boys. Harold said, "Lady, what else do these waryers put on?"

Tacha said she guessed anything they wanted. She opened a little sack and gave Raymond two strands of turquoise beads, a string for around his neck and another string, doubled, for around his right arm, up high.

She asked Harold if he wanted a ring for his nose. He said no, thank you, lady, but remembered Mr. Manly talking about the Zulus putting chunks of sugar cane in their ear lobes and he let Tacha pierce one of his ears and attach a single gold earring. It looked good with the tribal scars and the mustache that curved into a short beard. "All I need me is a lion to spear," Harold said. He was Harold Jackson the Zulu, and he could feel it without looking in the mirror.

He didn't talk to Raymond about the feeling because he knew Raymond, in a way of his own, Raymond the Apache, had the same feeling. In front of the convicts who watched them throw spears or in front of the two guards who took them out to run, Harold could look at Raymond, their eyes would meet for a moment and each knew what the other was thinking. They didn't talk very much, even to each other. They walked slowly and seemed to expend no extra effort in their movements. They knew they could do something no other men in the prison could do—they could run all day and go without water—and it was part of the good feeling.

They began to put fresh paint on their faces almost every day, in the afternoon before they threw the spears.

⟿ 10 ⟿

The evening Junior and Joe Dean came for them they were sitting out in front of the cells with Tacha. It was after supper, just beginning to get dark. For a little while Tacha had been pretending to tell them their fortunes, using an old deck of cards and turning them up one at a time in the fading light. She told Harold she saw him sleeping under a banana tree with a big smile on his face. Sure, Cuba, Harold said. With the next card she saw him killing a lion with his spear and Harold was saying they didn't have no lions in Cuba, when Junior came up to them. Joe Dean stood over a little way with his hands in his pockets, watching.

"Frank wants to see you," Junior said. "Both of you." He took time to look at Tacha while he waited for them to get up. When neither of them moved he said, "You hear me? Frank wants you."

"What's he want?" Harold said.

"He's going to want me to kick your ass you don't get moving."

Raymond looked at Harold, and Harold looked at Raymond. Finally they got up and followed them across the yard, though they moved so god-

damn slow Worley Lewis, Jr. had to keep waiting
for them with his hands on his hips, telling them
to come on, *move*. They looked back once and saw
Joe Dean still over by the cells. He seemed to be
waiting for them to leave.

Soonzy was in the passageway of the main cellblock, standing in the light that was coming from
No. 14. He motioned them inside.

They went into the cell, then stopped short.
Frank Shelby was sitting on his throne reading a
newspaper, hunched over before his own shadow
on the back wall. He didn't look up; he made them
wait several minutes before he finally rose, pulled
up his pants and buckled his belt. Junior and
Soonzy crowded the doorway behind them.

"Come closer to the light," Shelby said. He
waited for them to move into the space between
the bunks, to where the electric overhead light,
with its tin shield, was almost directly above them.

"I want to ask you two something. I want to
know how come you got your faces painted up like
that."

They kept looking at him, but neither of them
spoke.

"You going to tell me?"

"I don't know," Raymond said. "I guess it's hard
to explain."

"Did anybody tell you to put it on?"

"No, we done it ourselves."

"Has this Mr. Manly seen it?"

"Yeah, but he didn't say nothing."

"You just figured it would be a good idea, uh?"

"I don't know," Raymond said. "We just done
it, I guess."

"You want to look like a couple of circus clowns, is that it?"

"No, we didn't think of that."

"Maybe you want to look like a wild Indin," Shelby said, "and him, he wants to look like some kind of boogey-man native. Maybe that's it."

Raymond shrugged. "Maybe something like that. It's hard to explain."

"What does Mr. Jackson say about it?"

"If you know why we put it on," Harold said, "what are you asking us for?"

"Because it bothers me," Shelby answered. "I can't believe anybody would want to look like a nigger native. Even a nigger. Same as I can't believe anybody would want to look like a Wild West Show Indin 'less he was paid to do it. Somebody paying you, Raymond?"

"Nobody's paying us."

"See, Raymond, what bothers me—how can we learn people like you to act like white men if you're going to play you're savages? You see what I mean? You want to move back in this cellblock, but who do you think would want to live with you?"

"We're not white men," Raymond said.

"Jesus Christ, I know that. I'm saying if you want to live with white men then you got to try to act like white men. You start playing you're an Apache and a goddamn Zulu or something, that's the same as saying you don't want to be a white man, and that's what bothers me something awful, when I see that going on."

There was a little space of silence before Harold said, "What do you want us to do?"

"We'll do it," Shelby said. "We're going to re-mind you how you're supposed to act."

Soonzy took Harold from behind with a fist in his hair and a forearm around his neck. He dragged Harold backward and as Raymond turned, Junior stepped in and hit Raymond with a belt wrapped around his fist. He had to hit Raymond again before he could get a good hold on him and pull him out of the cell. Joe Dean and a half-dozen convicts were waiting in the passageway. They got Raymond and Harold down on their backs on the cement. They sat on their legs and a convict stood on each of their outstretched hands and arms while another man got down and pulled their hair tight to keep them from moving their heads. Then Joe Dean took a brush and the can of enamel Tacha had got from the sick ward and painted both of their faces pure white.

When R.E. Baylis came through to lock up, Shelby told him to look at the goddamn mess out there, white paint all over the cement and dirty words painted on the wall. He said that nigger and his red nigger friend sneaked over and started messing up the place, but they caught the two and painted them as a lesson. Shelby said to R.E. Baylis goddamn-it, why didn't he throw them in the snake den so they would quit bothering people. R.E. Baylis said he would tell Bob Fisher.

The next morning after breakfast, Shelby came out of the mess hall frowning in the sunlight and looking over the work details forming in the yard. He was walking toward the supply group when somebody called his name from behind. Bob Fisher was standing by the mess hall door: grim-looking tough old son of a bitch in his gray sack guard uniform. Shelby sure didn't want to, but he walked back to where the turnkey was standing.

"They don't know how to write even their names," Fisher said.

"Well"—Shelby took a moment to think—"maybe they got the paint for somebody else do to it."

"Joe Dean got the paint."

"Joe did that?"

"Him and Soonzy and Junior are going to clean it up before they go to work."

"Well, if they did it—"

"You're going to help them."

"Me? I'm on the supply detail. You know that."

"Or you can go with the quarry gang," Fisher said. "It don't make any difference to me."

"Quarry gang?" Shelby grinned to show Fisher he thought he was kidding. "I don't believe I ever done that kind of work."

"You'll do it if I say so."

"Listen, just because we painted those two boys up. We were teaching them a lesson, that's all. Christ, they go around here thinking they're something the way they fixed theirselves up—somebody had to teach them."

"I do the teaching here," Fisher said. "I'm teaching that to you right now."

Dumb, stone-face guard son of a bitch. Shelby said, "Well," half-turning to look off thoughtfully toward the work groups waiting in the yard. "I hope those people don't get sore about this. You know how it is, how they listen to me and trust me. If they figure I'm getting treated unfair, they're liable to sit right down and not move from the yard, every one of them."

"If you believe that," Fisher said, "you better tell them I'll shoot the first man that sits down, and if they all sit down at once I'll shoot you."

Shelby waited. He didn't look at Bob Fisher; he kept his gaze on the convicts. After a moment he said, "You're kneeling on me for a reason, aren't you? You're waiting to see me make a terrible mistake."

"I believe you've already made it," Fisher said. He turned and went into the mess hall.

Scraping paint off cement was better than working in the quarry. It was hot in the passageway, but there was no sun beating down on them and they weren't breathing chalk dust. Shelby sat in his cell and let Junior, Soonzy, and Joe Dean do the work, until Bob Fisher came by. Fisher didn't say anything; he looked in at him and Shelby came out and picked up a trowel and started scraping. When Fisher was gone, Shelby sat back on his heels and said, "I'm going to bust me a guard, I'll tell you, if that man's anywhere near us when we leave."

The scraping stopped as he spoke, as Junior and Soonzy and Joe Dean waited to hear whatever he had to say.

"There is something bothering him," Shelby said. "He wants to nail me down. He could do it any time he feels like it, couldn't he? He could put me in the quarry or the snake den—that man could chain me to the wall. But he's waiting on something."

Joe Dean said, "Waiting on what?"

"I don't know. Unless he's telling me he knows what's going on. He could be saying, 'I got my eye on you, buddy. I'm waiting for you to make the wrong move.'"

"What could he know?" Joe Dean said. "We don't know anything ourselves."

"He could know we're thinking about it."

"He could be guessing."

"I mean," Shelby said, "he could *know*. Norma could have told him. She's the only other person who could."

Junior was frowning. "What would Norma want to tell him for?"

"Jesus Christ," Shelby said, "because she's Norma. She don't need a reason, she does what she feels like doing. Listen, she needs money she gets herself a forty-four and pours liquor into some crazy boy and they try and rob a goddamn *bank*. She's seeing Bob Fisher, and she's the only one could have told him anything."

"I say he's guessing," Joe Dean said. "The time's coming to move all these convicts, he's nervous at the thought of it, and starts guessing we're up to something."

"That could be right," Shelby said. "But the only way I can find out for sure is to talk to Norma." He was silent a moment. "I don't know. With old Bob watching every move I got to stay clear of the tailor shop."

"Why don't we bring her over here?" Junior said. "Right after supper everybody's in the yard. Shoot, we can get her in here, anywhere you want, no trouble."

"Hey, boy," Shelby grinned, "now you're talking."

Jesus, yes, what was he worrying about that old man turnkey for? He had to watch that and never worry out loud or raise his voice or lose his temper. He had to watch when little pissy-ant started to bother him. The Indin and the nigger had bothered him. It wasn't even important; but goddamn-it, it had bothered him and he had done something about it. See—but because of it Bob Fisher had come down on him and this was not anytime to get Bob Fisher nervous and watchful. Never trust a nervous person unless you've got a gun on him. That was a rule. And when you've got the gun on him shoot him or hit him with it, quick, but don't let him start crying and begging for his life and spilling the goddamn payroll all over the floor—the way it had happened in the paymaster's office at the Cornelia Mine near Ajo. They would have been out of there before the security guards arrived if he hadn't spilled the money. The paymaster would be alive if he hadn't spilled the money, and they wouldn't be in Yuma. There was such a thing as bad luck. Anything could happen during a holdup. But there had been five payroll and bank robberies before the Cornelia Mine job where no one had spilled the money or reached for a gun or walked in unexpectedly. They had been successful because they had kept calm and in control, and that was the way they had to do it again, to get out of here.

It had surely bothered him though—the way the Indin and the nigger had painted their faces.

Junior pushed through the mess-hall door behind Norma as she went out, and told her to go visit Tacha. That's how easy it was. When Norma got to the TB yard Joe Dean, standing by the gate, nodded toward the first cell. She saw Tacha sitting over a ways with the Indian and the Negro, and noticed there was something strange about them: they looked sick, with a gray pallor to their skin, even the Negro. Norma looked at Joe Dean and again he nodded toward the first cell.

Soonzy stepped out and walked past her as she approached the doorway. Shelby was waiting inside, standing with an arm on the upper bunk. He didn't grin or reach for her, he said, "How're you getting along with your boyfriend?"

"He still hasn't told me anything, if that's what you mean."

"I'm more interested in what you might have told him."

Norma smiled and seemed to relax. "You know, as I walked in here I thought you were a little tense about something."

"You haven't answered my question."

"What is it I might have told him?"

"Come on, Norma."

"I mean what's there to tell him? You don't have any plan you've told me about."

"I don't know," Shelby said, "it looks to me like you got your own plan."

"I ask him. Every time he comes in I bring it up. 'Honey, when are we going to get out of this awful place?' But he won't tell me anything."

"You were pretty sure one time you could squeeze it out of him."

"I don't believe he knows any more than we do."

"I'll tell you what," Shelby said. "I'll give you three more days to find out. You don't know anything by then, I don't see any reason to take you with us."

Norma took her time. She kept her eyes on Shelby, holding him and waiting a little, then stepped in close so that she was almost touching him with her body. She waited again before saying, quietly, "What're you being so mean for?"

Shelby said, "Man." He said, "Come on, Norma, if I want to put you on the bunk I'll put you on the bunk. Don't give me no sweetheart talk, all right? I want you to tell me if you're working something with that old man. Now hold on—I want you to keep looking right at me and tell me to my face yes or no—yes, 'I have told him,' or no, 'I have not told him.'"

Norma put on a frown now that brought her eyebrows together and gave her a nice hurt look.

"Frank, what do you want me to tell you?" She spaced the words to show how honest and truthful she was being, knowing that her upturned, frowning face was pretty nice and that her breasts were about an inch away from the upcurve of his belly.

She looked good all right, and if he put her down on the bunk she'd be something. But Frank Shelby was looking at a train and keeping calm, keeping his voice down, and he said, "Norma, if you don't find out anything in three days you don't leave this place."

It was Sunday, Visiting Day, that Mr. Manly decided he would make an announcement. He called Bob Fisher into his office to tell him, then thought better of it—Fisher would only object and argue—so he began talking about Raymond and Harold instead of his announcement.

"I'll tell you," Mr. Manly said, "I'm not so much interested in who did it as I am in *why* they did it. They got paint in their eyes, in their nose. They had to wash theirselves in gasoline and then they didn't get it all off."

"Well, there's no way of finding out now," Fisher said. "You ask them, there isn't anybody knows a thing."

"The men who did it know."

"Well, sure, the ones that did it."

"I'd like to know what a man thinks like would paint another person."

"They were painting theirselves before."

"I believe you see the difference, Bob."

"These are convicts," Fisher said. "They get mean they don't need a reason. It's the way they are."

"I'm thinking I better talk to them."

"But we don't know who done it."

"I mean talk to all of them. I want to talk to them about something else any way."

"About what?"

"Maybe I can make the person who did it come forward and admit it."

"Mister, if you believe that you don't know anything a-tall about convicts. You talked to Raymond and Harold, didn't you?"

"Yes, I did."

"And they won't even tell you who done it, will they?"

"I can't understand that."

"Because they're convicts. They know if they ever told you they'd get their heads beat against a cell wall. This is between them and the other convicts. If the convicts don't want them to paint up like savages then I believe we should stay out of it and let them settle it theirselves."

"But they've got rights—the two boys. What about them?"

"I don't know. I'm not talking about justice," Fisher said. "I'm talking about running a prison. If the convicts want these two to act a certain way or not act a certain way, we should keep out of it. It keeps them quiet and it don't cost us a cent. When you push against the whole convict body it had better be important and you had better be ready to shoot and kill people if they push back."

"I told them they could put on their paint if they wanted."

"Well, that's up to you," Fisher said. "Or it's up to them. I notice they been keeping their faces clean."

When Mr. Manly didn't speak right away, Fisher said, "If it's all right with you I want to get downstairs and keep an eye on things. It's Visiting Day."

Mr. Manly looked up. "That's right, it is. You know, I didn't tell you I been wanting to make an announcement. I believe I'll do it right now— sure, while some of them have their relatives here visiting." Mr. Manly's expression was bright and cheerful, as if he thought this was sure a swell idea.

"I don't know what you're doing," Shelby said, "but so far it isn't worth a rat's ass, is it?" He sat facing his brother, Virgil, who was leaning in against the table and looking directly at Frank to show he was sincere and doing everything he could to find out when the goddamn train was leaving. There were convicts and their visitors all the way down the line of tables that divided the mess hall: hunched over talking, filling the room with a low hum of voices.

"It ain't like looking up a schedule," Virgil said. "I believe this would be a special train, two or three cars probably. All right, I ask a lot of questions over at the railroad yard they begin wondering who I am, and somebody says hey, that's Virgil Shelby. His brother's up on the hill."

"That's Virgil Shelby," Frank said. "Jesus, do you believe people know who you are? You could be a mine engineer. You could be interested in hauling in equipment and you ask how they handle special trains. 'You ever put on a special run? You do? Like what kind?' Jesus, I mean you got to use your head and think for a change."

"Frank, I'm ready. I don't need to know more than a day ahead when you leave. I got me some good boys and, I'm telling you, we're going to *do* it."

"You're going to do what?"

"Get you off that train."

"How?"

"Stop it if we have to."

"How, Virgil?"

"Dynamite the track."

"Then what?"

"Then climb aboard."

"With the guards shooting at you?"

"You got to be doing something too," Virgil said. "Inside the train."

"I'm doing something right now. I'm seeing you don't know what you're talking about. And unless we know when the train leaves and where it stops, we're not going to be able to work out a plan. Do you see that, Virgil?"

"The train goes to Florence. We know that."

"Do we know if it stops anywhere? If it stops, Virgil, wouldn't that be the place to get on?"

"If it stops."

"That's right. That's what you got to find out. Because how are you going to know where to wait and when to wait if you don't know when the train's leaving here? Virgil, are you listening to me?"

His brother was looking past him at something. Shelby glanced over his shoulder. He turned then and kept looking as Mr. Manly, with Bob Fisher on the stairs at the far end of the mess hall, said, "May I have your attention a moment, please?"

Mr. Manly waited until the hum of voices trailed off and he saw the faces down the line of tables looking toward him: upturned, solemn faces, like people in church waiting for the sermon. Mr. Manly grinned. He always liked to open with a light touch.

He said, "I'm not going to make a speech, if any of you are worried about that. I just want to make a brief announcement while your relatives and loved ones are here. It will save the boys writing to tell you and I know some of them don't write as often as they should. By the way, I'm Everett Manly, the acting superintendent here in Mr. Rynning's absence." He paused to clear his throat.

"Now then—I am very pleased to announce that this will be the last Visiting Day at Yuma Territorial Prison. A week from tomorrow the first group of men will leave on the Southern Pacific for the new penitentiary at Florence, a fine new place I think you all are going to be very pleased with. Now you won't be able to tell your relatives or loved ones what day exactly you'll be leaving, but I promise you in three weeks everybody will be out of here and this place will open its doors forever and become a page in history. That's about all I can tell you right now for the present. However, if any of you have questions I will be glad to try and answer them."

Frank Shelby kept looking at the little man on the stairway. He said to himself, It's a trick. But the longer he stared at him—the little fellow standing up there waiting for questions—he knew Mr. Manly was telling the truth.

Virgil said, "Well, I guess that answers the question, doesn't it?"

Shelby didn't look at his brother. He was afraid he might lose his temper and hit Virgil in the mouth.

⇒ 11 ⇒

For three sacks of Mail Pouch, R.E. Baylis told Shelby the convicts would be sent out in groups of about forty at a time, going over every other day, it looked like, on the regular morning run.

R.E. Baylis even got Shelby a Southern Pacific schedule. Leave Yuma at 6:15 A.M. Pass through Sentinel at 8:56; no stop unless they needed coal or water. They'd stop at Gila at 9:51, where they'd be fed on the train; no one allowed off. They'd arrive in Phoenix at 2:40 P.M., switch the cars over to a Phoenix & Eastern train and arrive at Florence about 5:30 P.M. Bob Fisher planned to make the first run and the last one, the first one to see what the trip was like and the last one so he could lock up and officially hand over the keys.

Shelby asked R.E. Baylis if he would put him and his friends down for the first run, because they were sure anxious to get out of here. R.E. Baylis said he didn't know if it could be done, but maybe he could try to arrange it. Shelby gave him fifty dollars to try as hard as he could.

The guard told Bob Fisher about Shelby's request, since Fisher would see the list anyway. Why the first train? Fisher wanted to know. What was the difference? R.E. Baylis asked. All the trains were going to the penitentiary. Fisher put himself in Shelby's place and thought about it a while. Maybe Shelby was anxious to leave, that could be a fact. But it wasn't the reason he wanted to be on the first train. It was so he would know exactly which train he'd be on, so he could tell somebody outside.

Fisher said all right, tell him he could go on the first train. But then, when the time came, they'd pull Shelby out of line and hold him for the last train. "I want him riding with me," Fisher said, "but not before I look over the route."

It bothered R.E. Baylis because Shelby had always treated him square and given him tobacco and things. He stopped by Shelby's cell that evening and said Lord, he could sure use that fifty dollars, but he would give it back. Bob Fisher was making them go on the last train. Shelby looked pretty disappointed. By God, he was big about it though. He let R.E. Baylis keep the fifty dollars anyway.

The next morning when he saw Junior and Soonzy and Joe Dean, Shelby grinned and said, "Boys, always trust a son of a bitch to be a son of a bitch. We're taking the last train."

All he had to do now was to get a letter of instructions to Virgil at the railroad hotel in Yuma. For a couple more sacks of Mail Pouch R.E. Baylis would probably deliver it personally.

Virgil Shelby and his three men arrived at Stout's Hotel in Gila on a Wednesday afternoon. Mr. Stout and a couple of Southern Pacific division men in the lobby got a kick out of these dudes who said they were heading south into the Saucedas to do some prospecting. All they had were bedrolls and rifles and a pack mule loaded with suitcases. The dudes were as serious about it though as they were ignorant. They bought four remount horses at the livery and two 50-pound cases of No. 1 dynamite at Tom Child's trading store, and on Thursday morning they rode out of Gila. They rode south two miles before turning west and doubling back to follow the train tracks.

They arrived in sight of the Southern Pacific water stop at Sentinel that evening and from a grove of trees studied the wooden buildings and frame structure that stood silently against a dark line of palo verdes. A water tank, a coaling shed, a section house and a little one-room station with a light showing in the window, that's all there was here.

As soon as Virgil saw the place he knew Frank was right again. Sometimes it made him mad when he sounded dumb in front of his brother. He had finished the sixth grade and Frank had gone on to the seventh or eighth. Maybe when Frank was looking at him, waiting, he would say the wrong thing or sound dumb; but Jesus, he had gone into places with a gun and put the gun in a man's face and got what he wanted. Frank didn't have to worry about him going in with a gun. He had not found out the important facts of the matter talking to the railroad people. He had not thought up the plan in all the time he'd had to do it. But he could sure do what Frank said in his letter. He had three good boys who would go with him for two hundred and fifty dollars each and bring the guns and know how to use them. These boys drank too much and got in fights, but they were the captains for this kind of work. Try and pick them. Try and get three fellows who had the nerve to stop a prison train and take off the people you wanted and do it right, without a lot of shooting and getting nervous and running off into the desert and hiding in a cave. He wished he had more like them, but these three said they could do the job and would put their guns on anybody for two hundred and fifty dollars.

He had a man named Howard Crowder who had worked for railroad lines in both the United States and Mexico, before he turned to holding up trains and spent ten years in Yuma.

He had an old hand named Dancey who had ridden with him and Frank before, and had been with them at the Cornelia Mine payroll robbery and had got away.

He had a third one named Billy Santos who had smuggled across the border whatever could be carried and was worth anything and knew all the trails and water holes south of here.

Five o'clock the next morning it still looked good and still looked easy as they walked into the little station at Sentinel with their suitcases and asked the S.P. man when the next eastbound train was coming through.

The S.P. man said 8:56 this morning, but that train was not due to stop on account of it was carrying convicts some place.

Virgil asked him if there was anybody over in the section house. The S.P. man said no, he was alone. A crew had gone out on the 8:45 to Gila the night before and another crew was coming from Yuma sometime today.

Virgil looked over at Billy Santos. Billy went outside. Howard Crowder and Dancey remained sitting on the bench. The suitcases and bedrolls and rifles and two cases of dynamite were on the floor by them. No, the S.P. man behind the counter said, they couldn't take the 8:56, though they could get on the 8:48 this evening if they wanted to hang around all day. But what will you do with your horses? he said then. You rode in here, didn't you?

Virgil was at the counter now. He nodded to the telegrapher's key on the desk behind the S.P. man and said, "I hope you can work that thing, mister."

The S.P. man said, "Sure, I can work it. Else I wouldn't be here."

"That's good," Virgil said. "It's better if they hear a touch they are used to hearing."

The S.P. man gave Virgil a funny look, then let his gaze shift over to the two men on the bench with all the gear in front of them. They looked back at him; they didn't move or say anything. The S.P. man was wondering if he should send a message to the division office at Gila; tell them there were three dudes hanging around here with rifles and dynamite and ask if they had been seen in Gila the day before. He could probably get away with it. How would these people know what he was saying? Just then the Mexican-looking one came back in, his eyes on the one standing by the counter, and shook his head.

Virgil said, "You all might as well get dressed."

The S.P. man watched them open the suitcases and take out gray and white convict suits. He watched them pull the pants and coats on over the clothes they were wearing and shove revolvers down into the pants and button the coats. One of them brought a double-barrel shotgun out of a suitcase in two pieces and sat down to fit the stock to the barrels. Watching them, the S.P. man said to Virgil Shelby, "Hey, what's going on? What is this?"

"This is how you stop a train," Virgil told him. "These are prisoners that escaped off the train that come through the day before yesterday."

"Nobody escaped," the S.P. man said.

Virgil nodded up and down. "Yes, they did, mister, and I'm the deputy sheriff of Maricopa County who's going to put them back on the train for Florence."

"If you're a deputy of this county," the S.P. man said, "then you're a new one."

"All right," Virgil said, "I'm a new one."

"If you're one at all."

Virgil pulled a .44 revolver from inside his coat and pointed it in the S.P. man's face. He said, "All you got to do is telegraph the Yuma depot at exactly six A.M. with a message for the prison superintendent, Mr. Everett Manly. You're going to say three escaped convicts are being held here at Sentinel and you request the train to stop and take them aboard. You also request an immediate answer and, mister," Virgil said, "I don't want you to send it one word different than I tell it to you. You understand?"

The S.P. man nodded. "I understand, but it ain't going to work. If three were missing at the head-count when they got to Florence, they would have already told Yuma about it."

"That's a fact," Virgil said. "That's why we had somebody wire the prison from Phoenix Wednesday night and report three missing." Virgil looked around then and said, "Howard?"

The one named Howard Crowder had a silver dollar in his hand. He began tapping the coin rapidly on the wooden bench next to him in sharp longs and shorts that were loud in the closed room. Virgil watched the expression on the S.P. man's face, the mouth come open a little.

"You understand that too?" Virgil asked him.

The S.P. man nodded.

"What did he say?"

"He said, 'Send correct message or you are a dead man.'"

"I'm happy you understand it," Virgil said.

The S.P. man watched the one named Dancey pry open a wooden case that was marked *High Explosives—Dangerous* and take out a paraffin-coated packet of dynamite sticks. He watched Dancey get out a coil of copper wire and detonator caps and work the wire gently into the open end of the cap and then crimp the end closed with his teeth. The Mexican-looking one was taking a box plunger out of a canvas bag. The S.P. man said to himself, My God, somebody is going to get killed and I am going to see it.

At six A.M. he sent the message to the depot at Yuma, where they would then be loading the convicts onto the train.

The Southern Pacific equipment that left Yuma that Friday morning was made up of a 4-4-0 locomotive, a baggage car, two day coaches for regular pas-

sengers (though only eleven people were aboard),
another baggage car, and an old wooden coach
from the Cannanea-Rio Yaqui-El Pacifico line. The
last twenty-seven convicts to leave the prison were
locked inside this coach along with Bob Fisher and
three armed guards. Behind, bringing up the rear,
was a caboose that carried Mr. Manly and three
more guards.

Bob Fisher had personally made up the list of
prisoners for this last run to Florence: only twenty-
seven, including Frank Shelby and his bunch. Most
of the others were short-term prisoners and trust-
ies who wouldn't be expected to make trouble.
A small, semi-harmless group which, Bob Fisher
believed, would make it easy for him to keep an
eye on Shelby. Also aboard were the TB convicts,
the two women and Harold Jackson and Raymond
San Carlos.

Harold and Raymond were near the rear of the
coach. The only ones behind them were Bob Fisher
and the guards. Ahead of them were the TB convicts, then two rows of empty seats, then the rest of
the prisoners scattered along both sides of the aisle
in the back-to-back straw seats. The two women
were in the front of the coach. The doors at both
ends were padlocked. The windows were glass, but
they were not made to open.

Before the train was five minutes out of Yuma
every convict in the coach knew they were going
to stop in Sentinel to pick up three men who had
escaped on Wednesday and had been recaptured
the next day. There was a lot of talk about who the
three were.

Bob Fisher didn't say a word. He sat patiently

waiting for the train to reach Sentinel, thinking about the message they had received Wednesday evening: *Three convicts missing on arrival Phoenix. Local and county authorities alerted.* Signed, *Sheriff, Maricopa County.* What bothered Fisher, there had been no information sent from Florence, nothing from Mr. Rynning, no further word from anybody until the wire was received at the depot this morning. Mr. Manly had wired back they would stop for the prisoners and Bob Fisher had not said a word to anybody since. Something wasn't right and he had to think it through.

About 7:30 A.M., halfway to Sentinel, Fisher said to the guard sitting next to him, "Put your gun on Frank Shelby and don't move it till we get to Florence."

Harold Jackson, next to the window, looked out at the flat desert country that stretched to distant dark mounds, mountains that would take a day to reach on foot, maybe half a day if a man was to run. But a mountain was nothing to run to. There was nothing out there but sky and rocks and desert growth that looked as if it would never die, but offered a man no hope of life. It was the same land he had looked at a few months before, going in the other direction, sitting in the same upright straw seat handcuffed to a sheriff's man. The Indian sitting next to him now nudged his arm and Harold looked up.

The Davis woman was coming down the aisle from the front of the coach. She passed them and a moment later Harold heard the door to the toilet open and close. Looking out the window again, Harold said, "What's out there, that way?"

"Mexico," Raymond answered. "Across the desert and the mountain, and if you can find water, Mexico."

"You know where the water is?"

"First twenty-five, thirty miles there isn't any."

"What about after that?"

"I know some places."

"You could find them?"

"I'm not going through the window if that's what you're thinking about."

"The train's going to stop in Sentinel."

"They open the door to put people on," Raymond said. "They ain't letting anybody off."

"We don't know what they going to do," Harold said, "till we get there." He heard the woman come out of the toilet compartment and waited for her to walk past.

She didn't appear. Harold turned to look out the window across the aisle. Over his shoulder he could see the Davis woman standing by Bob Fisher's seat. She was saying something but keeping her voice down and he couldn't make out the words. He heard Fisher though.

Fisher said, "Is that right?" The woman said something else and Fisher said, "If you don't know where what's the good of telling me? How are you helping? Anybody could say what you're saying and if it turns out right try to get credit. But you haven't told me nothing yet."

"All right," Norma Davis said. "It's going to be at Sentinel."

"You could be guessing, for all I know."

"Take my word," the woman said.

Bob Fisher didn't say anything for a while. The

train swayed and clicked along the tracks and there was no sound behind Harold Jackson. He glanced over his shoulder. Fisher was getting up, handing his revolver to the guard sitting across the aisle. Then he was past Harold, walking up the aisle and holding the woman by the arm to move her along ahead of him.

Frank Shelby looked up as they stopped at his seat. He was sitting with Junior; Soonzy and Joe Dean were facing them.

"This lady says you're going to try to escape," Fisher said to Shelby. "What do you think about that?"

Shelby's shoulders and head swayed slightly with the motion of the train. He looked up at Fisher and Norma, looking from one to the other before he said, "If I haven't told her any such thing, how would she know?"

"She says you're getting off at Sentinel."

"Well, if she tells me how I'm going to do it and it sounds good, I might try it." Shelby grinned a little. "Do you believe her?"

"I believe she might be telling a story," Fisher said, "but I also believe it might be true. That's why I've got a gun pointed at your head till we get to Florence. Do you understand me?"

"I sure do." Shelby nodded, looking straight up at Bob Fisher. He said then, "Do you mind if I have a talk with Norma? I'd like to know why she's making up stories."

"She's all yours," Fisher said.

Harold nudged Raymond. They watched Fisher coming back down the aisle. Beyond him they saw Junior get up to give the Davis woman his seat.

Tacha was turned around watching. She moved over close to the window as Junior approached her and sat down.

Behind Harold and Raymond one of the guards said, "You letting the woman sit with the men?"

"They're all the same as far as I can see," Fisher answered. "All convicts."

Virgil Shelby, holding a shotgun across his arm, was out on the platform when the train came into sight. He heard it and saw its smoke first, then spotted the locomotive way down the tracks. This was the worst part, right now, seeing the train getting bigger and bigger and seeing the steam blowing out with the screeching sound of the brakes. The locomotive was rolling slowly as it came past the coaling shed and the water tower, easing into the station, rolling past the platform now hissing steam, the engine and the baggage cars and the two coaches with the half-dozen faces in the windows looking out at him. He could feel those people staring at him, wondering who he was. Virgil didn't look back at them. He kept his eyes on the last coach and caboose and saw them jerk to a stop before reaching the platform—out on open ground just this side of the water tower.

"Come on out," Virgil said to the station house.

Howard Crowder and Dancey and Billy Santos came out into the sunlight through the open door. Their hands were behind their backs, as though they might have been tied. Virgil moved them out of the doorway, down to the end of the platform and stood them against the wall of the building: three convicts waiting to be put aboard a prison train, tired-looking, beaten, their hat brims pulled down against the bright morning glare.

Virgil watched Bob Fisher, followed by another guard with a rifle come down the step-rungs at the far end of the prison coach. Two more guards with rifles were coming along the side of the caboose and somebody else was in the caboose window: a man wearing glasses who was sticking his head out and saying something to the two guards who had come out of the prison coach.

Bob Fisher didn't look around at Mr. Manly in the caboose window. He kept his gaze on the three convicts and the man with the shotgun. He called out, "What're the names of those men you got?"

"I'm just delivering these people," Virgil called back. "I wasn't introduced to them."

Bob Fisher and the guard with him and the two guards from the caboose came on past the prison coach but stopped before they reached the platform.

"You the only one guarding them?" Fisher asked.

"Yes, sir, I'm the one found them, I'm the one brought them in."

"I've seen you some place," Fisher said.

"Sure, delivering a prisoner. About a year ago."

"Where's the station man at?"

"He's inside."

"Call him out."

"I reckon he heard you." Virgil looked over his shoulder as the S.P. man appeared in the doorway. "There he is. Hey, listen, you want these three boys or don't you? I been watching them all night, I'm tired."

"I want to know who they are," Fisher said. "If

you're not going to tell me, I want them to call out their names."

There was silence. Virgil knew the time had come and he had to put the shotgun on Fisher and fill up the silence and get this thing done right now, or else drop the gun and forget the whole thing. No more than eight seconds passed in the silence, though it seemed like eight minutes to Virgil. Bob Fisher's hand went inside his coat and Virgil didn't have to think about it any more. He heard glass shatter as somebody kicked through a window in the prison coach. Bob Fisher drew a revolver, half turning toward the prison coach at the same time, but not turning quickly enough as Virgil put the shotgun on him and gave him a load point-blank in the side of the chest. And as the guards saw Fisher go down and were raising their rifles the three men in convict clothes brought their revolvers from behind their backs and fired as fast as they could swing their guns from one gray suit to another. All three guards were dropped where they stood, though one of them, on his knees, shot Billy Santos through the head before Virgil could get his shotgun on the man and finish him with the second load.

A rifle came out the caboose window and a barrel smashed the glass of a window in the prison coach, but it was too late. Virgil was pressed close to the side of the baggage car, out of the line of fire, and the two men in prison clothes had the S.P. man and were using him for a shield as they backed into the station house.

Virgil could look directly across the platform to the open doorway. He took time to reload the shotgun. He looked up and down the length of the train, then over at the doorway again.

"Hey, Dancey," Virgil called over, "send that train man out with the dynamite."

He had to wait a little bit before the S.P. man appeared in the doorway, straining to hold the fifty-pound case in his arms, having trouble with the dead weight, or else terrified of what he was holding.

"Walk down to the end of the platform with it," Virgil told him, "so they can see what you got. When you come back, walk up by that first passenger coach. Where everybody's looking out the window."

Jesus, the man could hardly take a step he was so scared of dropping the case. When he was down at the end of the platform, the copper wire trailing behind him and leading into the station, Virgil stepped away from the baggage car and called out, "Hey, you guards! You hear me? Throw out your guns and come out with your hands in the air, or we're going to put dynamite under a passenger coach and blow everybody clear to hell. You hear me?"

They heard him.

Mr. Manly and the three guards who were left came out to stand by the caboose. The prisoners began to yell and break the windows on both sides of the coach, but they quieted down when Frank Shelby and his three boys walked off the train and wouldn't let anybody else follow.

They are going to shoot us, Mr. Manly said to himself. He saw Frank Shelby looking toward them. Then Frank was looking at the dead guards

and at Bob Fisher in particular. "I wish you hadn't
of killed him," he heard Shelby say.

"I had to," the man with the shotgun said.

And then Shelby said, "I wanted to do it."

Junior said that if he hadn't kicked out the window they might still be in there. That was all they
said for a while that Mr. Manly heard. Shelby
and his three convict friends went into the station
house. They came out a few minutes later wearing
work clothes and might have been ranch hands for
all anybody would know to look at them.

Mr. Manly didn't see who it was that placed
the case of dynamite at the front end of the train,
under the cowcatcher, but saw one of them playing
out the wire back along the platform and around
the off side of the station house. Standing on the
platform, Frank Shelby and the one with the shotgun seemed to be in a serious conversation. Then
Frank said something to Junior, who boarded the
train again and brought out Norma Davis. Mr.
Manly could see she was frightened, as if afraid
they were going to shoot her or do something to
her. Junior and Joe Dean took her into the station
house. Frank Shelby came over then. Mr. Manly
expected him to draw a gun.

"Four of us are leaving," Shelby said. "You can
have the rest."

"What about the woman?"

"I mean five of us. Norma's going along."

"You're not going to harm her, are you?" Shelby
kept staring at him, and Mr. Manly couldn't think
straight. All he could say was, "I hope you know
that what you're doing is wrong, an offense against
Almighty God as well as your fellowman."

"Jesus Christ," Shelby said, and walked away.

Lord, help me, Mr. Manly said, and called out, "Frank, listen to me."

But Shelby didn't look back. The platform was deserted now except for the Mexican-looking man who lay dead with his arm hanging over the edge. They were mounting horses on the other side of the station. Mr. Manly could hear the horses. Then, from where he stood, he could see several of the horses past the corner of the building. He saw Junior stand in his stirrups to reach the telegraph wire at the edge of the roof and cut it with a knife. Another man was on the ground, stooped over a wooden box. Shelby nodded to him and kicked his horse, heading out into the open desert, away from the station. As the rest of them followed, raising a thin dust cloud, the man on the ground pushed down on the box.

The dynamite charge raised the front end of the locomotive off the track, derailed the first baggage car and sent the coaches slamming back against each other, twisting the couplings and tearing loose the end car, rolling it a hundred feet down the track. Mr. Manly dropped flat with the awful, ear-splitting sound of the explosion. He wasn't sure if he threw himself down or was knocked down by the concussion. When he opened his eyes there was dirt in his mouth, his head throbbed as if he had been hit with a hammer, and for a minute or so he could see nothing but smoke or dust or steam from the engine, a cloud that enveloped the station and lay heavily over the platform.

He heard men's voices. He was aware of one of the guards lying close to him and looked to see if the man was hurt. The guard was pushing himself up, shaking his head. Mr. Manly got quickly to his feet and looked around. The caboose was no longer behind him; it was down the track and the prison coach was only a few feet away where the convicts were coming out, coughing and waving at the smoke with their hands. Mr. Manly called out, "Is anybody hurt?"

No one answered him directly. The convicts were standing around; they seemed dazed. No one was attempting to run away. He saw one of the guards with a rifle now on the platform, holding the gun on the prisoners, who were paying no attention to him. At the other end of the platform there were a few people from the passenger coach. They stood looking at the locomotive that was shooting white steam and stood leaning awkwardly toward the platform, as if it might fall over any minute.

He wanted to be doing something. He had to be doing something. Five prisoners gone, four guards dead, a train blown up, telegraph line cut, no idea when help would come or where to go from here. He could hear Mr. Rynning saying, "You let them do all that? Man, this is your responsibility and you'll answer for it."

"Captain, you want us to follow them?"

Mr. Manly turned, not recognizing the voice at first. Harold Jackson, the Zulu, was standing next to him.

"What? I'm sorry, I didn't hear you."

"I said, you want us to follow them? Me and Raymond."

Mr. Manly perked up. "There are horses here?"

"No-suh, man say the nearest horses are at Gila. That's most of a day's ride."

"Then how would you expect to follow them?"

"We run, captain."

"There are eight of them—on horses."

"We don't mean to fight them, captain. We mean maybe we can follow them and see which way they go. Then when you get some help, you know, maybe we can tell this help where they went."

"They'll be thirty miles away before dark."

"So will we, captain."

"Follow them on foot—"

"Yes-suh, only we would have to go right now. Captain, they going to run those horses at first to get some distance and we would have to run the first five, six miles, no stopping, to keep their dust in sight. Raymond say it's all flat and open, no water. Just some little bushes. We don't have to follow them all day. We see where they going and get back here at dark."

Mr. Manly was frowning, looking around because, Lord, there was too much to think about at one time. He said, "I can't send convicts to chase after convicts. My God."

"They do it in Florida, captain. Trusties handle the dogs. I seen it."

"I have to get the telegraph wire fixed, that's the main thing."

"I hear the train man say they busted his key, he don't know if he can fix it," Harold Jackson said. "You going to sit here till tonight before anybody come—while Frank Shelby and them are making distance. But if me and the Apache follow them we can leave signs."

Mr. Manly noticed Raymond San Carlos now behind Harold. Raymond was nodding. "Sure," he said, "we can leave pieces of our clothes for them to follow if you give us something else to wear. Maybe you should give us some guns too, in case we get close to them, or for firing signals."

"I can't do that," Mr. Manly said. "No, I can't give you guns."

"How about our spears then?" Raymond said. "We get hungry we could use the spears maybe to stick something."

"The spears might be all right." Mr. Manly nodded.

"Spears and two canteens of water," Raymond said. "And the other clothes. Some people see us they won't think we're convicts running away."

"Pair of pants and a shirt," Mr. Manly said.

"And a couple of blankets. In case we don't get back before dark and we got to sleep outside. We can get our bedrolls and the spears," Raymond said. "They're with all the baggage in that car we loaded."

"You'd try to be back before dark?"

"Yes, sir, we don't like to sleep outside if we don't have to."

"Well," Mr. Manly said. He paused. He was trying to think of an alternative. He didn't believe that sending these two out would do any good. He pictured them coming back at dusk and sinking to the ground exhausted. But at least it would be doing something—now. Mr. Rynning or somebody would ask him, What did you do? And he'd say, I sent trackers out after them. I got these two boys that are runners. He said, "Well, find your stuff and get started. I'll tell the guards."

They left the water stop at Sentinel running

almost due south. They ran several hundred yards before looking back to see the smoke still hanging in a dull cloud over the buildings and the palo verde trees. They ran for another half-mile or so, loping easily and not speaking, carrying their spears and their new guard-gray pants and shirts wrapped in their blanket rolls. They ran until they reached a gradual rise and ran down the other side to find themselves in a shallow wash, out of sight of the water stop.

They looked at each other now. Harold grinned and Raymond grinned. They sat down on the bank of the wash and began laughing, until soon both of them had tears in their eyes.

⊰ 12 ⊱

Harold said, "What way do we go?"

Raymond got up on the bank of the dry wash and stood looking out at the desert that was a flat burned-out waste as far as they could see. There were patches of dusty scrub growth, but no cactus or trees from here to the dark rise of the mountains to the south.

"That way," Raymond said. "To the Crater Mountains and down to the Little Ajos. Two days we come to Ajo, the town, steal some horses, go on south to Bates Well. The next day we come to Quitobaquito, a little water-hole village, and cross the border. After that, I don't know."

"Three days, uh?"

"Without horses."

"Frank Shelby, he going the same way?"

"He could go to Clarkstown instead of Ajo. They near each other. One the white man's town, the other the Mexican town."

"But he's going the same way we are."

"There isn't no other way south from here."

"I'd like to get him in front of me one minute," Harold said.

"Man," Raymond said, "you would have to move fast to get him first."

"Maybe we run into him sometime."

"Only if we run," Raymond said.

Harold was silent a moment. "If we did, we'd get out of here quicker, wouldn't we? If we run."

"Sure, maybe save a day. If we're any good."

"You think we couldn't run to those mountains?"

"Sure we could, we wanted to."

"Is there water?"

"There used to be."

"Then that's probably where he's heading to camp tonight, uh? What do you think?"

"He's got to go that way. He might as well."

"We was to get there tonight," Harold said, "we might run into him."

"We might run into all of them."

"Not if we saw them first. Waited for him to get alone."

Raymond grinned. "Play with him a little."

"Man, that would be good, wouldn't it?" Harold said. "Scare him some."

"Scare hell out of him."

"Paint his face," Harold said. He began to smile thinking about it.

"Take his clothes. Paint him all over."

"Now you talking. You got any?"

"I brought some iodine and a little bottle of white. Listen," Raymond said, "we're going that way. Why don't we take a little run and see how Frank's doing?"

Harold stood up. When they had tied their blanket rolls across one shoulder and picked up their spears, the Apache and the Zulu began their run across the southern Arizona desert.

They ran ten miles in the furnace heat of sand and rock and dry, white-crusted playas and didn't break their stride until the sun was directly overhead. They walked a mile and ran another mile before they stopped to rest and allowed themselves a drink of water from the canteens, a short drink and then a mouthful they held in their mouths while they screwed closed the canteens and hung them over their shoulders again. They rested fifteen minutes and before the tiredness could creep in to stiffen their legs they stood up without a word and started off again toward the mountains.

For a mile or so they would be aware of their running. Then, in time, they would become lost in the monotonous stride of their pace, running, but each somewhere else in his mind, seeing cool mountain pastures or palm trees or thinking of nothing at all, running and hearing themselves sucking the heated air in and letting it out, but not feeling the agony of running. They had learned to do this in the past months, to detach themselves and be inside or outside the running man but not part of him for long minutes at a time. When they broke stride they would always walk and sometimes run again before resting. At times they felt they were getting no closer to the mountains, though finally the slopes began to take shape, changing from a dark mass to dun-colored slopes and shadowed contours. At mid-afternoon they saw the first trace of dust rising in the distance. Both of them saw it and they kept their eyes on the wispy, moving cloud that would rise and vanish against the sky.

The dust was something good to watch and seeing it was better than stretching out in the grass and going to sleep. It meant Frank Shelby was only a few miles ahead of them.

They came to the arroyo in the shadowed foot-hills of the Crater Mountains a little after five o'clock. There was good brush cover here and a natural road that would take them up into high country. They would camp above Shelby if they could and watch him, Raymond said, but first he had to go out and find the son of a bitch. You rest, he told Harold, and the Zulu gave him a deadpan look and stared at him until he was gone. Harold sat back against the cool, shaded wall of the gulley. He wouldn't let himself go to sleep though. He kept his eyes open and waited for the Apache, listening and not moving, letting the tight weariness ease out of his body. By the time Raymond returned the arroyo was dark. The only light they could see were sun reflections on the high peaks above them.

"They're in some trees," Raymond said, "about a half-mile from here. Taking it easy, they even got a fire."

"All of them there?"

"I count eight, eight horses."

"Can we get close?"

"Right above them. Frank's put two men up in the rocks—they can see all around the camp."

"What do you think?" Harold said.

"I think we should take the two in the rocks. See what Frank does in the morning when nobody's there."

The grin spread over Harold's face. That sounded pretty good.

They slept for a few hours and when they woke up it was night. Harold touched Raymond. The Indian sat up without making a sound. He opened a canvas bag and took out the small bottles of iodine and white paint and they began to get ready.

There was no sun yet on this side of the mountain, still cold dark in the early morning when Virgil Shelby came down out of the rocks and crossed the open slope to the trees. He could make out his brother and the woman by the fire. He could hear the horses and knew Frank's men were saddling them and gathering up their gear.

Frank and the woman looked up as Virgil approached, and Frank said, "They coming?"

"I don't know. I didn't see them."

"What do you mean you didn't see them?"

"They weren't up there."

Frank Shelby got up off the ground. He dumped his coffee as he walked to the edge of the trees to look up at the tumbled rocks and the escarpment that rose steeply against the sky.

"They're asleep somewhere," he said. "You must've looked the wrong places."

"I looked all over up there."

"They're asleep," Shelby said. "Go on up there and look again."

When Virgil came back the second time Frank said, Jesus Christ, what good are you? And sent Junior and Joe Dean up into the rocks. When they came down he went up himself to have a look and was still up there as the sunlight began to spread over the slope and they could feel the heat of day coming down on them.

"There's no sign of anything," Virgil said. "There's no sign they were even here."

"I put them here," Frank Shelby said. "One right where you're standing, Dancey over about a hundred feet. I put them here myself."

"Well, they're not here now," Virgil said.

"Jesus Christ, I know that." Frank looked over at Junior and Soonzy. "You counted the horses?"

"We'd a-heard them taking horses."

"I asked if you counted them!"

"Christ, we got them saddled. I don't have to count them."

"Then they walked away," Frank Shelby said, his tone quieter now.

Virgil shook his head. "I hadn't paid them yet."

"They walked away," Shelby said again. "I don't know why, but they did."

"Can you see Dancey walking off into the mountains?" Virgil said. "I'm telling you I hadn't *paid* them."

"There's nothing up there could have carried them off. No animal, no man. There is no sign they did anything but walk away," Shelby said, "and that's the way we're going to leave it."

He said no more until they were down in the trees again, ready to ride out. Nobody said anything.

Then Frank told Joe Dean he was to ride ahead of them like a point man. Virgil, he said, was to stay closer in the hills and ride swing, though he would also be ahead of them looking for natural trails.

"Looking for trails," Virgil said. "If you believe those two men walked off, then what is it that's tightening up your hind end?"

"You're older than me," Frank said, "but no bigger, and I will sure close your mouth if you want it done."

"Jesus, can't you take some kidding?"

"Not from you," his brother said.

They were in a high meadow that had taken more than an hour to reach, at least a thousand feet above Shelby's camp. Dancey and Howard Crowder sat on the ground close to each other. The Apache and the Zulu stood off from them leaning on their spears, their blankets laid over their shoulders as they waited for the sun to spread across the field. They would be leaving in a few minutes. They planned to get out ahead of Shelby and be waiting for him. These two, Dancey and Crowder, they would leave here. They had taken their revolvers and gun belts, the only things they wanted from them.

"They're going to kill us," Dancey whispered.

Howard Crowder told him for God sake to keep quiet, they'd hear him.

They had been in the meadow most of the night, brought here after each had been sitting in the rocks, drowsing, and had felt the spear point at the back of his neck. They hadn't got a good look at the two yet. They believed both were Indians—even though there were no Indians around here, and no Indians had carried spears in fifty years. Then they would have to be loco Indians escaped from an asylum or kicked out of their village. That's what they were. That's why Dancey believed they were going to kill him and Howard.

Finally, in the morning light, when the Zulu

walked over to them and Dancey got a close look at his face—God Almighty, with the paint and the scars and the short pointed beard and the earring—he closed his eyes and expected to feel the spear in his chest any second.

Harold said, "You two wait here till after we're gone."

Dancey opened his eyes and Howard Crowder said, "What?"

"We're going to leave, then you can find your way out of here."

Howard Crowder said, "But we don't know where we are."

"You up on a mountain."

"How do we get down?"

"You look around for a while you find a trail. By that time your friends will be gone without you, so you might as well go home." Harold started to turn away.

"Wait a minute," Howard Crowder said. "We don't have horses, we don't have any food or water. How are we supposed to get across the desert?"

"It's up to you," Harold said. "Walk if you want or stay here and die, it's up to you."

"We didn't do nothing to you," Dancey said.

Harold looked at him. "That's why we haven't killed you."

"Then what do you want us for?"

"We don't want you," Harold said. "We want Frank Shelby."

Virgil rejoined the group at noon to report he hadn't seen a thing, not any natural trail either that would save them time. They were into the foothills of the

Little Ajos and he sure wished Billy Santos had not got shot in the head in the train station, because Billy would have had them to Clarkstown by now. They would be sitting at a table with cold beer and fried meat instead of squatting on the ground eating hash out of a can. He asked if he should stay with the group now. Norma Davis looked pretty good even if she was kind of sweaty and dirty; she was built and had nice long hair. He wouldn't mind riding with her a while and maybe arranging something for that night.

Frank, it looked like, was still not talking. Virgil asked him again if he should stay with the group and this time Frank said no and told him to finish his grub and ride out. He said, "Find the road to Clarkstown or don't bother coming back, because there would be no use of having you around."

So Virgil and Joe Dean rode out about fifteen minutes ahead of the others. When they split up Virgil worked his way deeper into the foothills to look for some kind of a road. He crossed brush slopes and arroyos, holding to a south-southeast course, but he didn't see anything that resembled even a foot path. It was a few hours after leaving the group, about three o'clock in the afternoon, that Virgil came across the Indian and it was the damnedest thing he'd ever seen in his life.

There he was out in the middle of nowhere sitting at the shady edge of a mesquite thicket wrapped in an army blanket. A real Apache Indian, red headband and all and even with some paint on his face and a staff or something that was sticking out of the bushes. It looked like a fishing pole. That was the first thing Virgil thought of: an Apache Indian out in the desert fishing in a mesquite patch—the damnedest thing he'd ever seen.

Virgil said, "Hey, Indin, you sabe English any?"

Raymond San Carlos remained squatted on the ground. He nodded once.

"I'm looking for the road to Clarkstown."

Raymond shook his head now. "I don't know."

"You speak pretty good. Tell me something, what're you doing out here?"

"I'm not doing nothing."

"You live around here?"

Raymond pointed off to the side. "Not far."

"How come you got that paint on your face?"

"I just put it there."

"How come if you live around here you don't know where Clarkstown is?"

"I don't know."

"Jesus, you must be a dumb Indin. Have you seen anybody else come through here today?"

"Nobody."

"You haven't seen me, have you?"

"What?"

"You haven't seen nobody and you haven't seen me either."

Raymond said nothing.

"I don't know," Virgil said now. "Some sheriff's people ask you you're liable to tell them, aren't you? You got family around here?"

"Nobody else."

"Just you all alone. Nobody would miss you then, would they? Listen, buddy, I don't mean anything personal, but I'm afraid you seeing me isn't a good idea. I'm going to have to shoot you."

Raymond stood up now, slowly.

"You can run if you want," Virgil said, "or you can stand there and take it, I don't care; but don't start hollering and carrying on. All right?"

Virgil was wearing a shoulder rig under his coat. He looked down as he unbuttoned the one button, drew a .44 Colt and looked up to see something coming at him and gasped as if the wind was knocked out of him as he grabbed hold of the fishing pole sticking out of his chest and saw the Indian standing there watching him and saw the sky and the sun, and that was all.

Raymond dragged Virgil's body into the mesquite. He left his spear in there too. He had two revolvers, a Winchester rifle and a horse. He didn't need a spear any more.

Joe Dean's horse smelled water. He was sure of it, so he let the animal have its head and Joe Dean went along for the ride—down into a wide canyon that was green and yellow with spring growth. When he saw the cottonwoods and then the round soft shape of the willows against the canyon slope, Joe Dean patted the horse's neck and guided him with the reins again.

It was a still pool, but not stagnant, undercutting a shelf of rock and mirroring the cliffs and canyon walls. Joe Dean dismounted. He led his horse down a bank of shale to the pool, then went belly-down at the edge and drank with his face in the water. He drank all he wanted before emptying the little bit left in his canteen and filling it to the top. Then he stretched out and drank again. He wished he had time to strip off his clothes and dive in. But he had better get the others first or Frank would see he'd bathed and start kicking and screaming again. Once he got them here they would probably all want to take a bath. That would be something, Norma in there with them, grabbing some of her under the water when Frank wasn't looking. Then she'd get out and lie up there on the bank to dry off in the sun. Nice soft white body—

Joe Dean was pushing himself up, looking at the pool and aware now of the reflections in the still water: the slope of the canyon wall high above, the shelf of rock behind him, sandy brown, and something else, something dark that resembled a man's shape, and he felt that cold prickly feeling up between his shoulder blades to his neck.

It was probably a crevice, shadowed inside. It couldn't be a man. Joe Dean got to his feet, then turned around and looked up.

Harold Jackson—bare to the waist, and a blanket over one shoulder, with his beard and tribal scars and streak of white paint—stood looking down at him from the rock shelf.

"How you doing?" Harold said. "You get enough water?"

Joe Dean stared at him. He didn't answer right away. God, no. He was thinking and trying to decide quickly if it was a good thing or a bad thing to be looking up at Harold Jackson at a water hole in the Little Ajo Mountains.

He said finally, "How'd you get here?"

"Same way you did."

"You got away after we left?"

"Looks like it, don't it?"

"Well, that must've been something. Just you?"

"No, Raymond come with me."

"I don't see him. Where is he?"

"He's around some place."

"If there wasn't any horses left, how'd you get here?"

"How you think?"

"I'm asking you, Sambo."

"We run, Joe."

"You're saying you run here all the way from Sentinel?"

"Well, we stop last night," Harold said, and kept watching him. "Up in the Crater Mountains."

"Is that right? We camped up there too."

"I know you did," Harold said.

Joe Dean was silent for a long moment before he said, "You killed Howard and Dancey, didn't you?"

"No, we never killed them. We let them go."

"What do you want?"

"Not you, Joe. Unless you want to take part."

Joe Dean's revolver was in his belt. He didn't see a gun or a knife or anything on Harold, just the blanket over his shoulder and covering his arm. It looked like it would be pretty easy. So he drew his revolver.

As he did, though, Harold pulled the blanket across his body with his left hand. His right hand came up holding Howard Crowder's .44 and he shot Joe Dean with it three times in the chest. And now Harold had two revolvers, a rifle, and a horse. He left Joe Dean lying next to the pool for Shelby to find.

They had passed Clarkstown, Shelby decided. Missed it. Which meant they were still in the Little Ajo Mountains, past the chance of having a sit-down hot meal today, but that much closer to the border. That part was all right. What bothered him, they had not seen Virgil or Joe Dean since noon.

It was almost four o'clock now. Junior and Soonzy were riding ahead about thirty yards. Norma was keeping up with Shelby, staying close, afraid of him but more afraid of falling behind and finding herself alone. If Shelby didn't know where they were, Norma knew that she, by herself, would never find her way out. She had no idea why Shelby had brought her, other than at Virgil's request to have a woman along. No one had approached her in the camp last night. She knew, though, once they were across the border and the men relaxed and quit looking behind them, one of them, probably Virgil, would come to her with that fixed expression on his face and she would take him on and be nice to him as long as she had no other choice.

"We were through here one time," Shelby said. "We went up through Copper Canyon to Clarkstown the morning we went after the Cornelia Mine payroll. I don't see any familiar sights, though. It all looks the same."

She knew he wasn't speaking to her directly. He was thinking out loud, or stoking his confidence with the sound of his own voice.

"From here what we want to hit is Growler Pass," Shelby said. "Top the pass and we're at Bates Well. Then we got two ways to go. Southeast to Dripping Springs and on down to Sonoyta. Or a shorter trail to the border through Quitobaquito. I haven't decided yet which way we'll go. When Virgil comes in I'll ask him if Billy Santos said anything about which trail's best this time of the year."

"What happened to the two men last night?" Norma asked him.

Shelby didn't answer. She wasn't sure if she should ask him again. Before she could decide, Junior was riding back toward them and Shelby had reined in to wait for him.

Junior was grinning. "I believe Joe Dean's found us some water. His tracks lead into that canyon yonder and it's chock-full of green brush and willow trees."

"There's a tank somewhere in these hills," Shelby said.

"Well, I believe we've found it," Junior said.

They found the natural tank at the end of the canyon. They found Joe Dean lying with his head and outstretched arms in the still water. And they found planted in the sand next to him, sticking straight up, a spear made of a bamboo fishing pole and a mortar trowel.

13

They camped on high ground south of Bates Well and in the morning came down through giant saguaro country, down through a hollow in the hills to within sight of Quitobaquito.

There it was, a row of weathered adobes and stock pens beyond a water hole that resembled a shallow, stagnant lake—a worn-out village on the bank of a dying pool that was rimmed with rushes and weeds and a few stunted trees.

Shelby didn't like it.

He had pictured a green oasis and found a dusty, desert water hole. He had imagined a village where they could trade for food and fresh horses, a gateway to Mexico with the border lying not far beyond the village, across the Rio Sonoyta.

He didn't like the look of the place. He didn't like not seeing any people over there. He didn't like the open fifty yards between here and the water hole.

He waited in a cover of rocks and brush with Norma and Junior and Soonzy behind him, and Mexico waiting less than a mile away. They could go around Quitobaquito. But if they did, where was the next water? The Sonoyta could be dried up, for all he knew. They could head for Santo Domingo, a fair-sized town that shouldn't be too far away. But what if they missed it? There was water right in front of them and, goddamn-it, they were going to have some, all they wanted. But he hesitated, studying the village, waiting for some sign of life other than a dog barking, and remembering Joe Dean with the three bullets in his chest.

Junior said, "Jesus, are we gong to sit here in the sun all day?"

"I'll let you know," Shelby said.

"You want me to get the water?"

"I did, I would have told you."

"Well, then tell me, goddamn-it. You think I'm scared to?"

Soonzy settled it. He said, "I think maybe everybody's off some place to a wedding or something. That's probably what it is. These people, somebody dies or gets married, they come from all over."

"Maybe," Shelby said.

"I don't see no other way but for me to go in there and find out. What do you say, Frank?"

After a moment Shelby nodded. "All right, go take a look."

"If it's the nigger and the Indin," Soonzy said, "if they're in there, I'll bring 'em out."

Raymond held the wooden shutter open an inch, enough so he could watch Soonzy coming in from the east end of the village, mounted, a rifle across his lap. Riding right in, Raymond thought. Dumb, or sure of himself, or maybe both. He could stick a .44 out the window and shoot him as he went by.

Except that it would be a risk. He couldn't afford to miss and have Soonzy shooting in here. Raymond let the shutter close.

He pressed a finger to his lips and turned to the fourteen people, the men and women and children who were huddled in the dim room, sitting on the floor and looking up at him now, watching silently, even the two smallest children. The people were Mexican and Papago. They wore white cotton and cast-off clothes. They had lived here all their lives and they were used to armed men riding through Quitobaquito. Raymond had told them these were bad men coming who might steal from them and harm them. They believed him and they waited in silence. Now they could hear the horse's hoofs on the hard-packed street. Raymond stood by the door with a revolver in his hand. The sound of the horse passed. Raymond waited, then opened the door a crack and looked out. Soonzy was nowhere in sight.

If anybody was going to shoot at anybody going for water, Soonzy decided, it would have to be from one of the adobes facing the water hole. There was a tree in the backyard of the first one that would block a clear shot across the hole. So that left him only two places to search—two low-roofed, crumbling adobes that stood bare in the sunlight, showing their worn bricks and looking like part of the land.

Soonzy stayed close to the walls on the front side of the street. When he came to the first adobe facing the water hole, he reached down to push the door open, ducked his head, and walked his horse inside.

He came out into the backyard on foot, holding a revolver now, and seeing just one end of the water hole because the tree was in the way. From the next adobe, though, a person would have a clear shot. There weren't any side windows, which was good. It let Soonzy walk right up to the place. He edged around the corner, following his revolver to the back door and got right up against the boards so he could listen. He gave himself time; there was no hurry. Then he was glad he did when the sound came from inside, a little creeking sound, like a door or a window being opened.

Harold eased open the front door a little more. He still couldn't see anything. The man had been down at the end of the street, coming this way on his horse big as anything, and now he was gone. He looked down half a block and across the street, at the adobe, where Raymond was waiting with the people, keeping them quiet and out of the way. He saw Raymond coming out; Harold wanted to wave to him to get inside. What was he doing?

The back door banged open and Soonzy was standing in the room covering him with a Colt revolver.

"Got you," Soonzy said. "Throw the gun outside and turn this way. Where's that red nigger at?"

"You mean Raymond?" Harold said. "He left. I don't know where he went."

"Which one of you shot Joe Dean, you or him?"

"I did. I haven't seen Raymond since before that."

"What'd you do with Virgil?"

"I don't think I know any Virgil."

"Frank's brother. He took us off the train."

"I haven't seen him."

"You want me to pull the trigger?"

"I guess you'll pull it whether I tell or not." Harold felt the door behind him touch the heel of his right foot. He had not moved the foot, but now he felt the door push gently against it.

"I'll tell Frank Shelby," Harold said then. "How'll that be? You take me to Frank I'll tell him where his brother is and them other two boys. But if you shoot me he won't ever know where his brother's at, will he? He's liable to get mad at somebody."

Soonzy had to think about that. He wasn't going to be talked into anything he didn't want to do. He said, "Whether I shoot you now or later you're still going to be dead."

"It's up to you," Harold said.

"All right, turn around and open the door."

"Yes-suh, captain," Harold said.

He opened the door and stepped aside and Raymond, in the doorway, fired twice and hit Soonzy dead center both times.

Shelby and Junior and Norma Davis heard the shots. They sounded far off, but the reports were thin and clear and unmistakable. Soonzy had gone into the village. Two shots were fired and Soonzy had not come out. They crouched fifty yards from water with empty canteens and the border less than a mile away.

Norma said they should go back to Bates Well. They could be there by evening, get water, and take the other trail south.

And run into a posse coming down from Gila, Shelby said. They didn't have time enough even to wait here till dark. They had to go with water or go without it, but they had to go, now.

So Junior said Jesus, give me the goddamn canteens or we will be here all day. He said maybe those two could paint theirselves up and bushwack a man, but he would bet ten dollars gold they couldn't shoot worth a damn for any distance. He'd get the water and be back in a minute. Shelby told Junior he would return fire and cover him if they started shooting, and Junior said that was mighty big of him.

"There," Raymond said. "You see him?"

Harold looked out past the door frame to the water hole. "Whereabouts?"

Raymond was at the window of the adobe. "He worked his way over to the right, coming in on the other side of the tree. You'll see him in a minute."

"Which one?"

"It looked like Junior."

"He can't sit still, can he?"

"I guess he's thirsty," Raymond said. "There he is. He thinks that tree's hiding him."

Harold could see him now, over to the right a little, approaching the bank of the water hole, running across the open in a hunch-shouldered crouch, keeping his head down behind nothing.

"How far do you think?" Raymond said.

Harold raised his Winchester and put the front sight on Junior. "Hundred yards, a little more."

"Can you hit him?"

Harold watched Junior slide down the sandy

bank and begin filling the canteens, four of them, kneeling in the water and filling them one at a time. "Yeah, I can hit him," Harold said, and he was thinking, He's taking too long. He should fill them all at once, push them under and hold them down.

"What do you think?" Raymond said.

"I don't know."

"He ever do anything to you?"

"He done enough."

"I don't know either," Raymond said.

"He'd kill you. He wouldn't have to think about it."

"I guess he would."

"He'd enjoy it."

"I don't know," Raymond said. "It's different, seeing him when he don't see us."

"Well," Harold said, "if he gets the water we might not see him again. We might not see Frank Shelby again either. You want Frank?"

"I guess so."

"I do too," Harold said.

They let Junior come up the bank with the canteens, up to the rim before they shot him. Both fired at once and Junior slid back down to the edge of the still pool.

Norma looked at it this way: they would either give up, or they would be killed. Giving up would be taking a chance. But it would be less chancey if she gave up on her own, without Shelby. After all, Shelby had forced her to come along and that was a fact, whether the Indian and the Negro realized it or not. She had never been really unkind to them in prison; she had had nothing to do with them. So there was no reason for them to harm her now—once she explained she was more on their side than on Frank's. If they were feeling mean and had rape on their mind, well, she could handle that easily enough.

There was one canteen left, Joe Dean's. Norma picked it up and waited for Shelby's reaction.

"They'll shoot you too," he said.

"I don't think so."

"Why, because you're a woman?"

"That might help."

"God Almighty, you don't know them, do you?"

"I know they've got nothing against me. They're mad at you, Frank, not me."

"They've killed six people we know of. You just watched them gun Junior—and you're going to walk out there in the open?"

"Do you believe I might have a chance?"

Shelby paused. "A skinny one."

"Skinny or not, it's the only one we have, isn't it?"

"You'd put your life up to help me?"

"I'm just as thirsty as you are."

"Norma, I don't know—two days ago you were trying to turn me in."

"That's a long story, and if we get out of here we can talk about it sometime, Frank."

"You really believe you can do it."

"I want to so bad."

Boy, she was something. She was a tough, good-looking woman, and by God, maybe she could pull it. Frank said, "It might work. You know it?"

"I'm going way around to the side," Norma said, "where those bushes are. Honey, if they start shooting—"

"You're going to make it, Norma, I know you are. I got a feeling about this and I *know* it's going to work." He gave her a hug and rubbed his hand gently up and down her back, which was damp with perspiration. He said, "You hurry back now."

Norma said, "I will, sweetheart."

Watching her cross the open ground, Shelby got his rifle up between a notch in the rocks and put it on the middle adobe across the water hole. Norma was approaching from the left, the same way Junior had gone in, but circling wider than Junior had, going way around and now approaching the pool where tall rushes grew along the bank. Duck down in there, Shelby said. But Norma kept going, circling the water hole, following the bank as it curved around toward the far side. Jesus, she had nerve; she was heading for the bushes almost to the other side. But then she was past the bushes. She was running. She was into the yard where the big tree stood before Shelby said, "Goddamn you!" out loud, and swung his Winchester on the moving figure in the striped skirt. He fired and levered and fired two more before they opened up from the house and he had to go down behind the rocks. By the time he looked again she was inside.

Frank Shelby gave up an hour later. He waved a flour sack at them for a while, then brought the three horses down out of the brush and led them around the water hole toward the row of adobes. He had figured out most of what he was going to say. The tone was the important thing. Take them by surprise. Bluff them. Push them off balance. They'd expect him to run and hide, but instead he was walking up to them. He could talk to them. Christ, a dumb nigger and an Indin who'd been taking orders and saying yes-sir all their lives. They had run scared from the train and had been scared into killing. That's what happened. They were scared to death of being caught and taken back to prison. So he would have to be gentle with them at first and calm them down, the way you'd calm a green horse that was nervous and skittish. There, there, boys, what's all this commotion about? Show them he wasn't afraid, and gradually take charge. Take care of Norma also. God, he was dying to get his hands on Norma.

Harold and Raymond came out of the adobe first, with rifles, though not pointing them at him. Norma came out behind them and moved over to the side, grinning at him, goddamn her. It made Shelby mad, though it didn't hold his attention. Harold and Raymond did that with their painted faces staring at him; no expression, just staring, waiting for him.

As he reached the yard Shelby grinned and said, "Boys, I believe it's about time we cut out this foolishness. What do you say?"

Harold and Raymond waited.

Shelby said, "I mean what are we doing shooting at each other for? We're on the same side. We spent months together in that hell hole on the bluff and, by Jesus, we jumped the train together, didn't we?"

Harold and Raymond waited.

Shelby said, "If there was some misunderstanding you had with my men we can talk about it later because, boys, right now I believe we should get over that border before we do any more standing around talking."

And Harold and Raymond waited.

Shelby did too, a moment. He said then, "Have I done anything to you? Outside of a little pissy-ass difference we had, haven't I always treated you boys fair? What do you want from me? You want me to pay you something? I'll tell you what, I'll pay you both to hire on and ride with me. What do you say?"

Harold Jackson said, "You're going to ride with us, man. Free."

"To where?"

"Back to Sentinel."

Norma started laughing as Shelby said, "Jesus, are you crazy? What are you talking about, back to Sentinel? You mean back to *prison*?"

"That's right," Harold said. "Me and Raymond decide that's the thing you'd like the worst."

She stopped laughing altogether as Raymond said, "You're going too, lady."

"Why?" Norma looked dazed, taken completely by surprise. "I'm not with him. What have I ever done to you?"

"Nobody has ever done anything to us," Raymond said to Harold. "Did you know that?"

The section gang that arrived from Gila told Mr. Manly no, they had not heard any news yet. There were posses out from the Sand Tank Mountains to the Little Ajos, but nobody had reported seeing anything. At least it had not been reported to the railroad.

They asked Mr. Manly how long he had been

here at Sentinel and he told them five days, since
the escape. He didn't tell them Mr. Rynning had
wired and instructed him to stay. "You have five
days," Mr. Rynning said. "If the convict pair you
released do not return, report same to the sheriff,
Maricopa. Report in person to me."

Mr. Manly took that to mean he was to wait here
five full days and leave the morning of the sixth.
The first two days there had been a mob here. Railroad people with equipment, a half-dozen guards
that had been sent over from Florence, and the
Maricopa sheriff, who had been here getting state-
ments and the descriptions of the escaped convicts.
He had told the Maricopa sheriff about sending
out the two trackers and the man had said, trackers? Where did you get trackers? He told him and
the man had stared at him with a funny look. It
was the sheriff who must have told Mr. Rynning
about Harold and Raymond.

The railroad had sent an engine with a crane
to lift the locomotive and the baggage car onto
the track. Then the train had to be pulled all the
way to the yard at Gila, where a new locomotive
was hooked up and the prisoners were taken on
to Florence. There had certainly been a lot of excitement those two days. Since then the place had
been deserted except for the telegrapher and the
section gang. They were usually busy and it gave
Mr. Manly time to think of what he would tell Mr.
Rynning.

It wasn't an easy thing to explain: trusting two
convicts enough to let them go off alone. Two murderers, Mr. Rynning would say. Yes, that was true;
but he had still trusted them. And until this morn-

ing he had expected to see them again. That was the sad part. He sincerely believed he had made progress with Harold and Raymond. He believed he had taught them something worthwhile about life, about living with their fellowman. But evidently he had been wrong. Or, to look at it honestly, he had failed. Another failure after forty years of failures.

He was in the station house late in the afternoon of the fifth day, talking to the telegrapher, passing time. Neither had spoken for a while when the telegrapher said, "You hear something?" He went to the window and said, "Riders coming in." After a pause he said, "Lord in heaven!" And Mr. Manly knew.

He was off the bench and outside, standing there waiting for them, grinning, beaming, as they rode up: his Apache and his Zulu—thank you, God, just look at them!—bringing in Frank Shelby and the woman with ropes around their necks, bringing them in tied fast and making Mr. Manly, at this moment, the happiest man on earth.

Mr. Manly said, "I don't believe it. Boys, I am looking at it and I don't believe it. Do you know there are posses all over the country looking for these people?"

"We passed some of them," Raymond said.

"They still after the others?"

"I guess they are," Raymond said.

"Boys, I'll tell you, I've been waiting here for days, worried sick about you. I even began to wonder—I hate to say it but it's true—I even began to wonder if you were coming back. Now listen, I want to hear all about it, but first I want to say this. For what you've done here, for your loyalty and courage, risking your lives to bring these people back—which you didn't even have to do—I am going to personally see that you're treated like white men at Florence and are given decent work to do."

The Apache and the Zulu sat easily in their saddles watching Mr. Manly, their painted faces staring at him without expression.

"I'll tell you something else," Mr. Manly said. "You keep your record clean at Florence, I'll go before the prison board myself and make a formal request that your sentences be commuted, which means cut way down." Mr. Manly was beaming. He said, "Fellas, what do you think of that?"

They continued to watch him until Harold Jackson the Zulu, leaning on his saddle horn, said to Mr. Manly, "Fuck you, captain."

They let go of the ropes that led to Frank Shelby and the woman. They turned their horses in tight circles and rode out, leaving a mist of fine dust hanging in the air.

If you liked *Gunsights* and
Forty Lashes Less One,
keep reading for a sneak peek
at another Western novel by
ELMORE LEONARD

VALDEZ IS COMING

Picture the ground rising on the east side of the pasture with scrub trees thick on the slope and pines higher up. This is where everybody was. Not all in one place but scattered in small groups, about a dozen men in the scrub, the front line, the shooters who couldn't just stand around. They'd fire at the shack when they felt like it, or when Mr. Tanner passed the word, they would all fire at once.

Others were up in the pines and on the road that ran along the crest of the hill, some three hundred yards from the shack across the pasture. Those watching made bets whether the man in the shack would give himself up or get shot first.

It was Saturday and that's why everybody had the time. They would arrive in Lanoria, hear about what happened, and shortly after, head out to the cattle company pasture. Most of the men went out alone, leaving their families in town, though there were a few women who came. The other women waited. And the people who had business in town and couldn't leave waited. Now and then a few would come back from the pasture to have a drink or their dinner and would tell what was going on.

No, they hadn't got him yet. Still inside the line shack and not showing his face. But they'd get him. A few more would go out from town when they heard this. Also a wagon from De Spain's went out with whiskey. That's how the saloon was set up in the pines overlooking the pasture. Somebody said it was like the goddam Fourth of July.

Barely a mile from town those going out would hear the gunfire—like a skirmish way over the other side of the woods, thin specks of sound—and this would hurry them. They were careful though, topping the slope, looking across the pasture, getting their bearings, then peering around to see who was there. They would see a friend and ask about this Mr. Tanner, and the friend would point him out.

The man there in the dark suit: thin and bony, not big especially, but looking like he was made of gristle and hard to kill, with a moustache and a thin nose and a dark dusty hat worn over his eyes. That was him. They had heard about Frank Tanner, but not many had ever seen him. He had a place south in the foothills of the Santa Ritas and almost to the border. They said he had an army riding for him, Americans and Mexicans, and that his place was like a barracks except for the women. They said he traded horses and cattle and guns across into Mexico to the revolutionary forces and he had all the riders in case the Federales came down on him; also in case his customers ever decided not to pay. Sure he had at least twenty-five men and he didn't graze a head of beef himself. Where were they? somebody wanted to know. Driving a herd south. That's what he had come here for, cattle; bought them from Maricopa.

Somebody else said he had brought his wife along—"God*dam*, a good-looking young woman, I'll tell you, some years younger than he is"—and she was waiting for him at the Republic Hotel right now, staying up in his room, and not many people had seen her.

They would look at Mr. Tanner, then across the cattle pasture to the line shack three hundred yards away. It was a little bake-oven of a hut, wood framed and made of sod and built against a rise where there were pines so the hut would be in shade part of the day. There were no windows in the hut, no gear lying around to show anybody lived there. The hut stood in the sun now with its door closed, the door chipped and splintered by all the bullets that had poured into it and through it.

Off to the right where the pine shapes against the sky rounded and became willows, there in the trees by the creek bed, was the man's wagon and team. In the wagon were the supplies he'd bought that morning in Lanoria before Mr. Tanner spotted him.

Out in front of the hut about ten or fifteen feet there was something on the ground. From the slope three hundred yards away nobody could tell what it was until a man came who had field glasses. He looked up and said, frowning, it was a doll: one made of cloth scraps, a stuffed doll with buttons for eyes.

"The woman must have dropped it," somebody said.

"The *woman*?" the man with the field glasses said.

A Lipan Apache woman who was his wife or his woman or just with him. Mr. Tanner hadn't

been clear about that. All they knew was that there
was a woman in the hut with him and if the man
wanted her to stay and get shot that was his business.

A Mr. Beaudry, the government land agent for
the county, was there. Also Mr. Malson, manager
of the Maricopa Cattle Company, and a horse-
breaker by the name of Diego Luz, who was big
for a Mexican but never offensive and who drank
pretty well.

Mr. Beaudry, nodding and also squinting so he
could picture the man inside the line shack, said,
"There was something peculiar about him. I mean
having a name like Orlando Rincón."

"He worked for me," Mr. Malson said. He was
looking at Mr. Tanner. "I mistrusted him and I believe that was part of it, his name being Orlando
Rincón."

"Johnson," Mr. Tanner said.

"I hired him two, three times," Mr. Malson said.
"For heavy work. When I had work you couldn't
pay a white man to do."

"His name is Johnson," Mr. Tanner said. "There
is no fuzzhead by the name of Orlando Rincón.
I'm telling you this fuzzhead is from the Fort Huachuca Tenth fuzzhead Cavalry and his name was
Johnson when he killed James C. Erin six months
ago and nothing else."

He spoke as you might speak to young children
to press something into their minds. This man
seemed to have no feeling and he never smiled, but
there was no reason to doubt him.

Bob Valdez arrived at the Maricopa pasture
about noon. He was riding shotgun on the Hatch

and Hodges run from St. David. He swung down from the boot, holding his sawed-off shotgun in the air, as the stage edged past the whiskey wagon.

Somebody standing at the tailgate with a glass in his hand said, "Hey, here's the town constable," and those nearby looked toward Bob Valdez in his dark suit and buttoned-up shirt, wearing a collar button but no tie or bandana; Valdez with his hat straight and slightly forward, the brim flat and the low crown undented.

"We'll get that nigger out of there now," somebody said, and a couple of others gave a little laugh to show they knew the person who said it was kidding.

Bob Valdez smiled, going along with it, though not knowing what they meant. "Out of where?" he said.

They explained it to him and he nodded, listening, his gaze moving over the shooters in the scrub, out to the line shack across the pasture and back to the slope, to the group of men a little way down from him. He saw Mr. Beaudry and Mr. Malson and Diego Luz, and the one they said was Mr. Tanner, there, talking to an R.L. Davis, who rode for Maricopa when he was working.

Bob Valdez watched the two men, both of them cut from the same stringy hide and looking like father and son: Mr. Tanner talking, never smiling, barely moving his mouth; R.L. Davis standing hip-cocked, posing with his revolver and rifle and a cartridge belt hanging over one shoulder, and the funneled, pointed brim of his sweaty hat nodding up and down as he listened to Mr. Tanner, grinning at what Mr. Tanner said, laughing out loud while Mr. Tanner did not show the twitch of a lip. Bob Valdez did not like R.L. Davis or any of the R.L. Davises in the world. He was civil, he listened to them, but God, there were a lot of them to listen to.

Well, all right, Bob Valdez thought. He walked down the slope to the group of men, nodding to Mr. Beaudry and Mr. Malson as they looked up. He waited a moment, not looking directly at Tanner, waiting for one of them to introduce him. Finally he held out his hand. "I'm Bob Valdez," he said, smiling a little.

Mr. Tanner looked at him, but did not shake hands. His gaze shifted as Mr. Malson said, "Bob's a town constable. He works a few nights a week in the Mexican part of town."

"The nights I'm here," Bob Valdez said. "Not on a stage run. See, I work for Hatch and Hodges too."

This time Mr. Tanner turned to say something to R.L. Davis, a couple of words that could have been about anything, and R.L. Davis laughed. Bob Valdez was a grown man; he was forty years old and as big as Mr. Tanner, but he stood there and didn't know what to do. He gripped the shotgun and was glad he had something to hold on to. He would have to stay near Mr. Tanner because he was the center of what was going on here. Soon they would discuss the situation and decide what to do. As the law-enforcement man he, Bob Valdez, should be in on the discussion and the decision. Of course. If someone was going to arrest Orlando Rincón or Johnson or whatever his name was, then he should be the one to do it; he was a town constable. They were out of town maybe, but where did the town end? The town had moved out here now; it was the same thing.

He could wait for Rincón to give up. Then arrest him.

If he wasn't dead already.

"Mr. Malson." Bob Valdez stepped toward the cattle company manager, who glanced over but looked out across the pasture again, indifferent.

"I wondered if maybe he's already dead," Valdez said.

Mr. Malson said, "Why don't you find out?"

"I was thinking," Valdez said, "if he was dead we could stand here a long time."

R.L. Davis adjusted his hat, which he did often, grabbing the funneled brim, loosening it on his head and pulling it down close to his eyes again and shifting from one cocked hip to the other. "Valdez here's got better things to do," R.L. Davis said. "He's busy."

"No," Bob Valdez said. "I was thinking of the one inside there, Rincón. He's dead or he's alive. He's alive, maybe he wants to give himself up. In there he has time to think, uh? Maybe—" He stopped. Not one of them was listening. Not even R.L. Davis.

Mr. Malson was looking at the whiskey wagon; it was on the road above them and over a little ways, with men standing by it being served off the tailgate. "I think we could use something," Mr. Malson said. His gaze went to Diego Luz the horse-breaker and Diego straightened up; not much, but a little. He was heavy and very dark and his shirt was tight across the thickness of his body. They said that Diego Luz hit green horses on the muzzle

with his fist and they minded him. He had the
hands for it; they hung at his sides, not touching or
fooling with anything. They turned open, gestured
when Mr. Malson told him to get the whiskey, and
as he moved off climbing the slope, one hand held
his holstered revolver to his leg.

Mr. Malson looked up at the sky, squinting and
taking his hat off and putting it on again. He took
off his coat and held it hooked over his shoulder by
one finger, said something, gestured, and he and
Mr. Beaudry and Mr. Tanner moved a few yards
down the slope to a hollow where there was good
shade. It was about two or two thirty then, hot,
fairly still and quiet considering the number of
people there. Only some of them in the pines and
down in the scrub could be seen from where Bob
Valdez stood wondering whether he should follow
the three men down to the hollow or wait for Diego
Luz, who was at the whiskey wagon now where
most of the sounds that carried came from: a voice,
a word or two that was suddenly clear, or laughter,
and people would look up to see what was going
on. Some of them by the whiskey wagon had lost
interest in the line shack. Others were still watching though: those farther along the road sitting in
wagons and buggies. This was a day people would
remember and talk about. "Sure, I was there," the
man in the buggy would be saying a year from now
in a saloon over in Benson or St. David or somewhere. "The day they got that Army deserter, he
had a Big-Fifty Sharps and an old dragoon pistol,
and I'll tell you it was ticklish business."

Down in that worn-out pasture, dusty and spotted with desert growth, prickly pear and brittle-

bush, there was just the sun. It showed the ground clearly all the way to just in front of the line shack where now, toward midafternoon, there was shadow coming out from the trees and from the mound the hut was set against.

Somebody in the scrub must have seen the door open. The shout came from there, and Bob Valdez and everybody on the slope were looking by the time the Lipan Apache woman had reached the edge of the shade. She walked out from the hut toward the willow trees carrying a bucket, not hurrying or even looking toward the slope.

Nobody fired at her, though this was not so strange. Putting the front sight on a sod hut and on a person are two different things. The men in the scrub and in the pines didn't know this woman. They weren't after her. She had just appeared. There she was; and no one was sure what to do about her.

She was in the trees by the creek awhile, then she was in the open again, walking back toward the hut with the bucket and not hurrying at all, a small figure way across the pasture almost without shape or color, with only the long skirt reaching to the ground to tell it was the woman.

So he's alive, Bob Valdez thought. And he wants to stay alive and he's not giving himself up.

He thought about the woman's nerve and whether Orlando Rincón had sent her out or she had decided this herself. You couldn't tell about an Indian woman. Maybe this was expected of her. The woman didn't count; the man did. You could lose the woman and get another one.

Mr. Tanner didn't look at R.L. Davis. His gaze

held on the Lipan Apache woman, inched along with her toward the hut; but he must have known R.L. Davis was right next to him.

"She's saying she didn't give a goddam about you and your rifle," Mr. Tanner said.

R.L. Davis looked at him funny. Then he said, "Shoot her?" like he hoped that's what Mr. Tanner meant.

"You could make her jump some," Mr. Tanner said.

Now R.L. Davis was on stage and he knew it, and Bob Valdez could tell he knew it by the way he levered the Winchester, raised it, and fired all in one motion, and as the dust kicked behind the Indian woman, who kept walking and didn't look up, R.L. Davis fired and fired and fired as fast as he could lever and half aim and with everybody watching him, hurrying him, he put four good ones right behind the woman. His last bullet socked into the door just as she reached it, and now she did pause and look up at the slope, staring up like she was waiting for him to fire again and giving him a good target if he wanted it.

Mr. Beaudry laughed out loud. "She don't give a goddam about your rifle."

It stung R.L. Davis, which it was intended to do.

"I wasn't aiming at her."

"But she doesn't know that." Mr. Beaudry was grinning, twisting his moustache, turning then and reaching out a hand as Diego Luz approached them with the whiskey.

"Hell, I wanted to hit her she'd be laying there, you know it."

"Well now, you tell her that," Mr. Beaudry said,

working the cork loose, "and she'll know it." He took a drink from the bottle and passed it to Mr. Malson, who offered the bottle to Mr. Tanner, who shook his head. Mr. Malson took a drink and saw R.L. Davis staring at him, so he handed the bottle to him. R.L. Davis jerked the bottle up, took a long swallow and that part was over.

Mr. Malson said to Mr. Tanner, "You don't want any?"

"Not right now," Mr. Tanner answered. He continued to stare out across the pasture.

Mr. Malson watched him. "You feel strongly about this Army deserter."

"I told you," Mr. Tanner said, "he killed a man was a friend of mine."

"No, I don't believe you did."

"James C. Erin, sutler at Fort Huachuca," Mr. Tanner said. "He came across a tulapai still this nigger soldier was working with some Indians. The nigger thought Erin would tell the Army people, so he shot him and ran off with a woman."

"And you saw him this morning."

"I had come in last night to see this gentleman," Mr. Tanner said, nodding toward Malson. "This morning I was getting ready to leave when I saw him, him and the woman."

"I was right there," R.L. Davis said. "Right, Mr. Tanner? Him and I was on the porch by the Republic Hotel and Rincón goes by in the wagon. Mr. Tanner said, 'You know that man?' I said, 'Only that he's lived up north of town a few months. Him and his woman.' 'Well, I know him,' Mr. Tanner said. 'That man's an Army deserter wanted for murder.' I said, 'Well let's go get him.' He had a

start on us and that's how he got to the hut before
we could grab on to him. He's been holed up ever
since."

Mr. Malson said, "Then you didn't talk to him."

"Listen," Mr. Tanner said, "I've kept that man's
face before my eyes this past year."

Bob Valdez, somewhat behind Mr. Tanner and
to the side, moved in a little closer. "You know this
is the same man?"

Mr. Tanner looked around. He stared at Valdez.
That's all he did, just stared.

"I mean, we have to be sure," Bob Valdez said.
"It's a serious thing."

Now Mr. Malson and Mr. Beaudry were looking up at him. "We," Mr. Beaudry said. "I'll tell
you what, Roberto. We need help we'll call you.
All right?"

"You hired me," Bob Valdez said, standing
alone above them. He was serious, but he shrugged
and smiled a little to take the edge off the words.
"What did you hire me for?"

"Well," Mr. Beaudry said, acting it out, looking
up past Bob Valdez and along the road both ways.
"I was to see some drunk Mexicans, I'd point them
out."

After that, for a while, the men with the whiskey bottle forgot Bob Valdez. They stayed in the
shade of the hollow watching the line shack, waiting for the Army deserter to realize it was all over
for him. He would realize it and open the door and
be cut down as he came outside. It was a matter of
time only.

Bob Valdez stayed on the open part of the slope
that was turning to shade, sitting now like an

Apache with a suit on and every once in a while making a cigarette and smoking it slowly and thinking about himself and Mr. Tanner and the others, then thinking about the Army deserter, then thinking about himself again.

He didn't have to stay here. He didn't have to be a town constable. He didn't have to work for the stage company. He didn't have to listen to Mr. Beaudry and Mr. Malson and smile when they said those things. He didn't have a wife or any kids. He didn't have land that he owned. He could go anywhere he wanted.

Diego Luz was coming over. Diego Luz had a wife and a daughter almost grown and some little kids and he had to stay, sure.

Diego Luz squatted next to him, his arms on his knees and his big hands that he used for breaking horses hanging in front of him.

"Stay near if they want you for something," Bob Valdez said. He was watching Beaudry tilt the bottle up. Diego Luz said nothing.

"One of them bends over," Bob Valdez said then, "you kiss it, uh?"

Diego Luz looked at him, patient about it. Not angry or stirred. "Why don't you go home?"

"He says get me a bottle, you run."

"I get it. I don't run."

"Smile and hold your hat, uh?"

"And don't talk so much."

"Not unless they talk to you first."

"You better go home," Diego said.

Bob Valdez said, "That's why you hit the horses."

"Listen," Diego Luz said. "They pay me to break horses. They pay you to talk to drunks and keep them from killing somebody. They don't pay you for what you think or how you feel. So if you take their money keep your mouth shut. All right?"

Bob Valdez smiled. "I'm kidding you."

Diego Luz got up and walked away, down toward the hollow. The hell with him, he was thinking. Maybe he was kidding, but the hell with him. He was also thinking that maybe he could get a drink from that bottle. Maybe there would be a half inch left nobody wanted and Mr. Malson would tell him to kill it.

But it was already finished. R.L. Davis was playing with the bottle, holding it by the neck and flipping it up and catching it as it came down. Beaudry was saying, "What about after dark?" And looking at Mr. Tanner, who was thinking about something else and didn't notice.

R.L. Davis stopped flipping the bottle. He said, "Put some men on the rise right above the hut; he comes out, bust him."

"Well, they should get the men over there," Mr. Beaudry said, looking at the sky. "It won't be long till dark."

"Where's he going?" Mr. Malson said.

The others looked up, stopped in whatever they were doing or thinking by the suddenness of Mr. Malson's voice.

"Hey, Valdez!" R.L. Davis yelled out. "Where you think you're going?"

Bob Valdez had circled them and was already below them on the slope, leaving the pines now and entering the scrub brush. He didn't stop or look back.

"Valdez!"

Mr. Tanner raised one hand to silence R.L. Davis, all the time watching Bob Valdez getting smaller, going straight through the scrub, not just walking or passing the time but going right out to the pasture.

"Look at him," Mr. Malson said. There was some admiration in his voice.

"He's dumber than he looks," R.L. Davis said, then jumped a little as Mr. Tanner touched his arm.

"Come on," Mr. Tanner said. "With the rifle." And he started down the slope, hurrying and not seeming to care if he might stumble on the loose gravel.

Bob Valdez was now halfway across the pasture, the shotgun pointed down at his side, his eyes not leaving the door of the line shack. The door was probably already open enough for a rifle barrel to poke through. He guessed the Army deserter was covering him, letting him get as close as he wanted; the closer he came the easier to hit him.

Now he could see all the bullet marks in the door and the clean inner wood where the door was splintered. Two people in that little bake-oven of a place. He saw the door move.

He saw the rag doll on the ground. It was a strange thing, the woman having a doll. Valdez hardly glanced at it but was aware of the button eyes looking up and the discomforted twist of the red wool mouth. Then, just past the doll, when he was wondering if he would go right up to the door and knock on it and wouldn't that be a crazy thing, like visiting somebody, the door opened and the Negro was in the doorway filling it, standing there in pants and boots but without a shirt in that hot place, and holding a long-barreled dragoon that was already cocked.

They stood twelve feet apart looking at each other, close enough so that no one could fire from the slope.

"I can kill you first," the Negro said, "if you raise it."

With his free hand, the left one, Bob Valdez motioned back over his shoulder. "There's a man there said you killed somebody a year ago."

"What man?"

"Said his name is Tanner."

The Negro shook his head, once each way.

"Said your name is Johnson."

"You know my name."

"I'm telling you what he said."

"Where'd I kill this man?"

"Huachuca."

The Negro hesitated. "That was some time ago I was in the Tenth. More than a year."

"You a deserter?"

"I served it out."

"Then you got something that says so."

"In the wagon, there's a bag there my things are in."

"Will you talk to this man Tanner?"

"If I can hold from busting him."

"Listen, why did you run this morning?"

"They come chasing. I don't know what they want." He lowered the gun a little, his brown-stained tired-looking eyes staring intently at Bob Valdez. "What would you do? They come on the run. Next thing I know they firing at us."

"Will you go with me and talk to him?"

The Negro hesitated again. Then shook his head. "I don't know him."

"Then he won't know you."

"He didn't know me this morning."

"All right," Bob Valdez said. "I'll bet your paper says you were discharged. Then we'll show it to this man, uh?"

The Negro thought it over before he nodded, very slowly, as if still thinking. "All right. Bring him here, I'll say a few words to him."

Bob Valdez smiled a little. "You can point that gun some other way."

"Well . . ." the Negro said, "if everybody's friends." He lowered the revolver to his side.

The wagon was in the willow trees by the creek. Off to the right. But Bob Valdez did not turn right away in that direction. He backed away, watching Orlando Rincón for no reason that he knew of. Maybe because the man was holding a gun and that was reason enough.

He had backed off six or seven feet when Orlando Rincón shoved the revolver down into his belt. Bob Valdez turned and started for the trees.

It was at this moment that he looked across the pasture. He saw Mr. Tanner and R.L. Davis at the edge of the scrub trees but wasn't sure it was them. Something tried to tell him it was them, but he did not accept it until he was off to the right, out of the line of fire, and by then the time to yell at them or run toward them was past. R.L. Davis had the Winchester up and was firing.

They say R.L. Davis was drunk or he would have pinned him square. As it was, the bullet shaved Rincón and plowed past him into the hut.

Bob Valdez saw Rincón half turn and he saw
Rincón's accusing eyes as Rincón pulled the long-
barreled dragoon from his belt.

"They weren't supposed to," Bob Valdez said,
holding one hand out as if to stop Rincón. "Listen,
they weren't supposed to do that!"

The revolver was free, and Rincón was cocking
it. "Don't!" Bob Valdez said. "Don't do it!" Looking right into the Negro's eyes and seeing it was
no use, that Rincón was going to shoot him, and
suddenly hurrying, he jerked the shotgun up and
pulled both triggers so that the explosions came
out in one blast and Orlando Rincón was spun and
thrown back inside.

They came out across the pasture to have a look,
some going inside where they found the woman
and brought her out, everybody noticing she would
have a child in about a month. Those by the doorway made room as Mr. Tanner and R.L. Davis approached.

Diego Luz came over by Bob Valdez, who had
not moved. Valdez stood watching them and he
saw Mr. Tanner look down at Rincón and after a
moment shake his head.

"It looked like him," Mr. Tanner said. "It sure
looked like him."

He saw R.L. Davis squint at Mr. Tanner. "It
ain't the one you said?"

Mr. Tanner shook his head again. "I've seen him
before though. I know I've seen him somewheres."

Bob Valdez saw R.L. Davis shrug. "You ask me,
they all look alike." He was yawning then, fooling
with his hat, and then his eyes swiveled over to Bob
Valdez standing with the empty shotgun.

"Constable," R.L. Davis said. "You went and killed the wrong coon."

Bob Valdez started for him, raising the shotgun to swing it like a club, but Diego Luz caught him from behind and locked a big arm around his neck, under his chin, until he was still and Mr. Tanner and the others had moved off.